Prai

“Putney offers a strong ing and memorable characters, and a portrayal of the London art world filled with jealousy and passion.”

—*Publishers Weekly*

"Mary Jo Putney once again sweeps readers into a story that captures and holds their hearts, introducing old friends and bringing us a new hero and heroine. She brilliantly captures the intricacies, mores, manners and wit of the era with panache, and with her special gift for story telling that brings readers great joy."

—*Romantic Times*

"*River of Fire* is intense and emotional, at times dark, but never depressing. Putney has done wonders at revealing the soul, creative insight, temperament, and world of visual artists. The novel so inspired me that I, not a visual artist, was moved to try to put my emotions on paper with color and form via a visual medium--and it was exhilarating. That's how exquisite *River of Fire* is."

—*Under the Covers*

"*River of Fire* delivers more than enough drama and romance to entertain historical romance readers and reinforce Mary Jo Putney's reputation as one of the best."

—*The Romance Reader*

The Fallen Angels Series
(in order)

Thunder & Roses

Dancing on the Wind

Petals in the Storm

Angel Rogue

Shattered Rainbows

River of Fire

One Perfect Rose

PANDAMAX
PRESS

RIVER OF FIRE

FALLEN ANGELS SERIES: BOOK 6

MARY JO PUTNEY

PANDAMAX
PRESS

To Binnie:
For support, boundless good nature—
and because she loves tortured heroes.

PROLOGUE

SUTTERTON HALL

BEDFORDSHIRE, ENGLAND, 1794

The boy's hand hovered over the paper, the fragile length of charcoal poised delicately as he thought. Starting the drawing of his pony had been easy, but what about the legs? How did they move when Albie trotted? Kenneth Wilding conjured up a precise mental image, then made a small sound of satisfaction and bent over his sketch. The right foreleg like that. The hindquarters *so.*

When he finished, he took the picture to his mother, who was rocking her infant daughter to sleep on the other side of the nursery. He knew she worried about the baby, but she looked up with a smile when he approached.

"Very good, Kenneth," she said after examining the picture. "This isn't just any horse, is it? It's Albie." When he nodded, Lady Kimball continued, "A wonderful likeness.

He looks ready to run off the page. I couldn't have done better myself."

It was a fine compliment, for his mother drew like an angel. Kenneth returned to his sketchbook with a proud smile. He was starting another drawing of Albie when the nursery door opened, admitting a blast of chilly air from the corridor. His fingers tightened around the charcoal when he saw that the newcomer was his father. Burly, forceful, as rooted in the earth as one of Sutterton Hall's famous oaks.

Lord Kimball frowned at his son. "I told you not to waste time drawing. You should be studying your Latin so you'll be ready for Harrow next year."

"Kenneth had finished his Latin lesson, so I told him it was all right to do some sketching," his mother said mildly. "He's really quite talented, Godfrey. When he goes on his Grand Tour, he'll be able to bring back wonderful views of the Continent."

Lord Kimball snorted. "Drawing is for girls. Gentlemen hire artists to sketch their travels." Swooping down on his son, he crumpled the picture of the pony in one hand and tossed it into the nursery fire. "Come with me. The cows are starting to calf and you're old enough to help."

Kenneth made an involuntary sound of protest before pressing his lips together and getting obediently to his feet. "Yes, sir." One day he'd be the fifth Viscount Kimball and he would be responsible for all of the livestock. He must know every inch of Sutterton, as his father did. Nothing mattered more than the land and the people. Nothing.

But before he followed his father from the room, he cast a last, regretful look at the drawing as it charred and fell into ash.

CHAPTER 1

SUTTERTON HALL, 1817

The situation was even worse than he had feared.

With a sigh of bone-deep weariness, Kenneth Wilding pushed away the account ledgers. He had known there would be serious financial problems when he inherited. But he'd thought there was hope—that years of hard work and frugality would be enough to preserve his heritage. The more fool he.

He rose from the desk and went to stare out the library window at the gentle hills of Sutterton. The beauty of the landscape was like a knife in his heart. For fifteen years he had yearned to come home. He had not expected to find that the once-rich fields were fallow and weed-choked, that the livestock had been sold to pay for the trumpery pleasures of an aging man and his heartless, extravagant young wife.

As he struggled to control his anger, he heard steps behind him, the irregular footfalls counterpointed by the tap of a cane. He schooled his face before he turned to his sister, Beth. She was all he had left, and he had loved her even when she was a colicky infant. But he didn't know how to talk to her. They had been apart too long.

Her dark hair and gray eyes were very like his, though her features were delicately pretty, nothing like his craggy, scarred visage. She settled into a chair and clasped the head of her cane loosely in her hands. She had a composure that made her look older than her twenty-three years. "I haven't heard a word from you since the solicitor left this morning. Shall I ring for some food? There's a rather nice pork pie."

"Thank you, but looking at the accounts has left me with no appetite."

Her expression became grave. "How bad is it?"

His first impulse was to make a soothing comment, but he rejected it. The grim truth could not be avoided. Besides, for all her air of fragility, Beth was strong. As a tiny child she had come to terms with a congenitally twisted foot, and as a young woman she had survived the waspish tongue of a spoiled, extravagant stepmother.

"We're completely ruined," he said bluntly. "Since Father drained Sutterton's resources while he lived in London with dear Hermione, the amount of the mortgages far exceeds what the property is now worth. Hermione has the family jewelry, and there is no chance of recovering it. The estate will have to be sold. There will be nothing left, not even your marriage portion. The creditors will probably evict us in a matter of weeks."

Beth's fingers clenched on the brass head of her cane. "I was afraid of that, but hoped I was wrong." She tried to smile. "Not that the dowry matters, since I'm a spinster by nature."

"Nonsense. If Father and Hermione hadn't kept you

buried in Bedfordshire, you'd be married with a baby on your knee." Then he wished he had not spoken, for her expression showed how much she wanted what she would probably never have.

She made a dismissive motion with her hand, as if marriage and family were of no interest. "I'm sorry, Kenneth. I did my best to manage the estate, but I wasn't good enough."

"Sutterton wasn't your responsibility," he said gruffly. "It was Father's and now mine. It is we who have failed you."

"Don't blame yourself. It was Papa who married a woman young enough to be his daughter, and it was Papa who threw away generations of stewardship to give Hermione the fashionable life she demanded." Beth stopped abruptly, tears glinting in her eyes. "It's almost a relief to know that the end has come, but I... I'll miss Sutterton."

Her refusal to blame made him feel worse. "I should have stayed instead of running away to enlist. If I'd been here, I might have been able to curb the worst excesses."

"I doubt it. If ever a man was besotted, it was Papa. Only Hermione's wishes mattered," Beth said dryly. "You would have gone mad here. Do you think I've forgotten the horrid fights you had with Papa before you left?"

Her words brought back stomach-turning memories of those last days at Sutterton. Beth was right; he could not possibly have stayed. Wanting to forget, he said reassuringly, "You needn't worry that we'll starve. I have some money from the sale of my commission. That will keep us until I find a suitable position. We shall be quite comfortable." His gaze went to the hills and he swallowed hard, hoping that the pain didn't show. "I'm going for a walk. After dinner tonight, we can make plans. I believe you'll be allowed to keep personal possessions."

"We'll manage very well." She got slowly to her feet. "Though I'm not much of a bailiff, I'm quite good at running a household. You'll see."

After a nod of acknowledgment, he made his escape, grateful to get out into the chill February air. He had spent the twenty-four hours since returning home indoors, examining the accounts and listening to the disastrous news from the family solicitor. He'd also fired the insolent, incompetent bailiff who had been hired after Kenneth's father lost interest in the estate.

Perhaps the late viscount had been ensorcelled by Hermione. He had seemed like a different man after his second marriage. As a boy, Kenneth had loved, feared, and respected his father in equal parts. Now only anger and contempt remained.

As his long strides took him down a lane that had been old when Henry VIII was on the throne, he began to relax. Every hill, every view, was as familiar as his own hands, yet at the same time new, because fifteen years had passed. Fifteen long years.

Some people would think the winter landscape bleak, but Kenneth loved the subtle colors. There were a thousand shades of gray in the trees, and the ever-changing clouds scudded across the sky like living beings. Soon the first buds of spring would unfurl in all their vivid green splendor. He paused at a brook, watching the crystalline splash of water over rippling weed and glossy stone. Home, and his, at least for the next month or two.

He hurled a stone into the brook and resumed walking. While he could keep his sister and himself from starvation, Beth's life had been ruined. She was pretty and clever and sweet-natured, and her clubfoot probably would not have proved an insurmountable barrier to marriage if she'd possessed a decent dowry. But the combination of penury and disability doomed her to spinsterhood.

He halted on the crest of Sutterton's highest hill. Above him, the leafless twigs of beech trees wove intricate patterns of marvelous complexity. He scooped up a handful of dry, crumbly soil. His ancestors had lived and worked and died on this land for centuries. Now, because of his father's criminal folly, the estate would be sold to strangers.

Though he was no agricultural genius, his earliest memories were of loving this land, much as he had loved his mother. With an anguished sound deep in his throat, he flung the handful of earth away. He'd forgo his chance of heaven to save Sutterton. Not that heaven would want a man who had spent half a lifetime committing the crimes of war.

The cold wind whipped at his hair as he stalked down the hill. With no real hope, he wondered if there was any chance he could borrow enough money to give partial payment to the mortgage holders. That might give him time to sell off some land and make the remaining acreage profitable.

But the amount needed would be staggering: at least twenty thousand pounds. He'd talked with several London bankers before coming home. They'd been polite, as befitted his noble rank, but it was clear that none would lend money to a man who had inherited nothing but debts. And that had been before he'd learned how bad the situation was.

Nor did he know anyone who might trust him for such an amount. His closest friends were in his former regiment, the Rifle Brigade. Though an elite fighting unit, it was far from fashionable. Most of the other officers had been the sons of doctors and vicars and country squires. Like him, they had had to live on their salaries, and sometimes send money home as well.

The exception had been his closest friend, Lord Michael Kenyon. But Michael, though aristocratic and possessor of a comfortable income, was a younger son. He was also recently married and with a baby on the way. It was unlikely that he would have twenty thousand pounds to spare even if Kenneth were able to bring himself to ask. And that he would never do. He had taken his troubles to Michael enough in the past.

By the time he reached the edge of the estate, he had mentally exhausted the possibilities for salvation. He turned back toward the house, his expression set. Sutterton was doomed. It was time to consider the future. With the war over, many former officers were searching for work. Luckily he had some family connections who might help him find some kind of position.

By the time he returned to the hall, he had achieved a degree of bleak acceptance. He went indoors and was greeted by the only male house servant left, the ancient butler, Harrod.

"You've a visitor, Lord Kimball." The butler proffered a tray with a card as elegantly as if Sutterton were a royal palace. "The gentleman chose to wait."

Lord Bowden. Kenneth frowned at the card, unable to place the name. "Where is he?"

Harrod gave a delicate cough. "I took the liberty of putting Lord Bowden in the library."

In other words, coal was expensive and the library was the only public room with a fire. Kenneth gave his hat and greatcoat to the butler, then walked down the icy hall to the library, which was only marginally warmer.

His guest rose from his seat by the fire at Kenneth's entrance. In his early fifties, Bowden had a spare, wiry frame and an air of cool self-possession. He might seem nondescript to anyone who didn't notice the intensity in his dark, assessing gaze.

Breaking the silence, Kenneth asked, "Have we met, Lord Bowden? Or were you a friend of my father's?"

"Your father and I were acquainted, though not close friends." Without waiting for permission, Bowden resumed his seat. "I came to discuss a matter of business with you."

Kenneth's face stiffened. "If you are a creditor, there is nothing I can do. The estate is about to go into bankruptcy."

"I know. The condition of the Wilding finances is common knowledge." Bowden's gaze went around the shabby library. "For that reason, I was able to purchase the outstanding mortgages at a substantial discount. The face value amounts to fifty thousand pounds, and all are overdue." He reached into an inside pocket and removed a sheaf of papers, then laid them on the desk.

Kenneth scanned the documents. They were quite genuine, including his father's scrawled signature. The end had come even sooner than he had expected. "You made a poor bargain, Bowden."

Trying to conceal his bitterness, he jerked open a desk drawer and removed the master keys for Sutterton. There were dozens strung on a massive, forged iron ring, jangling together like lengths of chain. "I wish you much joy of your new property. I suggest you consider retaining the servants. The few who are left are nothing if not loyal. My sister and

I will leave tomorrow. Though if you insist, I suppose we could be out tonight." He tossed the heavy ring to Bowden.

Caught by surprise, Bowden reacted too slowly to catch the keys. They bounced from the arm of his chair and crashed discordantly to the floor. He stared at the ring for a moment, then raised his gaze to Kenneth. "I didn't come to evict you. I want to make a proposal."

Refusing to allow himself to hope, Kenneth said, "Do you mean you're willing to extend the mortgages? Given the state of the property, it will be years before I would be able to pay anything more than the interest."

"I'm not here to negotiate new terms," Bowden said coolly. "If you can perform a service for me, I will cancel the debt and turn the mortgages over to you."

Stunned, Kenneth stared at his visitor. It sounded too good to be true, which in his experience meant that it was. "What do you want in return? My immortal soul?"

"I am not Mephistopheles, and your soul is your own business," Bowden said with a cool smile. "Sutterton can be yours. All you must do in return is destroy a man."

It *was* too good to be true. Obviously Bowden was mad. Kenneth's mouth twisted as he pushed the mortgage documents back across the desk. "Sorry. I'm a soldier, not an assassin. If you want a crime committed, you must find someone else."

Bowden's brows arched fastidiously. "If all I wanted was an assassination, I could find some scoundrel to do the job for a few shillings. What I want is more complicated. A man who is considered above suspicion has committed a great crime. I want to see him unmasked, imprisoned, and executed." A muscle in his cheek jerked. "I want to see his precious reputation annihilated so that everyone will know him for the swine he is. I believe you are the man who can do that for me."

A warning bell sounded in the back of Kenneth's mind. If he had any sense, he'd throw this lunatic out. Yet Bowden held Sutterton's future in his hands. Kenneth owed it to his sister and himself to listen. "Why me? We've never even met."

"I learned of you from a passing reference made by your father. I was intrigued and made further inquiries. It is unheard of for a young man of noble blood to conceal his rank and enlist in the army as a common soldier. Not only did you survive, but by courage and merit you earned an officer's commission." Bowden's gaze narrowed. "However, there are other brave men. You have two qualities that make you unique."

"Insanity is one or I wouldn't be listening to this," Kenneth said dryly. "What is the other?"

Ignoring the interruption, Bowden continued, "You were a reconnaissance officer in Spain, which means you must be ruthless, resourceful, and have the ability to ferret out information. You were known as the Demon Warrior, I understand."

Kenneth grimaced. "That was merely a nickname given to me after I hunted down a band of French deserters who had been terrorizing the Spanish peasants. I did what any officer would do."

"Perhaps, but you did it with remarkable efficiency." Bowden's gaze became speculative. "After three years as an intelligence officer, you were captured by the French and held for several days. After you escaped, you returned to regular duty with your regiment. No one seemed to know why."

Kenneth thought of Maria, and knew he would see

Bowden in hell before he would explain why he had given up intelligence work. "If you need a personal spy, why not hire a Bow Street Runner? They are far more qualified to investigate a crime."

"I did hire one, but he was unable to discover anything important. I need someone who can enter the villain's household and investigate from within. That is where you come in." Bowden studied Kenneth's craggy face and broad, muscular figure. "I admit you don't look the part, but I have it on good authority that you're a talented artist."

"I'm no artist," Kenneth said stiffly. "I merely have a knack for drawing."

Bowden's brows rose again. "As you wish. In any event, I'm told that you took advantage of your years on the Continent to study art and architecture whenever your military duties permitted. You have seen the treasures of Spain, France, and the Low Countries, viewed masterpieces that few Englishmen of the last generation have seen. That fact will help you get into the villain's household."

The conversation was getting stranger by the second. "You need a brave, ruthless spy who knows art, and you're willing to spend a fortune to get one," Kenneth said without inflection. "Why?"

"The man I wish to unmask is a painter. Anyone ignorant of art is unlikely to be able to get close enough to investigate him." Bowden gave a chilling smile. "You see why I consider you uniquely suited to the task."

A painter? Kenneth said warily, "Who is your quarry?"

Bowden hesitated. "Before I reveal that, you must give your word to speak of this to no one even if you decide to refuse my proposal. I want justice, Kimball, and I will not be denied!"

"You have my word."

Bowden's eyes became slits. "The man is Anthony Seaton."

"Sir Anthony Seaton!" Kenneth stared at his visitor. "Bloody hell, surely you're joking!"

"I would not joke about such a thing," Bowden snapped. "Your reaction demonstrates why he is such a difficult man to bring down. No one wants to believe him a criminal."

Kenneth shook his head in disbelief. Though known particularly for his portraits, Sir Anthony had produced vast, magnificent historical paintings as well. Kenneth had seen engravings of his work. The power of them had struck him to the heart. "He is one of Britain's foremost painters."

"So he is." Bowden flattened a wrinkle in his immaculate buckskin breeches. "He is also my younger brother."

CHAPTER 2

After another stunned moment, Kenneth said, "I will not get involved in a family feud."

"Not even to trap a murderer, and save your heritage in the process?" Bowden said softly. "This is no simple family feud. It is a matter of justice."

Feeling a sudden, overpowering need for a drink, Kenneth rose and went to his father's lovingly stocked liquor cabinet. He poured two measures of brandy, gave a glass to his visitor, and took his seat again. After a deep swallow, he said, "You're going to have to tell me the whole story before I can decide on this insane proposition of yours."

"I suppose I must," Bowden said reluctantly. He studied his brandy without drinking. "Twenty-eight years ago I was betrothed to a young lady named Helen Cosgrove. She had flaming hair and was... very lovely. The banns had been cried and we were within a week of the wedding when she eloped with my brother Anthony."

Kenneth caught his breath. No wonder there was bad

blood between the men. "Twenty-eight years is a long time to wait for revenge."

Bowden's eyes flashed. "Do you think I am so petty? I was furious at the betrayal and never spoke to either of them again. Yet even though I could not forgive, I could understand how it happened. Helen was enough to tempt any man, and Anthony was a dashing, romantic young artist. Society eventually accepted their misconduct and called it a great love match."

He stopped speaking. When the silence had gone on too long, Kenneth prompted, "You spoke of murder."

Bowden resumed in a clipped voice. "Helen died last summer at their house in the Lake District. It was called an accident, but I know better. For years, there had been talk of Anthony's affairs. The knowledge must have been shattering to a woman of Helen's refinement. At the time of her death, it was rumored that Anthony had tired of Helen and wanted to marry his current mistress. He always was a selfish devil." Bowden leaned forward, his gaze fierce. "I believe that he either murdered Helen himself or made her so wretched that she took her own life. That would make him as responsible for her death as if she died by his hand."

Driving a woman to suicide might be the moral equivalent of murder, but the law would take a different view. Kenneth said bluntly, "You want to believe the worst of your brother, but apparently everyone else thought Lady Seaton's death was an accident. Perhaps it was."

Bowden snorted. "Healthy women don't walk over cliffs when the weather is fair and they know the country intimately. One thing the Bow Street Runner did learn was that after her fall there were signs of struggle at the top of the cliff. But because my brother is 'above suspicion,' it did not occur to anyone to accuse him."

This was a bad business. Yet if Bowden was mad, it was an ice-cold, controlled mania. "Perhaps you're right and Seaton did murder his wife," Kenneth said slowly. "Yet given how she died, the best investigation in the world may be unable to prove conclusively what happened."

"I understand," Bowden said, his eyes flat as slate. "But I will not rest until her death has been thoroughly investigated. I sought you out because I think you have the best chance of accomplishing the task. If you will give your word as an officer and a gentleman to use your best efforts to determine the circumstances of Helen's death, I will cancel the mortgages when you are finished. If you provide conclusive evidence of Anthony's guilt, I will give you a bonus of five thousand pounds to help you put your estate on its feet again."

It was an incredible offer. Miraculous, in fact. Kenneth set down his empty brandy glass and got to his feet, moving tensely around the library. Bowden's proposal was mad and bordered on the illegal. If Kenneth had any sense, he would show Bowden the door. Yet he had never lived life sensibly.

If he accepted, Sutterton would be saved. Beth could have the life she deserved, with a Season in London and a dowry if she wished to marry. The estate would become profitable and the servants and laborers provided for after years of neglect.

As for himself...

He stopped by the fireplace and ran his palm over the exquisitely carved mantelpiece. As a child, he had imagined stories about the oaken figures.

Sutterton would give meaning to his life. In muddy billets and baking Spanish heat, before battles and during shivering winter nights, he had dreamed of what he would do when the house came to him. He had made elaborate plans for modernizing the drafty old building without destroying its Tudor character. If he agreed to Bowden's proposition, someday he would be able to realize those dreams.

And who would be injured? If Sir Anthony was guilty, he deserved to be punished even if he was the finest painter in England. If he was clearly innocent, perhaps the truth would relieve Lord Bowden's anguished obsession. And if nothing could be proved either way—Kenneth would still save Sutterton.

He felt a superstitious prickle at his nape when he remembered that an hour before, he'd told himself he would give up his chance of heaven to save his heritage. But Bowden was no demon, merely a troubled English gentleman.

Kenneth turned to his visitor. "We must draw up a contract detailing our agreement."

Triumph glowed in Bowden's eyes. "Of course. Bring out ink and paper and we shall do it now."

After half an hour of discussion and writing, each of the men possessed a copy of their compact. It was not a matter that either of them would want made public, but its existence should keep both sides honest.

Kenneth rose and replenished the brandy after they had each signed. "Let us drink to a mutually successful mission."

Bowden raised his glass. "To success." Instead of sipping, he drained his goblet, then hurled it into the fireplace. It smashed, droplets of brandy flaming blue among the coals. Fury throbbing in his voice, he said, "And may my brother burn in hell for what he has done."

The words hung fever-heavy in the air until Kenneth said, "You spoke of my entering Sir Anthony's household.

Since you've worked out everything else, I assume you have a plan for that."

Bowden nodded. "My brother's secretary is about to leave for a better position. Morley was a kind of general factotum who ran the whole establishment. The household leans toward the chaotic at the best of times and without Morley, it will deteriorate swiftly. Go to my brother and ask for the position."

Startled, Kenneth said, "Why would he want me for his secretary? There are bound to be better-qualified candidates."

"Anthony will not advertise the position if someone suitable appears first. Your army service will help, since my brother has a romantic reverence for the military, but your knowledge of art will be the deciding factor." Bowden considered. "Present yourself at Anthony's house and say that a friend of his who wishes to remain anonymous sent you because he knows your organizational skills are desperately needed. My brother will find that amusing."

Kenneth hoped it would be that easy. "What of the rest of the household? Has Sir Anthony married his mistress?"

Bowden hesitated. "Not yet. He may have thought it would look too suspicious if he remarried right away."

Kenneth took another sip of brandy. "Does Sir Anthony have children?"

"A daughter named Rebecca. She's twenty-seven, I believe. A ruined spinster."

"Can a woman be a spinster if she has been ruined?"

Bowden shrugged. "You can call her a slut if you prefer. At the age of eighteen, she ran off with a self-proclaimed poet, then didn't have the decency to marry him."

Elopement seemed to be a family trait, Kenneth thought dryly. "Does she live with her father?"

"Yes. It's a mark of his own low morals that he took her back into his household."

Kenneth did not agree; for a man to turn his only daughter away because of a youthful mistake would have been even more immoral. Keeping the thought private, he said, "She would be the logical person to run the household instead of her father's secretary. I wonder why she doesn't."

"She's probably either lazy or incompetent. I assume that you'll find out which." Bowden got to his feet and gave a cold smile. "After all, I am paying you a fortune to learn every single thing about my brother's life."

As Kenneth escorted his visitor out, he wondered wryly whether the faint scent in the hall was mildew or brimstone.

Before changing for dinner, Kenneth went to tell his sister the good news. She was sitting by her bedroom window, taking advantage of the last of the light to do mending.

He frowned and crossed the room to the fireplace. "It's freezing in here, Beth. You must take better care of yourself."

She glanced up from the pillowcase she was darning. "No need to waste coal. I'm used to the cold."

He knelt and laid a generous scoop of coal on the feeble fire. A few pumps with the bellows created a warm blaze. He rose and was about to speak when he saw a small painting. "Good God, the Rembrandt! I thought it was gone."

"I'm sorry, I should have told you yesterday, but I forgot in the excitement of your arrival." Beth began stitching again. "Whenever Hermione came to Sutterton, she looked for valuables to take to London. I knew that picture was your favorite, so I switched frames with that awful little landscape in the hall and brought the Rembrandt in here. Hermione did come in once, but didn't give the picture a second glance."

"Thank heaven for that. The painting isn't a major work, but it's worth a hundred pounds or so. Enough for Hermione to covet." Pulse quickening, Kenneth went to the small still life of fruits and flowers. It was easy to overlook in its new plain frame, yet to a discerning eye, it was unmistakably the product of a master. He had always loved the sensual colors and forms. How was it possible to get such depth, such richness?

Touched by the knowledge that his sister had cared enough to save the painting for his sake, he glanced up and was struck by how much she resembled their mother. "Bless you, Beth," he said quietly. "I thought I'd never see this again."

She smiled. "I'm glad you're pleased." Her smile vanished. "We won't lose the picture to bankruptcy, will we?"

Remembering why he had come, he said, "Our luck may have turned. A gentleman called this afternoon and asked me to do some work that might save Sutterton."

Beth gasped and her darning dropped forgotten into her lap. "Good heavens, what kind of position could do that?"

"It's an odd business, and I'm not at liberty to discuss it yet. But if all goes well, next year you can be presented at court as Miss Wilding of Sutterton." Forestalling the questions he saw in his sister's face, he added, "What I'm doing isn't dangerous or illegal, merely odd. However, I'll have to go to London for a time—anywhere from several weeks to several months. I'll leave some of the money I got from the sale of my commission to cover the household expenses."

"You're going away so soon?" Though she tried, Beth couldn't keep the disappointment from her voice.

Kenneth shifted uncomfortably. His sister had already been alone too much. A thought occurred to him. "When I came through London last week, I saw my friend Jack Davidson. I've mentioned him in letters. He lost the use of his left arm at Waterloo and has been rather at loose ends ever since. However, he's the younger son of a squire and quite knowledgeable about agriculture. If you don't object, I'll ask him to come to Sutterton. I think he'd be willing to act as a temporary steward. He can survey what will be needed if we're able to keep the estate."

Beth glanced wryly at her cane. "Mr. Davidson should fit in very well here. I'll have to find a chaperone, though." She thought a moment. "I'll write Cousin Olivia. She'll come if I let her stay in the Royal Suite."

Kenneth smiled. "Done. Let's hope everything else falls into place as easily." But as he left to dress for dinner, his good spirits faded. He wondered how long it had taken Faust to develop doubts about his bargain with Mephistopheles.

CHAPTER 3

Sir Anthony Seaton cast a disapproving eye on the dishes laid out in the breakfast room. "The cook calls this a meal? That idiot Frenchman deserves to be discharged."

"He *was* discharged, Father," Rebecca Seaton said without raising her gaze from the sketchbook beside her plate. "You got rid of him yesterday."

Her father frowned. "So I did. The insolent devil deserved it. Why hasn't he been replaced?"

"Finding a new cook takes time, particularly when all of the registry agencies shudder at my approach." She paused for a bite of toast. "We've become notorious for the frequency with which servants leave. Luckily, the kitchen maid can cook a little."

"How would you know? Half the time, you don't notice what you're eating." Sir Anthony scowled at her. "Why aren't you doing a better job of running this place?"

Knowing her father's temper would not improve until he had his morning tea, Rebecca laid down her pencil and went to pour a cup. She stirred in milk and sugar and handed him the steaming beverage. "If I spent my time on such things, I would be unable to help in your studio."

"There is that." Her father swallowed a scalding mouthful. "Damn Tom Morley for leaving. He wasn't particularly skilled at domestic management, but he was better than nothing."

Without much hope, she asked, "Did you interview that young man Mr. Morley suggested as a replacement?"

Her father made a disgusted gesture. "He was an ignorant puppy. Quite unsuitable."

Rebecca sighed. Advertisements for a new secretary would have to be run in the newspapers. Because her father had no patience for interviewing, she would be the one to weed through the hordes of applicants. She hoped someone acceptable appeared quickly. "Two of the registry offices promised to send over cooks today. With luck, one of them will do."

He put two slices of ham on his plate. "Make sure you don't hire another temperamental artist."

"I'll do my best," she said dryly. "No household can survive more than one temperamental artist."

Her father gave the sudden smile that made even his enemies forgive his high-handedness. "Quite right—and I'm it." He paused to look over her shoulder. "What are you working on?"

She tilted the sketchbook toward him. "I'm considering the Lady of the Lake. What do you think of this composition?"

Her father studied it. "Interesting how you've made her half nymph and half warrior. I like the way her hair is drifting in the water as she raises Excalibur."

High praise from Sir Anthony Seaton, who didn't believe in tact when it came to art. Rebecca got to her feet.

She hoped her father found a secretary soon so she would be able to begin the new painting.

Rebecca had intended to spend only a few minutes sketching studies for the Lady of the Lake, but the next time she glanced up, it was early afternoon and she still hadn't written the advertisement for a new secretary. By now, it was too late to make the following day's newspapers. Drat. Worse, she was not satisfied with the Lady of the Lake.

She stood and stretched her cramped muscles, then wandered across the slant-ceilinged room with her sketchbook. Her studio took up half of the attic, and was her sanctuary. No one came in without her permission, not even her father.

She perched on the window seat and glanced outside. The house stood on a corner, which gave her a good view of traffic on both streets. Below her on Hill Street, she recognized two neighborhood servants pausing in their errands to flirt. The pert maid made a slight, preening gesture as her gaze slanted up at the handsome young footman.

Rebecca flipped to a fresh page of her sketchbook and quickly recorded the arch of the girl's neck and the teasing angle of her eyes. Someday she wanted to do a series on lovers. Maybe she would learn something about love in the process.

When she glanced up again, she saw a costermonger pushing his battered wheelbarrow around the corner into Waverton Street. The weathered old man was a regular in the area. Her father had several times lured the fellow away from his barrow to pose for minor characters in large-scale paintings. The costermonger was delighted to be made "forever famous."

She was about to move away from the window when a man turned the corner from Waverton. He caught her attention because of the way he moved. Erect, confident, almost arrogant. Though he wore the garb of a gentleman, his broad, muscular build was that of a laborer. An interesting contradiction.

The fellow hesitated on the corner and glanced down Hill Street. She caught her breath when he turned his head and she saw his face. He wasn't handsome—quite the contrary. His features were harsh, almost brutal, and a thin scar curved across his cheek and into his dark hair. Yet at the same time, he gave an impression of feral intelligence. A pirate in Mayfair. She could not take her eyes off him.

The spell broke when he lowered his head and began walking again. She dropped back onto the window seat and began to draw, her pencil racing to record the man while he was vivid in her mind. A few quick lines caught his physical features, but the expression eluded her. She tried again, then again, but couldn't capture that air of lethal unpredictability.

She raised her hand and looked out the window. Might the man be persuaded to pose for her? But of course he had long since gone. She sighed. Once, she would have chased him down the street to get a better view of that face. Perhaps someday that creative passion would return. She certainly hoped so.

~

Kenneth paused across the street from Seaton House. Being a society portrait painter obviously paid well. The wide

Mayfair residence, so convenient for fashionable clients, must have cost Sir Anthony a fortune.

He wondered what he would find inside. Though Lord Bowden had called him a spy, the chief skills of a reconnaissance officer were riding and the ability to make maps and sketches of French positions. He had never had to infiltrate the enemy as he was doing here.

Mouth tight, he crossed the street to the house. He didn't like the prospect of what he must do, but for the sake of Beth and Sutterton, he could lie and betray. He just hoped to God that Seaton's guilt or innocence could be established quickly.

It took so long for Kenneth's knock to be answered that he began to wonder if Seaton had left London and forgotten to take the knocker down. He knocked again, harder. After another two minutes, the door was opened by a young maid.

"Yes, sir?" she said, panting as if she had run from the farthest corner of the house.

"I'm Captain Wilding," Kenneth said in his best commanding voice. "I wish to see Sir Anthony."

Responding to his authority, the girl bobbed a curtsy. "This way, sir." She led him upstairs to a salon at the back of the house and announced, "Captain Wilding to see you, Sir Anthony." Then she scampered away.

Kenneth walked through the doorway and was assaulted by the pungent, mingled scents of linseed oil and turpentine. Though comfortable chairs and sofas furnished the nearer half of the room, the true function was not salon but studio. Tall windows on two walls admitted great swaths of light. The other walls were covered with a jumble of paintings in all sizes and shapes, casually hung as if to keep them out of the way.

He would like to have studied the paintings in more detail, but business came first. At the opposite end of the room, a scantily draped lady reclined on a velvet sofa. Her bored expression brightened when Kenneth entered.

His gaze passed over the model to focus on his quarry. Impeccably dressed in a gentleman's morning attire, Sir Anthony Seaton stood at an easel in the center of the studio with a palette in one hand and a long brush in the other. His wiry build and coloring were like those of his older brother, but he was a far more vivid, compelling figure.

Ignoring the newcomer, Seaton continued to make delicate brush strokes on his canvas. Kenneth quietly cleared his throat. Without looking up, Sir Anthony said irritably, "Who the devil are you, and what are you doing in my studio?"

"My name is Kenneth Wilding. A friend of yours sent me because he said you're in dire need of a new secretary."

The artist glanced up with amusement in his eyes. "Who had the infernal cheek to do that? Frazier? Turner? Hampton?"

"The gentleman preferred to remain anonymous."

"Probably Frazier." Sir Anthony cast an assessing glance over his visitor. "What are your qualifications, Mr. Wilding?"

"I think he looks *very* well qualified," the model purred, her gaze fastening on Kenneth's groin.

"He's not applying for that sort of position, Lavinia," the artist said dryly. "The requirements for a secretary are organization and the ability to write a good, clear hand."

Having decided not to use his title but be otherwise as honest as possible, Kenneth replied, "Until a fortnight ago, I was a captain in the Rifle Brigade. That gave me experience in command and organization. I've also been aide-de-camp to a general and can write a fair hand."

"You begin to interest me, Captain Wilding." Sir Anthony set his palette and brush on the small table to his left. "Lavinia, go downstairs and have a cup of tea while I talk to this fellow."

The model rose and languidly donned a silk robe. Then she strolled for the door, passing so close to Kenneth that her trailing draperies touched his leg. The carefully arranged robe did little to conceal her lush breasts. She gave him an enticing smile, then swayed from the room. His bemused glance went after her. Working for an artist might have unexpected benefits.

When the door closed behind the model, Seaton asked, "Why would an army officer wish to become a secretary?"

"Because I need work," Kenneth said tersely. "Now that the wars are over, the army needs fewer officers."

Sir Anthony's expression kindled. "It's a disgrace the way the nation is treating the soldiers who saved civilization from the Corsican monster." He hesitated and his doubtful gaze went over his visitor's broad frame again. "However, I really can't hire a secretary who doesn't have some knowledge of art."

Kenneth was used to people assuming he was ignorant of anything more complex than laying bricks. "I've always been interested in art, and during my years on the Continent I was fortunate enough to see many great works. The churches of the Low Countries are a feast for the eyes. I was also in Paris during the occupation. The Louvre contained perhaps the finest collection in the world until the stolen masterpieces were sent back to the original owners."

"That must have been a sight to behold." The painter

shook his head. "Still, a man can look at the sea without learning to swim. You must demonstrate your knowledge. Come." He strode across the room to a pair of double doors and threw them open to reveal a formal drawing room.

Kenneth followed Seaton into the room, then stopped, frozen in his tracks. Directly in front of him was the huge canvas of Sir Anthony's most famous painting.

"Do you recognize that, Captain Wilding?" Seaton asked.

Kenneth swallowed back the dryness in his throat. "Everyone in Britain has probably seen a print of *Horatius at the Bridge.* But no black and white copy could ever do full justice to this. It's magnificent." His awed gaze went over the canvas. The left side was dominated by the figure of Horatius. Behind him was the bridge over the Tiber. At the far end, the tiny figures of two fellow Romans worked frantically to cut the supports so that the enemy could not cross. Sweeping toward the bridge was a troop of savage warriors, with only Horatius to block their path.

"Tell me about the picture," Sir Anthony ordered.

Uncertain what the artist wanted to hear, Kenneth said tentatively, "Technically it's brilliant—your mastery of line is equal to that of Jacques-Louis David."

Seaton sniffed. "Not equal. Superior. David is nothing but an overrated French revolutionary scribbler."

No one would ever accuse Seaton of false modesty. Kenneth continued, "The power of the painting comes from the composition. There's great tension in the angle of Horatius's raised sword. That diagonal dominates the picture and brings it to life."

Encouraged by the artist's nod, Kenneth went on, "I once saw another treatment of this subject that showed Horatius as a seasoned warrior, but the fact that you made him a boy lends great poignancy to the picture. There is fear in him, for he's never seen battle. In his eyes is a terrible regret that he might lose his life before he has had a chance to really experience it. Yet it's clear in every line of his body that he will stand fast no matter what the cost."

"Very good, Captain." Sir Anthony's gaze went from the painting to Kenneth. "What is the picture's underlying meaning?"

If this was a test, it wasn't a difficult one. "You were using the historical tale of Horatius as a parallel with Britain standing alone against the French. A more obvious painter might have used Napoleon's face on the leader of the charging enemies, but you gave only a hint of Bonaparte—just enough to make a viewer think of the French without knowing why."

"They say more prints of this painting have been sold than any other British picture in history." Sir Anthony stared broodingly at his work. "Historical paintings are the finest flower of art. They are uplifting. Educational. An inspiration to the viewer. I wish to God I could spend all my time on such pictures, but if I did, I would starve."

The artist spun on his heel and stalked back into his studio. "All the average Englishman wants is portraits and landscapes. It's a disgrace."

He led the way to an easel in the corner of the room and flipped back the covering cloth to reveal an almost completed family portrait of a handsome, hawk-faced man and his lovely golden-haired wife. Between them stood a small boy, one hand clutching his mother's hand and the other curled into the fur of a spaniel. "What do you think of this, Captain Wilding? I'm the finest painter England has ever produced, yet in order to keep myself and my daughter from poverty, I must prostitute my talent on rubbishy pictures of dukes and duchesses."

In spite of his words, it was obvious that Seaton expected praise for his work. Taking a calculated risk, Kenneth said, "I think you are a fraud, Sir Anthony."

Seaton's jaw dropped. "How dare you, sir!"

"Oh?" Kenneth indicated the portrait. "You call this rubbish, yet look at the quality. It isn't only that the drawing and colors are superb—one can feel the tenderness between the people, the protectiveness of the man for his wife and son. No one could paint with such sensitivity and power if he truly despised what he was doing. I think you have a secret fondness for portrait work, but you don't wish to admit it because it's an article of faith among your fellow artists that only historical paintings are worthy."

Sir Anthony looked as if he had been hit by a club. Then he gave a slow, crooked smile. "Caught out, by God. Even my daughter has not guessed that, I think. You have passed the test, Captain—almost too well."

Kenneth knew he had made an impression, and his flattering remarks were all the more powerful for coming from an unexpected direction. But in the pleasure of talking art, he was in danger of going too far. He blanked his expression and said, "Forgive my insolence, Sir Anthony. I should not have spoken as I did."

The painter gave him a keen glance. "Don't overdo the humility, Captain. It's not convincing."

Clearly the observational powers that made Seaton such a fine portrait artist made him difficult to deceive. Making a mental note to watch his tongue, Kenneth replied, "I'll admit I'm not good at humility, sir, but I usually try to avoid rudeness."

"Good. I'm the only one in this house who is allowed to

be rude." Seaton covered the portrait again. "I dislike domestic chaos—it interferes with my work. Since I've never found a butler or housekeeper capable of managing my household, my secretary must do that as well as the usual business matters. Not to mention exercising my horse when I'm too busy to ride. For all these reasons, you must live in. The salary is two hundred pounds a year. When can you begin?"

Glad that the matter had been settled without references or other delays, Kenneth said, "As soon as I've collected my belongings from the inn where I spent last night."

"Send a footman for your bags." Sir Anthony yanked at one of the two heavy bellpulls. "My daughter, Rebecca, will instruct you in your duties. When possible, ask questions of her rather than me. However, she dislikes interruptions almost as much as I do, so the sooner you master the work, the better. Every morning, I will spend an hour with you going over business and dictating letters. After that, I do not wish to think again of business until the next day. Is that clear?"

"Blindingly so," Kenneth said, unable to keep a trace of irony from his tone.

The other man gave him a gimlet stare. "I am in a mood to tolerate sarcasm today. That will not always be the case."

"I'm sure that my desire to be sarcastic will moderate after I become accustomed to your household," Kenneth said blandly.

"You are unlike any of my previous secretaries, Captain," Sir Anthony said with a faint smile. "I foresee an interesting relationship. But not, I think, a smooth one."

The door to the hall opened and a small female swept in. She was dressed casually, with a mass of auburn hair knotted untidily at her nape and a smudge of soot accenting a high cheekbone, but her manner was that of the daughter of the house. "You rang for me, Father?"

"Yes, my dear. Meet my new secretary, Captain Wilding."

Rebecca Seaton turned to Kenneth and a skeptical gaze examined him from head to foot. He felt as if he had been skewered. Though not a conventional beauty, the "ruined spinster" had shrewd hazel eyes and a vivid individuality that was far more memorable.

She was going to be trouble. Serious trouble.

CHAPTER 4

Good heavens, it was the pirate! Rebecca stared at the broad figure beside her father. Every impression she had received when looking down at him in the street was magnified close up. He looked powerful and dangerous, a wolf among the Mayfair lambs. "This man, a secretary? Surely you're joking."

Her father's brows arched. "I had thought you would be pleased that the position has been filled."

Realizing how rude she had sounded, Rebecca said, "Excuse me, Captain... Wilder, was it? It's simply that you don't look like any secretary I've ever seen."

"Wilding, Miss Seaton. At your service." He bowed courteously. "I fear I can do nothing about the fact that I look more like a pugilist than a gentleman."

His voice was distractingly deep, but his accent was well-bred. So why did she distrust him? Perhaps it was the coolness of his ice-gray eyes. Or perhaps it was because a man of action seemed so out of place in a house devoted to art and ideas. His mere presence was disruptive. She gave her father a troubled glance.

"Don't worry, Captain Wilding is quite qualified. He'll start right away. Show him the house and explain his domestic duties. Captain, meet me in the office at four o'clock and I will explain my business papers." Sir Anthony turned back to his easel. "Send Lavinia up so I can resume work."

If the pirate weren't present, Rebecca would have argued with her father, but apparently it was too late to prevent the hiring. Damn Sir Anthony's impulsiveness. She guessed that his patriotic desire to employ a veteran of the wars had overcome his sense. With ill grace, she said, "Very well. Come with me, Captain Wilding. I'll show you your room first."

He silently followed her from the studio. As she led the way upstairs, she said, "You were in the army, Captain?"

"Yes, the Rifle Brigade."

She glanced back over her shoulder. "Did my father explain that a large portion of your work will be domestic? Very different from the military. You may not find it to your taste."

"Not so different. Both jobs involve commanding men."

"Commanding women may prove more difficult," she said dryly.

"I'll manage."

He did look like a man who had had his share of experience with women. The knowledge did not raise her opinion of him. She thought wistfully of her father's previous secretaries. All had been pleasant young men of good family. Civilized. Easy to have around the house. Not a pirate in the lot.

The captain said, "While I don't mind acting as a general factotum, I'm curious about why I'm needed for such work when you are so obviously competent."

"I don't choose to spend my time as a housekeeper," she said in a clipped voice.

Responding to her tone rather than her words, he remarked, "You don't like me very much, do you, Miss Seaton?"

Good God, had the man no discretion? Well, if he preferred bluntness, she would oblige. She halted on the landing and turned to face him. He stopped a step below her, putting their eyes almost level. For some reason, that made her even more aware of his physical power. She repressed the urge to back away. "We've only just met, so how can I either like or dislike you?"

"Since when is it necessary to know someone to dislike him? It's clear that you wish your father hadn't engaged me."

"You look more like a marauder than a secretary," she said tartly. "And knowing my father, he didn't bother to ask for references. How did you learn about the position?"

His gaze became opaque. "A friend of your father's told me."

"Who?"

"The gentleman preferred to remain anonymous."

It was undeniably the sort of thing one of Sir Anthony's eccentric friends might do. "Do you have any letters of reference?" she asked. "Anything to suggest that you're not a fraud or a thief?"

There was a faint tightening at the corner of his eyes. After a moment, he said, "No, though if you don't mind waiting, I suppose I could get one from the Duke of Wellington. He's known me for years, and I think he considers me respectable."

The matter-of-fact answer was quite convincing. Tacitly

conceding the point, she said, "God forbid we should bother the duke over something so trivial."

It was hard to concentrate this close to his face, which was even more fascinating than it had seemed at a distance. Piercing, charcoal-edged eyes that had seen sights she couldn't imagine. Skin tanned by a harsher sun than that of England. Lines of sternness and possibly humor. Once there must have been youthful softness over the hard planes of bone, but that had long since been scourged away. He made her think of a volcano: calm on the surface, but with unknowable depths of hidden fire.

The captain said, "Am I missing any of the usual features?"

"Faces interest me, especially those that have been well lived in." Her gaze went to the scar that curved from his cheek into the thick, dark hair at his temple. There was no puckering, only a pale, slightly raised line. She wanted to touch it, to find if it felt as smooth as it looked. Restraining herself, she asked, "Was that scar made by a saber?"

It was not a tactful question, but he took it in stride, saying, "Yes, at Waterloo."

So he had fought in that ghastly carnage. She had a vague recollection that the Rifle Brigade had been in the thick of the battle. "You were lucky not to lose your eye."

"Very true," he agreed. "Since I wasn't handsome to begin with, I lost nothing of value."

She wondered if he was trying to disconcert her. That was not easily done to a woman who had grown up in an artist's unconventional household. "Quite the contrary," she said thoughtfully. "The scar adds interest and emphasis to your face, like a highlight on a painting. Quite artistic, really. The Frenchman did a good job of cutting."

She turned and resumed her ascent of the stairs. At the top, she led the way along the corridor. "The family bedrooms are on this floor. My father's is behind us, mine is to the left, and yours is here, overlooking the garden." His room shared a wall with her own chamber. That seemed far too close.

She swung the door to his room open, then winced when she saw its state. "Sorry. This should have been cleaned after Tom Morley left." She should have known that one of the housemaids never did a lick of work if she could avoid it. The other, Betsy, was willing, but couldn't do everything. Rebecca had known, actually, but hadn't cared. She had an almost infinite capacity to overlook subjects that didn't interest her.

Unperturbed, Wilding said, "Introduce me to the staff, and I'll arrange for the work to be done."

"I'll take you down to the servants' hall in a few minutes." She drew a finger along the edge of the wainscoting and frowned at the thick dust that accumulated on the tip. The housekeeping really was disgraceful. "I look forward to seeing you turn them into models of hard work and efficiency."

"If any of your present servants are irredeemable, I presume I have the right to discharge them and hire new ones."

"Of course." Rebecca turned and headed to the stairs. "No need for you to see the attics. The servants' quarters are there, and my private workroom. If you wish to speak with me, pull on one of the red bell cords. They ring into my workroom."

"So that is how your father summoned you," he murmured as he followed her. "Will you respond to me as quickly?"

For some reason, her face heated. "No," she said

brusquely, "so I hope you're resourceful at solving problems on your own."

Gloomily she led the way downstairs. The captain was going to be every bit as disruptive as she had feared. She hoped he would soon decide that the life of a secretary was not for him.

Kenneth found it hard to keep his attention on the house tour and Rebecca Seaton's crisp description of his duties. The lady was quite a distraction in herself, with her tart tongue and her penetrating gaze. Equally distracting was the art that was everywhere—paintings, watercolors, etchings, even sculpture.

The visual richness left him as dazed as a daylong French cannonade. Works by Sir Anthony were intermixed with paintings by other masters. No wonder Rebecca had wanted proof that he wasn't a thief. Luckily, she seemed to have accepted his honesty, even if she liked nothing else about him.

The next stop was on the first floor. She opened the door of a small chamber at the rear of the house. "This is my father's office, though you'll spend more time here than he does. The desk in the corner is yours. As you can see, business has accumulated since Tom Morley left."

An understatement; the secretary's desk was completely covered with untidy piles of paper. "I see why your father was eager to hire the first available candidate."

"Actually, Papa turned down the replacement Tom suggested. Said he was an ignorant young puppy."

"I'm glad to know that Sir Anthony rates me more highly than that," Kenneth said gravely.

She gave him a sharp glance. Mentally he kicked himself. His job was to be an efficient, unobtrusive secretary. If he didn't learn to hold his tongue, he'd end up on the street and Sutterton would be lost.

She continued, "Father's solicitor handles major financial affairs, but you will be responsible for correspondence and the household accounts. Ledgers and writing supplies are kept in this cabinet." She took a key from the secretarial desk and opened the cabinet. Kenneth glanced at a ledger. It was similar to an army captain's company accounts. He'd manage well enough.

Rebecca handed him the key and turned to go. He locked the cabinet and started to follow, then stopped when he saw the portrait above Sir Anthony's desk. A striking woman of mature years was posed in front of a misty landscape, her gaze mischievous and her red hair tumbling over her shoulders.

He glanced at his guide, then back to the painting. The woman looked like a wanton, sensual Rebecca Seaton. It had to be the late Lady Seaton, and Kenneth was willing to swear that Sir Anthony had painted the picture with love. Could the caring visible in every stroke really have turned to murderous hatred?

Rebecca looked back to see why he wasn't following. Thinking it was time to start gathering information, he said quietly, "Surely this must be your mother."

Her fingers whitened on the doorknob as she nodded. "It was done at Ravensbeck, our house in the Lake District."

Even more quietly, he said, "I've heard no mention of Lady Seaton. I gather she is dead."

Rebecca looked away and said tightly, "Last August."

"I'm sorry." He studied the painting. "What happened—some sudden disease? She seems so vital. So alive."

"It was an accident," Rebecca said harshly. "A horrible, stupid accident." She pivoted and went out the door. "I'll take you down to meet the servants now."

He followed, wondering if her response was straightforward grief, or if she had secret doubts about the circumstances of the death. If her father had really murdered her mother, it would be a horror almost beyond imagining.

He took a last glance at the portrait. Seeing it made him recognize the latent sensuality in Rebecca Seaton. Unlike her mother, she rigidly suppressed that aspect of her nature. He wondered what she would look like with her glossy auburn hair cascading lushly around her piquant face and slim body....

Damnation! He yanked the door closed behind him. He could not afford an attraction to the prickly daughter of the man he had come to destroy. Luckily, she wasn't the flirtatious sort. Quite the contrary. Nonetheless, there was something very appealing about her.

On the way to the back stairs that led to the kitchen and servants' hall, they passed through the main dining room. Rebecca said with delicate sarcasm, "Since secretaries are gentlemen, naturally you will share meals with my father and myself."

It was blazingly clear that the lady thought Kenneth fit only for mucking out stables. What had Lord Bowden said about her elopement? The fellow had been a self-proclaimed poet. Presumably that meant Miss Seaton preferred men who were weedy and wordy—if indeed the experience hadn't put her off men entirely, which seemed quite possible from her behavior.

The painting above the sideboard interrupted his

musings and brought him to an abrupt halt. Catching Rebecca's impatient glance, he said apologetically, "I'm sorry. It's hard not to become diverted. I feel as I did the first time I went to the Louvre. How can anyone eat when there is this to look at?"

Apparently the idea that he might appreciate art surprised her, but her tone was milder when she said, "For the first week after the picture was hung, I didn't notice a single bite I ate. It's called *Charge of the Union Brigade* and it's part of a four-painting Waterloo series Father has been working on for the last year and a half. He hopes to exhibit all four pictures at the Royal Academy this year."

The enormous canvas depicted half a dozen cavalry horses and riders racing directly toward the viewer. The lethal hooves and glittering sabers seemed ready to explode from the canvas. Kenneth suppressed a shiver. "Magnificent. Though it's not realistic, it certainly brings back memories of having the French cavalry thundering down on me."

She frowned. "What do you mean, not realistic? Father arranged for troopers of the Household Cavalry to charge right at him again and again so he could get accurate sketches. A miracle he wasn't crushed beneath their hooves."

"He's jammed the horses together until they're virtually touching, which would be impossible in battle," Kenneth explained. "But the painting would have less power if the horses were spread out more naturally. This captures the essence of what it's like to be attacked by cavalry."

"Father always says that in painting, the illusion of reality is more important than technical accuracy." She cocked her head thoughtfully, then gestured for him to follow her into the adjoining breakfast parlor. "Here's a different kind of battle picture. Boadicea, the warrior queen, just before her final battle with the Romans. What do you think?"

Kenneth studied the painting, which depicted a barbaric, auburn-haired woman with a spear in one hand and a raised sword in the other. Her back was arched and the wind whipped her white draperies and wolfskin cloak about her as she commanded her troops to follow her to death. She reminded him of a fierce, uncompromising Rebecca. It must be the red hair. "Though she's not a convincing warrior, as a symbol of courage and the passion for freedom she's splendid."

"Why isn't she convincing?"

"Too slender. It takes muscle to wield such weapons. And too unscarred. Anyone who had been fighting the Romans regularly would probably have acquired some marks of battle."

Rebecca's gaze went from his marred face to his hands and wrists, where the faint scars of half a dozen minor wounds were visible. "I see what you mean. At least you'll be useful as a battle consultant."

He supposed he should take her left-handed compliment as a step in the right direction. His gaze went back to the picture. Thinking out loud, he said, "It's very fine, but the style is rather different from the other examples of Sir Anthony's painting I've seen. Was this an experimental work? The dramatic composition and richness of color are characteristic, but the lines are softer, with a quality that is almost poetic."

Rebecca didn't answer, merely watched him from narrowed eyes. Perhaps this was another test. He glanced at the corner of the picture, where Sir Anthony marked all of his work with a small AS. This time, however, the initials looked like RS. He stared. "Good God, did you paint this?"

"Why the shock?" she said waspishly. "Are you one of those men who think women can't paint?"

Stunned, he looked at the picture with new eyes. "Not at all. It's only that I had no idea you are also an artist."

And what an artist! Technically she was very nearly her father's equal, with a distinctive style that was simultaneously akin and different. He supposed he shouldn't be surprised; historically, female artists were usually daughters or wives of male painters. It was the only way a woman would have the chance to learn the necessary skills. "No wonder you don't want to spend your time on housekeeping. That would be a criminal waste of your talent."

For a moment Rebecca looked almost bashful at the praise, but her voice had its usual bite when she said, "I couldn't agree more. That's why it's essential to have someone capable to run the household." Her expression made it clear that she doubted he was up to the job.

It was time to prove his competence. "Before I meet the staff, I need to know more. How many servants do you have?"

She thought a moment. "There are currently four female and three male servants."

"Have they been with you for a long time?"

"Only the coachman, Phelps. The rest have been here only a few months."

A pity. Servants could have been a prime source of information. Kenneth would have to cultivate the coachman. "Why so many new people? And why hasn't it been possible to keep a capable housekeeper?"

"My mother preferred to manage the household herself. Since her death, everything has been chaotic. My father has not... been himself. I tried two different housekeepers, but neither understood the requirements of running an artist's house. Father would become provoked and discharge servants who irritated him. The ones he didn't fire soon left for more orderly establishments. Then Tom Morley began overseeing the servants. That worked fairly well, though the dusting suffered."

"Are there any positions currently vacant?"

"We're in dire need of a cook and a butler." A wicked gleam showed in her eyes. "Two applicants for cook should be here soon. You may do the interviewing and selection."

He nodded as if that were the most natural thing in the world. But as he followed her downstairs, he wondered wryly what the men in his regiment would think if they could see him now.

CHAPTER 5

The servants were relaxing over tea and buttered bread in their sitting room off the kitchen when Rebecca arrived with Captain Wilding. The buzz of conversation died down and six pairs of eyes swiveled toward the new arrivals. Everyone but Phelps, the groom, was present.

"This is Sir Anthony's new secretary, Captain Wilding," Rebecca said tersely. "You will be taking your orders from him." She made an ironic gesture that transferred all responsibility to the captain.

As he surveyed the group, the maid who flirted with everyone glanced slyly at her favorite footman and gave a knowing giggle. Wilding's calm gaze went to her face. Her expression instantly sobered. Not a word was spoken. Then the smaller maid, the hardworking one, got to her feet. One by one, the other servants followed her lead. Before Rebecca's bemused eyes, the casual group began to resemble a squad of well-disciplined soldiers.

Captain Wilding said in a cool voice, "Standards have been lax. That will change. Anyone who considers the work too burdensome is welcome to seek employment elsewhere.

Problems and complaints are to be brought to me. Under no circumstances are Sir Anthony and Miss Seaton to be disturbed unnecessarily. Is that clear?"

It was clear. The captain went around the room and learned the names and duties of everyone before he dismissed the group. The servants filed out, looking not precisely intimidated, but certainly impressed. Rebecca had to admit that she was impressed, too.

The captain had interviewed the two candidates for cook with equal efficiency. The first applicant was a very grand Frenchman. After examining the letters of recommendation, Wilding asked the Frenchman to prepare something for himself and Miss Seaton. Offended at the idea of having to prove himself in such a lowly manner, the applicant had stalked out.

The next candidate was also French, but female, plump and placid. Her references were not quite as glowing as those of her predecessor. However, when asked to prove her skill, she had merely raised her brows for a moment, then set to work. Twenty minutes later, she sent her judges a tantalizing dessert omelette and a pot of steaming coffee.

Rebecca's doubts about the hiring process vanished with her first bite. "Lovely." She took another bite. "Clever of her to use brandied cherries for a quick sauce. Will you hire her?"

Captain Wilding, who sat on the opposite side of the breakfast room table, swallowed a substantial bite of omelette. "Yes. Madame Brunei passed all three tests very well."

Rebecca cut another bite. "What three tests?"

"First and most important was attitude. She was willing to do what was necessary." The captain drank some of the excellent coffee. "Secondly, she was ingenious. In a matter of minutes, she determined what she could make from available ingredients that would be swift and impressive. Lastly, her results were delicious."

Rebecca's fork paused in midair. "Shouldn't her ability to cook come first?"

"All the skill in the world is wasted if someone is too temperamental to do the job. A cooperative nature is doubly important in a household where there have been problems."

Thoughtfully Rebecca finished her omelette. The new secretary had a better understanding of human nature than his stevedore's appearance implied. He also seemed fond of art. Perhaps Sir Anthony hadn't chosen so badly after all. She got to her feet. "You're off to a good start, Captain. I will see you at dinner."

His dark brows rose. "So I've passed *your* tests?"

Uncomfortably aware of how skeptical she had been, she said, "You were hired by my father. It is not my place to test you."

"You are too modest, Miss Seaton," he said with a hint of irony. "I'm sure your father would not retain a secretary whom you found disagreeable."

"True. But I would not quickly complain of a man who pleases my father." She found herself staring at him again. What really went on behind those craggy features? He had been a model of courtesy, but she felt sure that blandness was not his real nature. What had made him so different from the other men she knew? She would never find out as long as he felt constrained to watch every word for fear he would be discharged.

On impulse, she said, "No one should have to be always circumspect, so I give you leave to speak freely around me.

I won't use your words to persuade my father to get rid of you."

His brows rose. "You're giving me carte blanche to be a crude, tactless soldier?"

"Exactly."

A mischievous light glinted in his clear gray eyes. "You wouldn't object even if I expressed a desire to kiss you?"

She stared at him, hot color rising in her face. "I beg your pardon?"

"Excuse me, Miss Seaton. I didn't meant that I actually do want to kiss you," he said smoothly. "I was merely trying to establish the boundaries of permissible remarks."

"You have just exceeded them. Don't do it again." She spun on her heel and stalked out of the breakfast parlor. He certainly wasn't bland. But for the life of her, she wasn't sure what bothered her most: his outrageous comment about kissing her—or his claim that he had no desire to do any such thing.

~

With half an hour to spare before meeting with Sir Anthony, Kenneth went to his room. The maids had cleaned the place until it sparkled, and the footman had retrieved his baggage from the inn where he had spent the previous night. He; guessed that most of the servants would prove to be satisfactory; they merely needed a firm hand.

It took only a few minutes to unpack his belongings. For some obscure reason, he had brought a portfolio of his drawings. He tucked it in the back of the wardrobe, safe from the eyes of servants. Then he drifted across the room, feeling as tired as if he had marched thirty miles. Deceit took energy.

He halted at the window and looked out at the small garden. Beyond were the houses and rooftops of Mayfair, the most fashionable neighborhood in the city that was the heartbeat of Britain. Though he had gone to school at Harrow, only a dozen miles away, he had never spent more than a few days at a time in London proper. At the age when he might have started to know the city's delights, he had left the country.

He wondered what this visit would bring. Somewhere nearby, Hermione, the widowed Lady Kimball, was living in comfort on the money plundered from her late husband. Kenneth hoped to God that their paths would not cross. Even after fifteen years, he would have trouble being civil to his stepmother.

Lord Bowden was also living nearby, and he wanted regular reports from his investigator. With a sigh, Kenneth settled down in the armchair to define his first impressions of Sir Anthony's household. This investigation was going to be an even uglier business than he had guessed. Though Sir Anthony might be volatile and sometimes arrogant, he was not unlikable. It was going be difficult to work daily with the man while trying to find evidence to destroy his life.

He reminded himself that if Seaton had murdered his wife, he deserved whatever happened to him. But was Sir Anthony capable of murder? Perhaps. He was an intense, forceful man, used to getting his own way. In a moment of rage, he might turn violent. A single angry shove when he and his wife were walking near a cliff could have had lethal consequences. That would send him to prison even if murder had not been his intent.

But how could such a crime be proved without witnesses? Kenneth must learn exactly what had been going on in the Seaton household at the time of Helen's death—not only the events, but the emotions.

He thought back to Rebecca Seaton's behavior when she had said her mother had died in a "horrible, stupid accident." Her reaction had seemed like more than simple sorrow. It implied that Bowden's suspicions might be justified. He wondered what she had meant when she said her father had not "been himself" since the death. Grief—or guilt?

Thinking of Rebecca Seaton made Kenneth wince. He never should have made that idiotic remark about kissing her. She had stalked away like an angry cat. But damn the woman, something about her attracted him intensely. It certainly wasn't love at first sight; he wasn't sure he even liked her. Nonetheless, her sharp edges and individuality were intriguing, which was why he'd spoken so imprudently. He had been away from civilized society too long. He must relearn manners.

Even though a couple of hours in the Seaton household had underlined the fact that his artistic skills were strictly amateur, he lifted a pencil and began idly sketching on a tablet. He'd always found drawing relaxing. Often it was useful for clarifying his thoughts and feelings.

He did a thumbnail sketch of Sir Anthony's voluptuous Lavinia. She would make a good model for a decadent Venus. With two swift strokes, he crossed her out. Odd that even though he had always loved beauty, he had never fallen in love with a beautiful woman. Catherine Melbourne, an army wife who had followed the drum through Spain and Belgium, was one of the most stunning women on God's earth, and as loving and good as she was beautiful. He would have laid down his life for her and her young daughter, yet his feelings had always been those of friendship, even after she was widowed. It was Maria, a fierce Spanish guerrilla fighter, whom he had loved.

Thinking of Maria made him recognize that there were similarities between her and Rebecca. Neither woman was conventionally beautiful, but each was striking in an uncommon way. Each had blazed with single-minded passion. For Maria, the cause had been Spain. Rebecca Seaton's passion, he guessed, was art. Talent alone could not account for the quality of her painting; she must also be dedicated to the point of obsession.

It was that single-minded fierceness that aroused him. Maria had lived and died for Spain, but when she had the time and inclination, she had made love like a wildcat. Mating had been tempestuous and satisfying. He had been unable to imagine a normal, mundane life with her, though that hadn't kept him from asking her to marry him.

If she had accepted, would it have made a difference? Might she still be alive today?

For an instant, the image of how he had last seen Maria rose in his mind. He shoved it away, his stomach knotting. The past could not be changed. He must think of the present, of Sutterton and Beth and their future.

His investigation would not be easy. The coachman might be helpful, and he would try to locate the previous secretary, Tom Morley. But he was not optimistic. His intelligence work in Spain had taught him that the overall picture was usually painstakingly constructed from numerous tiny pieces contributed by many informants. Here he would have few sources.

He recognized uneasily that Rebecca was probably the best source of information about her mother's death. She would know things no servant could know. He was going to have to cultivate her friendship—and then betray it.

He swore to himself as he prepared to go down to Sir Anthony's office. War was cleaner and more honorable than what he was doing here.

"Send polite dunning letters to everyone in this pile." Sir Anthony tapped a stack of letters. "Most of 'em are aristocrats. Cits are much better at paying their bills." He dug into the mess of the secretary's desk and pulled out a leather-bound notebook. "Another of your tasks is to maintain my daybooks. I jot down what I want recorded on scraps of paper." He opened the volume, revealing a dozen scribbled sheets tucked inside the front cover. "These need to be transcribed."

Kenneth took the daybook and scanned a page. Listed in Tom Morley's neat hand were notations such as "5th February, 10:00-11:00, Duke of Candover & family, first sketches. Hazy sunshine." Two more sittings were listed on the same day, with other entries for visits from friends and a meeting of the Council of the Royal Academy. He felt a stir of excitement; the daybook from the summer of Lady Seaton's death would give invaluable information about Sir Anthony's activities.

Masking his reaction, he remarked, "You have a very full schedule."

"Too full. Last year I had three hundred and six sittings. Didn't leave me enough time for my historical paintings." Seaton sighed elaborately. "But it's hard to turn down a lady when she pleads for a portrait, saying that no one else can possibly paint her as well."

Kenneth was tempted to point out that Seaton had already admitted to enjoying portrait work, and that the income from it maintained this expensive household, but he restrained himself. "Is there anything else you wish to explain, sir?"

"That's enough for today." Sir Anthony got to his feet. "I'll save dictation of letters for tomorrow morning. You have enough to keep you busy."

An understatement; it would take Kenneth days to catch up on the accumulated work. He was about to ask what Sir Anthony wanted done first when footsteps sounded in the hall. After a perfunctory knock, the door opened to reveal three fashionably clad people. The taller of the two men, a handsome fellow about Seaton's age, said, "What, not at your easel, Anthony?"

"I'm training the new secretary who has providentially appeared." Seaton gestured toward Kenneth. "Captain Wilding was sent by a nameless friend who knew I was in dire need of a secretary. Are you the one I should thank, Malcolm?"

Malcolm gave Kenneth a sharp, curious glance. "Surely I wouldn't admit it if I wish for anonymity."

Sir Anthony gave an amused nod, as if the answer were confirmation. "Captain Wilding, these are some of my scapegrace friends, who like to use my studio as a salon."

"But only in the late afternoons," said the woman standing slightly behind Malcolm. To his surprise, it was the voluptuous Lavinia, now dressed in the height of flamboyant fashion.

"If a man can't be a tyrant under his own roof, where can he be?" Sir Anthony said before making the introductions.

Kenneth stood and murmured greetings to the visitors. The elegant Malcolm turned out to be Lord Frazier, a fairly well-known gentleman painter. The second man, a short, stocky fellow with an easy smile, was George Hampton, an engraver and owner of the best-known print shop in Britain. Lavinia was introduced as Lady Claxton. Kenneth spoke little but studied everyone closely. These people must have known Helen Seaton.

After several minutes of general talk, Malcolm Frazier said, "I was hoping to see how your new Waterloo picture is progressing. May we have a view?"

Sir Anthony shrugged. "I've had little time to work on it since your last visit, but you can see it if you wish." He offered his arm to Lavinia.

Before the group could leave, Rebecca Seaton appeared in the doorway, her hair even untidier than it had been earlier. She paused at the sight of the visitors. Lord Frazier drawled, "How is the best-looking artist in London?"

"I have no idea," she replied. "How *are* you feeling?"

He laughed, unaffected by her implication of vanity. "You're the only woman I know who refuses to accept compliments."

"If you didn't give them to so many, I might be more willing to keep one for myself," Rebecca said sweetly as she greeted Lavinia and George Hampton.

After the visitors left to see Sir Anthony's painting, Rebecca closed the door and said to Kenneth, "I see you've met your first members of Seaton's Salon."

His brows rose. "Sir Anthony said people use the house as a gathering place, but I thought he was joking."

"Father won't admit casual visitors early in the day, but in the late afternoon he rather enjoys having people drop in to see his work and chat with his sitters. Sometimes it's a nuisance." Her searching gaze went around the office. "Have you seen a cat?"

"A cat?"

"A small animal with four feet, whiskers, and a tail." She

peered behind her father's desk. "This room is one of my cat's preferred hiding places."

Kenneth thought back. Though most of his attention had been on Sir Anthony, he seemed to recall seeing a small shadow from the corner of his eye. He went to the stationery cabinet and peered beneath. A pair of large yellow eyes opened and regarded him unblinkingly. "I assume this is your feline friend."

Rebecca dropped to her knees beside Kenneth. "Come out, Ghostie. It's almost dinnertime."

The cat oozed from beneath the cabinet and stretched languorously. It was a lean, rangy gray tom with battle scars on its ears and an unnaturally shortened tail. Rebecca made cooing noises and scooped the cat onto her shoulder. Kenneth was interested to see that her usual tart expression had become doting. He asked, "Is the correct name Ghost or Ghostie?"

"He's the Gray Ghost." She stroked her palm down the cat's spine and was rewarded with a deep, rumbling purr. "He was a starving alley cat who used to beg at the kitchen door. I started feeding him, but it was months before he would let himself be touched. Now he's turned into a proper house puss."

Kenneth found her care for a wild, hungry creature unexpected but endearing. Wanting to take advantage of her relaxed mood to further their relationship, he scratched the Gray Ghost between the ears. "He's a fine fellow. Well behaved, too. He slept through the invasion of the fashionables."

"He's used to such onslaughts. There are dozens who call regularly, but the three who were just here are the most frequent visitors. Father and George and Malcolm have been friends since they were students at the academy school. George is my godfather. He does the engravings of Father's pictures."

"The prints are marvelous, and they've contributed greatly to your father's fame." Kenneth stroked the cat again, his fingertips almost touching Rebecca's cheek. He wondered if the delicate skin was as flawlessly smooth as it appeared. He withdrew his hand before he was tempted to find out. "I met Lavinia earlier and thought she was a professional model. It was a surprise to learn she is Lady Claxton."

Rebecca moved to a chair and settled down with the cat still draped over her shoulder. "Did you have any trouble recognizing her with her clothes on?"

He suppressed a smile. "I did have to look twice to be sure it was the same woman."

"Lavinia was a minor actress and artist's model who married an elderly baronet. Now she's a wealthy widow who delights in being outrageous. She isn't received in the best society, but she's very popular among the artistic set." Rebecca rubbed her cheek against the cat's soft fur. In a voice that was too casual, she added, "She is Father's current mistress, I believe."

Kenneth came instantly alert. Seeing his expression, Rebecca said coolly, "Have I shocked you, Captain?"

He collected himself. "Perhaps I've been out of England for too long. When I left, it would have been considered improper for a young lady to speak of illicit affairs."

She smiled with self-mockery. "But I am not young, nor am I a lady. I've been officially ruined for years. The art world is unconventional enough to accept me, if only because I'm Sir Anthony Seaton's daughter, but I would never be allowed into a respectable drawing room."

Knowing his response would have a critical effect on

how well she accepted him, he said, "Are you stronger or weaker for having been ruined?"

She looked startled by the question, then thoughtful. "Stronger, I suppose. I had not realized how much I valued my reputation until I lost it, but in some ways, I've found the situation rather liberating."

He nodded as he took his seat again. "It is not our triumphs that define us, but our failures."

Her stroking hand stilled on the cat's back as she studied his expression. "You have an interesting mind."

"I've been told that before," he said dryly. "It wasn't usually intended as a compliment."

She gave a smile that lit her face to vivid prettiness. "From me, it's a compliment, Captain." She rose, the cat twining around her neck like a scarf. "I'll see you at dinner. An unbreakable law of the house is that everyone dines together." Her gaze went to the portrait of Lady Seaton. "My mother knew that Father and I often become lost in our work, so she insisted that we behave as civilized people for one meal a day."

"You look very like her," he observed.

"Not really. We have the same coloring, but she was much taller, almost Father's height." Rebecca turned from the portrait, cradling the cat against her. "And of course Mother was beautiful."

Kenneth considered saying that Rebecca was also beautiful, but refrained because she would surely think him a flatterer. Yet as he watched the setting sun turn her hair to silky fire, he saw that there was true beauty there for anyone with the eye to see it. Reminding himself to keep his mind on business, he said, "Was Lady Seaton as charming as she appears in the portrait?"

"When she was happy, the whole house glowed. And when she was sad..." Rebecca hesitated. "We all knew it."

"She was moody?"

Rebecca's face froze and she began moving toward the door. "Who isn't sometimes?"

He had touched some kind of nerve. He thought for a moment, wondering how to recover from his slip. Reluctantly he recognized that if he was to win Rebecca's trust, he would have to reveal something of himself. Quietly he said, "My mother died when I was sixteen. Nothing else has ever hurt as much."

Rebecca paused and swallowed hard. "It... it leaves an unfillable hole in one's life." She closed her anguished eyes for a moment. "How did your mother die?"

"Slowly and painfully, of a wasting disease." A sharp memory of that terrible year struck him. He began straightening papers on his desk. Gruffly he said, "I've seen great courage in battle, but none greater than hers as she faced death."

While Kenneth resembled his father physically, in temperament he was very much Elizabeth Wilding's son. One of his first memories was of his mother's long, graceful fingers clasping his chubby hand as she guided him in writing his own name. It was from her that he had learned drawing and how to truly see the world around him.

Though her bluff husband had loved her in his way, he had been unable to deal with Elizabeth's slow dying. It was to her son that she had turned for comfort and support. Kenneth had been forced into adulthood that year. He and his small sister had drawn together in their grief, and the bond had never really been broken during his long years away.

The Gray Ghost gave a soft meow, which pulled

Kenneth from his reverie. He realized that his unmoving hands rested on the piled papers in front of him. Uneasily he looked up and saw that Rebecca was regarding him with compassionate eyes.

His intention had been to show sympathy, not weakness. "Your father explained about the daybook. Are the earlier ones kept here in the study? I thought it might help me understand the business better if I glanced through the last several years' worth."

"You'll have to ask Father. I'm not sure where he keeps them. Until dinner, Captain." She turned and left the study.

He watched her go, knowing that his first instinct had been correct. She was trouble.

~

Rebecca petted the Gray Ghost for comfort as she went downstairs to the kitchen. It had been upsetting to discuss her mother, and Captain Wilding's sorrow when he talked of his mother's death had triggered her own grief. Still, his sensitivity had shown an unexpected side of his character. For a moment, the stern army officer had revealed the boy he had been.

He was an intriguing puzzle. Her first impressions of him had included both harshness and intelligence. Those qualities were certainly part of him, but he was also tolerant and surprisingly philosophical. She had deliberately revealed her ruined reputation to see his reaction. To his credit, he had shown neither shock nor lewd speculation.

After feeding her cat, she headed purposefully up to her studio again. She had half an hour before she must dress for dinner. Time enough to try another sketch or two of the captain.

CHAPTER 6

As they had agreed beforehand, Kenneth visited Lord Bowden to make a report after his first week at Seaton House. He was promptly shown into Bowden's study. At Kenneth's entrance, Bowden set his newspaper aside and gestured for the visitor to take a seat. "Good day, Lord Kimball. What have you to report?"

Kenneth studied the older man's face. Having met Sir Anthony, he could see how strong the physical resemblance between the two men was. The same spare figure, the same medium height, the same chiseled facial bones. But Sir Anthony's vitality, his flashes of charm and occasional petulance, made him seem much younger than the two years that actually separated the brothers. "I've not made as much progress as I would like," he said as he took a seat. "This will be a slow investigation."

Briefly he explained about the lack of long-term servants, and how much of his time had been taken in dealing with Sir Anthony's accumulated work. Then he described how he intended to proceed. He ended by saying, "Sir Anthony keeps detailed daybooks that could reveal a great deal about the critical time period. Unfortunately, I've learned that the relevant volume was left at his country house in the confusion after Lady Seaton's death. I won't get to see it unless I'm still part of the household this summer, when Sir Anthony retires to the country again. Given the difficulties of this investigation, it may come to that."

Bowden listened with a frown. "I had hoped you would have results before then."

"A certain amount of progress is being made, though it isn't of an obvious sort. I'm becoming familiar to Sir Anthony's friends. Soon I can start to question them about the past. Also, I want to speak with the previous secretary, Morley."

"That will be simple." Bowden reached into his desk for a pen and wrote down a name and address. "He is now secretary to a member of Parliament, a friend of mine."

Kenneth gave a nod as he accepted the paper. "You arranged that? I suspected it was no accident that the position in Sir Anthony's house became available when it did."

"I learned that Morley has political ambitions. It was simple to see that he was offered a situation that would further them." Bowden leaned back in his chair and steepled his fingers. "Granted you haven't had the time to find real evidence, but what are your impressions so far?"

Kenneth spent a moment marshaling his thoughts. "Lady Seaton's death is like an open wound that is felt but never acknowledged. Sir Anthony hasn't once mentioned his wife, yet sometimes he stares at the portrait of her that hangs in his study. His daughter can barely endure talking about her mother's death. I wish I could read their thoughts, but I can't." Kenneth gave Bowden a quizzical glance. "Is Lady Claxton the mistress whom he was rumored to want to marry? Certainly they are involved, but the affair seems casual."

"Lavinia Claxton?" Bowden snorted. "I suppose that was to be expected. She spreads her favors rather widely. It was for someone else's sake that Anthony murdered Helen, but I was unable to learn the woman's identity. In his way, he is discreet."

Kenneth frowned as he thought about that. If Sir Anthony loved another woman enough to kill for her, it seemed odd that he would be carrying on with Lavinia rather than his prior mistress. He wondered what had ended the earlier affair.

That is, if there really *was* a significant earlier affair. He felt as if he were chasing shadows.

Bowden said unexpectedly, "What is my niece like?"

Kenneth found himself reluctant to discuss Rebecca. "I scarcely see Miss Seaton except at dinner. She's rather quiet and spends all her time in her studio. Did you know she's a gifted painter?"

The other man's brows arched. "I had no idea. Perhaps that explains her immorality. Artists seem to feel that the laws of God and man don't apply to them."

Kenneth found that he had to clamp down on his temper. "Miss Seaton may have made a foolish mistake when she was young, but I've heard no rumors about misbehavior since."

"Try harder," Bowden said coolly. "I'm sure the rumors will be there. I hope the next time you will have more to report."

Disliking the pressure, Kenneth said, "It's a mistake to insist on weekly reports. You will become frustrated at the apparent lack of progress, and it does me no good to feel that you are looking over my shoulder."

Bowden's face clouded. After a long silence he said reluctantly, "Perhaps you are right, but I must insist that we meet at least once a month."

"Very well, but future meetings shouldn't be held here. We're less than a mile from Sir Anthony. If he hears I've been seen entering your house, I'd be out on the street five minutes later. For the same reason, don't write me at Seaton House unless it's an emergency." Kenneth handed Bowden a piece of paper with an address scribbled on it. "I'm using this postal receiving station for personal correspondence. I'll stop and check for messages every day or two."

Bowden put the address in a desk drawer. "Now that you are established, I trust matters will proceed more quickly."

"Perhaps, but I suspect this investigation will take longer than either of us wishes." Kenneth got to his feet. "I'll see myself out. Good day to you, Lord Bowden."

He left the study, then paused, hidden in the shadowed hall, as the butler admitted a small, graceful woman with silvery hair. From the way the butler greeted her, it was clear that she was the lady of the house. So Bowden had married, if only to keep the title out of his despised brother's hands.

As Lady Bowden went to the stairs, she noticed Kenneth and gave an absent nod. Kenneth wondered what kind of marriage had been possible when Bowden was obsessed with his former fiancée.

On the walk back to Seaton House, he thought about how his secretarial position was turning out to be rather enjoyable. Both Sir Anthony and Rebecca were so involved in their painting that they didn't question his activities as long as his work got done. Sir Anthony's friends had accepted the new secretary with careless good humor and talked freely in front of him. He had already learned some useful facts that way.

It had taken longer to establish his authority over the servants, but they'd settled down nicely after he discharged the laziest maid and hired a butler, an efficient man called Minton. Soon the household would be running with silken smoothness.

In Kenneth's rare free moments, there were marvelous works of art to admire. His chief regret was that he saw so little of Rebecca. After the talk they'd had his first day, he'd thought it would be easy to win her confidence and learn more about her mother's death, but as he'd told Lord Bowden, he scarcely ever saw her. Guests were usually present at dinner, which made serious conversation impossible. She would eat quietly, then excuse herself from joining the company in the drawing room.

He had wondered once or twice if she was deliberately avoiding him, but that seemed unlikely. It was merely that her interests were elsewhere. Having accepted Kenneth as part of the household, she paid no more attention to him than she would a piece of furniture. He must find excuses to talk with her.

The devil of it was that his interest in seeing more of Rebecca was not solely because of his mission. He wanted to know more about her talent and her sharp edges and her hidden sensuality. The fact that she intrigued him increased his distaste for his deception. If Sir Anthony was eventually charged with murder, Rebecca would surely learn that Kenneth had entered the house under false pretenses. He didn't like to think what her reaction would be.

His route took him by the postal receiving station he was using. It was part of a stationer's shop, which meant it would be easy to find excuses to visit. He stopped and found that a letter from his sister had arrived. Beth must have written back as soon as she received his note. He broke the wafer and read the single, closely written sheet.

Dear Kenneth,

I'm glad your work is going well. Matters are in surprisingly good heart here, largely because of the arrival of your friend Lieutenant Davidson. As you implied, he was rather subdued at first, but his mood has improved markedly. His sense of humor is really quite droll. Cousin Olivia and I are both very fond of him.

Because of Lieutenant Davidson's crippled left arm, I find that with him I am not self-conscious about my clubfoot the way I am with most strangers. Each morning we ride together about the estate. He has a number of ideas for improving crop yields without having to invest much money. The tenants and laborers are impressed with his good sense. Sutterton seems a different place from when it was run by the old bailiff.

Beth went on to describe Davidson's suggestions. All were clear proof that his friend knew more about agriculture than Kenneth. If Sutterton was saved, he hoped Jack would stay on as steward permanently.

He refolded the letter and tucked it into his coat. Beth's buoyant tone assuaged his guilt over leaving her so soon after returning to England. But his good mood faded when he left the shop. Even the knowledge that he was working to save Beth and Sutterton could not mitigate his distaste for what he was doing.

As soon as Rebecca entered her father's studio, she saw that he was on the verge of a major explosion. Society knew Sir Anthony as one of its own, an aristocrat of impeccable wit and dress who happened to have a gift for painting. Only his closest associates saw the fiercely disciplined, intense artist that existed beneath the surface.

As a girl Rebecca had once sketched her father as a smoldering volcano on the verge of boiling over. He'd laughed in rueful acknowledgment when she showed it to him. When Sir Anthony encountered problems with a project he cared about deeply, the volcano erupted. Rebecca always tried to avoid him during such episodes.

The state of his dress was a good indicator of his mood. Usually he was as elegant as if he had just stepped out of a St. James club, but today his coat was tossed on the floor, his sleeves rolled up, and his graying hair disordered. All were clear signs that she should leave before he noticed her.

But it was too late. He set down his palette and brush and snapped, "Where the devil is Wilding?"

Resigned, she entered the studio. "I believe he went out this morning." Not that she had seen the captain go, but she'd noticed that the house felt different when he was home. More charged with energy.

Her father went back to glaring at the large canvas propped on his easel. "What's wrong with this damned picture?"

Though she'd watched the painting develop from sketches to nearly finished oil, Rebecca dutifully approached and studied it again. The last of her father's Waterloo series, it showed the Duke of Wellington on horseback, standing in his stirrups and waving his cocked hat forward in the signal for his army to advance against the

French. The heroic figure of the duke dominated the canvas, with battered regiments in the background.

It was a good painting. Nonetheless, she understood her father's dissatisfaction. In some indefinable way, the picture lacked soul. But she knew no way to remedy such a failing.

Since an answer was expected, she said hesitantly, "There is nothing really wrong. It's a fine likeness of Wellington, and the battlefield looks very convincing. The forward sweep of his arm is very dynamic."

"Of course the composition and likeness are good—mine always are," her father said with exasperation. "But it's not a great painting—merely a good one." He frowned at the canvas again. "Maybe Wilding can tell me what is lacking. After all, he was there." His voice turned querulous. "Why isn't he *here?*"

"I'm sure he'll be back soon." Seizing the excuse to leave, she continued, "I'll tell the footman to send the captain up as soon as he comes in."

Before she could start for the door, it swung open and Captain Wilding entered. His blue coat and buff breeches were subdued, yet he drew the eye as surely as if he were dressed in a scarlet uniform. He nodded to Rebecca and set a parcel on the table. "Here are the pigments you ordered, Sir Anthony. Since I was near the colorman's shop today, I picked them up myself."

Instead of taking the opportunity to leave, Rebecca stepped back and scrutinized the newcomer, trying to analyze what gave him that air of command. His aura of physical strength was part of it, but only a small part. Intelligence was also there, and a hint of flinty integrity, yet none of those qualities fully defined his essence.

Instead of being gratified by the captain's presence, Sir Anthony growled, "Where have you been?"

"Interviewing wine merchants," Wilding said mildly. "You may recall that we discussed yesterday how your present supplier is inadequate. I believe I've found a better one."

"So I suppose you've been sampling and are now three sheets to the wind," Sir Anthony said sarcastically.

"Naturally I tasted some wine, but I'm certainly not drunk," the captain said, refusing to be baited. "I'm sorry if my absence was a problem. I didn't know you would need me here."

Furiously Sir Anthony picked up a bladder of white lead paint and flung it at his secretary. "You should have been here when I wanted you!"

"What the devil?" Wilding swiftly sidestepped the missile. The bladder hit the door with a soggy sound and splashed white paint in an arc across the oak panels.

All vestiges of control gone, Sir Anthony began hurling other objects around the room. The white lead was followed by bladders of Naples yellow and Prussian blue paint. A handful of his special long-handled brushes separated in midair and flew in all directions before clattering to the floor. With a sweep of his arm, he knocked everything from the table beside him before flinging his palette knife wildly. It whizzed by Rebecca, just missing her shoulder before bouncing off the wall.

Shaking inside, she prepared to take shelter behind the sofa. Then Captain Wilding bounded across the room and caught Sir Anthony's wrist in one powerful hand. "You may destroy your whole studio if you wish," he said in a dangerously soft voice, "but don't throw things at a lady."

Her father tried to wrench free. "That's not a lady, that's my daughter!"

The captain's fingers locked harder around her father's wrist. "All the more reason to control yourself."

For a moment the men were silhouetted motionless against the windows. The slighter figure of Sir Anthony crackled with furious emotion, but he was helpless against the captain's implacable strength. Rebecca had a swift mental image of lightning fruitlessly striking a mountain.

Her father's left arm jerked, and for a sickening moment she thought he was going to strike the captain. Then, in one of his swift mood changes, Sir Anthony's arm dropped.

"You're right, damn you." He glanced at Rebecca. "I've never once hit you, have I?"

She unclenched her fists. "Only with splashing paint," she said, trying to sound light. "Your aim is terrible."

The captain released her father, but his face was set and his gray eyes looked like flint. "You make a habit of such tantrums, Sir Anthony?"

"Not precisely a habit, but they're not unknown." Her father rubbed his right wrist where the captain had held it. "These furnishings have been chosen because they clean easily and are forgiving of minor stains."

"Very amusing," Wilding said dryly. "Nonetheless, you owe your daughter an apology."

Sir Anthony's face tightened at the implied rebuke from an employee. "Rebecca doesn't take my moods seriously."

"No? Then why does she look as pale as if she's just risen from a sickbed?"

Both men's heads swung toward her. She froze, knowing that her distress was visible to anyone who looked closely.

With his artist's perception, her father saw her state clearly. "It bothers you so much when I get angry, Rebecca?" he said with surprise.

She almost lied to ease his conscience, but she couldn't,

not with Captain Wilding's probing gaze on her. "Your explosions always upset me," she admitted uncomfortably. "When I was little, they made me fear that the world was about to end."

Her father drew a sharp breath. "I'm sorry, Rebecca. I didn't know. Your mother—" He stopped speaking abruptly.

Her mother had never minded the explosions; she was capable of being equally explosive. It was Rebecca who had run and hid under the bed when her parents roared, singly or at each other.

She filled the awkward silence by saying quickly, "My father has been having trouble with this picture, Captain Wilding. He thought you might have some useful insights. It's the last of his Waterloo series. Wellington posed for it himself."

Wilding turned to look at the painting. Because she was watching him closely, she saw the skin over his cheekbones tauten. Though she'd initially thought him cool and passionless, she was learning to recognize subtle signs of emotion.

"Wellington ordering the general advance," the captain murmured. "Rather unnerving to see it again."

"You saw him give the signal to attack?" she asked.

"Yes, though I was much farther away, of course." He studied the canvas. "Sir Anthony, do you want this to be a classical, idealized portrait of a hero, or a realistic rendition of the actual battle?"

Her father opened his mouth to reply, then closed it again. "Wellington is a great man, and I want viewers to see that greatness," he said finally. "I want this picture to live in their minds forever. Two hundred years from now, I want people to speak of Seaton's Wellington."

"Perhaps your rendition is too classical and restrained to

create that sort of power," the captain said slowly. "The duke and his horse look as neat as if they were trotting across a parade ground. Waterloo wasn't like that. After a day of fierce fighting, soldiers and their mounts were exhausted and filthy with mud and sweat and black powder. Even as far away as I was, I could see lines of strain and fatigue in the duke's face."

"What was his expression like?" Sir Anthony asked.

Wilding thought before answering. "The sun was low in the sky and a ray of light struck his face as he swept his hat forward. His expression can't really be described—but remember how many years he had been fighting to reach this point. In Spain, he faced overwhelming odds for years on end. Inadequate supplies, a much smaller army than the enemy. Unbreakable will has put victory within his grasp—yet he has seen many of his dearest friends die. The steel inside the man should be visible."

"Stupid of me to draw the duke as he appeared in the studio," Sir Anthony muttered to himself. "I should have tried to imagine him as he was then." He gave the captain a quick glance. "Is there anything else I should consider."

Wilding gestured toward the background of the painting. "The soldiers are as clearly visible as on a fine day in May. That's wrong—the battlefield was a stinging hell of black powder smoke. Sometimes it was impossible to see a hundred yards away."

Sir Anthony's eyes narrowed in thought as he studied his painting. "I can use transparent gray glazes to get that effect. But Wellington is the key. The steel. I must show the steel."

The captain asked Rebecca, "What pictures are in the series besides this and the cavalry charge in the dining room?"

She went to a portfolio and removed two drawings. "The finished paintings aren't here, but these sketches are fairly accurate. This first one shows the allied regiments lined up along the ridge as far as the eye can see."

Wilding came to look over her shoulder. She was intensely aware of the warmth of his body, mere inches behind her. This man had been through the hells of the Peninsula and Waterloo, and survived. Like Wellington, he must be pure steel within. She asked, "Where were you positioned?"

He pointed. "About there, a little left of center. I spent most of the day skirmishing around a sand pit."

"For me, what makes the painting is these men in the foreground." Rebecca indicated the figures of a young ensign and a grizzled sergeant who were guarding their regimental colors. Above them, the Union Jack curled and snapped in the wind, defying the French army that stood in silent ranks on the opposite side of the valley.

"It's always the particular that moves us, not the general," the captain said reflectively. "A youth on the verge of his first battle who wonders if his courage will be equal to the challenges of the day. A battle-scarred veteran who has faced death again and again and wonders if this time his luck will run out. Any viewer who looks at this must wonder if these two men will survive what lies ahead."

From his voice, Rebecca knew he had been both of those men at different times in his career. As a youth he had found the courage, as an experienced officer his luck had held, and the forge of battle had tempered him into what he was now. He was utterly different from anyone she had ever known, and that difference fascinated her. She wanted to lean back against him, to absorb his warrior power and determination.

Mouth dry, she pulled out the second drawing. "The second picture is the defense of the Chateau de Hougoumont." The fight for the chateau had become a vicious battle-within-a-battle, with a small number of allied troops withstanding two and a half French divisions. Her father had chosen the moment when the French had broken into the courtyard and the defenders were fighting savagely to push them out before it was too late. "He wanted a scene of furious hand-to-hand combat."

"Soldiers at their most primal. It's a fitting companion to the grandeur of the cavalry picture."

She nodded, impressed. Not only was he a warrior, but he was very perceptive about paintings.

Her father looked over from the Wellington picture. "Do you think this series will tell the story of Waterloo?"

To Rebecca's relief, the captain moved away from her. "It says as much as four pictures can," he replied.

"I hear a reservation in your voice," Sir Anthony said shrewdly. "I've done the beginning, the end, the infantry, and the cavalry. What other scenes do you think should be included?"

"If I were you," Wilding said hesitantly, "I would do two more. The next would be Wellington shaking hands with Prince Blücher when the British met up with the Prussians near La Belle-Alliance. The Waterloo campaign is the story of many nations standing against a common enemy. If the Prussians hadn't arrived late in the day, the victory would not have been decisive."

"Mmm, an interesting possibility," Sir Anthony mused. "And what would be as the final painting?"

"Show the price of victory," the captain said flatly. "Show exhausted, wounded soldiers sleeping like the dead around a campfire. In the darkness beyond them, show the tangled corpses and broken weapons. Show how all the victims of battle lie together in the democracy of death."

There was a long silence before Rebecca said softly, "You have a vivid way with words, Captain."

"And a good mind for pictures," her father added. "I shall consider what you have suggested. Indeed I shall."

In the pause that followed, a surge of desire swept through Rebecca, the most powerful emotion she had felt in months. She must possess Captain Wilding, capture his essence so that something of him would always belong to her.

Beyond caring for propriety, she crossed the room and touched his cheek, her fingertips skimming along the scar. It was smooth and hard to her touch. "I surrender, Captain," she said huskily. "I'm afraid that I simply must paint you."

CHAPTER 7

Rebecca's words and light, sensual touch startled Kenneth so much that all he could manage was a feeble, "I beg your pardon?"

"I've been yearning to have you for a model since you came here." She moved back a step. "You're quite irresistible."

The words would have sounded suggestive coming from most women. Rebecca Seaton, however, looked more like a frugal housewife eyeing a chicken and deciding it would do nicely for Sunday dinner. Dryly he said, "Should I be honored or alarmed?"

"Oh, certainly alarmed." She glanced at her father. "Do you mind if I borrow Captain Wilding for an hour or two a day?"

Sir Anthony smiled. "I understand perfectly—in fact, I'm tempted to repaint the sergeant in my prebattle scene to look like Kenneth." His keen gaze went to his secretary. "They say a soldier's eyes show how much combat he has seen. Everything I wanted to say about that sergeant is in Kenneth's face. But you can have him first, if he's willing."

Rebecca asked, "Are you willing, Captain?"

Kenneth shifted uncomfortably under the twin scrutiny of father and daughter. These damned artists saw too much. However, he'd wanted more time with Rebecca and this opportunity was too good to pass up. "Your wish is my command, Miss Seaton."

"Then come along to my workroom."

"Give me a few minutes." He indicated the disordered studio. "First I must detail a maid to clean up before the spilled paint ruins the carpet and furniture."

"Make sure whoever you send works quietly," Sir Anthony ordered. He got a tablet and pencil, then sat and began to sketch with swift, sure strokes.

Kenneth opened the door for Rebecca. As she passed, he noticed that her knot of hair was starting to come unmoored from its pins. The silky auburn strands didn't take kindly to discipline. The tousled result made her look as if she had just emerged from a bed.

For the hundredth time since entering Seaton House, he reminded himself to concentrate on business. He checked on the servants to see what had transpired while he was out and sent Betsy, the most careful maid, to Sir Anthony's studio. Then he went up to Rebecca's sanctum sanctorum.

He knocked and entered when she called permission, looking around with interest. Where Sir Anthony's studio had the elegance of a drawing room, Rebecca's lair had whitewashed walls, slanted ceilings, and the casual comfort of a farmhouse kitchen. The windows that faced the street were the usual size, but large, open windows across the back wall of the house admitted a soft, even north light. An artist's light.

And everywhere, there were paintings. Some were hung,

others were unframed canvases tilted against the walls. The lavishness of image and color stunned his senses.

Rebecca was curled up in a large chair, a sketchbook in her lap and a pencil in her hand. She waved at the sofa opposite. "Make yourself comfortable, Captain. Today I'll just do a few studies. I need to decide how best to portray you."

"If we're going to be in each other's pockets every day, you really should call me Kenneth," he said as he took his seat.

She gave him a swift smile. "Then you must call me Rebecca." The hazel of her eyes was flecked with green, giving her penetrating gaze a feline quality.

"I've never modeled before. What should I do?"

"For now, just relax and try not to move your head."

As her deft fingers sketched, his gaze went to the paintings within his field of vision. Her style had some of her father's classical precision, but with a softer, more emotional quality. Many pictures portrayed women as famous figures from history and legend. Without moving his head, he could see half a dozen paintings that equaled the splendid Boadicea hanging downstairs. "Have you ever exhibited at the Royal Academy?"

"Never," she said without looking up.

"You really should submit your work." His gaze went to a powerful Judith and Holofernes. "Show them what a woman can do."

"I feel no need to prove that," she said coolly.

Silence reigned for a time, broken only by the faint scratch of her pencil. After admiring the paintings within view, Kenneth's attention went to Rebecca. Her wrists were delicate, almost fragile, yet there was strength in her long, supple fingers. She was twisted sideways in her chair, which hitched her muslin gown several inches above her ankles. They were as slender and shapely as her wrists.

Though Rebecca lacked Maria's voluptuousness, she was every bit as sensually alluring. Whenever she bent her head over her sketchbook, he got a tantalizing glimpse of her nape. The pale skin seemed almost translucent next to her richly colored tresses. He wondered what she would do if he kissed her there. Probably tell him to sit down so she could finish her sketches.

The room seemed warmer than could be accounted for by the small coal fire. Shifting his gaze away from her didn't help; he was as conscious of her body as if she were nestled in his lap. Under the scents of linseed oil and coal smoke, he detected a light floral fragrance. Rosewater, he thought. Elusive, feminine. Not unlike the lady herself.

What would she look like wearing nothing but rosewater and a shimmering veil of auburn hair? His heartbeat quickened and perspiration began to film his forehead.

Damnation! He was unused to idleness; no wonder his imagination was spinning erotic fantasies. It didn't help that it had been months since he had lain with a woman. He had found the lightskirts of Paris much like French pastries: sweetly enjoyable and quickly forgotten. Rebecca Seaton would be a very different dish.

Knowing he must distract himself before he started to smolder, he commented, "Sir Anthony in a rage is an alarming sight. I don't blame you for being frightened."

"I wasn't afraid," she said with mild surprise. "Father would never hurt anyone. I just don't like shouts and flying objects."

Her faith in her father was rather touching, but Sir Anthony's outburst had convinced Kenneth that the painter was capable of doing grievous harm. Had Helen Seaton challenged her husband about his mistress and become a victim of the kind of fury displayed today? What kind of woman had Helen been?

Now seemed a good time to learn more. He asked, "How did your mother like being surrounded by mad artists?"

"She loved it." Without looking up, Rebecca tore off a page of her sketchbook and set it aside, then resumed drawing on the sheet below. "Friends called her the queen of the London art world. Every poor artist in the city knew she could be relied upon to lend a few pounds to keep starvation at bay."

"Did they ever pay her back?"

"Occasionally." Rebecca smiled reminiscently. "Some painters repaid her with specimens of their work. Usually bad ones, since first-rate artists are less likely to need loans."

"That explains the dreadful landscapes in my room. She must have been trying to hide them."

"Very likely," Rebecca agreed. "If they offend you, something better can be found. Heaven knows there are plenty of paintings in this house."

"Could you lend one of yours?" He scanned the ones he could see. "Perhaps that marvelous one opposite me. Diana the Huntress, I think." The goddess was standing quietly, her hand on a bow as tall as she, and a pensive expression on her face. It reminded him a little of Rebecca.

"If you like." She flipped to another page of the sketchbook. "I have a frame that will suit it nicely."

"Before you continue, do you mind if I take a break?" he asked. "I'm not used to sitting still for so long."

"Oh, of course. I'm sorry." She smiled ruefully. "When I work, I forget how much time is passing. Would you like tea? I usually make a pot about this time every day."

"That would be much appreciated." Kenneth stood and stretched to loosen the tightness in his shoulders.

Rebecca rose and went to the fireplace, bending gracefully to hang the kettle over the fire. "Give thanks that you're modeling for me instead of my father. He's even more ruthless than I am." She examined him with eyes that seemed to slice through to the bone. "Father was right—you would make a wonderfully formidable sergeant in the prebattle picture."

"I should look the part. I was a sergeant for years."

"A sergeant? You?" She stared at him.

"I took the king's shilling and enlisted when I was eighteen," he explained. "Later I was promoted from the ranks."

"For conspicuous bravery," she said softly. "That's always the reason, isn't it?"

"That's part of it, but a certain amount of luck is involved." He smiled a little. "One must be brave within sight of an officer who will recommend the commission."

"You're a man of surprises, Captain. From your speech, I assumed you were..." She paused, disconcerted.

"You assumed I was a gentleman," he said helpfully.

Her eyes dropped. "I'm sorry. Obviously you are a gentleman, and all the more credit to you for earning what is usually an accident of birth."

He shrugged. "Actually, my birth is respectable, but I was estranged from my father, so I had no money to buy a commission. That meant enlistment."

"What caused the estrangement?"

Feeling uncomfortable, he began strolling the length of the attic, staying in the center to avoid banging his head on the angled ceiling. He was supposed to be probing Rebecca; how had things become reversed? "A year after my mother's death, my father took a seventeen-year-old wife. We... didn't get along."

"It would have been hard to accept any stepmother so soon after your mother's death," Rebecca said sympathetically. "A girl your own age in her place must have seemed indecent."

Far worse than indecent. For an instant, remembered rage and revulsion reared their ugly heads. Kenneth clamped down on the feelings, reminding himself that he had not been without fault in what had happened.

"It didn't help that she wasn't a particularly nice person. However, my father was in love. Or in heat, to be more accurate. I could not stay under his roof." Turning the conversation, he continued, "Do you think your father will remarry? And if he does, how will you feel about it?"

She looked startled, as if she had not yet considered the possibility. "That would depend on whom he marries," she said without enthusiasm. "I'll have to wait and see."

"Is Lavinia hoping to be the next Lady Seaton?"

Rebecca bent to take a jar of tea from a small cabinet. "I doubt it. Under her brash exterior she's really quite sweet, but I think she's too fond of a widow's freedom to give it up. Father will probably remarry someday, though. He likes having a wife to pamper him." The kettle began steaming, so she lifted it from the fire and poured hot water to warm the teapot. "There's a picture of Lavinia behind you."

He turned and quickly found Lavinia among the unframed canvases leaning against the wall. Clad in revealing classical draperies, she reclined on a Greek sofa, her gaze a cool invitation. In the eternal struggle between the sexes, Lady Claxton would be hunter, not quarry. "Let me guess," he said. "She's portrayed as Messalina, the Roman empress who defeated the chief prostitute of Rome in a fornication marathon that exhausted half the men in the city."

Rebecca chuckled as she spooned tea leaves into the pot and added boiling water. "Actually, she's supposed to be Aspasia, the most beautiful and learned courtesan in Athens. I've painted Lavinia several times. She enjoys modeling."

But she would probably not be Sir Anthony's next wife. If that was true, who was the mistress that might have been the cause of Lady Seaton's death? Thinking he had asked enough questions for the time being, Kenneth strolled toward the far end of the long attic. Small windows opened onto the street, bright southern light illuminating a utilitarian table and chairs.

This was Rebecca's workshop, with rolls of canvas and stacked frames in the corners. The Gray Ghost slept on the table between a picture frame and a mortar and pestle. The cat opened his eyes a slit at Kenneth's approach, then resumed snoozing.

To the left, an alcove contained a massive piece of furniture that resembled an elaborate Italianate building. Faint lines showed where drawers had been cunningly concealed among pretend pilasters. He stroked the curve of an arch, which framed a pigeonhole containing brushes and small tools.

Seeing his interest, Rebecca called from the other end of the attic, "That storage cabinet was made specially for a seventeenth century Flemish artist called Van Veeren."

"I'm afraid I've never heard of him."

"No reason why you should have." She assembled a tea tray, then brought it to the workshop. "He was a not very talented painter of portraits and genre still lifes."

Kenneth grinned. "Vegetables and dead rabbits?"

"Exactly. But he must have made a good living at it." She set the tray on the table. The Gray Ghost instantly rose and came to investigate. "There are some rather nice currant cakes in the tin, if you can get them before the Ghost does."

She gently pushed the cat away from the tray. The Ghost hunkered down like a stone lion, his avid gaze fixed on the cake tin while Rebecca poured tea. She handed a cup to Kenneth, then sat in one of the well-worn wooden chairs.

He had not expected this quiet domesticity from Rebecca, but it suited her well. Very well. His willingness to model for her had changed their relationship, putting her more at ease with him. He should feel satisfied; he'd wanted her trust and confidence so he could extract information from her. A pity that success was tempered with shame.

The army had taught him to set aside what couldn't be helped, so he might as well enjoy his tea. Between his legitimate tasks and his visit to Lord Bowden, he'd not eaten since breakfast. He added an irregular chunk of sugar to his cup and settled in the other chair.

There was silence as they ate the excellent currant cakes. When Rebecca leaned over to pour more tea, he said, "I gather that you stretch your own canvases here?"

She offered a fragment of cake to the Gray Ghost, who daintily nipped it from her fingers. "Yes, and most of my father's as well. I also make our pastel crayons and mix some special pigments that the regular colorman doesn't make."

He looked at her quizzically. "Surely Sir Anthony could find someone else for such menial tasks."

"Ah, but would the tasks be done as well? Though painting is now called art, it was first of all a craft. The better one understands the materials, the more effectively they can be used." She caressed the smooth stone mortar. "There is something wonderfully satisfying about blending the pigments and medium together to the perfect consistency, in the perfect color. It's the first step in creating a picture that successfully captures one's inner vision."

The sensuality so clear in her mother's portrait was now visible in Rebecca's dreamy face. He wanted her to touch him the same way she touched the mortar. He wanted her...

He looked away, not completing the thought. "When did you start to draw?"

She made a wry face. "According to family legend, one day in the nursery I broke a soft-boiled egg and used the yolk to draw a recognizable cat on the wall."

He smiled at the image. "So you were always an artist. I assume Sir Anthony taught you?"

"Not really. Father was always so busy. Whenever I could escape my nanny, I would slip into his studio and watch him work. He didn't mind as long as I wasn't in the way. Soon I had my own pastel crayons and charcoal." She chuckled. "Mother made sure I had paper so I wouldn't ruin any more walls. When she had time, she sometimes gave me lessons."

"Did your mother have artistic ability beyond the standard accomplishments of a lady?"

Rebecca gestured to a small watercolor hanging in a corner. "She did that of me when I was four years old."

The picture showed Rebecca as a happy, laughing child, her baby curls a shining copper. She looked open and eager for life, not like the wary woman she had become. He wondered if her disastrous elopement had been the cause of her losing that openness. "It's lovely. With both parents artists, it's not surprising you have such talent."

Rebecca shook her head. "Mother had talent—her

watercolors were exquisite—but she wasn't really an artist. Marriage got in the way, I think."

"What does it take to be a real artist?" he asked curiously.

"Selfishness." Rebecca gave a self-mocking smile. "One must believe one's work is the most important thing in the world. Putting other people and their needs first can be crippling."

He wondered if her statement was an oblique criticism of her father. A painter as successful as Sir Anthony might have had little time for his family. "Must an artist always be selfish?"

"Perhaps not quite always, but most of the time." She brushed an unruly lock back from her cheek.

He watched, thinking that artifice might counterfeit that rich auburn hair, but no cosmetic could ever duplicate her complexion, which had the translucent fairness of a true redhead.

With sudden anger, he wished they had met in some other time and place, where she was not the daughter of a murder suspect and he was a gentleman of means, not a penniless spy. A place where he could explore the complexities of her mind and spirit. A place where he could kiss her, and persuade her to kiss back.

He drew a deep, slow breath. Anger at the unjustness of fate subsided, but not his powerful desire to touch her. He leaned forward and took her hands in his, turning them palm up. They were capable hands, the fingers long and elegant, like those of a Renaissance saint. "Such strength and skill," he murmured. "What splendors will these create in the future?"

Her hands quivered within his. "The real skill lies in the

mind, not the fingers," she said huskily. "The spirit must see the picture before the body can create it."

"Wherever it comes from, you have a great gift." He traced the lines in her palm with his fingertip. "I wonder if it's really possible to read the future in a hand. Will your talent bring you fame? Wealth? Happiness?"

She pulled away, her fingers curling shut. *"A* creative gift guarantees none of those things. If anything, it interferes with happiness. The work itself is the only sure reward. It is a shield against loneliness, a passion safer than human love."

He raised his head and their gazes met. The tension that had been slowly building rose to choking intensity. He sensed that they were both vulnerable, terribly so, and on the edge of doing something that could not be undone.

Fearing her hazel eyes would see into the depths of his deceitful soul, he got abruptly to his feet. "I really must return to my regular work. Do you want me to model tomorrow?"

She swallowed. "Not... not tomorrow. The day after."

He nodded and left, wondering how the devil he would survive more such intimate sessions. Rebecca might be the best source of information about her mother, but he might not be able to keep his hands off her long enough to learn what he sought.

~

Rebecca managed to remain impassive until she heard the door shut behind the captain. Then she closed her eyes and pressed her right palm to her cheek. Where he had touched her, the skin tingled as if she had stroked fur in winter.

Damn the man! What right did he have to come here and

crack the shield that had protected her for so long? She had been in control of her life, grateful for the freedom to paint as she chose with few distractions. She'd needed nothing else.

Exhaling roughly, she got to her feet and stalked the length of the attic. She'd always loved the slanting ceilings because she could walk erect where most people would have to bend. The captain had been able to stand straight only in the center. His vitality and powerful frame had filled the room to overflowing. Everywhere she turned, she saw him.

She had been wise to admit few people into her sanctuary. Even wiser would have been not to allow Kenneth in.

Allow? She'd practically dragged him up the stairs.

She ran a hand through her hair, inadvertently loosening the pins so that the heavy mass fell loose to her waist. Impatiently she tied her hair into a knot and resumed her pacing.

Kenneth's military past intrigued her, as did the contrast between his rugged form and his keen, perceptive mind. He was a magnificent subject for painting. Yet what drew her most was the way she could talk to him. No one had ever been so interested in what she had to say. The time with him had affected her like spring rain on flowers. She had not realized how lonely she was.

No, perhaps not lonely, but certainly alone. She and her father shared a ruling passion and a house, and they understood each other well. Yet he was a famous man with a full life, and she was only a minor part of it.

Absorbed in her art, she had never had close friends, and more casual acquaintances had dropped her after the idiotic elopement with Frederick had exiled her from respectable society. The members of her father's inner circle treated her with careless good nature, but only Lavinia and her honorary Uncle George were truly fond of her. To the others, she was merely Sir Anthony's eccentric daughter.

It had been the same with her father's previous secretaries. All had been polite and respectful, but she guessed they saw her as some kind of freak, a disgraceful painting female who must be tolerated as part of the job. No wonder she was susceptible to Kenneth's wholehearted attention.

Heaven knew they were very different, yet there was an unexpected empathy between them. Perhaps it was simply their aloneness. Certainly Kenneth could not be attracted to her; she wasn't the sort to inspire a man to unruly passion. Frederick had been in love with the idea of love, not with her.

A thought struck her. Kenneth's tension probably stemmed from his awareness that any sort of relationship with his employer's daughter was fraught with potential hazards. She shouldn't have insisted that he sit for her. Though she hadn't intended coercion, he'd probably felt he had no choice. It might have been better for them both if he had felt free to refuse. Yet she could not regret having him for a model.

Her pacing had brought her to the studio end of the attic. She picked up her sketchbook to study her drawings. Several were quite good, though well short of what she wanted to accomplish.

Slowly she paged through the sketches, wondering what would be the best way to capture his essence, the mingled qualities of warrior fierceness and sensitive observer. Perhaps she should paint the captain in his army uniform. She had a vague recollection that Riflemen wore dark green. That would be more interesting than the usual scarlet uniform, and the color would not dominate the canvas. She could show him after a battle, weary to the soul, yet unbroken.

Dissatisfied, she shook her head. Though it would be effective, such a picture belonged in her father's Waterloo series. It would not have quite the mythic quality she wanted.

That led her to imagine Kenneth in a mythic white toga. She smiled at the fanciful thought. Women often looked splendid in classical garments; the gowns of the French Revolution had been fashioned after antique clothing. However, the style did not suit modern men nearly so well.

She considered other possible compositions without finding one that seemed suitable. Then she flipped a page too far and unexpectedly found one of her falling woman sketches. Jolted by pain, she ripped the drawing out and threw it into the fire with a muttered oath. Kenneth Wilding might be a problem, but at least with him there was pleasure mingled with the pain.

CHAPTER 8

Kenneth woke gasping from a restless sleep. Nightmares again.

He'd always had an excellent visual memory. He could recall the exact colors of a sunset or sketch the face of someone he had seen for only a few minutes. Having looked at Rebecca's hand earlier, he could have drawn the pattern of lines if he wished. He'd thought his ability a blessing until he entered the army. It was far more pleasant to remember sunsets than battles.

The last image of Maria flared in his mind again. Stomach churning, he sat up and lit his bedside candle, forcing himself to think of other things. He visualized how Rebecca's eyes narrowed when she was studying an object. The hint of a dimple in her left cheek. Her delightfully free-spirited hair.

She was only ten feet away, on the other side of the wall.

As his pulse quickened, he acknowledged that thinking of her was not without its own kind of hazards. Still, arousal was far more pleasant than images of death and desolation.

Knowing he would not sleep again, Kenneth rose and

quietly donned his worn robe. He would do some sketching; he'd learned very young that for him, drawing was a better escape from grim reality than drink or mindless fornication. Creating peaceful, empty landscapes was very soothing. After the horrifically bloody siege of Badajoz, he'd done a series of Spanish flowers in watercolor. Waterloo had been the spark for some rather decent pastel sketches of children at play.

He went for his sketchbook and drawing supplies, which were concealed in the back of his wardrobe. As he felt behind the hanging garments, he touched a smooth, metallic object wedged down into a crack. A sharp tug freed a handsome silver card case. Inside, the top card read, "Thomas J. Morley."

Perfect; he'd wanted an excuse to call on Tom Morley so he could discreetly probe for information. Now he had it.

Taking the find as a good omen, he brought out his drawing materials and settled into a chair. A moment's thought gave him a good subject. A few days earlier, Beth had forwarded a letter from his friends Michael and Catherine. They had announced the birth of a son and invited him to a week-long christening party to be held on an island off Cornwall. A pity he could not afford the time or money to attend. He couldn't even afford a proper christening gift. A picture would have to do.

He set to work, using pencil to lightly block in a family group standing beside a baptismal font. In the center was Michael, delighted and a little nervous to be holding his infant son in his arms. To his left was Catherine, her head inclined toward her husband as she made a gentle maternal adjustment to the sweeping folds of the christening gown.

On the right Catherine's daughter Amy was beaming at her new brother. Amy must be all of thirteen now. Kenneth hadn't seen her since before Waterloo, so he would have to guess at how much she had grown. She was almost a young lady and must look even more like her beautiful mother.

The final drawing was laid in with pen and India ink. Sometimes his fingers seemed divinely guided, and this was one of those occasions. Ink was unforgiving of errors, but every stroke went in exactly right. He took particular care with the expressions, wanting to portray the love that had created a new life. Since he did not know the actual setting, he made several vague, curved strokes in the background to imply churchly arches.

The picture pleased him, and he thought it would please Michael and Catherine as well. Yet when he set it aside, he felt sadness. For years, he had dreamed of his return to Sutterton. Eventual marriage had been part of the dream. He had never imagined that he would be too poor to support a wife and family. Even if Lord Bowden cleared the mortgages, years of struggle lay ahead. Capital would have to be invested in Sutterton, and whatever money could be spared must go to provide for Beth.

Forcibly he reminded himself that his situation was far brighter than before Bowden had entered his life. It might take ten years before he would be in a position to marry, but with luck and hard work, the time would come.

He glanced at the drawing, and for an instant he saw the figures of himself and Rebecca instead of Michael and Catherine.

Rubbish! Rebecca might be intriguing, but she was the least wifely female he'd ever met. If and when he settled down, it would be with a warm, loving woman like Catherine, not a sharp-edged spinster who preferred painting to people.

Feeling depressed, he set his sketchbook aside. Outside,

the sun was creeping above the horizon. Perhaps taking Sir Anthony's horse out for exercise would improve his mood.

Kenneth spent a moment studying the young man working diligently inside the small office. Thin, neatly dressed, an intelligent face, and a faint but unmistakable air of self-importance. Here was someone who looked like a private and personal secretary.

A rap on the door frame brought the young man's head up. "Come in, sir," he said politely. "I'm Thomas Morley, Sir Wilford's secretary. He is not available, but may I help you?"

Kenneth advanced into the room. "Actually, I came to see you. I'm Kenneth Wilding, Sir Anthony Seaton's new secretary."

A flicker of surprise implied that Morley was another who didn't think Kenneth looked right for the job. Concealing the reaction, he rose and offered his hand. "A pleasure to meet you. I'd heard Sir Anthony finally found someone. It's *Captain* Wilding, isn't it?"

Kenneth agreed to the title. After shaking hands, he produced the silver card case. "I'm in your old room, and yesterday I found this wedged in a corner of the wardrobe. Sir Anthony told me your current address, and since I was coming to Westminster anyhow, I thought I'd drop it by in person."

Morley's face lit up as he took the case. "Splendid! This was a present from my godmother when I finished at Oxford. With all the confusion of moving and starting a new position, I feared it was lost for good." He slipped it into a pocket. "I was about to dine at the tavern down the street. Will you join me, Captain? I should like to buy you a dinner to show my gratitude. You can tell me the news from Seaton House."

Since Kenneth had timed his visit with the idea of inviting Morley out, he accepted immediately. Soon they were eating excellent beefsteak at opposite sides of a table in the nearby tavern. The fact that both of them had worked for Sir Anthony created a bond that caused Morley to talk easily.

After half an hour of describing his political work, Morley broke off with a laugh. "Sorry for running on so, but I am enjoying my position greatly. What do you think of Seaton House?"

Kenneth swallowed a mouthful of ale. "Different."

Morley smiled. "A tactful description. One could meet the most prominent people in Britain at Sir Anthony's, but I'm not sorry to be gone. There's something a bit too chaotic about artists, don't you think? Trying to make that household efficient was an uphill battle, as I'm sure you've learned."

"Commanding a company under battle conditions was good preparation," Kenneth said with a faint smile. "Things got into a sad state after you left, but I'm beginning to sort them out. Sir Anthony hasn't thrown anything at anyone for days."

The other man gave an elaborate shudder. "I liked the old boy, but I don't miss his tantrums. I never could understand why he carried on so when he's the most fortunate man I know. Have you ever watched him work? He stands back from his easel with a long-handled brush and hardly seems to watch where he's slapping the paint. A few days of that and voila! A portrait someone will pay hundreds of guineas for." Morley sighed. "Hardly seems fair the way fame and fortune have fallen into his lap, while men like you and me must work for our livings."

"Sir Anthony may make painting look easy," Kenneth said dryly, "but it took years of discipline and hard work for him to know where and how to 'slap paint.'" Wondering what the other man thought of Rebecca, he continued mendaciously, "When Miss Seaton heard I might see you, she sent her greetings."

"That was good of her." Morley poured more ale from the pitcher. "I'm surprised she noticed I was gone. An odd sort of girl, don't you think? I never understood what she did with her time. Moped upstairs in her room, I suppose. She committed a..." he paused a moment to come up with an appropriate phrase, "grave indiscretion some years ago, which is why she isn't received in polite society. It soured her disposition, I think."

Kenneth resisted—barely—the impulse to empty his tankard on the other man's head. "I've found Miss Seaton to be a remarkably interesting and intelligent young woman."

Morley's brows rose. "She must talk to you more than she did me." He leaned forward confidentially. "I considered trying to fix her interest. After all, someday she'll be a considerable heiress, and with her age and reputation she can't be too choosy about a husband. But I decided against it. She would not make a suitable wife for a man with ambitions."

Presumably Morley's idea of a perfect mate was a simpleminded doll who knew how to pour tea and not ask questions. Deciding he'd better begin serious probing before he lost his temper, Kenneth asked, "How long were you with Sir Anthony?"

"Three years. I went to him a month after coming down from university."

"Three years," Kenneth repeated as if he hadn't already known the answer. "Then you must have been well acquainted with Lady Seaton. What was she like?"

Morley's amiable expression went rigid. "She was a charming and beautiful lady," he said after a long silence. "Her death was a great tragedy."

Suspecting that the younger man had been at least half in love with his employer's wife, Kenneth asked, "How did she die? No one will speak of her, and I've been reluctant to ask."

Morley stared into his tankard. "She fell from a cliff while walking near their country home, Ravensbeck House. I'll never forget that day. My office overlooked the drive. I was working on Sir Anthony's correspondence when George Hampton, the engraving fellow, came galloping up to the house." A spasm crossed his face at the memory.

In the pause that followed, Kenneth asked, "What was Hampton doing in the neighborhood?"

"He was on holiday. It's the Lake district, you know. Very popular with the artistic set." His voice dropped to a whisper. "Hampton looked frantic, so I went out to find what was wrong. He said he'd seen someone falling from Skelwith Crag, so he'd come to Ravensbeck for help." Morley swallowed hard, his Adam's apple bobbing. "I asked what the person was wearing. As soon as Hampton said green, I knew. Lady Seaton had worn the loveliest green gown that morning. She looked so beautiful..." His voice broke.

Kenneth gave the other man time to compose himself before saying, "So you collected Sir Anthony and the male servants and a rope and went to investigate."

"More or less, except for Sir Anthony. He was out. So was Miss Seaton, so it was up to me to deal with what had happened."

"Sir Anthony and his daughter were together?"

"No, they'd gone off separately. Miss Seaton had been out walking. She joined us as we were... were bringing up her mother's body."

"How ghastly for her," Kenneth murmured. "And for you. Having a weeping female on your hands must have made everything more difficult."

Morley shook his head. "Miss Seaton didn't weep. Her face was bone white, but she didn't say a word or shed a tear. Seemed damned unnatural to me."

"Very likely she was in a state of shock." Kenneth poured more ale into the other man's tankard. "When did Sir Anthony learn about the tragedy?"

"When he came home to dress for dinner." Morley's face twisted. "I think he'd been with another woman. It's common knowledge that he has a roving eye."

"Were you the one who had to break the news to him?"

Morley nodded. "It was the strangest thing. He snarled, 'Damn her!' Then he pushed by me and went to Lady Seaton's bedroom, where we had laid her out. It was as if he didn't believe she was dead. I went with him. She... she looked as if she were only sleeping. He told me to get the hell out. He spent the whole night there. The next morning he emerged as calm as you please and began giving orders for the funeral." Morley's fingers whitened around his tankard. "The selfish bastard never showed any sign of caring that his wife was dead."

Kenneth had seen enough of grief to know that it took many forms. Spending a night by a dead wife's side did not sound like lack of caring. "How did Lady Seaton come to fall? Was there a storm, or did the earth at the edge of the cliff crumble away?"

Morley looked troubled. "Neither. There was a wonderful prospect from Skelwith Crag. It was a favorite spot of hers. It's hard to understand how she could have fallen."

Putting shock into his voice, Kenneth said, "Surely foul play was not suspected."

"Of course not," Morley said, a little too quickly. "The inquest was merely a formality."

"If everyone is so sure Lady Seaton's death was an accident, why the universal reluctance to talk about it?" Kenneth said, trying to look innocently puzzled. "What is the mystery?"

"There is no mystery," the other man said sharply. "Merely regret, that her life was cut off too soon." He got to his feet. "I must return to my work now. It was a pleasure to meet you, Captain. Sir Anthony will be in good hands with a secretary who is so thorough." He made a brisk exit from the tavern.

Kenneth finished his ale slowly, considering what he had learned. Morley's uneasy manner supported the possibility that Helen Seaton's death was not a simple accident. If George Hampton and the mystery mistress were in the area at the time, perhaps other members of their social circle were also there. He made a mental note to find out.

What could Sir Anthony have meant when he said "Damn her"? The curse might have been the anger of someone who felt abandoned by a loved one's death. But he might also have been damning another woman. Could the mystery mistress have murdered her lover's wife in the hope that Sir Anthony would marry her? If that had happened and Sir Anthony suspected it, that would explain why the affair had ended. It would also explain guilt if Sir Anthony knew who had committed the murder, but could not bring himself to give the evidence that would send his paramour to the gallows.

Reminding himself that such thoughts were highly speculative, Kenneth finished his ale and left the tavern. Using their mutual interest in horses, he had been cultivating the longtime Seaton groom, Phelps. Sometime in the next few days, he would start asking serious questions of the man.

As for Rebecca, he hoped that in the intimacy of the studio she could be persuaded to tell him her version of her mother's death.

CHAPTER 9

Rebecca set her sketchbook on her desk and leaned back, stretching her arms over her head. Though she was no stranger to obsession, sometimes it was a damned bore. It was not uncommon for her to spend days or weeks trying to decide how best to paint a subject. Images would fill her mind by day and haunt her sleep at night until she found the right solution. Though she often felt like a dog gnawing at a bone, the pleasure of a good idea compensated for the tiresome process of getting there.

No idea had really possessed her since her mother's death—until she'd seen Kenneth Wilding. Now, she was a woman obsessed. Such intensity made it hard to decide the best way to do his portrait. She wanted something special, something that would capture his unique qualities of body and soul. Then in a small way—a safe way—he would be hers forever.

It didn't help that he slept in the room next to hers. She glanced across her bedroom at the common wall. She'd scarcely ever been aware of the other secretaries who had lived there, but she thought of Kenneth often. Did his sternness relax in sleep? How did he spend his private time? In reading and correspondence, she supposed. He was almost spookily quiet.

With a sigh of irritation, she rubbed her stiff neck. She'd done literally dozens of sketches showing the captain in different poses and costumes. Nothing seemed right. Tomorrow he was going to sit for her for the second time. If she didn't have a good concept by then, she would have to cancel the session rather than waste his time.

The Gray Ghost, who was lying at the foot of her bed, opened his eyes and gave her a look of feline contempt. "It's easy for you to criticize," she said accusingly. "But I notice you don't have any useful suggestions."

Treating her remark with the disdain it deserved, he gave a weary sigh and closed his eyes again. "You think I should go to bed?" she asked. "I doubt I would sleep."

From experience, she knew she would lie awake for hours while visions of Kenneth Wilding danced in her head. Perhaps a glass of sherry would help. She'd get one from the dining room.

After lighting a candle, she opened her door and stepped into the hall—and almost crashed into the object of her obsession, who was emerging from his own room. She stopped just short of banging her nose into Kenneth's collarbone, almost losing her balance in the process.

"Sorry!" He steadied her with a hand on her elbow. "I was heading to the kitchen to find something to eat. I didn't think anyone else was awake at this hour."

He'd removed his coat and cravat and undone the top buttons of his shirt. Sharply aware of the strength in the hand holding her arm, Rebecca raised her gaze from the solid wall of his chest to his face. The candlelight cast dramatic shadows across his strong features. There was something about the lighting, the way he was dressed... the white line of his scar. His mesmerizing eyes. Damnation, she almost had it....

His brows drew together. "Is something wrong?"

Her fragmented ideas coalesced into sizzling unity. *"The Corsair!"* she burst out. "Come here."

She grabbed his wrist and towed him into her bedroom. He'd always reminded her of a pirate, and Byron's corsair was the quintessential pirate, brave and bold and wildly romantic. She'd been a blasted fool not to see that right away.

After setting down the candle, she put her hands on Kenneth's shoulders to press him into a sitting position on the sofa. Intently she studied the rugged planes of his face. "A little too civilized," she muttered to herself.

She ran both hands through his hair, loosening the dark waves. The texture was thickly silken on her palms. After brushing a length rakishly across his forehead, she reached for his shirt and unfastened two more buttons. The white fabric fell back to reveal a tantalizing glimpse of bare flesh and dark, curling hair. "Perfect," she said with satisfaction.

"Perfect for what?" he inquired.

There was humor in the smoky depths of his eyes. Humor, and something more. Abruptly she recognized the wild impropriety of dragging a man into her bedroom and attacking his clothing. A good thing she didn't have a reputation to lose. "I've been toying with how to do your portrait, and inspiration just hit," she explained. "Lord Byron wrote a poem called 'The Corsair' three years ago. It was a great success—all about a dashing, Oriental, wildly romantic pirate. A perfect way to paint you."

"Surely you're joking. I'm neither dashing nor romantic, and certainly not Oriental." He smiled suddenly. "If I were a real pirate, I'd do this." He slid a hand around her neck and pulled her down for a kiss.

His tone was teasing, but the meeting of their lips was deadly serious. She felt a physical shock as his mouth moved against hers. The blaze of creative energy she'd been experiencing transmuted into fierce desire. Her hands were still resting on his chest, and her fingertips tingled from the accelerating beat of his pulse. She wanted to climb into his lap and rip off his shirt. She wanted to explore every inch of his powerful, masculine body. She wanted... she wanted...

He released her and pulled his head back, ending the kiss. She saw in his eyes that he was as stunned as she.

After a long moment, he said with a credible attempt at calm, "But I am not a corsair. Merely a secretary."

"Once a captain, always a captain," she said, as eager as he to pretend that nothing important had happened.

She dropped her hands from his chest and stepped unsteadily away. "You positively radiate romance and dashingness. When I've finished with your portrait, you'll look at it and see yourself for the first time."

"I'm not sure I want to see myself that clearly!"

"You don't have to look at the results if you don't want to." Her eyes narrowed as she retreated into the safety of professional judgment. "I want to play with this for a bit. Lean back. Relax. Lay your arm along the back of the sofa."

She gave a nod of satisfaction when he obeyed. A pose like this, languid but latent with power, would be exactly right. What else should be used? She didn't want to clutter the painting with an elaborate costume, so she must create a sense of Oriental mystery more subtly.

She paused, then gave a crow of triumph and seized a small carpet that lay by the far side of the bed. "This will make a perfect background. I'll drape it over the sofa behind you."

He turned to examine the carpet as she spread it over the sofa back. "This is superb." He ran his palm lovingly across the lustrous, exquisitely patterned surface. "I suppose it's Persian, but I've never seen a carpet with such rich burgundy colors. And the texture... it feels like the Gray Ghost's fur."

"It's made from silk. A gift from the Persian ambassador."

Kenneth's brows rose. "Surely there's a story behind that."

She shrugged. "Nothing terribly exciting. Mirza Hassan Khan decided that while he was in London he would commission a European-style portrait, so he came to Father. He liked the results so much that he also wanted a picture of the two wives he'd brought to keep him company. Since a strange man could not be allowed to see their unveiled faces, Father suggested me for the commission. The carpet was Mirza Hassan Khan's gift when I refused to accept money for the portrait."

"He must have been very pleased with your work. This is worth a king's ransom." Kenneth caressed the luxurious pile. "And I get to touch it for however long it takes you to paint me. I feel privileged."

The carpet provided exactly the sensual richness that she wanted. Her pulse quickened, fueling the exhilaration that came when the pieces began to click into place.

Now to find the right pose. Usually she directed her subjects, but she suspected that Kenneth would need no more than a suggestion. "Take a comfortable position that you can maintain for long periods," she ordered. "I want you to look relaxed but alert. A lounging lion rather than an upright soldier."

He turned and leaned against the back of the sofa, then drew his left leg up so that his booted foot rested on the edge of the sofa seat. When he draped his arm casually across his raised knee, the effect combined the ease of total confidence with a menacing sense that he could spring into action on an instant's notice.

"Excellent," she said. "Now look at me as if I'm a lazy, insolent soldier in your company."

His expression hardened, the scar becoming more prominent. He looked every inch the pirate captain who would loot or love with equal ease.

She bit her lip as she studied the overall composition. She would use dramatic lighting on his features and leave the rest of the scene shadowed to add to the air of mystery. So far, so good. Yet there was still something missing. Making Kenneth look fierce would be easy. But how could she convey the perceptive, contemplative side of his nature?

She stalked around him, trying to find the perfect angle. A shimmer of movement caught her eye. It was Kenneth's reflection in the mirror on her dressing table. Her eyes flicked from him to the mirror as an idea crystallized.

Eureka! Her excitement blazed higher. She would do a double portrait. The focus would be on him staring challengingly from the picture. But on the right side would be a reflection of his profile. There she could convey his haunted, weary intelligence. The reflection could not be as bright as if it were in a real mirror—that would be too strong, too distracting. She would use a wall of polished black marble so viewers would have to look closely to see the captain's hidden side.

As she reached for her sketchbook, the Gray Ghost

came awake and leaped from the bed to the sofa, landing with an audible thump. Then he sprawled alongside the captain's thigh. Kenneth began idly stroking the cat's head. "Will the Ghost interfere with your drawing?"

Rebecca laughed aloud, intoxicated by the rightness of it all. To think she'd just told her pet that he'd never given her any good ideas! "On the contrary, the Gray Ghost is the crowning touch. I'll make him larger and turn him into some kind of wild Asiatic hunting cat. Just the kind of barbaric pet one would expect of a pirate chief."

She bent her head and set her charcoal flying across the page. This was going to work. It was going to work *well*.

The ensuing silence was broken only by the rasp of charcoal and the faint, distant sounds of a sleeping city. She had finished the main figures and was roughing in background when Kenneth said wistfully, "Will I ever be allowed any food?"

Startled, she glanced at the clock and saw that it was after one o'clock. "I'm so sorry—I had no idea how much time had passed. I'm afraid I got carried away."

"An understatement. If a fire-breathing dragon had fallen down the chimney, you wouldn't have noticed." He stood and rolled his shoulders to loosen them.

She watched the fabric of his shirt tighten over his taut muscles and made mental notes of how to imply that power in her painting. Then she set aside her sketchbook and got to her feet. "You're going to make a splendid corsair, Captain."

"If you say so." He lifted the sketchbook and studied her work, his brows knit. "Do I look that ferocious?"

"Sometimes. It's no accident that the household staff has become so well behaved." She yawned, suddenly tired.

"They're terrified you'll sell them into slavery in High Barbary."

He began flipping through the earlier pages. "You certainly tried a variety of different compositions." He paused at a drawing that portrayed him as a weary soldier in a shabby uniform, his expression stark as he gazed over a harsh Spanish landscape. "Are you sure you aren't clairvoyant?"

"Just an artist's imagination." She regarded the sketch thoughtfully. "Is the sunlight really different in Spain?"

"There's a bright clarity very unlike England. We're much farther north here, and the moist air makes the light softer, almost hazy." He began paging through the sketches again.

Content with her progress, Rebecca picked up a fresh stick of charcoal to set into the holder. Then the silence caught her attention. She looked up to see that Kenneth had stopped again and was staring at the sketchbook.

Feeling her gaze, he raised the book to show the drawing of a woman tumbling headlong through the air, her expression a silent scream of horror. "What's this?"

The fragile stick of charcoal snapped between Rebecca's fingers as her elation crashed into grief. She had forgotten the drawing was in this particular sketchbook. "It's... it's a study of Dido hurling herself from the towers of Carthage when Aeneas abandoned her," she improvised, her mouth dry.

"In modern dress?" he said skeptically. "A change for you. Your other classical studies celebrate women who are heroic, not those who die of thwarted love. Besides, I thought Dido killed herself with a sword."

She stared at him mutely, unable to come up with another lie. Quietly he said, "The woman looks rather like the portrait of your mother. Did Lady Seaton die in a fall?"

Heart pumping as if she'd been caught stealing, Rebecca dropped into her chair again. "Yes, and ever since then, I've been obsessed by images of her falling," she said haltingly. "I suppose I've done at least fifty sketches like that one. I keep wondering how she felt, what she thought in the last moments. It must have been ghastly to die alone, in terror."

There was a long silence. Then Kenneth said slowly, "I've been afraid often, particularly before battles. Fear can be a lifesaver by increasing one's strength and alertness. Yet oddly, on two occasions when I've *known* beyond any shadow of a doubt that I would die, I felt no fear. Instead, there was a strange kind of peacefulness.

"Both times, I survived through a miracle. After the second incident, I became curious and talked to friends and found that others had had the same experience. Perhaps peace is nature's last gift when nothing can be done to stave off an inevitable fate." Expression compassionate, he set down the sketchbook. It's quite possible that your mother felt no terror before the end. Only a few fleeting moments of acceptance."

Rebecca bent her head as she struggled to master her emotions. "You're not making that up to make me feel better?"

"It's God's own truth." He sat opposite her on the sofa again and enfolded her hands in his, the warmth dispelling some of her chill. "If you tell me what happened, it might exorcise a few demons."

Perhaps he was right. Though she had tried never to think of that day, she forced herself to cast her mind back. "We were at Ravensbeck, our home in the Lake District," she said, praying that her voice wouldn't break. "It was a lovely, sunny day—one could see for miles. I had been walking in the hills and was returning home when I saw several men on a cliff where Mother often went to enjoy the views. Even though I was far away, I knew something was very wrong. I began to run. By the time I reached the cliff, they were... were bringing up her body."

"How dreadful for you." His hands tightened comfortingly. "Perhaps the worst thing about a lethal accident is the sheer suddenness. There is no time for friends and family to prepare."

That wasn't quite true in this case, but she said only, "Even now, I sometimes forget she is gone." Her throat closed and she could say no more.

His thumbs stroked gently over the back of her hands, sending pleasant tingles through her fingers and wrists. "I wonder how the accident happened," he said thoughtfully. "Had your mother been upset about anything? Unhappiness or worries could have distracted her to cause a fatal misstep."

"No," Rebecca said sharply. "There was nothing like that." She pulled her hands away. "One of the men who went down the cliff said that flowers were scattered all around her. Mother loved wildflowers and picked them often. The cliff slants gradually before dropping sharply. I think she simply went too close to the edge while gathering a bouquet, then lost her balance and fell."

"A tragic irony," he murmured, his keen gaze on her face.

Rebecca looked at the picture of the falling woman. "When I'm upset, I draw pictures about what is bothering me," she said haltingly. "Like lancing an infected wound to release the poison. It worked for everything from a dead pet to a broken heart. But this time, drawing hasn't helped."

"You draw what distresses you?" he asked curiously. "I dr... I would have thought it would make more sense to escape the pain by drawing other subjects."

She smiled without humor. "I've done that, too." Drawing and painting had been her life. And a rich and rewarding life it had been, but art was not enough. Not this time.

"If lancing doesn't work, perhaps cauterization will." Kenneth took the sketchbook from her and ripped out the picture of her mother. Then he held the corner in the candle flame. "From what I've heard about Lady Seaton, she would not have wanted you to be crippled by grief. Let her go, Rebecca."

Heart aching, Rebecca watched the flames consume the drawing. Smoke spiraled upward before dissipating into the darkness. She appreciated his desire to help, but he didn't understand. Not really. Because he was strong, he didn't know what it was like to be so filled with grief that her spirit was paralyzed. He couldn't know that if she ever cried, she would never be able to stop. That she would cry until she died.

He tossed the burning remnant of paper into the fireplace before it singed his fingers. They watched silently as the paper and image crumbled into ash and the yellow flame died away. Then he said, "Drawing so furiously must have required a great deal of energy. You should eat. Join me in my raid on the kitchen."

He smiled, and her heart lifted. He might not fully understand, but he had known pain of his own. He was also kind and a good companion. She smiled back. "You're right. I'm ravenous and hadn't noticed."

As she took a candle and moved toward the door, she thought of the swift, searing kiss they had exchanged.

Though a mistake, it had made her feel more alive than she had since her mother's death. Perhaps there really was life beyond sorrow.

Who would have thought that a pirate would show her the way?

Kenneth did his best to amuse Rebecca during their midnight feast. By the time they retired to their respective bedrooms, some of the shadows had left her eyes.

Unfortunately, he could not share her lightened mood. Her version of her mother's death left him convinced that she was suppressing something significant. She had been too quick to reject the possibility that the death had been anything but a random accident. Perhaps her grief was mixed with a fear too ugly to face—one that involved her father.

There were other reasons for his restlessness. The shock of that kiss, for one. Obviously his primitive male self had been waiting for a halfway decent excuse to act on the attraction he had felt from the first. One short embrace had confirmed everything he had suspected about Rebecca's latent sensuality. The fire that made her an artist could flare into fierce passion.

Under ordinary circumstances, he would not have stopped kissing her. But these circumstances were not ordinary.

Physical yearning was matched by mental turmoil. He had been fascinated by Rebecca's comment that she drew pictures about what upset her. It was so different from his own habit. He had drawn compulsively his whole life, even when he had had to do it in secret to prevent his father from knowing. Even when it had become clear that he would never be an artist. When he was unhappy, sketching had been an escape, an opportunity to create a wall of safety between himself and the unbearable.

He took out his sketchbook and stared at it as if the sheets of paper were a ticking bomb. What would happen if he dared draw one of the images that lacerated his mind? Part of him feared that doing so would open Pandora's box, releasing anguish that he would never be able to control again.

Yet her words haunted him. *Like lancing an infected wound to release the poison.* Perhaps escape was not the best remedy for suffering. If he had the courage to confront his private demons, perhaps they would lose some of their power to wound.

But to draw them well, he would have to face the pain. Tear down the mental walls that had made it possible for him to continue living.

Steeling himself, he reached for pen and India ink. He would start with an image that had been burned into his brain during his first battle. If drawing that reduced the remembered ache, he would try other, more difficult scenes.

He opened his mind to the shock he had felt when he saw that first image. To the pain that surrounded the scene in his nightmares.

Then he dipped his pen into the ink bottle, and prayed that Rebecca's method would also work for him.

CHAPTER 10

The next afternoon, Kenneth was working in the office when Lavinia Claxton sauntered into the room, a golden-haired picture in blue silk and a dashing, feather-trimmed bonnet. "Good day, Captain," she said in a deep, purring voice. "I decided to seek you out in your mysterious lair."

He looked up from his desk, his pulse quickening. Though Lavinia was a frequent visitor to Seaton House, this was the first time he'd had a chance to question her. Casually he said, "There's nothing mysterious about doing one's job, Lady Claxton."

She smiled with the confidence of a woman who knew the power of her beauty. "Then the mystery must come from you. You don't belong here, Captain. You're like a tiger among the lambs. You should be leading armies or exploring wild corners of the earth. Not sitting at a desk writing letters."

He smiled a little. "Even tigers need to earn a living. Some hunt game. Others take dictation."

"How mundane." She crossed the room, her lush figure

swaying provocatively. "I prefer to think of you as a heroic warrior who has turned from the violence of battle to the boudoirs of art."

"Boudoirs?" He pushed back from his desk. "You have a fine imagination, my lady. Most would think this only an office."

"Call me Lavinia. Everyone does." She perched on the edge of his desk, her skirts brushing his knee. Then she reached out and caressed his cheek. "And you can call me anytime."

Even though she had been giving him alluring smiles ever since they first met, he was startled by the blatantness of her advance. Perhaps she and Sir Anthony were at odds. Against his will, his body tightened in response. But it really wouldn't do to bed someone connected to his murder investigation. "Such familiarity would be wrong, my lady." He caught her hand and pressed a light kiss on the back before returning it to her lap. "Sir Anthony would think me impertinent, and justly so."

"He wouldn't mind. Everyone knows what a great whore Lavinia is," she said self-mockingly. She slid from the desk and strolled across the room, halting under the portrait of Lady Seaton. "Not like Helen. Anthony once did a picture of us entitled *The Saint and the Sinner.* Naturally I was the sinner."

"Was Lady Seaton such a saint?"

Lavinia glanced at the painting. "Like most of us, she could be generous or selfish, wise or foolish. Sometimes she was very difficult. But she was my closest friend and I miss her greatly. As much as Anthony and George do."

"George?"

"George Hampton. Helen was his mistress, you know."

Masking his surprise, he said, "Really? Or are you just trying to shock me?"

"I doubt you are so easily shocked, Captain," she said dryly. "Helen was discreet, but she had her share of lovers over the years. Only George was significant, though."

Startled by the possibilities this opened up, he asked, "Did Sir Anthony know his wife was having an affair with one of his closest friends?"

"Oh, yes. Their marriage was terribly immoral, but very civilized. Anthony approved of George, knowing he would never hurt Helen. And she didn't mind her husband's little flings. She knew she was the only one who really mattered."

"I'd heard that he was involved in a more serious affair at the time Lady Seaton died."

"Don't believe everything you hear, Captain." Lavinia untied the ribbons of her bonnet and took it from her head, giving a shake to her golden ringlets. "Anthony and I have been friends for a long time. I think I would have guessed if he'd really fallen in love with someone."

There was a brittle note in her voice. Under Lavinia's sophistication was more vulnerability than she might want to admit. Kenneth wondered if she was in love with Sir Anthony. "Do you think Sir Anthony is likely to remarry?"

She hesitated. "I really don't know. Helen's death still hangs over him like a dark cloud."

"Was there something suspicious about how she died?"

Lavinia curled a bonnet feather around her forefinger. "No doubt it was an accident. And yet..." Her voice trailed off.

Quietly he said, "I've heard that there were signs of a struggle where Lady Seaton fell."

She gave him a sharp glance. "Merely broken plants and scuff marks, probably a result of Helen slipping, then trying to catch something to prevent herself from going over the cliff."

It was a logical explanation, yet Lavinia still seemed troubled. "Whenever the subject of Lady Seaton's death is raised, the people who knew her become very evasive," he said thoughtfully. "What is the great mystery? Did Sir Anthony or George Hampton push her over the cliff?"

"Rubbish," Lavinia retorted. "There is no mystery. It is merely that death is so much less amusing than lust."

Seeing that she would reveal no more, he said equably, "Then by all means let us discuss lust. What you've been saying supports the common view of artists as wild and dissolute."

"No more dissolute than the fashionable world. Merely more honest." She gave a slow, provocative smile. "And to be honest, I find you very attractive, Captain."

He had a sudden craving for the soft sweetness of female flesh, but despite Lavinia's assurances, he doubted that Sir Anthony would appreciate sharing his current mistress with his secretary. "The feeling is mutual, but I don't think it would be wise for me to act on it."

"I shall hope that spending time with artists will soon undermine your wisdom." She crossed the room and slipped her gloved hand behind his neck as she bent to give him a leisurely kiss. Her eyes were a cool, pale green. She kissed very skillfully, yet he did not feel a fraction of the response he had experienced with Rebecca.

He saw a movement from the corner of his eye. A moment later, an icy female voice said, "Much as I dislike interrupting this tender scene, I have some business to transact."

Kenneth glanced up to see a smoldering Rebecca standing in the doorway. With her untidy auburn hair haloing around her head, she looked like a fierce ginger kitten.

While he uttered a mental curse, Lavinia straightened unhurriedly. "Hello, my dear." Her interested gaze went from Rebecca back to Kenneth. "I hope your work is going well. I've received a number of compliments on that last picture you did of me. If you would allow me to reveal the name of the artist, you'd have as many commissions as you could handle." She smiled and glided from the room.

Rebecca let Lavinia pass, then stepped into the office and slammed the door behind her. "My father expects his secretaries to be versatile, Captain, but you exceed what he had in mind."

"If you overheard the last of the conversation," Kenneth said mildly, "you know that I politely rejected her hints."

"But not her kiss."

"I could hardly use physical violence against the lady."

"A spanking would not have been out of place," Rebecca said tartly. "Lavinia is overdue for one."

Watching her closely, he said, "Based on what Lady Claxton was saying, illicit kisses should not be so shocking in this house. In the course of our discussion, she mentioned your mother's relationship with George Hampton."

Rebecca's face went rigid, but not with surprise. She had known about the affair. "I would have thought you were above such gossip, Captain," she snapped.

"I don't gossip, merely listen." He hesitated. "Was it upsetting to know how... unconventional your parents were?"

"How promiscuous, you mean." Her gaze touched the portrait of her mother before moving to the safety of the window. "How could I be upset? The apple didn't fall far from the tree. I ruined myself at eighteen. Wantonness is in the blood."

"I don't believe that," he said gently. "Did you really elope because of the example of your parents? Or was it because you were looking for love?"

After a long silence, she said, "Just before my come-out, I met a young viscount who came to Father for a portrait. I mistook his flirtation for serious interest and agreed to go riding in the park. He tried to maul me when we stopped to walk. When I resisted, he said that since I'd grown up with artists, I had no right to play Miss Propriety."

"I'm sure you didn't let that pass without comment."

"I pushed him into a fountain and left, resenting both him and my father, whose way of life had laid me open to such insult. Not very reasonable, perhaps, but I was young and hurt."

A hard pulse beat in her throat. "Then I was presented to society, and met Frederick. He sighed and wrote poems and told me he loved me, which was balm to my bruised heart. My parents didn't like him, and probably nothing would have come of it if I hadn't learned about Mother and Uncle George. Though I'd known about Father's affairs, it was a shock to find that my mother was no better. Three days later, I eloped." She gave a twisted smile. "I quickly realized that my parents were right and that marrying Frederick would be disastrous. Luckily, I found that out before tying myself to him for life."

Privately thinking that the elder Seatons should have given their daughter less freedom and more guidance, Kenneth said, "I presume that an advantage of having liberal parents was their willingness to take you back in spite of the scandal."

She nodded. "The only lectures I got were on my judgment, not my morality. My father said he was glad I had the sense not to marry such a loose fish, my mother said she was sure that I wouldn't make such a mistake again, and that was that."

"And she was right—you didn't repeat the mistake."

"Nor will I in the future," she said in a tone that said the subject was closed. "I came down to ask what happened to the roll of canvas I ordered. I'm almost out."

"Yesterday I wrote the supplier and received a note from him in this morning's post. He apologized for the delay and said the canvas would be delivered day after tomorrow. Is there anything else you wished to inquire about?"

"Oh. No. That was all." She turned to leave.

"Is this afternoon's painting session still on, or are you too irritated with me for that?"

She gave him an ironic glance. "Not at all. Being assailed by lusty females like Lavinia is in the best tradition of Byronic heroes. Exactly right for a corsair."

As he chuckled, she exited and closed the door. His smile faded as he evaluated what he had learned. The Helen Seaton described by Lavinia might have had several potential murderers. Sir Anthony's superficial complaisance about her affairs might have masked festering rage. Perhaps the mystery mistress had yearned to have the painter for herself, or Helen had decided to dismiss George Hampton from her life and he had killed her in a jealous fury. Or there might be other, unknown lovers.

Passion and gain were the most likely reasons for murder, if indeed there had been a murder. Kenneth sighed with frustration. The longer he spent in Seaton House, the more he appreciated the difficulties of determining the truth about Helen Seaton—and the more he disliked his own duplicity. Becoming Rebecca's confidant when he was here under false pretenses was a kind of betrayal. If she ever learned what he was doing...

It wasn't a thought he wanted to complete.

Rebecca mentally berated herself as she made her way back to the safety of her studio. When she found Lavinia kissing Kenneth, she should have quietly left and returned at a later time. Instead, she'd felt a surge of jealousy. Worse, she had showed it even though she had no right to be jealous where he was concerned. The one impulsive kiss they had shared had meant nothing, even though it had affected her down to her toes. Kenneth was her father's employee, not her suitor.

Nonetheless, even though she and Lavinia always got on well, she felt like scratching the other woman's eyes out. Rebecca blushed when she remembered Lavinia's speculative gaze. Had she guessed that Rebecca had more than a casual interest in her father's secretary?

To relieve her feelings, Rebecca did a quick sketch of what Lavinia would look like if she weighed twice as much and had acquired a good set of wrinkles. The childish exercise cheered her no end. Reminding herself that Kenneth had given Lavinia no encouragement, she prepared for the afternoon painting session. It took only a few minutes to arrange the sofa, Persian carpet, and mirror that would be used for the shadow portrait.

Kenneth wouldn't come until after luncheon. She glanced restlessly around the studio. There were a dozen things she could do, none of which interested her.

Her gaze fell on the painting of Diana the Huntress. Drat, she had promised to frame it and replace the dreadful paintings in Kenneth's room.

Thinking that changing the pictures would be a subtle way of apologizing for her bad temper, she mounted Diana in a suitable frame. Then she selected two other paintings, a large Lake District landscape and a study of the Gray Ghost stalking a bird with panther wildness in his amber eyes.

She carried the two smaller pictures downstairs and knocked on Kenneth's door, entering when she received no answer. The existing paintings made her winkle her nose. All were an insult to anyone who appreciated good art. In Kenneth's place, she would have pitched them out the window.

She was hanging the Diana when her foot grazed a portfolio propped against the armoire. It tipped open, spilling drawings across the carpet. Wondering what the captain was doing with an artist's portfolio, she bent to close it.

She stopped, frozen. On top was a pen and ink sketch of a battle scene. Soldiers lunged with raised bayonets, smoke drifted, and horses reared in the background.

But what riveted her attention was the figure at the center of the page. Defined entirely by the dark lines of the background, it was a pure white silhouette of a man jerking in agony. Without a shred of detail, the outline conveyed the lethal strike of a bullet ripping into fragile human flesh. Shock and death, a moment of eternal silence set amid the horrors of hell. It was an image of profound, visceral power.

She dropped cross-legged to the floor and began paging through the portfolio. Charcoal and pastel portraits, precise topographical renderings of buildings, a handful of lovely watercolor landscapes. Though none matched the drama of the first picture, all were skillfully executed.

The last sketch was of a couple clinging urgently together. The scrawled legend said "Romeo and Juliet." Though the man and woman wore medieval garb, the aching emotion in the picture made her suspect that the two were real lovers, perhaps on the verge of a wartime separation.

She was studying the picture when the door opened and Kenneth stepped in. He stopped dead when he saw her, his expression turning thunderous. Then he slammed the door shut and advanced into the room, his usual quiet deference vanishing in a blaze of anger. "What the bloody hell are you doing?"

Repressing the urge to cower, she laid a hand on the portfolio in her lap. "You drew these pictures?"

He leaned down and snatched the portfolio away. "You have no right to pry among my possessions."

"I wasn't prying," she protested. "I accidentally knocked the portfolio over when I was hanging new paintings." Wondering why he was so upset, she asked again, "This is your work?"

He paused, as if considering a lie, then reluctantly nodded.

At a disadvantage on the floor, she scrambled to her feet. Unfortunately, Kenneth still towered over her. He was a fearsome sight; she sympathized with any unfortunate Frenchmen who had encountered him on the field of battle.

Curiosity overcoming caution, she said, "Why have you been hiding the fact that you're an artist?"

"I'm not an artist," he snapped.

"Of course you are!" she retorted. "No one learns to draw this well without years of practice. Why is your work such a secret? And why are you acting like a raging bull?"

He drew a deep breath. "Sorry. My drawing isn't exactly a secret, but I'm a mere dilettante. It would be presumptuous to mention my sketches to you or your father."

She made a rude noise. "Rubbish. You're very talented.

No wonder you were able to impress Father with your understanding of painting." She smiled a little. "I've been surrounded by artists my whole life, and you're the only one I ever met who wanted to hide his light under a basket."

Raw vulnerability in his voice, he said furiously, "*I am not an artist!*"

Startled by his vehemence, she set her hands on his shoulders and pressed him to a sitting position on the bed. Eyes almost level and hands resting lightly on his shoulders, she asked, "What's wrong, Kenneth? You're behaving very strangely."

The muscles under her palms tensed, and he dropped his gaze. After a long silence, he said, "My father hated my interest in art and tried to beat it out of me. He didn't consider drawing and painting a proper pursuit for his only son."

"Yet you didn't stop."

"I couldn't," he said simply. "It was like a fire inside me. In pictures, I could say things that I could never put into words. So I learned to conceal or destroy whatever I did. To pretend that it didn't matter."

"How ghastly for you!" No wonder he had been so disturbed by her discovery. Resisting the desire to kiss the shadows from his eyes, she brushed his cheek with the back of her hand, then stepped away. "I would have gone mad if my parents had tried to stop me from drawing."

"Instead, you had the good fortune to live with one of the finest painters in England." He gave a twisted smile. "When I was young, my secret dream was to study at the Royal Academy Schools to become a professional artist. It's too late for that now. I became a soldier, which is the antithesis of art." He glanced at his portfolio. "Being surrounded by so many wonderful paintings makes me want to burn my own feeble efforts."

"You *are* an artist, Kenneth," she said emphatically. "You already draw better than half the professionals in London. With some concentrated effort, you could become outstanding."

"I have a knack for drawing, and I do decent watercolors," he agreed, "but those are standard accomplishments for all young ladies and a good few gentlemen. I'm thirty-three. The time when I might have learned to be a real artist has passed."

Curiously she said, "How do you define an artist?"

"Someone who goes beyond rendering a likeness to reveal something new or hidden about the subject," he said slowly. "This picture of the Gray Ghost is pretty and amusing and painted with great fondness. Yet at the same time, it reveals his feral side—the wildness that lurks within the heart of every plump hearthside tabby. Similarly, your painting of Diana the Huntress shows her strength and pride in her skills, but also the loneliness that comes from being set apart. The yearning to be like other women. She reminds me of you a little."

Damn him! It was all very well to be perceptive about paintings of cats, but not about her. Ignoring the comment about the Diana, she said, "I merely painted the Ghost as I saw him."

"You saw him that way because you have an artist's vision." He went to study the painting more closely. "Your unique, individual view of the world infuses everything you do. I think I would recognize anything done by your hand."

The thought that he could so clearly recognize her in her work was as intimate as a kiss. Preferring to keep the discussion about him, not her, she removed several pictures from his portfolio. "You have the same ability." She indicated the pastel portrait of a dark Spanish beauty. "This woman is not only lovely but driven. Fiercely dedicated. Dangerous, even."

The tightening of Kenneth's face confirmed her description. She lifted the picture of the bullet-struck soldier. "If it's unique vision that makes an artist, you've got it. This is brilliant, and wholly original."

He shrugged. "That's a fluke. I did it last night because of what you said about drawing pictures of what upset you. Since for me drawing was always an escape, I decided to see if one of my milder demons could be safely released."

She glanced down at the drawing. If this was a mild demon, she'd love to see a major one. "Did it work?"

"Actually, it did. That image scorched my mind like a brand during my first battle. Drawing it made the memory seem..." he frowned, trying to define his thought, "not less clear, but farther away. Safer."

"It also gave me a chance to see and understand something I will never see in reality." She closed the portfolio again. "If that doesn't make you an artist, what would?"

He smiled faintly. "The ability to paint with oils. No other medium can match the intensity, the richness of color, of oil painting. The charcoal and watercolors I use are wielded by every schoolroom dauber."

"Then learn to use oils," she said tartly. "It's no great trick. In many ways, watercolor is far more difficult, and you've mastered that."

The scar on his face whitened. When he didn't speak, she said quietly, "You don't think you're capable of it."

His eyes fell. "I... I want it too much to believe it's possible."

The words said a great deal about how life had treated

him. Knowing he would loathe pity, she said briskly, "I'll teach you. Once you get past the foolish conviction that oils are beyond your capabilities, you'll do very well."

Seeing that he was on the verge of protest, she said with steel in her voice, "You have a great many foolish ideas about what it takes to be an artist. Forget them. The truth is that an artist is no more, and no less, than someone who creates art. You have the gift. Honor it."

Then she turned and marched to the door, throwing over her shoulder, "Be in my studio at two o'clock."

Her steps slowed after she closed the door and turned toward the stairs. She felt drained, and not only because of her sympathy for what Kenneth had endured. His talk of what it meant to be an artist stirred thoughts of her own life. She had been lucky, so lucky.

Sir Anthony might have been a casual parent in many ways, but he had always respected and encouraged her talent. What would it be like to have the strength and lethal skills of a warrior and the soul of an artist?

Poor damned pirate.

Face set, she opened the door to her studio. By the time she was through with Kenneth Wilding, he would know he was an artist. Either that, or they would both die trying.

CHAPTER 11

After Rebecca left, Kenneth sank into a chair, shaking as if with fever. He felt like a walnut that had been smashed open with a hammer.

She had said that he had talent. That he was already an artist. And Rebecca Seaton was not a woman for idle flattery.

He drew a ragged breath, wondering if what she had said was true: that it was not too late. Unconsciously he had always put oil painting on a pedestal, a skill more of gods than mortals. Now that Rebecca had made him aware of that assumption, he saw the absurdity. Granted, most artists began working with oils at a much younger age. Rebecca had started in the nursery. But he did draw well. He had a feel for composition and color.

Perhaps... perhaps he could learn to be a real painter. Not one on the level of Sir Anthony and Rebecca, but good enough to sometimes find satisfaction in his own efforts.

The prospect filled him with an unholy mixture of fear and excitement. The sensation, he realized wryly, was not unlike a young man's response to unchaste thoughts.

It was only when he got to his feet that he remembered why he had come to Seaton House: to investigate a mysterious death. Now his suspect's daughter was offering him the deepest wish of his soul. To accept her gift when his mission might destroy the person she loved most would be despicable. Yet God help him, he was unable to refuse.

For the first time, he considered abandoning Lord Bowden's assignment. An angry Bowden would immediately foreclose on Sutterton, but Kenneth might be able to endure that if he had a chance for the life he had always longed for. He could continue as Sir Anthony's secretary and devote his private time to study and painting. Someday, perhaps, he would be able to support himself as an artist. Plenty of people wanted portraits, and most of them couldn't afford Sir Anthony Seaton. Anyone who had lived as a common soldier could manage with little money and no comforts; it would not take many commissions for him to survive.

But what of Beth? She was his responsibility. He had no right to buy his own happiness at the cost of her future. Though starving in a garret might suit him, his sister deserved better.

His mouth tightened as he thought of Beth's uncomplaining good nature. It was impossible to withdraw, and equally impossible to resist Rebecca's offer to teach him to paint. His only choice was to go forward and pray that his investigation produced nothing to incriminate Sir Anthony in his wife's death.

Unfortunately, he had little faith in prayer.

Before going to Rebecca's studio, Kenneth stopped by the

office to take care of a few small matters of business. To his surprise, his employer was there, gazing at the magnificent portrait of his wife and drinking what appeared to be brandy.

As Kenneth hesitated, Sir Anthony glanced over and said musingly, "It was twenty-eight years ago today that I met Helen. Sometimes it's hard to believe she's gone." A faint slur in his speech showed that the drink he held was not the first.

Kenneth entered the office. "Lady Seaton was beautiful. Your daughter is very like her."

"In appearance, but Rebecca's temperament is more like mine." Sir Anthony smiled ironically. "In some ways, she's even more like my older brother. Marcus would hate knowing that."

Curious to hear his employer's side of the family feud, Kenneth said untruthfully, "I didn't know you had a brother."

"Marcus is a baron and very starchy. Doesn't approve of me. Never did." Sir Anthony took a deep swallow of brandy. "He and my father were both convinced that for me to become a painter would be the shortest way to Hades. On the rare occasions when our paths cross, he always gives me the cut direct."

So Kenneth was not the only hopeful artist to face family opposition. Sir Anthony, however, had done a better job of surmounting it. "Why does your brother disapprove of you?"

Sir Anthony snorted. "To Marcus, painting is no better than being in trade. He must have been appalled when I was knighted five years ago. It put the seal of respectability on my disreputable career."

"Most men would consider an artist of your stature a credit to the family name."

"There were... other reasons for our estrangement." Sir Anthony's gaze went to his wife's face. "Helen was Marcus's fiancée. When we met, it was like being swept up by wildfire. She tried to resist, to do the honorable thing. I didn't even try. I knew the result was foreordained. Within a fortnight, we ran off together. Gretna Green was only a day's ride to the north. We were married before anyone could stop us."

"I assume your brother was not pleased."

"Marcus never spoke to me again, except to send a note saying I wasn't welcome at the funeral when my father died." Sir Anthony smiled without humor. "I can't blame him. In his place, I'd have been murderous if someone had taken Helen from me."

Wondering if the comment might be literally true, Kenneth asked, "He loved her?"

"Losing her might have hurt his pride, but not his heart. To him, Helen was a pretty, docile girl who would have made a conformable wife. He never really knew her. God knows, he replaced her quickly enough. He was married within the year and immediately fathered a couple of sons to ensure that the title would never come to me."

"Lady Seaton wasn't sweet and docile?"

"She was a hellcat when her temper was up, but that was all right—I have a temper, too." Sir Anthony shook his head. "She was all fire and shadow. She would have died a slow death with Marcus. He is all honor and tradition. Worthy, but dull."

"He sounds very unlike you," Kenneth remarked. "You must not have minded being cut out of his life."

The other man stared down at his brandy glass. "He wasn't so bad. I quite admired him when I was a boy. He was a gentleman to the bone. I was the one who was a freak. My father was devoutly grateful that I was the second son, not the heir."

Kenneth's empathy increased. He, too, had been a freak, and it had cost him his father. At least he and Beth were on good terms. "Lady Seaton obviously didn't mind the fact that you were different from most members of the nobility."

"She didn't mind at all." Sir Anthony's gaze went to the portrait again. "I don't know how I would have survived after Helen's death if it hadn't been for Rebecca. She was like a rock. Strong. Steady. Enduring."

Surely a man who cared so much for his wife could not have murdered her. If there was some way to prove that, Kenneth could honorably fulfill his obligation to Lord Bowden without losing Rebecca's regard.

Sir Anthony's brows drew together. "Aren't you supposed to be posing for Rebecca now?"

Kenneth glanced at the clock. "Yes, sir. I came down to do some work, but it can wait." He headed toward the door.

His hand was on the knob when he heard Sir Anthony say in a barely audible voice, "Now she's gone, and may God forgive me—because it was my fault."

For an instant, Kenneth became rigid. Then he left the room, feeling sick to his stomach. If what Sir Anthony said was true, may God help them all.

~

By the time Rebecca reached her studio after discovering Kenneth's artwork, her fatigue had been replaced by brimming excitement. The picture of the mortally wounded soldier showed remarkable assurance, especially for a man who was essentially self-taught.

No wonder she had felt drawn to him from the beginning. Under his brawn and military bearing, he was as much an artist as she. Shared interests could become the basis of a deep friendship.

She went to her worktable and began to mix the tints that she would use in her afternoon's work. It was a process that she had done so often that her mind was free to question if it was really friendship that she wanted from Kenneth.

For a moment, the thought of marriage flickered through her mind. She instantly dismissed it. Marriage was not for her. Even if Kenneth was interested and willing to overlook her lack of reputation, she would never surrender her freedom. The selfishness essential to an artist would be fatal in a wife.

She supposed they could become lovers. The London art world was a tolerant one. If she and Kenneth were discreet, they could carry on as they pleased. Absorbed in his own business, her father wouldn't object. He probably wouldn't even notice.

But while her upbringing had given her a liberal outlook, her observations had convinced her that affairs could be a messy business. No doubt Lavinia could explain how to prevent pregnancy, but there were other hazards. The fact that a relationship was illicit would not make it any less painful when it ended. And end it would. Kenneth seemed to find her attractive, but she would be of more value to him as a teacher than as a not-very-skilled mistress. And they both knew it.

With a sigh, she finished mixing her tints. Friendship

was clearly the best possible relationship. She would simply have to repress any lustful thoughts.

There was a gift she could give Kenneth, as a friend, that would help him develop as a painter. With a smile, she got to her feet. She would have just enough time to arrange it.

Kenneth arrived for his modeling session dressed in the boots, breeches, and open-throated shirt she had requested. Rebecca caught her breath when he entered the room. There was a darkness in his expression that made him an utterly convincing pirate, a man who lived by his own rules alone. Merciful heaven, how she wanted to capture that!

Wanting to put him at ease, she said lightly, "You needn't look as if you're going to be made to walk the plank." She dusted off her hands. "Before we start, I have something for you."

"A pirate parrot to carry on my shoulder?" he said dryly.

She laughed. "It's a thought, but the Gray Ghost would make short work of a parrot. Come with me."

She led him from her studio to the hall that went to the other end of the attic. They passed the closed doors of half a dozen servants' rooms before she halted and unlocked the final door. After swinging it open, she stood aside so that Kenneth could enter what had been an empty servants' room.

His gaze went over the simple furnishings and single window and came to rest on the easel that stood in the center of the room. Beside the easel a battered pine table held a selection of different-sized brushes and a box containing plump bladders of paint. He glanced at her, his brows lifted questioningly.

"If you're going to paint seriously, you need a studio," she explained. "This is private, and it has a north light. You can take whatever materials you need from my workroom." She handed him the heavy iron key. "It's yours for as long as you want."

His hand closed convulsively over the key, the warm fingertips brushing her palm. "I don't deserve this," he said tightly. "Why are you so good to me, Rebecca?"

Sensing that the question wasn't rhetorical, she thought a moment before answering. "I suppose this is a kind of thanks offering for the fact that my creative path was so smooth. Or perhaps it's what I would have hoped to find if I'd had to face the obstacles to painting that you have."

"I don't deserve it," he said again, something very near pain in his eyes. "If you only knew..."

It was a moment that could easily slide into dangerous emotion. She tried not to stare at the rapid pulse beating at the base of his throat. He was surprised. Grateful that she took his dreams seriously.

What would happen if she stepped forward and lifted her face to his?

Clenching her hand into a fist, she turned away. "By the time you've finished posing for me, you'll have earned your painting lessons," she said briskly. "Come. It's time to begin."

~

Emotions taut, Kenneth followed Rebecca back to her studio. Several minutes were spent in duplicating the pose of the night before. As she began sketching on the canvas, he thought about the fact that in a matter of hours, he had acquired a teacher, a studio, someone to whom he could speak of his deepest longings. Everything would be perfect —if Sir Anthony hadn't just revealed that he felt responsible for his wife's death. Would the painter have said more if pressed? Probably not; his words had not been intended for other ears.

With grim honesty, Kenneth recognized that he had not wanted to know more. It was quite possible that an argument between two hot-tempered people might have escalated to unexpected violence.

The Seatons' love affairs had provided an abundance of motive. Perhaps George Hampton had persuaded Helen to leave her husband and live openly with her lover, and Sir Anthony had turned "murderous" at the news. Or perhaps Helen had become jealous of the mystery mistress in a way that she had not been of her husband's passing affairs. Or perhaps the mistress had decided to do away with her rival, and Sir Anthony had found out after the fact and ended the relationship, unable to turn his lover over to the law but blaming himself for the death.

Why couldn't these blasted people restrict themselves to sleeping with their own mates?

His reverie was interrupted when Rebecca glanced up from her drawing. "The dangerous expression is good, but try to relax. If you don't, you'll feel tied in knots within a half hour."

He did his best to obey. A more pleasant subject to ponder was whether Rebecca's casually knotted hair would stay pinned up or come tumbling down. Or he could think about her incredible generosity in finding a private space for him to work, except that the topic induced as much guilt as pleasure.

The sofa sagged under the weight of the Gray Ghost, who had materialized from some hidden lair. As the cat flopped alongside Kenneth's thigh in a perfect pose, he remarked, "The Ghost is a born artist's model."

"He's certainly very good at holding one position." Brows knit, Rebecca donned a paint-marked smock. "I've never taught painting, and I'm not sure quite where to start. As I've said before, art is a craft, like making watches or shoeing horses. A painter who is a great craftsman is not necessarily a great artist—but talent without craft will never be great."

"With that explanation, you've already taught me something," Kenneth said. "Assume I know nothing about working with oils, which isn't far wrong."

"Very well." She thought a moment. "The wonderful pictures of the old masters were done with painstaking care, building the final result through many layers of paint. Undercolors often glow through transparent upper layers. Marvelous effects were possible, but it was very slow. The fashion now is for direct painting—using the colors you want from the beginning. It's much faster, and what is lost in depth is gained in spontaneity."

"Is that why your father can be so prolific?"

"That's one of the reasons," she agreed. "He's also very well organized. Before starting work, he mixes the tints, halftones, and highlights the subject is likely to need. That means he seldom has to stop and mix colors. I've seen him do wonderful informal portraits in a single sitting."

"I assume you use the same approach."

She nodded and came over to display her oval palette.

"Every artist develops a particular system for laying out colors. It's usual to put white lead nearest the thumb hole because white is used the most. Apart from that, setting the palette is very personal. I generally use a dozen pure pigments and lay them along the edge. Then I do another row of tints that vary depending on what I'm painting. I mixed this set for flesh tones and a dark interior. I would use a very different range of colors for a landscape."

He studied her palette, committing the arrangement to memory. It made such beautiful sense.

Rebecca returned to her easel. "Later I'll explain how to prepare a canvas in detail, but for now, I'll just say that it's usual to start by laying down a ground—a solid color that covers the whole surface. The ground will affect the finished picture, even if it's completely covered. Dark brown is common because it adds richness to the painting. I generally use lighter colors for the brightness they create."

She brushed impatiently at an auburn lock that had fallen untidily over her eyes. It was the last straw needed to bring down the precariously balanced mass of her hair. Lushly sensual, it fell to her waist in a cascade of russet and chestnut and red-gold. Kenneth caught his breath at the sight. There was more provocation in that molten sweep of hair than most women had in their whole bodies.

Trying to sound detached, he said, "It would be a crime to cut hair like yours, but considering how it gets in the way, you must be tempted sometimes."

"Father won't let me. Whenever he does a subject with lots of hair, he likes to use me as a model." With the nonchalance of long practice, she swept up the fallen tresses, swirled them into a knot, and stabbed the wooden handle of a paintbrush through the middle to hold the mass in place. Then she lifted the palette in her left hand. "The ground was already laid in, and I just did a preliminary sketch that blocks out the major forms in the picture. It's time to begin to paint."

She dipped a wide brush into a daub of paint, then stroked the canvas, still talking about what she was doing. Kenneth listened intently as the accumulated knowledge of her and her father poured forth like a golden river. He tried to memorize every word, knowing that even the Royal Academy Schools could not have matched instruction like this.

Her words slowed, then stopped altogether as her concentration narrowed to the canvas in front of her. Kenneth didn't mind. She'd given him plenty to absorb already.

He found that an advantage of his pose was that he could watch her. With her intensity and delicate, steely strength, she was a wonderful subject for a study of an artist at work. Perhaps someday he would be able to do justice to such a portrait.

Better yet, he could paint her as a nude veiled only in a shimmering mantle of her splendid hair. It was a distracting thought. He found himself imagining the slim body beneath her shapeless protectiveness, and wondering how, exactly, her breasts were shaped.

A wave of heat spread through him. Damnation! He would go up in flames if he didn't think of something else. He forced himself to look past her. Soon it would be planting time at Sutterton. He must write and learn what Jack Davidson was planning to put in. He really ought to take his seat in Parliament, though of course he couldn't until this mission was completed. Would the paintbrush keep Rebecca's hair in place for the rest of the session?

His mind continued to skip around. Holding one position went from easy, to uncomfortable, to excruciating. When the pose became unendurable, he said, "Time for a break."

He stood and stretched his shaking muscles, his hands grazing the slanting ceiling. At least an hour had passed. Probably two. "Don't you ever tire when you work?"

Rebecca looked up, blinking as if coming out of a trance. "Yes. But I never notice until later."

"The Gray Ghost is better at posing than I. I swear he hasn't moved a whisker." Kenneth went to the hearth and swung the kettle over the fire. Then he ambled toward the easel, rubbing his stiff neck. "May I see what you've done?"

"I'd rather not until the picture is more advanced." She tugged the easel around so that the canvas faced the wall. "It's time for your first painting lesson."

While they drank tea, she talked about stretching and sizing, grounds and varnishes, scumbles and glazes. Then she set down her cup and got to her feet. "That's enough talk for one afternoon. If I'm not careful, I'll drown you in theory."

She indicated a box set by the wall. "Choose several objects and set up a still life on that small table."

Obediently he dug into the box. Aided by her suggestions, he settled on a graceful goblet, a cast of an antique Greek head, and half a dozen other items. Then he arranged them on a sweep of velvet drapery. When he was satisfied, she set another easel by the table, saying, "I've prepared canvases with different-colored grounds for you to experiment with."

She lifted a brush and ceremoniously offered it to him, handle first. "The time has come to start putting paint on canvas," she said with an encouraging smile.

As a newly enlisted soldier, he had been handed a rifle in a very similar fashion. The gun had led him down a long and harrowing road. He wondered where this new tool would take him.

Heart hammering, he accepted the brush.

CHAPTER 12

The empty trail stretched ahead between rows of trees, disappearing into the dawn mists. Kenneth called, "Go!" and gave his mount its head. They leaped forward.

For a few minutes, his mind was blessedly free of everything but the pleasure of a fine horse between his legs and the sting of a wintry wind. Reality returned when he reluctantly reined in his mount and turned toward Seaton House again.

Usually he was refreshed after exercising Sir Anthony's horse. Not today. The previous day's painting lesson was painfully vivid in his mind. It had not gone well. The feel, the weight, the flow of oils were entirely different from watercolors, and they'd demonstrated an infuriating reluctance to do as he wished.

Though he had always deprecated his artistic ability, he saw now how accustomed he'd become to the praise of his army friends. Catherine Melbourne and Anne Mowbry had loved his sketches of their families. Though he knew they overrated his work, he had found their compliments gratifying.

With Rebecca, however, he was unable to forget how amateur his efforts were compared to hers. He'd felt like a clumsy oaf. That wasn't her fault; her calm comments had not contained a hint of scorn. Nonetheless, he'd been tempted to kick the easel over. The experience made him sympathize with the occasions when Sir Anthony hurled objects in all directions.

Things had gone no better later in the evening, when he had ascended to his new studio and set up another still life so he could paint in private. He'd thought his second attempt would go a little better.

He had been appallingly wrong; he couldn't even paint a simple bowl decently. The flat, muddy result had made him ashamed of his own arrogant dreams. He'd ended the session by furiously scraping the paint from his canvas because he could not bear the sight of his own failure.

He reminded himself forcefully that he had only had one lesson. Surely he would get better. Yet he could not shake the bitter belief that his small talent for sketching was utterly inadequate when it came to creating real art.

Arriving back at Seaton House, he dismounted and led the chestnut into the stable. He was rubbing the horse down when Phelps, the groom and coachman, emerged from his small apartment above the stable, a clay pipe clamped between his teeth. After nodding a greeting, Phelps went to stand in the doorway and gaze out at the courtyard.

The groom was the only long-term Seaton servant. His taciturn nature made him a poor source of information, but Kenneth enjoyed his company. When he finished rubbing down the horse, he went to join the groom in the doorway. "Cold this morning. Hard to believe it will be spring soon."

"Not soon enough." Phelps drew in a mouthful of pipe smoke, then slowly exhaled it. "Be glad to leave London for the Lakes."

"When does Sir Anthony usually go?"

Another puff of smoke spiraled into the mist. "*A* fortnight or so after the Royal Academy Exhibition begins."

Since the exhibit opened the first Monday in May, the journey north would be in mid-May. More than two months away. Kenneth wondered if he would still be part of the household then. "Does Miss Seaton enjoy going to the country?"

"Oh, aye. 'Tis good for her. In London, Miss Rebecca scarcely ever sets foot out of the house."

Kenneth realized that Phelps was right. He made a mental note to try to coax Rebecca out for some fresh air.

Since the groom was in a relatively talkative mood, Kenneth remarked, "From what I've heard, a good part of Sir Anthony's circle also goes to the Lakes."

"Aye, that's true enough. Lady Claxton, Lord Frazier, and half a dozen others have places near Ravensbeck." Phelps made a face. "As if we didn't see enough of 'em in London."

"George Hampton also summers there, doesn't he?"

"With his print shop to run, Mr. Hampton only takes a few weeks of holiday," Phelps explained. "Usually August."

Kenneth wondered if it was significant that Helen had died during the time when George Hampton was in the neighborhood. As her lover, he must be considered a suspect. "I heard that Hampton discovered Lady Seaton after her accident."

The groom's teeth clicked tight on his pipestem. After a

long silence, he said, "Aye, you heard rightly. That was a bad day. A very bad day."

"Her death must have come as a great shock."

"Mebbe not so great as all that," Phelps said cryptically.

Startled, Kenneth studied the other man's expression. "Were you expecting such a tragedy?"

"Not expecting, no. But not surprised."

Sensing that the groom would not elaborate, Kenneth said, "I've heard that Mr. Hampton and Lady Seaton were... very close."

Phelps spat onto the cobbles. "Too close. Sir Anthony should've taken a horsewhip to Hampton, but no, they were the best of friends. Still are. Shameless, the lot of 'em."

"Such goings-on aren't what I'm used to," Kenneth agreed. "What about Lord Frazier? He seems like a man who might have an eye for the ladies."

"Aye. Gets particular pleasure in taking women away from Sir Anthony." The groom smiled a little. "Not that Sir Anthony cares. He's got more important things on his mind."

So there might be undercurrents of rivalry between the two men. The same could be true with Hampton; Sir Anthony's fame greatly exceeded that of his two old friends. Kenneth considered asking more questions, but restrained himself. One thing he had learned in his intelligence work was to stop before his subjects became suspicious.

He let the conversation drift into horse talk before excusing himself and going into the house. It was the most Phelps had ever said about the family tragedy. Interesting, his comment that Lady Seaton's death had not been entirely a surprise. Perhaps Helen had been the sort of woman who didn't look as if she would make old bones. Kenneth had met such people; in some invisible fashion, they carried the mark of doom on them. In the army, they often became heroes and martyrs. Perhaps they lived life too quickly, consuming their share of mortality in fewer years than the common run of humankind.

Maria had been like that. On some level, he had always known that her time was limited. Perhaps that had added to the sorrowful intensity of their affair.

Kenneth washed and changed, then went down for breakfast. Uncharacteristically, Rebecca was in the breakfast parlor, yawning over toast and coffee. She had slumberous bedroom eyes, and her wonderful hair was tied back loosely with a green ribbon. She looked adorable. His somber mood began to lift. "Good morning. You're up earlier than usual."

"Not by choice." She gave him a pained glance. "I loathe people who are cheerful at the crack of dawn."

He grinned. "Dawn cracked some time ago. It was quite lovely in the park with the sun glowing through the mist."

"Paint it." She spread a spoonful of marmalade over her toast. "That will be close enough to dawn for me."

He picked up a plate and helped himself to eggs, ham, and fried oysters. "A cruel comment. My painting would not do justice to the subject."

She came alert. "It will. Give it time."

He set his plate opposite her, poured coffee, then took his seat. "Patience has never been my strong point."

"I never would have guessed," she said dryly.

He chuckled. "When you're irritated, you look like a furious ginger kitten."

She smothered a smile. "My hair is not gingery. It's a decorous shade of auburn."

"Almost decorous. Incidentally, your father has asked me to meet with his solicitor this afternoon, so I won't be able to sit for you until after three o'clock." He tackled his food with gusto. After clearing his plate, he said, "It really was lovely in the park. You don't get out enough. Shall I escort you to see the Elgin marbles?"

"No!" she said sharply. "I have no desire to be marched around London like a schoolgirl."

"You'll wither away if you don't get some fresh air and sunshine."

"Both of which are almost nonexistent during March in London," she pointed out.

He abandoned his teasing manner. "I know you're devoted to your work, but you really should get out more. In the heart of one of Europe's most exciting cities, you live like a hermit."

Her gaze dropped. "During the summer, I'm often out of doors. London is too dirty and noisy."

Following his intuition, he asked, "Is that the real reason, or is it because you feel like a social outcast?"

She began shredding her toast into damp pieces. After a long silence, she said, "It isn't so bad going to places where no one would know me. Fashionable destinations, like the park during the promenade hour, or visiting the Elgin marbles, are different. I suppose it's very feeble of me, but I would not be comfortable."

He frowned. "It's been almost ten years since your elopement. Surely the scandal has been forgotten by now."

She smiled humorlessly. "You underestimate the memories of the socially righteous. Not six months ago, I was given the cut direct by an old schoolmate when our paths crossed in the British Museum. It was not an experience I enjoyed."

"I would have thought your father's position would provide some protection if you wished to go out in society."

"He is a famous artist, knighted by the king. I'm a disgraced spinster, which is quite a different matter. I have no place in normal society, except at the fringe of the art world." She slanted him a glance. "Surely when you were commissioned from the ranks, you learned something about social ostracism. Or were you accepted because your birth was obviously respectable?"

He gave a wry half-smile. "From sheer stubbornness, I didn't even try to convince other officers that I was their social equal. It was quite educational. A few despised me for my presumed vulgarity. Most accepted me once I proved my competence." He thought of Michael Kenyon. "And a few took me exactly as I was. They became friends."

She sighed. "You're braver than I. I prefer to avoid society rather than challenge it."

It was probably easier to ignore social barriers in the army, where war was the ultimate test, than in the artificial world of London, where status was all. Even so, he'd experienced enough snubs to know how uncomfortable they could be.

If he took the social position to which his birth and rank entitled him, he should be able to help Rebecca as well as Beth. Once Rebecca began going out and making friends, she would no longer be self-conscious about the past. She could build a fuller, more satisfying life.

In fact, if Michael and Catherine came to London for the Season, they would surely be willing to receive Rebecca. The two women would like each other very well. The thought vanished as soon as it appeared. Nothing could be done while Kenneth was acting as Sir Anthony's secretary. Damn his present deceptions.

But there might be another, better way for Rebecca to become established. "You could create your own place in society if you exhibited your work. As a respected artist, Angelica Kauffmann was received everywhere, even though she generated a few scandalous rumors of her own."

Rebecca's expression tightened. "I have no desire to exhibit my paintings."

"At least consider submitting something to this year's exhibition," he said coaxingly. "You have dozens of pieces that are suitable."

She crushed her napkin into a ball and stood, her eyes snapping. "You don't listen very well, Captain. I said that I am *not* interested." She turned and exited the breakfast room.

He frowned after her. A pity she was afraid to go outside the bounds of her safe, narrow world. He must do something about that. As he rose and headed to the office for his morning business session with Sir Anthony, he wondered why he felt so compelled to help Rebecca. His desire went beyond the need to return some of what she was giving him.

He had the uncomfortable suspicion that he was trying to make amends for the hurt he would surely inflict on her.

Rebecca stalked into her studio, slamming the door behind her. She should have breakfasted from a tray in her room, as she usually did. Having to face an insufferable, arrogant male first thing in the morning was a terrible way to start the day.

Especially when he was right.

Damn the man! She grabbed a pillow from the sofa and hurled it across the room. Before his arrival, she had been content with her life. She had her work, she had... she had...

Very little else.

Her experience had never been broad. What worldly knowledge she possessed came from observing the people who sought out her father. Always shy, after her disgrace she had withdrawn completely, concentrating on her painting and relying on her parents for companionship.

Then Helen Seaton had died, and something vital had been broken deep inside her daughter.

Rebecca went to her desk and brought out the gimmal ring that had been her mother's. After a long, brooding study, she scowled and put it away again. She was as flawed and incomplete as the ring, and the proof was in her work. She hadn't done a first-class painting since her mother's death. All of the pieces Kenneth had singled out for special comment had been done earlier.

Oh, she'd kept busy and painted a number of pictures in the last months, all of them technically sound. Most people would think them very fine. But her fatal weakness was reflected in her paintings, and was a compelling reason for not submitting to the Royal Academy. To have older pictures accepted would be a farce when she could no longer match that quality.

With a sigh, she dropped onto the sofa. The Persian carpet was silky behind her back. She could almost imagine that she felt her corsair's warmth lingering there.

The portrait of Kenneth was the first project she had really been excited about since her mother had died. Perhaps painting him would infuse her with some of his valor.

A painful thought crossed her mind. She became very still. There was another picture that she should paint, one that would require all her courage.

Before her nerve could fail, she lifted a sketchbook and began to draw a falling woman.

Kenneth's meeting with Sir Anthony's solicitor involved only routine financial matters. He took advantage of the occasion to make oblique inquiries about Helen's death, but learned nothing of interest. He was unsurprised; there really didn't seem to be much to learn.

Even though a chilly rain was falling when he left the solicitor's office, he decided to walk back to Seaton House. On the way, he stopped at his postal receiving station. A letter from Jack Davidson was waiting. Jack described his plans for the spring planting and gave an estimate of the cost. Kenneth paused to calculate. With the money left from the sale of his commission, plus what he had saved of his salary, there should be enough, barely. God help them if an unexpected emergency arose.

He looked back at the letter. In the last paragraph, Jack switched from business to personal.

Kenneth, I can't thank you enough for bringing me to Sutterton. During the years in the Peninsula, then in hospital after Waterloo, I had forgotten the pleasures of living close to the land. I had also forgotten the gentle charm of a true English lady. Your sister has been everything kind and amiable.

A sentence was scratched out. Then:

It is too soon to speak of paying my addresses to Miss Wilding—but I mention the subject now so that you might consider what your answer would be when the day comes that I can honorably ask.

Respectfully yours,
John Davidson

Kenneth smiled as he tucked the letter inside his coat. He'd already guessed from Beth's letters that she was equally taken with Jack. The two were very good for each other.

But his expression was somber when he resumed his walk. He'd asked his friend to Sutterton with the knowledge that Jack and Beth might suit very well. However, matchmaking was a chancy business and he'd had no real expectation of success.

Now he had mixed feelings about the results. Not about the relationship itself. Though a match wouldn't be brilliant in worldly terms, he could not ask for a more worthy husband for his sister. But there could be no marriage without enough money for a couple to live on, and Beth and Jack were dependent on him. If Sutterton was lost, Jack would have to seek employment elsewhere. It might be years before he could support a wife.

That meant Kenneth could not walk away from Lord Bowden's investigation. His personal desires could be indulged only to the extent that they did not interfere with his mission.

~

Given the gloom of the weather and his thoughts, Kenneth was glad to reach Seaton House. He hung up his wet cloak and hat, then went to the studio to let Sir Anthony know he'd returned.

He walked into an oasis of warmth and laughter.

Kenneth halted in the doorway, fascinated. He'd known from the appointment book that Sir Anthony was scheduled to begin a complicated group portrait involving two earls and their countesses. What he hadn't known was that the ladies were lovely identical twins. Sir Anthony had posed the women sitting slightly turned away from each other, like mirror images. The two husbands, one blond and one dark, framed them on each side.

Kenneth was intrigued by the way the grouping subtly delineated the relationships. The twins, the same only different, close to each other and closer still to their respective husbands. The men, friends as well as brothers-in-law.

While Kenneth tried to analyze why the arrangement worked so well, Sir Anthony glanced up and said whimsically, "When you make the daybook entries, be sure to note that the Countesses of Strathmore and Markland are *extremely* identical."

"An interesting painting challenge, sir."

"Particularly since I'm going to be doing two portraits, one for each household." Sir Anthony studied his clients. "The arrangement will be different for the second, though."

One of the countesses said with a chuckle, "Identicalness can be overdone."

"Anything worth doing is worth overdoing," the dark husband said with a private smile for his wife. "That is definitely true when it comes to beautiful women."

There was a ripple of laughter from several friends who had come to keep the principals company. The group of them had turned a gray day into a party.

After checking to see that the servants had provided refreshments, Kenneth withdrew and headed toward his room to change into corsair clothing for his session with Rebecca. Just before ascending the stairs, he paused, his attention caught by a painting he had never particularly noticed before.

It was a rendition of the death of Socrates, a popular classical subject. The large canvas depicted the noble philosopher holding aloft the cup of hemlock while his heartbroken disciples wept around him. It was not really a bad painting, but neither was it especially good. While the underlying drawing was technically sound, the poses were stiff and conventional, the composition and color undistinguished. Worst of all, it had no soul.

Dryly he reminded himself that the execution was better than anything he could do. He was about to go upstairs when a male voice drawled, "Do you like the Socrates, Captain?"

Kenneth turned to see the debonair figure of Sir Anthony's friend Lord Frazier, who had just arrived. Noticing the intentness of Frazier's gaze, Kenneth said tactfully, "Yes, my lord. A very powerful subject. Is it your work?"

Looking gratified, Frazier removed his hat and shook the rain off. "I painted it five years ago. After it was exhibited at the academy, I received several very flattering offers, but of course I turned them down. I'm a gentleman, not a tradesman. Since Anthony admired the picture, I gave it to him."

If Sir Anthony had expressed admiration, it had been out of politeness for a friend; the picture was unremarkable. Keeping the thought to himself, Kenneth said, "Naturally I knew of your reputation before I came here, but this is the first example of your work I've had the privilege to view. Do you do many historical pictures?"

"Of course. They're the only worthwhile subjects for a serious painter. Are you familiar with Sir Joshua Reynolds's writings on painting in the Grand Manner? He discourses beautifully on how art must be on an elevated plane, purged of the gross human element." Frazier pursed his lips. "A pity that Anthony must do portraits to earn a living. He's really quite good at historical painting, when he has the time for it."

The veiled cattiness of the remark confirmed what the groom, Phelps, had implied. Though Lord Frazier and Sir Anthony were friends of long standing, Frazier also nourished some resentment for the other man's greater success.

"His portraits may not have the sweep of historical works, but they are very good in their own right," Kenneth said. "The one of Lady Seaton in the office is truly splendid."

"I remember the day he started that picture," Frazier said, a faraway look in his eyes. "A dozen of us were picnicking on the lawn at Ravensbeck. After consuming a bottle of champagne, Anthony said Helen looked so lovely that he must immortalize her. He immediately went for paint and canvas, claiming he had to work outside to capture the light properly. We all laughed at him, of course—only a fool would choose to paint outdoors rather than in the controlled conditions of a studio. Still, the portrait came out well." He shook his head regretfully. "Only a few weeks later, Helen was dead. I can't think of Anthony's comment about immortalizing her without feeling a pang."

"You were in the Lake District when Lady Seaton's accident took place?"

"Yes. In fact, she and Anthony were engaged to dine with me that evening." Frazier's expression became troubled. "Anthony's work has suffered since Helen's death. I worry that he may never fully recover from the loss."

"Really?" Kenneth said innocently. "I think his Waterloo pictures are the equal of anything he's ever done."

"Certainly they are competent," Frazier said with a touch of hauteur, "but if you were an artist, you would see the subtle deficiencies, the loss of power."

Trying to look properly impressed at the other man's superior knowledge, Kenneth said, "If grief has affected Sir Anthony's work that way, the tragedy is twice as great."

"His reaction seems like more than grief," Frazier said, half to himself. "It's almost like... like guilt."

Kenneth's gaze intensified. "What do you mean?"

The other man's face blanked. "I meant nothing. I should not have spoken." He bent his head and brushed an imaginary wrinkle from his sleeve. "Is Anthony free? I stopped by to see if he wished to go to Turner's gallery with me."

"He's in the middle of a portrait session, but I'm sure he wouldn't mind if you looked into his studio to say hello."

"No need." Frazier donned his damp hat again. "Just tell him that I called, and I'll see him this evening at the club."

Kenneth frowned after the departing Frazier, wondering what the devil the man had meant. Though he might envy his friend's success, he'd been quick to retreat from the suggestion that Sir Anthony might have something to be guilty about.

The painter's friends were admirably loyal to him. But in the process, perhaps they were being disloyal to Helen Seaton.

CHAPTER 13

By chance, Rebecca glanced out her window and saw Kenneth return to the house. Naturally she hadn't been watching for him, but she was glad to know that he would soon be up for his sitting. The strain of starting her falling woman picture had left her craving company.

When Kenneth did not appear, she decided to wander downstairs and see what was delaying him. She was at the top of the staircase that led to the main hall when she saw him ending a conversation with Lord Frazier. She drew back, preferring not to be seen. Not that Frazier was ever less than polite, but she'd always known that he had no real interest in her. The feeling was mutual. Of her father's old friends, George Hampton had always been the best company.

Kenneth's face had an odd expression as he watched Lord Frazier leave. It wasn't precisely calculating. Analytical, perhaps. Frazier had probably made some pompous statement about Art, and Kenneth was trying to decide if there was any truth to it. She smiled. There was more genuine artistic feeling in Kenneth's little finger than in the whole of Lord Frazier's highly polished person.

She was about to descend the stairs when the front door opened again, admitting a gust of damp, chilly air. Probably people coming to visit her father's current sitters. She paused to allow the newcomers to be guided to the studio.

Then a rich contralto exclaimed with delight, "Kenneth!"

A woman moved gracefully into Rebecca's field of vision, her garnet-colored cloak glittering with raindrops. "What a splendid surprise!" She threw herself into Kenneth's arms and kissed him. As she did, her hood fell back onto her shoulders.

Rebecca's fingers whitened on the banister. The woman was the most beautiful creature she had ever seen, a stunning brunette with a marvelously expressive face.

And Kenneth was not exactly fighting her off. Quite the contrary. After a swift, almost furtive glance around the hall, he embraced the brunette, murmuring something in her ear. Her beauty and Kenneth's strength would make them perfect models for Venus and her husband Vulcan. Rebecca might have wanted to paint such a picture, except that her desire to stab the woman with a paintbrush was much stronger.

"You should have let us know you were in London, Kenneth." The brunette stepped back, laughing. "Or should I call you Lord Kimball now?"

Rebecca gasped and sank to the floor, clinging to the railings for support. *Lord Kimball?*

"Don't you dare," Kenneth said easily. "We've known each other too long for such formality, Catherine."

A distinguished gentleman appeared behind the lady and caught Kenneth's hand in both of his. "Lord, how long has it been?" he said with a broad smile. "Almost two years."

"Don't remind me, Michael." Kenneth clapped his free hand on the other man's shoulder. "At our last meeting, you were so near dead as to make no difference."

"As you can see, I'm as good as new." The newcomer put his arm around the woman's waist. "Much better than that, actually."

"We're just back from the christening," Catherine said. "I'm so sorry you couldn't come—it was almost as warm as summer in Cornwall. But the drawing you sent was wonderful. It looked as if you had been right there in the church with us."

Rebecca listened numbly as the people below continued their conversation. Clearly the man and woman were married, and Catherine's effusive greeting was that of a friend, not a lover. But still—Lord Kimball? Knowledge of what that meant knotted her stomach. She peered through the railings, glad that the people below were too busy to glance upward.

Kenneth was asking, "What brings you to Seaton House?"

The man, Michael, said, "Some friends are having a portrait done and they invited us to keep them company." He gave his wife a fond look. "It seemed fortuitous, since I've been thinking of commissioning a portrait of Catherine. I like Sir Anthony's work, and this is a good chance to meet him."

"No portrait unless it is of the whole family," Catherine said firmly. "Are you also here about a portrait?"

"I'm working for Sir Anthony," Kenneth said without inflection. "As his secretary."

His friends were obviously surprised, but recovered

quickly. "It must be sheer heaven to be surrounded by so much wonderful art," Catherine said warmly.

Her husband added, "Can you dine with us tomorrow? There is much to catch up on."

"I'm not sure." Kenneth shifted from one foot to the other. "I'll let you know. Where are you staying?"

"Ashburton House." Michael took Kenneth's hand again. "If you can't come tomorrow, name a time. Amy will be furious if you don't call as soon as possible."

Dully, Rebecca huddled in a ball against the railings while the people below took their leave of each other. Under her shock was a deep ache for what she had learned. She had thought there was a special kinship between her and Kenneth. Instead, she hadn't even known his name, or other vital facts. Once again, she had been a fool about a man.

Too late, she heard the footsteps coming up the stairs. Instinctively she froze, like a mouse faying to hide from a hawk.

An instant later, Kenneth's head appeared, his eyes almost level with hers. He stopped dead, his expression going rigid.

After a long, tense moment, he said, "I assume you overheard the conversation with my friends."

Anger began to stir. "Lord Kimball?" she said icily.

He winced at the note in her voice. "Let's go to your studio. It's a better place to talk than the stairs, and I think we could both use a cup of tea."

He ascended the remaining steps and caught her hand to help her up. As soon as she was on her feet, she jerked her hand away. Then she turned and wordlessly led the way to the attic.

When they reached her studio, he went immediately to

the hearth. The kettle was already simmering on the hob. Knowing that he would be chilled after his errands, she had set out a tea tray and cakes so they could refresh themselves before starting work. Cozy. Romantic. She had been a *fool.*

Her anger grew as he poured the steaming water into the teapot. What right did he have to make himself so much at home in her private sanctuary? Damn, and damn again!

After setting the tea to steep, he straightened and gave her a tentative smile, as if hoping he could tease her out of her mood. "You're looking like an outraged ginger kitten again."

"Do you blame me?" she snapped. "You're an endless source of surprises. First a secret artist, now a secret nobleman. What the devil are you doing in this house, Lord Kimball?"

"Working as a secretary," he said peaceably. "Given your reaction to my title, do you blame me for not mentioning it?"

She wanted to throw something at him. Instead, she lashed out with the source of her deepest pain. "Last year my father did a portrait of Lady Kimball. The picture turned out very well, but of course you must know that. Your wife is a beautiful woman, Lord Kimball."

Kenneth stared at her. "Christ, no wonder you're upset!" he swore. "The woman in question is neither a lady nor my wife, Rebecca. She's my stepmother."

It was Rebecca's turn to stare. Then she sank onto the sofa, remembering that Kenneth had mentioned his father's marriage to a girl the same age as Kenneth. Thinking back, she vaguely recalled that an older man with a broad, powerful build sometimes escorted Lady Kimball to sittings. She scarcely noticed him because her attention had been on her ladyship's sulky beauty.

"I see," she said more moderately. "But that really doesn't explain why you're working as a secretary and why you've been concealing your rank."

He dropped his eyes and poured her tea. "There's no great mystery. When my father died several months ago, I inherited nothing but debts. I needed work and someone referred me to your father." After mixing in sugar and milk, exactly as she liked it, he handed her the teacup. "I was afraid that if I presented myself as a lord, it would interfere with my hope of getting the position. Besides, I prefer being called captain. That title I earned. The viscountcy is an accident of birth."

"Your financial state is so desperate that you must take such a humble position?" she said, unconvinced. "I remember that Lady Kimball was draped in really magnificent jewels in her portrait. Surely some of them are family pieces."

He poured tea for himself and sat at the opposite end of the sofa. "No doubt." His mouth twisted bitterly. "But the will didn't specifically mention the jewelry, and Hermione claims that my father gave the whole collection to her. I'm sure she's lying—my father had a strong sense of tradition, and he had already provided for Hermione very generously. Since he was both honest and besotted, it didn't occur to him that his little darling would try to steal the family heirlooms as well."

"Do you have any legal recourse?"

He shook his head. "My solicitor says that in the absence of written proof of my father's wishes, it would be virtually impossible to get the jewelry back. I don't have the money to pursue a lawsuit, especially with so little chance of winning. It's a great pity. Besides the jewels that should have gone to the next viscountess, there were a number of pieces that my mother intended for my younger sister."

So he had a sister. Another significant fact she hadn't known. "The jewels may be a lost cause, but surely your father would have left any estates to you."

"I did inherit the family seat, Sutterton in Bedfordshire," he agreed. "When my mother was alive, the estate was well run and prosperous. My father lost interest in the place after she died. When Hermione demanded to live in London, he took out a series of mortgages to buy a town house and pay for her other extravagances. By the time he died, everything of value had been shifted to the town house, which was left to Hermione."

Seeing the pain in his eyes dispelled the last of her anger. "Can nothing be done to save the estate?"

"There... may be a way." He set his cup aside and got to his feet to pace restlessly. "A possibility is being explored. I won't know the results for a while."

She saw the deep tension in his body and knew that he was telling her the truth, but not the whole truth. "You're still concealing something important."

A muscle jumped in his jaw before he looked away. "I'll admit to a secretive streak. It developed as soon as I was old enough to recognize that drawing, the thing I loved most, was utterly unacceptable in a viscount's heir. Being an intelligence officer in Spain made me even more evasive, I'm afraid."

"Don't try to play on my sympathies." Her eyes narrowed. "You're hiding something very specific, and it bothers you."

"I should know better than to try to lie to an artist." He went to the window and gazed out at the gray rain, his face haggard. "You're quite right. I am involved in something I cannot discuss. I'm sorry. Please believe that I don't like being less than truthful, Rebecca."

"Saying you dislike a sin doesn't exonerate you if you go ahead and commit it anyhow."

"I don't suppose it does." He ran his hand through his damp hair, tangling it hopelessly. "Sometimes one must act against one's nature, even though it will produce grief and regret."

She rose from the sofa and went to stand beside him at the window, where she could watch his profile and the subtle changes in his expression. "Have you come here to hurt me or my father?"

The lines at the corners of his eyes deepened. "As a soldier, I hurt far too many decent people because our countries were at war," he said haltingly. "I swore I would never again injure the innocent."

No doubt she was being foolish again, but she believed him. Perhaps his secret had no direct bearing on the Seatons. If his primary reason for being in London was to salvage his family from disaster, he might feel that he was not wholeheartedly fulfilling his duties to his employer. For someone as scrupulous as Kenneth, such a situation could be a source of guilt. Or perhaps he was wrestling with his conscience whether he should burgle Hermione's house. Personally, Rebecca thought that would be a fine idea.

A more serious thought struck her. "Are you concealing a wife who isn't Hermione, or a fiancée?"

"No," he said immediately. "Nothing like that."

The shocking intensity of her relief revealed how much she wanted him to be free. Hoping he was too absorbed in his own thoughts to recognize her reaction, she said, "Surely there has been some woman who mattered."

He swallowed hard, his Adam's apple jerking under his dark skin. "There... there was a woman in Spain. Maria had joined a guerrilla band to fight the French. I met her because my intelligence work often took me to the guerrillas. In theory, she refused my proposal because I wasn't Catholic. But the real reason was that the needs of her country came first."

Rebecca thought of the fierce beauty whose portrait she'd seen in Kenneth's portfolio. Surely that had been his Maria. And they had been lovers, not merely sweethearts.

"Spain is free now," she said without inflection. "Perhaps it is time to ask Maria again."

The scar on his face whitened. "She was captured and killed by the French."

Rebecca sensed he would rather not have revealed such a painful piece of his past. Perhaps he felt the need to compensate for the other secrets he was keeping. The man was like a Chinese puzzle, made of layers of mysteries. Yet in some strange way, they did understand each other.

"I'm sorry," she said softly. She laid a hand on his arm and lifted her face to brush his lips with hers.

He turned toward her and slipped his hand behind her head, and suddenly sympathy flared into desire. He deepened the kiss, his long fingers kneading the sensitive nape of her neck. Her hairpins slipped loose, and her hair spilled down her back. She pressed against him, molding herself against the hard planes of his body, feeling the pulse of his strength and desire.

His arms came around her hard, and for a few wild moments passion reigned supreme. She ran her hands hungrily up and down his spine. Marvelous muscles, marvelous bones, Michelangelo would have *killed* to sculpt a body like this.

Then he broke the kiss and lifted his head away. "You shouldn't have done that," he said hoarsely.

"No, I shouldn't." She rose on her tiptoes and lightly nipped his lower lip with her teeth.

He groaned and captured her mouth again. Their tongues mated, hot and deep. His hand went to her breast, teasing the nipple through her gown. She gasped as sensation burned through her. She should be concerned about where this was going, but at the moment she didn't give a damn about what was wise and proper.

He swept her up in his arms and carried her across the room. She clung to him, licking his throat and the line of his jaw, loving the taste and feel of him.

Then he dumped her onto the sofa and stepped back, panting. "Ginger, you're a menace."

For a moment she lay still, numbed by the shock of separation. Then she grinned up at him, feeling blessedly, wickedly alive. "A menace. I rather like that. It's time I started enjoying the fact that I'm ruined."

He smiled ruefully. "Driving me mad may be enjoyable for you, but I don't want to add seducing my employer's daughter to the list of my sins."

Rebecca swung her legs to the floor and sat up, moving with provocative slowness. Though she might not be a beauty, she could see in his eyes how much he wanted her. The thought was intoxicating. "But you weren't seducing me. Quite the contrary. Since that's settled, shall we continue?"

"No!" He ran a hand through his dark hair again and turned away. "If you only knew..."

"So we're back to secrets again," she said, her levity fading. "It's hard to imagine what mischief a man so doggedly honorable might be up to."

"Then let's not imagine," he said with sudden vehemence. "God willing, what I fear will never come to pass."

She watched the smooth power of his movements as he paced the length of the studio. He was feral as a jungle cat, a warrior with an artist's soul. Dear Lord, but she wanted to capture those qualities on canvas. She certainly wasn't having much luck with capturing him physically.

"If you took the position with my father temporarily while you wait for the verdict on your estate, you won't be here long," she said with regret. "I'd better get busy with my painting."

She went to her easel, absently tying a knot in her hair to get it out of the way. Interrupted passion burned in her veins, sharpening her vision and making her impatient to begin. "Whenever you are ready, Lord Kimball."

He walked to the sofa, stripping off his coat and cravat and unbuttoning his shirt as he went. "My name is still Kenneth."

But he was also a viscount. An obvious solution to his financial problems occurred to her. Wondering how he would react, she said, "If you wish to preserve Sutterton, marry an heiress. You have a title, and"—she surveyed him with frank appreciation—"you're presentable. There must be plenty of rich merchants who would be willing to hand over their well-dowered daughters in order to acquire a viscount for a son-in-law."

He stared at her, his expression genuinely appalled. "Believe it or not, I never thought of that. Probably because it's such a revolting idea."

"Such marriages are a time-hallowed tradition."

"And they say that men are cold-blooded," he muttered. "Go back to your painting, Ginger."

She was beginning to like the nickname; there was

something intimate and playful about it. Her gaze went to her canvas. So far, the picture was only rough shapes that she had blocked in at the first session. The proportions of mass and space worked well. Today she would firm up the areas of light and dark, and perhaps start to stroke in some detail. She daubed her brush on the palette and laid swath of shadow along the side of his face. She was adding another shadow when she recognized the logical corollary to the semi-serious suggestion she had made.

She was an heiress herself. Not only was she her father's sole heir, but she had received a sizable fortune from her mother, and she controlled the money herself.

Kenneth obviously hated the idea of marrying a stranger for a fortune. Might he be more willing to marry her? If he were interested, would *she* be willing? The prospect produced a giddy mixture of excitement and alarm. She truly didn't want to give up her freedom, but she hated to think of Kenneth being reduced to penury because of a feckless father and greedy stepmother.

"Is something wrong?" Kenneth asked.

She realized that she had lowered her palette and was staring holes in him. Glad he couldn't read her mind, she bent her gaze to her canvas again. "Just evaluating the light," she said gruffly.

She would have to do some serious thinking about Kenneth, marriage, and what she wanted for herself. But not now.

Now it was time to paint.

~

The stillness of posing helped Kenneth gather the frayed threads of his composure. Rebecca's uncanny ability to read him was harrowing. Luckily she seemed to have accepted his carefully worded statement that he had vowed never to injure the innocent. He just hoped to God that Sir Anthony *was* innocent.

Her unabashed sensuality was as unnerving as her razor-sharp perception. She was a captivating blend of shyness and audacity, and he deserved a damned medal for stopping when he did.

He thought about her suggestion that he marry an heiress. It was hard to explain his deep-seated revulsion to what was a common enough occurrence. Obviously he'd rather act as a spy than become a fortune hunter.

The minutes passed and peace became boredom. He amused himself by watching the knot in Rebecca's silky hair slip slowly downward. Whenever she turned her head, he could see how the knot had dropped a fraction of an inch. Finally it reached the ends of her hair and dissolved, releasing her shimmering tresses into a waist-length mantle that would have done a princess proud.

Not long after, he got to his feet with a groan. "Enough, Ginger. It's almost time for dinner. You have no mercy."

She blinked as his words snapped her from her creative haze. "You are allowed to take breaks, you know." She set down her palette and stretched like a cat. "Was the gentleman you met downstairs an army friend? He had the look of a military man."

"Michael was the officer who recommended me for a commission. He truly didn't care about my background, so he was the only one to whom I told the truth." Kenneth chuckled. "As an old Etonian, Michael took a dim view of the fact that I went to Harrow, but he was willing to overlook even that."

"He seemed equally tolerant of the fact that you are

now working as a mere secretary." She knotted her hair again. "Who is the Amy they mentioned?"

Though her manner was casual, he was amused to hear a hint of jealousy in her voice. "Catherine's thirteen-year-old daughter. I used to give her drawing lessons."

He crossed the room and helped himself to one of the almond cakes on the tea table. His gaze returned to Rebecca. "Since the cat is out of the bag about my title, we might as well take advantage of it."

"In what way?" she asked warily.

"To reestablish your reputation. Michael Kenyon is a war hero, the brother of a duke, and has impeccable social standing. I'm sure he and Catherine would be happy to receive you themselves, and sponsor you with their friends. You'd be respectable again in no time."

She bit her lip, not looking pleased at the prospect. "Why would they be willing to receive a stranger of bad reputation?"

"They would do it the first time because I ask it." He finished his cake. "And after they've met you, they will accept you for your own sake. You'll like them both, I think."

She dropped her eyes and began wiping excess paint from her brushes with a rag. "How could any woman possibly like a female as beautiful as Catherine Kenyon?"

"Because she is the warmest, most generous woman you will ever meet," he said mildly. "In the army, she was known as Saint Catherine for her battlefield nursing."

"A paragon." Scowling, Rebecca plopped her brushes bristle first into a jar of turpentine. "She would despise me on sight."

"Will it help if I say that she shamelessly wore breeches

when it was convenient, or that she adopted the most peculiar low slung dog and named him Louis the Lazy?"

"She does sound rather interesting," Rebecca agreed with a reluctant smile. "But I don't know if I *want* to be reestablished. Social life is usually a flat bore."

"True." He took another almond cake. "But being an outcast must be rather tedious as well. Think of the pleasure you'll feel if you meet one of your dreadful schoolmates when you're an honored guest of Lord and Lady Michael Kenyon."

"You're trying to appeal to my lower nature."

"You're the one who's the expert at appealing to lower nature," he said with dry humor.

She blushed and looked down at her clean-up rag. "I'll think about what you've suggested."

He hoped she would agree. She needed friends, and helping her find them would ease his conscience a little.

But not enough. Not enough.

CHAPTER 14

Rebecca started the next day with a tray in her room.

She didn't want to face Kenneth over breakfast again. Her will was weak in the morning and she might be tempted to take a bite or two out of him.

Later, after she knew her father would have finished his morning business session with his secretary, she descended to his studio. She had learned early that if she wanted to talk, she must catch her father before he started working.

He was studying his Wellington picture when she arrived. Glancing up at her entrance, he said, "What do you think?"

She examined the canvas critically. "I can almost smell the smoke and hear the thunder of the guns. The duke looks like a man who has been tempered in the fires of hell and emerged an invincible leader of men."

"Kenneth's advice made all the difference. Before, the picture was good. Now it is great." Sir Anthony regarded the painting with pride. "My Waterloo series will be the sensation of this year's academy exhibition."

"Without question," Rebecca said with a smile. Sometimes her father was like a child in his artless arrogance. "By the way, Kenneth turns out to be a viscount."

"Oh?" At first her father barely registered the statement. Then he frowned. "Wilding. Is he Viscount Kimball?"

She nodded. "You did a portrait of his stepmother."

"I remember," Sir Anthony said dryly. "Wonderful bones, and a truly stunning degree of self-absorption."

Deciding it was time to mention the real purpose of her visit, Rebecca said, "Kenneth has suggested using his connections to reestablish me socially. What do you think?"

Her father looked a little blank. "Is that necessary?"

"I was ruined, remember? I haven't been welcome in respectable drawing rooms since I was eighteen."

Her father opened his mouth to reply, then shut it again as color slowly rose to his face. "Are you saying that you haven't mingled with society because you couldn't?"

She looked at him in surprise. "Exactly. Have you forgotten my scandalous behavior?"

"Not forgotten, but I didn't really consider the implications. I left that sort of thing to your mother. I guess I assumed that after the scandal died down, you stayed close to home by choice." His mouth twisted. "I know I'm not a very good father, but it's unpleasant to be reminded of that."

Touched, she said, "You're the right father for me. Who else would have taught me how to be an artist, and given me such freedom to do as I pleased?"

"You were born an artist—I didn't teach you that." He sighed. "You and Helen always made it easy for me to be selfish. It's a fine line between freedom and neglect, and too often I've crossed it. I should have paid more attention. Set more rules."

"Surely you're not going to start now," she said, alarmed. "I'm too old to train to obedience."

He smiled a little sadly. "There's no need. You've turned out rather well, small thanks to me."

She said crisply, "Don't brood, Father. If social life was important to me, I could have found a way to have one years ago. I'm only considering it now because of Kenneth's desire to introduce me to society. To be honest, I'd really rather not."

"Do what Kenneth suggests," her father ordered. "Your birth entitles you to move in the highest circles, and that's a resource that shouldn't be wasted. I'll ask Kenneth if I can help, but I imagine he has matters well in hand. He's the best secretary I've ever had."

She wasn't sure she liked her father's answer. Secretly she had hoped he would say that she shouldn't waste her time on socializing. Was her reluctance shyness, or fear?

It was fear. The dark side of an artist's perception was painful sensitivity. At least that was the case for her. Being a recluse was far easier than venturing into an abrasive world.

But she ran the risk of withering away personally and creatively. She'd be a fool to turn down this chance to expand her horizons.

Decision made, Rebecca strolled over to another work in progress and flipped back the cloth that covered it. "So this is the portrait of the twins. It's coming nicely."

"The challenge is to show the differences in the women's personalities when their features are so similar." Her father came to stand beside her. "Lady Strathmore is on the right and Lady Markland on the left. What are their temperaments?"

Rebecca studied the portrait. "Lady Markland is more

outgoing. There's mischief in her eyes. Lady Strathmore is quieter, more reflective. A little shy."

"Good, good," her father murmured. "Then I got it right."

"You need to work on the dark-haired gentleman." She pointed. "The left leg is a bit off."

"Mmm, so it is. I'll fix it at the next session." He covered the canvas again. "How is Kenneth's portrait coming?"

"Quite nicely." She started to elaborate, then settled for saying, "He has such an interesting face."

Her father also had an artist's perception. She didn't want to risk the chance of him seeing things she wasn't willing to admit even to herself.

~

Rebecca descended from the carriage with trepidation. Then she started up the marble steps of Ashburton House, glad rain made the steps slippery enough to give her an excuse to cling to Kenneth's arm. "I'm going to regret this," she muttered as he rapped the door with a lion-head knocker.

"No, you won't," he said reassuringly. "It's only an informal dinner with two very pleasant people."

Perhaps, but her heart was beating at a rate just below terror. She thought of every leer and sneer and lifted eyebrow that had ever been directed her way, and was tempted to bolt. God help her, when it was time for the ladies to withdraw, she would be alone with Catherine the Paragon!

Too late. The door was opened by a horribly superior butler. After removing their cloaks, the guests were ushered into an elegant drawing room. Rebecca's gaze went to the man and woman who rose and came to greet their guests. Even though the two weren't touching, they were *together* in a way that was almost palpable. They made a striking couple. Close up, Catherine Kenyon was even more beautiful than at a distance.

Kenneth gently urged her forward with a large hand on her lower back. "Michael, Catherine, this is my friend Miss Seaton."

Catherine smiled and clasped Rebecca's hand. "I'm so happy to meet you," she said, and seemed to mean it.

"The pleasure is mine, Lady Michael," Rebecca murmured.

"Please, call me Catherine."

Impossible to resist such warmth. "My name is Rebecca."

Lord Michael greeted her and made his bow. His eyes were a clear, true green. Even more interesting was what she saw in their depths. Her father had said that a soldier's eyes revealed how much combat he had seen, and it was true. The same steely strength that marked Kenneth was in his friend.

Thinking aloud, she said, "You'd make a wonderful model for Alexander the Great." Then she colored as she realized how inappropriate the comment was.

Lord Michael merely grinned. "Kenneth said you were an artist to the bone. He didn't exaggerate."

She smiled ruefully. "If Kenneth meant I don't know how to say hello like a normal person, I'm afraid he was right."

"I think that normality is greatly overrated," Catherine said as she led her guests to the fire. "Don't you?"

Rebecca smiled, and began to relax. By the time they

went in to dinner, she was enjoying herself. The Kenyons were as nice as Kenneth had promised. The pleasure they felt in Kenneth's company was unhesitatingly extended to her. By the time she and her hostess left the gentlemen to their port, she was no longer alarmed at the thought of being alone with Catherine.

After they left the dining room, Catherine said, "This is horribly rude of me, but I need to go upstairs to feed my son." She pulled her Indian shawl more closely, unconsciously brushing one of her breasts. "Will you mind dreadfully if I leave you alone in the library for a few minutes?"

To her surprise, Rebecca found herself saying, "If it wouldn't be an intrusion, I'd like to come and see your baby."

Her hostess beamed. "It's impossible to insult a mother by wanting to meet her children. I'm only sorry that my daughter is staying with friends tonight."

They went up to the nursery, where a middle-aged nurse was rocking the baby by the fire. "You're just in time, my lady," she said placidly. "Young master is getting right peckish and no mistake." After handing the baby to Catherine, she went downstairs for a cup of tea.

The infant began to nuzzle his mother hungrily. Rebecca studied him with fascination, trying to remember if she had ever been this close to a baby. She didn't think so. Such tiny hands. Such gossamer hair. "He's beautiful. What is his name?"

"Nicholas, after one of Michael's oldest friends. He looks very like his father, don't you think?" Catherine said fondly as she lowered herself into the rocking chair.

Under the soft drape of her shawl, she unbuttoned the front of her specially designed gown with one hand. Then she cradled her son to her breast. The infant's soft mouth greedily fastened onto his mother's nipple and he began to nurse with furious intensity, his miniature hands locking into fists.

Once the baby was properly settled, Catherine said to her guest, "Please, do sit down. This will take a bit of time."

Rebecca obeyed, moving with a quietness that seemed natural in the nursery. "I'm woefully ignorant about babies, but isn't it rare for a woman of your station to nurse her own child?"

Catherine laughed softly. "I may be Lady Michael now, but when my daughter was born, I was merely an army wife looking for the best way to care for my baby. After nursing Amy, I decided that only a fool would surrender such joy to a wet nurse."

The sight of mother and child made Rebecca ache with tenderness. Kenneth had said he wanted to broaden her life, and in a single evening he had already succeeded. For the first time she recognized what she was losing by turning her back on marriage and the chance of children.

The women talked in a desultory fashion until Nicholas had nursed his fill. Catherine deftly redid her gown, then tilted the baby against her shoulder and gently patted his back.

Rebecca remarked, "The two of you would make a magnificent Madonna and Child painting."

"I suppose seeing the world as potential pictures is part of what makes an artist," Catherine said thoughtfully. "I envy your talent. I've no special abilities, except perhaps for nursing the ill and wounded."

Catherine was wrong, Rebecca thought. She had the most precious talent of all: the courage to freely give and receive love. It was a gift greater even than her beauty.

Rising from the rocking chair, Catherine asked, "Would you like to hold Nicholas?"

"Me?" Rebecca's voice was a squeak. "What if I drop him?"

Catherine transferred the baby to Rebecca's nervous grasp. "You won't."

The infant opened his eyes and blinked sleepily at her. He did look like his father, but like his mother as well. His skin had the delicate tints of the finest watercolors.

What would it be like to hold a child of her own like this? To look for signs of family resemblance, and for features that were uniquely the infant's own?

What would it be like to hold a baby that had been made by her and Kenneth?

The thought touched something unbearably vulnerable inside her. If she and Kenneth had a child, it probably wouldn't be so beautiful as this one, but she wouldn't mind. She wouldn't mind at all.

With infinite care, she handed the baby back to his mother. "He's going to be a heartbreaker when he grows up."

"He already is." Catherine laid her son into a cradle that boasted a carved and gilded Ashburton crest on the side. Before straightening, she brushed his cheek with a feather-light kiss. "Everyone in the family adores him, especially my daughter."

Rebecca glanced around the nursery. "Does Nicholas have any cousins his age?"

"I'm afraid not. Michael's brother, Stephen, was married for many years, but he and his wife never had children." Catherine's brow furrowed. "Stephen is in the country now, in mourning because his wife died last year. I hope he remarries and has better luck. Nicholas is in line to inherit the dukedom someday, and I'd rather that didn't happen. Being a duke doesn't seem to have brought Stephen much happiness."

The nurse returned from her tea and resumed her vigil with the baby. But as Rebecca left the room she cast one last look at the sleeping infant, and thought of Kenneth.

What was happening to her?

After the ladies withdrew, Michael Kenyon indicated the two decanters that the butler had set out. "What will it be —my brother's excellent port, or some ferocious Scottish whiskey?"

Kenneth grinned. "A wee dram of whiskey, of course. For old times' sake."

After his host poured the drinks, they settled back to talk. Michael said, "Your young lady is delightful. She makes me think of a shy sword, if there is such a thing."

"It's not a bad description, but she's not my young lady."

Michael cocked a skeptical brow but didn't pursue the point. "What kind of painting does she do?"

"Oil portraits, usually of women. On one level they're wonderfully individual, yet at the same time they have a mythic, larger-than-life quality that is uniquely hers. I've suggested she submit to the Royal Academy, but she won't hear of it."

"It must be hard for her, knowing she will inevitably be judged as her father's daughter," Michael observed. "You said she needs social rehabilitation. What happened?"

"An elopement when she was eighteen. Luckily she had the sense to back out before it was too late, but of course there was a scandal." Kenneth frowned. "Her parents should have waited two or three years, then quietly brought her out among their own friends. She could have moved from artistic circles into broader society. Instead, she was allowed to burrow into her attic studio and become completely isolated. Even though you and Catherine aren't much for grand society, I hope you have friends who will receive her. She needs to meet more people."

Michael considered. "My friend Rafe—the Duke of Candover, you know—is giving a ball next week. I'll ask him to send cards to you and Rebecca."

Kenneth shook his head, impressed. "Knowing the right people makes it so easy. Once she's seen at Candover's, almost all doors will be open to her. I doubt she'll ever be a social butterfly, but at least she'll have choices." He made a face. "Unfortunately I'll have to go, too."

"A ball will be good for you," Michael said callously. "But tell me more about your work. Somehow I don't think you became Sir Anthony Seaton's secretary merely to meet artists."

Kenneth hesitated only a moment before abandoning discretion. "You're right. I was sent there to investigate a mysterious death, but it's the most bloody maddening job I've ever been given." Tersely he explained Lord Bowden's offer, and the complications he had met while trying to learn about how Helen Seaton had died. It was an immense relief to express some of his frustration to a trustworthy friend.

After listening in silence, Michael said, "I understand Bowden's desire to learn the truth, but the situation must be damnably awkward. Obviously you like Rebecca, and it sounds as if you like Sir Anthony, too."

Kenneth thought of all the murky undercurrents he had discovered in Seaton House. "Awkward is an understatement. I've considered backing out, but I really can't. I've given Bowden my word. There is also the question of justice."

"It would be nice to think you could find some evidence to exonerate Sir Anthony, but more likely nothing conclusive will turn up. Maddening for you, and for Lord Bowden."

"At least I'll benefit financially." And in other ways. But Kenneth could not escape the superstitious belief that he was going to pay a high price for what he was getting.

"Speaking of justice, I'd like to hear more about your wicked stepmother. I gather that since there are no documents assigning ownership of the family treasures, her only real claim is that she is in possession."

"True, but in this case, possession is conclusive." Kenneth smiled wryly. "God knows that if I had the jewels, I wouldn't give them up."

"Interesting," Michael said, a speculative look in his eyes.

"More depressing than interesting." Kenneth poured another dram of whiskey. "Your turn. Tell me about the joys of marriage and fatherhood."

Michael needed no encouragement. The only drawback was that he made marriage seem altogether too appealing. Kenneth reminded himself that Rebecca, with her tart tongue and fierce creative drive, would be a very different kind of wife from serene, loving Catherine. Always assuming that Rebecca would even consider becoming any man's wife.

A pity that he found that fierce creativity so alluring.

When Rebecca and Catherine returned to the drawing room, they found that the men had not yet emerged. Catherine said philosophically, "Kenneth and Michael will be over the port for some time tonight. They have a lot of catching up to do."

Rebecca didn't mind. She couldn't remember when she had enjoyed a woman's company so much.

They both took seats by the fire. A moment later, a hound so short that its legs seemed cut in half oozed from the shadows and flopped by Rebecca, resting his muzzle on her slippered foot.

Catherine rolled her eyes. "Sorry. Our dog likes you. If you can't bear his way of showing it, I'll remove him."

Rebecca leaned over and ruffled the long ears. "I wouldn't dream of disturbing him. I assume this is Louis the Lazy?"

The other woman laughed. "I see that his reputation has preceded him. My daughter cherishes the sketch that Kenneth drew of Louis the winter we shared a billet in Toulouse."

Rebecca leaned comfortably into her chair. "I was immensely impressed when Kenneth told me that you followed the drum through Portugal and Spain. I can't imagine what it must have been like to maintain a household and raise a child under such conditions."

"It was often difficult, yet my daughter, Amy, thrived in circumstances that would have made a mule complain." Drolly, Catherine described incidents that sounded hilarious in retrospect but which must have been dreadful at the time.

Rebecca noted that her hostess's first husband was seldom mentioned. The fellow never seemed to have been around when needed. Lord Michael, she suspected, would not have such a failing. Nor would Kenneth.

Thinking of him made her ask, "How did you first meet Kenneth?"

"We were traveling with the baggage train when a squad of French cavalry attacked. Amy and I became separated from the main group and several French troopers cornered us. I was frantically wondering whether it would do any good to dig the pistol out of my saddlebag when Kenneth and some of his men appeared and drove the troopers off. He brushed the incident off as part of a day's work, but as you might imagine, I've never forgotten." She gazed absently into the fire. "It wasn't the only time he came to the rescue."

Once more a picture clicked into Rebecca's mind: the Indomitable Beauty rescued by the Noble Warrior. Very dramatic. Far more romantic than the Mousy Painter making acid remarks to the Retired Hero. Repressing a sigh, she said, "You've led an exciting life. I don't know whether to be envious or to fall on my knees and give thanks that I've been spared such delights."

"By all means, be thankful." Catherine fingered the fringe of her shawl. "Have you ever seen any of Kenneth's drawings?"

"Yes, though it was largely by accident. He didn't volunteer the fact that he drew."

The other woman gave her a slanting glance. "His work seemed very, very good to me, but I know little about art." There was a question in her voice.

"He's extremely talented, and very original," Rebecca replied. "I've started to give him painting lessons. Even though he is starting late, he has the potential to become a really fine artist."

A smile lit Catherine's lovely face. "I'm so glad. He always acted as if his drawing was a trivial matter, but I suspected that was because art meant too much for him to talk about it casually."

Catherine was as perceptive as she was beautiful. If Kenneth wasn't in love with the woman, he had less sense than Rebecca gave him credit for.

Reminding herself that she was his teacher, not his sweetheart, she asked her hostess what Brussels had been like during the heady days before Waterloo.

War was a much safer topic than love.

CHAPTER 15

Rebecca slept later than usual the next morning.

After deciding to eat in the breakfast room, she was disappointed to learn that Kenneth had already gone out. Still, she would see him later. The certainty of that made her smile.

She was stirring her tea when Lavinia drifted into the room, looking absurdly glamorous for such an early hour. Her presence meant she had spent the night with Sir Anthony. It was not the first time, though naturally the fact would not be mentioned.

Rebecca poured another cup of tea. "Good morning, Lavinia. You take two spoons of sugar, don't you?"

"Yes, thank you." Lavinia accepted the cup and took a deep swallow. "You're looking lovely this morning, my dear. Does that mean your work is going well?"

"Yes, but that's not the reason I feel mellow. Kenneth decided I should go out more, so he took me to dine with some friends from his army days." She gave a self-deprecating smile. "Even though I practically had to be dragged, I must admit I had a very enjoyable evening."

"I knew that young man had good sense the first time I met him." Lavinia served herself a soft-boiled egg and toast from the sideboard, then took a seat. "You're alone far too much."

Rebecca gave her a quizzical glance. "I'm surprised that you noticed."

"Of course—you're the daughter of two of my dearest friends. I've been rather concerned about you, especially since Helen's death. You've been the next thing to a hermit." Lavinia cracked the top off her egg. "However, it wasn't my place to speak. You'd have bitten my head off if I'd tried."

"Very likely," Rebecca admitted. "I don't take direction very well."

One of the footmen entered and laid an elaborately sealed letter by Rebecca's plate. Curious, she slit the seal with her knife and opened the missive. Then she gasped.

Lavinia glanced up from her egg. "Is something wrong?"

Rebecca swallowed. "Not exactly. This is a card for a ball that the Duke and Duchess of Candover are giving."

Lavinia's brows arched. "Your social life is progressing by leaps and bounds."

"The couple we dined with last night are close friends of the Candovers. They must have written the duke first thing this morning." She bit her lip as she reread the card. A quiet dinner was one thing, but a ball given at one of the grandest homes in London?

Accurately interpreting her expression, Lavinia said, "Don't panic. You couldn't pick a better occasion to be introduced to the world. The Candovers entertain wonderfully. They never invite so many people that it becomes a hideous crush, so there is actually room to dance."

"I haven't danced a step in nine years. I won't remember

how." A welcome thought struck her. "I'm in mourning for my mother. I'll have to decline."

"Nonsense," Lavinia said briskly. "It's been more than six months, which is adequate mourning time for a parent. Nor does the fact that it's a ball mean you have to dance. I plan to spend at least half my time talking."

"You're going to this affair?"

"I never decline any of Rafe's invitations." Lavinia smiled reminiscently. "I've known him for years. He was always fond of slightly wicked females, but I feared I would be purged from the Candover guest list after his marriage. I should have known he wouldn't marry a prude. You'll like his wife, Margot."

For the first time, it occurred to Rebecca that there were similarities between her situation and Lavinia's. "It's horribly rude of me to ask, but how did you manage to become accepted everywhere when you were once considered very..." she sought for a tactful word, "very fast."

Lavinia laughed. "You mean how did I go from being a vulgar theatrical slut to a semi-respectable lady?"

Rebecca gave an embarrassed nod.

"For the record, I should mention that I'm not received everywhere. If I tried to enter Almack's, they would pitch me down the stairs. But that's all right—Almack's is a flat bore." She neatly scooped out a spoonful of egg. "I was able to overcome my disreputable past because I was beautiful and amusing, and because I made a good marriage."

"I am neither beautiful nor amusing, and I have no desire to marry anyone," Rebecca said gloomily. "Clearly I'm beyond hope of redemption."

"Ah, but you are Sir Anthony Seaton's daughter, and you have rare talent. That will be enough, particularly if you submit your work to the academy. Good artists are forgiven their little lapses of propriety."

Rebecca said suspiciously, "Have you and Kenneth been talking behind my back? You sound just like him."

Lavinia laughed. "No, we haven't discussed you. A simple case of great minds reaching similar conclusions. If you exhibit, you'll become an overnight sensation. The Prince Regent will invite you to Carlton House. Say what you will about Prinny, the man cares about art."

"You're not persuading me to exhibit. Quite the contrary." Another objection occurred to her. "I have nothing suitable to wear. I don't even know what the current styles are. I'll have to decline." She set the invitation down with relief.

"You'll do no such thing. Three days is difficult, but not impossible. In fact..." Lavinia hesitated. "I have an idea. The odds are about even whether you'll love or hate it."

When Rebecca gave her an encouraging glance, she continued, "You could alter one of your mother's gowns. Helen had wonderful taste, and since you have the same coloring, her gowns would suit you equally well...." Her voice trailed off. "Of course, you may not like to wear something that was hers."

Rebecca's first reaction was to reject the idea violently. As she hesitated, Lavinia said quietly, "It wouldn't be a bad thing if the thought of Helen became a part of your life again instead of being an aching wound that can't be touched."

Rebecca bit her lip, surprised that Lavinia understood so well. She made a wary attempt to consider Lavinia's suggestion, and realized there was something comforting about the idea of wearing a garment of her mother's. It would be like having Helen's silent support. "I... I think I would like that. Shall we go look? Her clothing is packed in trunks in the attic." She got to her feet. "I haven't the least notion of how to turn myself out fashionably. I'm going to need help."

"Approach your appearance the same way you would a portrait," Lavinia said shrewdly as she finished her tea and stood. "Don't look in the mirror and think, 'shy, unfashionable Miss Seaton.' Think of what you would do if you were painting that person and wanted to make her look lovely and elegant."

Rebecca looked at the other woman with new respect. "Lavinia, you're a godsend."

"Helen had an amber silk gown that will suit you right down to the ground. Shall we see if we can find it?"

As the two women went upstairs, Rebecca realized that her relationship with Lavinia had passed a watershed. They had gone from being friendly to being friends.

As usual, Kenneth stopped at his postal receiving station on his way back to Seaton House after finishing Sir Anthony's errands. The only letter waiting was from Lord Bowden. He frowned as he read it. Bowden was becoming impatient and wanted a report. Rather than arranging a meeting, Kenneth decided to write. He tucked the letter away and resumed walking, mentally composing a reply that would sound more substantial than it was.

It was more pleasant to think of Rebecca. By the end of the previous evening, she had been laughing and exhibiting her tart humor. She would have more confidence at her next engagement.

He could use some confidence himself, for the ball

would be his own first venture into London society. He had joined the army before he'd had a chance to descend on the town as most young gentlemen did. If not for Hermione...

He suppressed the thought. Though his stepmother had been the serpent in Eden, his own weakness had turned the situation from difficult to impossible. He had got what he deserved.

It was almost noon by the time he got back to Seaton House. An invitation to the Candovers' ball awaited him on a side table in the hall. Michael and his friends were most efficient.

He went up to the office and found Sir Anthony conferring with George Hampton. His employer said, "Ah, Kenneth, just in time to help George find a picture in the vault."

"The vault, sir?"

"It's a storeroom on the ground floor that has been fitted out for keeping paintings. George will show you. I'd go myself, but a client is here for a sitting." He gave Kenneth a key, then left.

Hampton picked up a lit oil lamp, explaining, "I need to get the original of one of Anthony's paintings so I can make an engraving of it."

Thinking it was fortunate to have this chance to talk with Hampton privately, Kenneth said as they descended the stairs, "Is the picture you're engraving one of the Waterloo series?"

"Yes, the Chateau de Hougoumont painting. The first two are completed, and I'll engrave the Wellington picture as soon as Anthony finishes it. The series will cause a sensation when they're exhibited together, and we want to have the prints ready for sale when the show opens."

"That sounds like good business."

"As the son of a Kentish shopkeeper, I was born to trade," Hampton said with unmistakable dryness. "Which is just as well. If it was up to gentlemen to run the world, mankind would still be living in caves."

"I meant no insult. Quite the contrary."

"Sorry," Hampton said apologetically. "I've been oversensitive on the subject ever since I left the country to attend the Royal Academy Schools. It was frequently pointed out to me that I was not a gentleman and never would be."

"Surely few of the students at the academy are gentlemen by birth. Wasn't Mr. Turner's father a barber?"

"Yes," Hampton said, dry again, "but I don't think he made the mistake of becoming friends with his more aristocratic classmates."

Did Hampton resent Sir Anthony for his superior birth? Kenneth doubted that his employer would deliberately insult a man of lower rank, but he did have a natural arrogance that could be irritating. Hoping to elicit more, Kenneth said, "You couldn't have been accepted at the academy without talent and drive."

Hampton's broad face relaxed into nostalgia. "The day I was admitted was the happiest of my life. I'd always loved to draw. Even my father admitted that I was good. I went to London with great dreams. I was going to become the finest painter England had ever known, better than Reynolds and Gainsborough put together." He sighed. "Foolish, youthful fantasies."

The words hit uncomfortably close to home, for Kenneth's boyhood dreams had been much the same. Even now, he could not stop himself from secretly hoping that he would prove to have a natural genius for oil painting. That he would be able to create works that would become immortal. Instead, he couldn't even paint a still life worthy of the name.

They reached the ground floor and passed the kitchen and servants' hall to reach the back corner of the house. Kenneth had noticed the door before, but vaguely assumed it opened to an ordinary storeroom. As he turned the key in the lock, he said, "Perhaps you didn't achieve your earliest goals, but you have become the finest engraver in England. Surely there is satisfaction in that."

"There is," Hampton agreed as he went into the vault. "And a very good living as well. But it was a bitter blow when I started at the academy school and for the first time was among others whose gifts exceeded my own. Even at sixteen, Anthony's talent was so great as to break the spirit of lesser mortals. When I saw his work, I knew that I could never be his equal."

"Yet you became friends."

"Our talents might not be equal, but our love of art is," Hampton said musingly. "It's the same with Malcolm Frazier. Under his aristocratic hauteur, he has a fierce passion for art. For over thirty years, that bond has kept the three of us friends, despite all our other differences."

That shared passion had even preserved their friendship through Hampton's affair with Helen Seaton. Kenneth would not have been so tolerant if the woman in question were his wife. He wondered if the engraver had found secret satisfaction in cuckolding his more successful friend. Jealousy could take many forms.

He glanced around the vault. Cool and dry with high, narrow windows, it was filled with racks specially designed to hold paintings. He slid the nearest canvas from its slot. Both disturbing and lovely, it depicted a seductive water nymph drawing a vain youth to his doom in a forest pool.

He remarked. "Surely this is by Rebecca, not Sir Anthony."

Hampton gave him a look of mild surprise. "She's showed you her work? A rare mark of favor. Yes, it's one of hers. That was done not long after her elopement." Humor glinted in his eyes. "The chap being dragged into the water bears a distinct resemblance to the young swine who seduced her."

Kenneth returned the canvas to its slot, glad that Rebecca had found a small way to even the score. "Is the Chateau de Hougoumont painting the same size as the others in the series?"

"Yes, which means it's probably in this rack." Hampton pulled a large canvas out, then caught his breath, pain on his face.

Kenneth understood the reaction when he saw the painting. It was a swiftly executed oil sketch of Helen Seaton, but not the laughing Helen of the portrait in the study. Instead, she was dressed in Greek draperies and wailing to the sky with grief, her auburn hair streaming over her shoulders like old blood. "Good God," he said involuntarily. "What is this supposed to be—a Trojan woman after the destruction of her city?"

"Perhaps. Or perhaps it was... simply Helen." Expression bleak, Hampton shoved the picture back into the rack and reached for another canvas.

Wondering what the devil that meant, Kenneth said, "I heard you were the one who discovered her body after the accident."

Hampton nodded somberly. "I was taking a ride through the hills that day, following one of my usual trails and thinking of nothing in particular. Then from the corner of my eye I saw an odd motion, out of keeping with the setting. I turned to look more closely just in time to catch a glimpse of a green shape tumbling from Skelwith Crag."

"You actually saw her fall?" Kenneth said, startled. When the engraver nodded, he continued, "Was there anything else strange about the scene?"

Hampton frowned. "What do you mean?"

"Was someone with her at the top of the cliff?"

"Of course not," he said, puzzled. "Though my distance vision is so poor that I suppose a coach and four could have been on the cliff without me noticing. I simply saw that frighteningly human shape fall. Then I galloped to Ravensbeck, which was the nearest house. I was hoping against hope that Helen would be there and laugh at me for my fears, but... but I was not surprised when she was not."

A pity that Hampton's vision wasn't better. "Why weren't you surprised?"

"Why are you asking so many questions?" Hampton countered, his gaze sharpening to hostility.

Making his expression earnest and uncomplicated, Kenneth replied, "Everyone acts so strangely about her death. I've been concerned because I know that Rebecca is still troubled."

The hostility faded, but Hampton's reminiscences were over. "Everyone was troubled by Helen's death, Captain. Pull out that picture on the end. I believe it's the one we're looking for."

Silently Kenneth obeyed. He had been given another puzzle piece—and it was just as useless as all the others.

Kenneth helped Hampton crate the picture for transport to the engraver's studio, then headed upstairs. On the second floor, he encountered Rebecca and Lavinia, their arms overflowing with colorful fabrics.

"You two look pleased with yourselves," he observed. "What have you been up to?"

"Finding me something to wear to the ball," Rebecca explained. "Lavinia suggested altering one of my mother's gowns." She caressed a shimmer of amber silk that spilled from the top of her pile. "This one, I think."

Kenneth lifted the trailing hem and held it alongside her face. "Perfect. The color makes your eyes seem the exact same shade of amber."

Her lashes fluttered when he inadvertently brushed her cheek with the silk. She glanced away, a pulse visible in her throat. "I assume that you've also received an invitation to the ball?"

He nodded. "Luckily I had some evening wear made up when I was stationed in Paris, but I warn you, there is no chance whatsoever that I will steal your thunder."

"I'll have no thunder to steal," she said dryly. "However, Lavinia assures me that I shall not be a disgrace."

"Will you be too busy to paint this afternoon?"

Rebecca glanced at Lavinia. "Am I going to be too busy?"

"I'm afraid so," Lavinia said, smiling like a fond aunt. "We must go to my house so my maid can start the alterations. Then we'll have to choose your accessories. But it can all be completed today. Tomorrow you can return to your work."

As he watched the two women, he realized how much Lavinia was enjoying herself. She liked being helpful. A pity that she had never had children. He remarked, "There seem to be quite a pile of garments there."

"Lavinia wants me to be prepared in the unlikely event

that I behave well enough to get invited somewhere else," Rebecca replied before the two women proceeded on their way.

As he watched the graceful sway of Rebecca's figure, he thought of a small gift that he could make for her in honor of her first ball. And unlike oil paintings, it was something he knew he could do.

Between the frustrations of his investigation and his painting, he would welcome a project that went well.

CHAPTER 16

Lavinia's maid, Emma, made a final adjustment to Rebecca's hair before whisking away the cloth that protected the amber gown. Then Emma and Lavinia studied their handiwork.

"You'll do very well," Lavinia announced. "You may now look in the mirror."

Rebecca obeyed, then inhaled in surprise, causing the crystal beads on her bodice to glitter with light. She hardly recognized herself. Emma had altered the gown to fit perfectly, and the braids and waves of her coiffure lent her a much-needed air of sophistication. "I think you two have finally succeeded in the ancient task of making a silk purse out of a sow's ear."

While Emma giggled, Lavinia said sternly, "Nonsense, my dear. You've always had looks, despite your best efforts to obscure them. All you need now is some jewelry."

Rebecca opened the lacquered box that had belonged to her mother and was now hers. Swallowing against the lump in her throat, she selected several pieces, all of them gold. A necklace and bracelet of intricately woven links, delicate swinging earrings, a filigreed comb. "These."

Lavinia frowned. "Aren't they a bit plain?"

"No." Rebecca slid the comb into the heavy coil of hair at her nape, then donned the other pieces. She turned her head to study the effect. The gold was a dramatic complement to the shimmer of amber and auburn.

"Splendid," Emma said with a sigh of satisfaction.

"It's a pleasure working with an artist," Lavinia agreed. "You look wonderful, my dear. Now it's time for Emma to render me presentable. A much harder task at my age, I fear."

Rebecca laughed. "None of this nonsense about your age. You look at least a decade younger than you are, and you have a presence that a queen would envy."

"No queen would want to look like me, but a really successful courtesan might," Lavinia said breezily. "*Au revoir.* I shall see you at the ball."

After the other women left, Rebecca analyzed her appearance with the detachment she would use on one of her paintings, but she could find no flaw. She looked as good as she was capable of looking. After picking up her chocolate-brown velvet cloak, she left the room and went to tap at her father's door. "Father? I'm going down now."

When Sir Anthony opened the door, his face went blank. Then he drew a shaky breath. "You look almost eerily like Helen."

"I'm smaller and not beautiful." She turned in a circle so that he could get the whole effect.

"Smaller, anyhow." His perceptive gaze went over her. "Colors suit you much better than those white muslins you had to wear for your come-out. I'm sorry I won't see your triumph."

"You received a card for the ball, didn't you? Surely you could change your mind and come."

He shook his head. "I've lost my taste for grand affairs. With Kenneth, you'll be in safe hands."

"I'd better be. This was all his idea," she said darkly. She turned and went down the stairs to the drawing room, where they would wait to be picked up by Michael and Catherine Kenyon in the spacious Ashburton coach.

Kenneth was already in the drawing room. He turned at her entrance. She was surprised at how well formal dress suited him. Since he was too broadly built for fashion, he had wisely chosen stark simplicity. The cream-colored pantaloons, plain buff waistcoat, and dark blue coat made him look every inch a gentleman without obscuring his physical power and natural authority. All in all, he was a most impressive sight. But this time she didn't want to paint him; she wanted to kiss him.

He came forward to take her hand. "You look magnificent, Rebecca. You'll be as grand as any lady there."

The admiration in his eyes sent a tingle up her spine. She thought more seriously about kissing him, but heaven knew where that would lead. "I'll settle for fitting in unobtrusively." She squeezed his hand lightly, then released it. "All things being equal, I really would rather stay home and paint."

He laughed. "You will have a splendid, memorable evening. I promise it." He crossed the room and lifted something from the table, then turned to her hesitantly. "I have a trifling present for you. A memento of your first ball."

He gave her a fan. She spread the ivory sticks, then burst into laughter. The silk fabric was hand-painted with a lovely, rather oriental design of leaves and flowers—and lurking under a blossom was a playful ginger kitten. "You painted this yourself, didn't you? No one else would create this design." She held the open fan against her gown. "And exactly the right colors."

"Not difficult since I had seen your gown." His tone was casual, but she could see how pleased he was at her reaction.

This time she did kiss him, standing on her toes to touch her lips swiftly to his before retreating even more swiftly. She set aside the fan she had purchased two days before and studied Kenneth's gift more closely. Though custom-painted fans were not unusual, this one was exceptional. "Your watercolor technique is really excellent. You have the knack of layering the washes to take full advantage of the transparency of the medium."

"Painting the fan was a welcome change from the problems of working with oil," he said wryly.

"If you decide to abandon oils, you could do very well as a watercolorist. Watercolor paintings can be submitted to the Royal Academy, you know."

He looked surprised. "I don't think I did know that. I've never been to one of the exhibitions."

She snapped the fan shut and slipped the loop over her wrist. "You should submit some of your watercolors to be hung."

"I can't submit to the Royal Academy!" he said, appalled.

"You most certainly can," she retorted.

He was still looking dumbfounded when the rattle of hooves and wheels sounded in the street. Visibly relieved, he went to the window and drew back one of the draperies. "The Kenyons are here. Time to go."

He took her cloak and held it for her. She slipped into

the garment, her heightened senses making her extra aware of the lush velvet and Kenneth's warm, solid body behind her. She yearned to lean back against him. His arms would come around her, and perhaps he would kiss the side of her throat....

A little breathlessly, she said, "It must be convenient to have a duke for a brother. Michael and Catherine can enjoy all of the amenities of Ashburton House without any of the costs."

"It's more than convenient—in this case, it's a minor miracle." Kenneth donned his own cloak, then opened the drawing room door for her. "For most of the years I've known him, Michael was as estranged from his family as I was from mine. In some ways, more so—at least I was in communication with my sister. It's to his brother's credit that when Stephen inherited the dukedom last year, he took steps to mend the breach."

She found the story interesting. Was there any chance her father and his brother might end their feud? Probably not. Lord Bowden would have to make the first move, and he was obviously not a forgiving sort. With a sigh, she went outside to the coach. There were too many feuds in the world.

A ball was a marvelously visual event. The lacquered shimmer of carriages, the torches flaring against the night, the sumptuous shine of rich fabrics. Unfortunately, Rebecca's desire to bolt interfered with her appreciation. She felt overpowered by the sights and sounds around her. Realistically she knew that few people were likely to notice or care that she was present, but her hand locked on Kenneth's arm as they advanced through the receiving line. She hated crowds. She really, really hated them.

Just ahead, Michael and Catherine greeted the Candovers. She recognized the host and hostess from her father's recent portrait: the duke, tall and dark and commanding and his lovely blond duchess, who managed to be both regal and vivacious.

As the duchess and Catherine hugged, Michael said, "I'd like to present two particular friends of mine. Lord Kimball, a fellow officer of the 95th, and Miss Seaton."

Rebecca wanted to vanish. But the gazes that turned to her showed only friendly interest, without the condemnation she had come to expect after her disgrace.

The duke shook Kenneth's hand warmly. "Welcome. Michael has spoken often of you." Then he bowed to Rebecca, a playful light in his eyes. "It's a pleasure to meet Sir Anthony Seaton's most beautiful creation."

As Rebecca colored, the duchess said, "I'm so glad to finally meet you, Miss Seaton. I don't blame you for avoiding your father's studio when we were having the portrait done—my son was in a dangerous state the whole time!"

Remembering how Catherine had liked hearing a compliment about her baby, Rebecca said shyly, "It's hard for a young child to sit still for so long, but I thought the picture of your son came out very well. He's a beautiful little boy."

The duchess glowed. "Thank you. I think so, too. He looks very like his father, doesn't he?"

Rebecca wondered if that was the answer all proud mothers gave. Perhaps only those who adored their husbands; the same kind of subtle bond that joined Michael and Catherine also connected the duke and duchess. If these people weren't careful, they would give marriage a good name.

As their party moved into the ballroom, Kenneth murmured, "How are you managing?"

She made a face. "Overwhelmed."

He patted her hand where it curved over his arm. "Not surprising. To someone who is intensely aware of colors and forms and motion, a scene like this has entirely too much going on. Rather like drowning in a flood of visual stimulation."

"Good heavens," she said, surprised. "Do you think that's why I've always disliked crowds?"

"It's probably a good part of the reason. Add in natural shyness and"—he smiled teasingly—"a wicked past, and it's not surprising that you've avoided the social gatherings."

"But if I find a ball overwhelming because I'm an artist, it must have a similar effect on you."

"I generally avoid such events if possible," he admitted, "but I'm inured. This is almost restful compared to the average battlefield."

She smiled. "I take your point."

The orchestra began to play a waltz. "May I have this dance, Miss Seaton?" he asked formally.

"It will be my pleasure, Lord Kimball."

She was glad to have an excuse to move into the safety of Kenneth's arms. Even through gloves, she was keenly aware of his touch, and the seductive feel of his hand resting on her waist. She sighed with pleasure as they swirled into the music.

"Does that sigh mean I've stepped on your foot already?" he asked with foreboding.

"Not at all." She smiled at him with deep affection. "It

means that if you don't stray more than a yard from me for the rest of the night, I might actually enjoy this ball."

He smiled back. His calm flowed through her, dissolving her fears and creating a warm glow of desire. An afternoon's lesson with her old dancing instructor had helped her confidence. Her body not only remembered the steps, but took wordless pleasure in the rhythm and movements. She also found that, for someone who claimed an aversion to balls, Kenneth was a very capable dancer. Yes, this occasion would be a success.

Their party's corner of the ballroom became a gathering place. The Kenyons brought over friends and introduced them to her and Kenneth. She met the identical twin countesses and their handsome husbands; a petite, exotic-looking American woman who was married to a wickedly charming blond man who had met Kenneth on the Peninsula; a dark gypsy earl and his serene wife; other guests who knew and respected her father and his work.

She danced with the men and laughed with the women, fully aware that she was being cocooned with warmth and protection. All a result of Kenneth invoking Michael's help on her behalf. She had not known how great a gift he was giving her.

After a reel with Michael, she fanned herself and chatted with her partner while waiting for Kenneth to return from dancing with Catherine. Then Lord Strathmore, one of Michael's friends, approached with a young man in tow. "I've been asked to make an introduction," he announced.

She smiled encouragingly, wondering if she had made a conquest. Not that she wanted one, of course. Especially one who must be younger than she. But he did look pleasant.

Strathmore continued, "Miss Rebecca Seaton, please meet the Honorable Henry Seaton."

"Good heavens," she exclaimed. "Are we related?"

"I'm your cousin Hal," he said with an engaging smile. "Lord Bowden's heir. Just because our fathers haven't spoken in donkey's years, I see no reason why we should be enemies."

"Nor do I." She gave him a dazzling smile, amazed at her pleasure in discovering a new relative. His compact build, the cast of his features, were very similar to her father's. "Just this evening, I was thinking how tragic family feuds are."

"Particularly one that began like the Seaton feud." His eyes twinkled. "I can understand my father being upset at having his fiancée swept away by his younger brother, but I happen to be quite fond of the mother he chose for me. The old boy seems rather fond of her himself."

She knew that Lord Bowden had married and had two sons, and it sounded as if the marriage was a successful one. A pity that had not been enough to mitigate her uncle's hurt pride and sense of betrayal. "I don't suppose my uncle would ever wish to meet me," she said with regret, "but perhaps someday I might make the acquaintance of Lady Bowden."

"No sooner said than done. It was she who sent me to find you." He offered his arm. "Shall I take you to meet her?"

She asked Michael to tell Kenneth where she had gone. Then she took her cousin's arm and accompanied him across the ballroom. Lady Bowden was sitting with a group of older women, but she stood and came forward when she saw her son and Rebecca approaching. She was even smaller than Rebecca, not beautiful but with lovely silver hair and a fine-boned elegance.

"Mother, meet Cousin Rebecca," Hal said.

"A pleasure, my dear." She glanced at her son. "Off with you, Hal. Fetch us some lemonade or something." He chuckled and went to do her bidding.

Lady Bowden turned back to Rebecca, her soft blue eyes studying her husband's niece with undisguised interest. "I knew you must be Helen's daughter as soon as you entered the room."

"You knew my mother?"

"Oh, yes. My father's property marched with the Bowden estate. Marcus and Anthony and I grew up together. Our fathers had some vague idea of a marriage between the families. Then Marcus met Helen and went head over heels." Lady Bowden smiled a little sadly. "I could hardly blame him. She was the most ravishing creature. All the young men were in love with her. But of course you know what she was like. My condolences on your loss."

"Thank you. She is much missed," Rebecca said quietly. "You are very good to talk to me when there has been such a schism between our families."

"I have nothing against you, child," Lady Bowden said with wry humor. "I owed Helen a great debt. If not for her elopement with Anthony, I would never have married Marcus."

In a flash of insight, Rebecca understood what had happened: Lady Bowden growing up loving Marcus and thinking she would be his bride. Silently enduring first the pain when he lost his heart to another woman, then his anguish when Anthony and Helen had run away. In the end, Marcus had turned to the girl next door—but in her secret heart, Lady Bowden carried the sorrowful knowledge that she had been second best.

Instinctively concealing her understanding, Rebecca asked, "Is Lord Bowden here tonight?"

"No. If he were, I could not have met you." A flicker of a smile crossed Lady Bowden's face. "I would do nothing that my husband forbade. But what he doesn't know won't hurt him."

Rebecca laughed. "I wish we could become better acquainted, Lady Bowden, but I don't suppose that is possible."

"Please call me Aunt Margaret." Her ladyship pursed her lips. "Naturally we cannot exchange calls. But perhaps, on occasion, I might send you a note mentioning some unfashionable time when I might be strolling in the park."

"I should like that." She took the older woman's hand for a moment. "Until next time, Aunt Margaret."

Smiling, Rebecca made her way around the edge of the ballroom. After the current quadrille ended, it would be time for the supper dance. Kenneth would be her partner. She looked forward to telling about her aunt and cousin.

Then, between one step and the next, her happiness shattered as she came face-to-face with the two sisters who had been Rebecca's chief tormentors during the one long, miserable year she had spent at a school for young ladies. Charlotte and Beatrice had been smugly self-righteous ten years earlier, and time had not improved them.

As Rebecca stared, her stomach churning, Charlotte said spitefully, "Merciful heaven, Beatrice, you were right—it really is Rebecca Seaton. Who would have believed that she would have the barefaced gall to try to force herself into decent society?"

"Obviously the dear duke and duchess don't know about

her past," Beatrice said, her nostrils pinched as if she were smelling rotten fish. "It is our duty to inform them."

They both turned ostentatiously in the gesture of contempt known as the cut direct. Rebecca stood trembling, knowing that she should simply walk away, but unable to move. Their malice was all the worse for the fact that she had ceased to expect it.

Then a deep voice said, "There you are, Miss Seaton. I have someone I wish you to meet."

It was the Duke of Candover himself. He brushed by Charlotte and Beatrice as if they were invisible. Then he took Rebecca's hand and tucked it in his elbow. "Margot and I are so pleased that you have finally consented to attend one of our balls. I trust you are enjoying yourself?"

Unable to speak, Rebecca nodded. Her old schoolmates were watching the duke, their eyes wide with shock. Candover turned his head with cool deliberation and looked at them. Whatever was in his face made the sisters turn white. Then he led Rebecca away. She clung to his arm, grateful for the support.

When they were out of earshot, she said unevenly, "What did you do, your grace—turn them to stone?"

He chuckled. "My wife calls that my Medusa stare. It's a modest talent, but useful."

"I'm very grateful for being rescued, but why did you do that for a woman you've only just met?"

He regarded her with thoughtful gray eyes. "The general reason is that I don't approve of intolerance, perhaps because it has been one of my own failings. The specific reason is that Kimball wants you to be accepted socially. Since he saved my friend Michael's life, I shall do my best to oblige him."

"I didn't know that," she said, surprised. "Is that why

you've all gone to such lengths to welcome Kenneth and me?"

"The initial reason." The duke smiled at her with masculine appreciation. "But it's no great hardship, you know."

As they reached the corner where her new friends were gathered, Candover said, "I hope that encounter didn't ruin your evening."

"It made me appreciate how fortunate I am," she said with a smile. "Thank you, your grace."

Kenneth had been in a group with several other men, but he broke away and came to join Rebecca. "You're looking a little strained." He put her arm on his hand and led her into a promenade about the ballroom. "Did something happen?"

Tersely she described her meeting with her relatives and the unpleasant incident with her old schoolmates. When she finished, Kenneth said, "A good thing Candover was there. Since he has conspicuously championed you, your problems should be over."

With her free hand, she used the fan to waft cooler air to her face. "The duke said you saved Michael's life."

"Perhaps I did." His expression darkened. "But Michael saved my sanity, which was rather more difficult."

She made a note to ask what that meant at some later time.

Kenneth continued, "I should have thought of this earlier. Is there any chance you'll meet your despicable poet here?"

"None at all. A year or so after our ill-fated affair, he ran away to Italy with a married woman. There he expired, very poetically, of a fever," she said dryly.

"Proving that there is poetic justice in the world."

She smiled. She had shed no tears for Frederick, whose self-love had greatly exceeded his talent.

Beginning to feel tired, she asked, "How late will we stay?"

"Michael ordered the carriage to be ready after supper. Catherine needs to get back to her baby, and I imagine that by then you'll have had your fill of socializing."

"You're a genius. After supper will be perfect." She stood on her toes to search the ballroom. "Have you seen Lavinia? She must have arrived, but I haven't found her yet."

"I saw her in the distance, dazzling several cabinet ministers." He gave Rebecca a teasing glance. "Your problem is that you need to be a foot taller."

He scanned the crowd as they continued their slow progress about the room. She held his arm and mentally did a pastel sketch of her surroundings, content to let him do the serious looking. Then an eddy of the crowd brought them face-to-face with a woman whose blond beauty and lavish jewels were familiar.

The woman halted, then gave a slow, malicious smile. "Kenneth, darling. How wonderful to see you again after so many years."

He whipped his head around to stare at her, the blood draining from his face. "I can't say this is an unexpected pleasure," he said in a voice as brittle as glass, "so I will settle for saying that it is unexpected."

Her eyes narrowed. "Your wit has quickened, darling. It becomes you." She laid a hand on her magnificent diamond necklace. "Almost as much as this becomes me."

With sudden deep foreboding, Rebecca realized that the woman was Hermione, Lady Kimball.

CHAPTER 17

After her first shock, Rebecca examined Kenneth's stepmother with clinical detachment. Though most would call her beautiful, an unmistakable hardness marred the handsome features.

"I didn't expect to see you here tonight," Kenneth said coolly, his hand tightening protectively on Rebecca's arm. "If memory serves me, it is still customary to spend a year in mourning after the death of a spouse."

"I'm wearing black, darling, and diamonds rather than colored stones." Hermione gestured at her low-cut, clinging gown and the king's ransom in gems draped over her voluptuous body. "And of course I'm not dancing. But I know that your father would not have wanted me to spend a whole year in isolation. He was the most generous and indulgent of husbands."

Kenneth surveyed her costume with contempt. "Perhaps, but he was also a great believer in tradition."

Ignoring the remark, Lady Kimball said to Rebecca, "You're Anthony's girl, aren't you? I sometimes saw you scurrying around Seaton House. You look quite sweet in your mother's cast-offs."

"That's enough, Hermione," Kenneth said sharply. "Save your insults for me, not innocent bystanders."

"If you think little Miss Seaton is innocent, you haven't been listening to enough gossip, but no matter." She studied his face critically. "A pity about the scar. However, it wasn't as if you were good-looking to begin with. At least you survived. I was rather glad to hear that, for sentiment's sake."

For a moment, Rebecca feared that Kenneth might do murder, but he managed to retain his control. "Good-bye, Hermione," he snapped. "We have nothing to say to each other."

Before he could take Rebecca away, Hermione raised her hand and cupped his cheek with provocative intimacy. "Ah, Kenneth, darling. Still troubled by that boring conscience of yours. I rather hoped you had overcome it by now." Her malicious gaze slanted over to ensure that Rebecca was listening. "If you had, we could have resumed where we left off all those years ago."

The implication was unmistakable. Rebecca stared at Kenneth in shock, but there was no denial in his eyes. Only the sick horror of someone who had been dealt a mortal blow. Knowing she must get him away, Rebecca grasped his arm hard, but she spared a last glance for his stepmother. "Have a care, Lady Kimball," she said with icy fury. "Your face is beginning to reflect the ugliness of your spirit."

As Hermione gasped, Rebecca turned and guided her companion into the crowd. A dozen steps brought them to the end of the ballroom and a pair of open double doors that led into a corridor. She led Kenneth through the doors. He went without resistance, his expression numb.

Half a dozen dimly lit alcoves opened off the passage, each furnished with chairs and lamps so guests could converse in relative peace. Most were occupied, but the last was blessedly empty. She led him inside and pressed him into a chair.

Remaining standing, she rested her hand on his shoulders as she studied his face. His tanned skin was stretched taut over the underlying bones, and the scar was dead white. Quietly she said, "You and she were lovers."

His eyes closed and he drew a long, shuddering breath. "What... what happened had nothing to do with love. My father married Hermione when I was in my last year at Harrow. When I returned to Sutterton, I did my best to be civil even though I suspected that under her facade of proper young wife beat a heart of pure brass. Yet while I couldn't like her, I... I was attracted to her. She had a sexual aura no man could ignore."

Rebecca nodded. She had seen that sexuality in Hermione and could easily imagine how disturbing it must have been for a vigorous, impressionable young man.

He drew another deep breath. "Over the summer, things went well enough. Though Hermione must have realized that I disapproved of her, there was no open friction. My father was starting to neglect the estate, but I was able to take care of what needed to be done. Then I learned that he was going to mortgage Sutterton to buy a London house. I was badly worried, but decided that rather than start a row, I would tell him I didn't want to go to Cambridge. Instead, I would stay in Bedfordshire and act as his steward.

"I thought he would be glad—he'd spent years training me to manage the estate. But he guessed that I'd made the offer because I disapproved of his plans. He became enraged by my impertinence, and we had a blazing great row—the worst ever. After he slammed out of the house, I decided that for the first time in my life, I was going to get roaring drunk. I grabbed a bottle of brandy and went up to my room. About the time I emptied it, Hermione came in, crying and saying how distressed she was to have caused trouble between my father and me."

His voice broke off. When the silence had gone on long enough, Rebecca said in a matter-of-fact voice, "She fell weeping into your arms and nature took its course."

"There's nothing natural about bedding your father's wife." His mouth twisted. "I did it from an unholy combination of anger and lust and drink, coupled with a desire to prove to myself that Hermione was as vile as I suspected. Yet in doing so, I behaved with equal vileness."

His eyes opened, pain clouding the smoky depths. "After that, I couldn't possibly stay at Sutterton. I said good-bye to my sister, Beth, took what little money I had, and left. Two days later, I enlisted. Partly because it was a practical way to support myself, but more as a kind of self-punishment for what I had done. God knows, I'd never had any desire to be a soldier."

"You shouldn't have been so hard on yourself." Rebecca's hands tightened on his shoulders. "Hermione did it deliberately, you know. She knew you would be crippled by guilt. The bitch probably hoped you'd hang or shoot yourself, but leaving was good enough. With you gone, there was no one to oppose her wishes."

"Good God," Kenneth said, startled. "You think she was that cold-blooded?"

"I'm sure of it—she reeked of smug triumph."

"And well she should," he said bitterly. "Because of my

weakness, she was left unchecked to rip the heart out of Sutterton. In the process she destroyed the livelihoods of dozens of people and deprived my sister of the life she should have had. If I had controlled my anger and lust, I would have been able to stay. I had some influence with my father. I could have prevented the worst excesses."

"Don't count on it," Rebecca said slowly. "I think Hermione would go to any lengths to get her own way. If you had resisted her that time, she would have tried other methods to get rid of you. Perhaps she would have arranged a little scene where your father would find the two of you together, her with ripped clothing and screaming rape."

"Christ," Kenneth said, shaken. "I hadn't thought of that, but it sounds horribly plausible."

"Because of that woman, you spent a dozen years in hell, fighting and killing when that was the last thing on earth you should have chosen." Rebecca slid her arms around his neck and pressed her cheek to his, aching. "Oh, my dear."

"Rebecca. God, Rebecca." He pulled her down into his lap and crushed her in his embrace, his breathing harsh. "I'm sorry for falling to pieces. Most of the time, I've been able to bury what happened in some dark corner of my mind, but seeing her unexpectedly... it brought the whole hellish business back."

"She knew you were honorable, and she used that against you." Rebecca buried her face against his neck, feeling the hard rhythm of his pulse. It was sheer madness to sit in his lap when they were visible to anyone who might walk down the corridor and glance their way. Yet she could not bring herself to move.

He held her for the space of a dozen heartbeats. Then he turned his head and captured her mouth in a kiss that she guessed was fueled more by a need to drown his haunted memories than by passion. Yet passion followed in an instant, swift and hot. She kissed him back, hungry for the taste of his mouth, the melting surrender and fierce pleasure she had known with him before.

It was all there, and more. Sensual heat, living fire. His hand slid to her hip and crushed the amber silk as he drew her hard against him. Beneath her the muscles of his thighs tensed, subtle and erotic, as she twisted in his lap to bring herself closer. When they were pressed breast to breast, she slipped her arms under his coat, cursing the fabric that separated them.

Then a female voice behind her gasped, "Shameless! Utterly *shameless."*

Rebecca froze and Kenneth muttered a curse under his breath. She pivoted in his lap to see that a whole group of people were staring into the alcove. Sickly she realized that the dance music had stopped and guests were coming down the corridor to the supper room. The cry had come from an aging dowager who stood with her hand pressed to her mouth in disgust. Flanking her were the Duke and Duchess of Candover, Michael and Catherine Kenyon, and a dozen other guests, all of them riveted by the scandalous sight of Rebecca sitting on Kenneth's lap.

Rebecca began to shake. After a mere three hours of respectability, she had ruined herself again, this time forever. Worse, people like Catherine and Michael who had offered their support in spite of her past were going to feel that she had betrayed their trust. She wished the floor would open and swallow her.

Then Lavinia pushed to the front of the group. "Well, my little lovebirds, you won't be able to keep your betrothal private any longer," she said with indulgent humor. "Sir Anthony will be glad to finally send out the notices."

Kenneth caught Rebecca in his arms and got to his feet, then smoothly set her beside him, wrapping his left arm around her waist for support. "Please forgive us," he said disarmingly. "Ever since Rebecca agreed to be my wife, I've been behaving like a mooncalf. I still have trouble believing my good luck." He smiled dotingly into her eyes. Under his breath, he whispered, "Play along, Ginger, and we'll survive this skirmish."

Jarred out of her paralysis, she tilted her head and gave him a slightly shaky smile. "It is I who am the lucky one."

Catherine stepped forward, Michael just behind her. As Michael shook Kenneth's hand, Catherine exclaimed, "How wonderful! Mind you, I suspected an engagement the first time I saw you together." She kissed Rebecca's cheek. "You're the only woman I know who is good enough for Kenneth."

An instant later the duke and duchess were offering their best wishes, quickly followed by others, even the dowager who had been so outraged. A little hysterically, Rebecca realized that Lavinia's quick thinking had transformed them from outrageous sinners into a charmingly romantic betrothed couple. Her reputation had been saved—but dear God, at what price?

Though the next hour passed with ghastly slowness, Kenneth managed to keep up the facade of proud newly engaged man. Rebecca stayed close, smiling shyly and accepting good wishes. But he didn't like the brittle expression in her eyes. They must talk before she shattered.

Luckily they had already arranged to leave right after supper, but Michael and Catherine's presence in the carriage prevented private conversation. He suspected that his old friends guessed that no betrothal had existed. However, with exquisite tact, they asked no questions.

He breathed a sigh of relief when they were finally set down at Seaton House. Rebecca held on to his arm as they climbed the steps and he unlocked the front door. She even waved good-bye to the Kenyons, but the instant they entered the dimly lit foyer she jerked away. Under her glowing auburn hair, her face was white.

Wanting to ease the distress in her eyes, he said, "We got out of that rather lightly. All we have to do is maintain the pretense of a betrothal for several months, then quietly let it be known that we decided we wouldn't suit."

"So in addition to my previous reputation as a slut, I will now be known as a jilt." She yanked off her cloak and hurled it onto a chair. "Wonderful."

"Ending the engagement will cause only a mild ripple compared to the scandal that would have erupted if Lavinia hadn't thought so quickly." He sighed as he removed his hat and set it on the hall table. "I'm sorry, Rebecca. I swear that you won't have to marry me because of a stupid accident."

"Was it an accident, Captain?" She peeled off her kid gloves and said in a voice that trembled, "You have access to most of my father's papers. Did you learn that my mother's death made me a considerable heiress? I imagine there is enough to save your precious estate, with some left over to start your own private art collection."

"Christ, do you think I engineered that wretched scene to trap you into marriage?" he asked incredulously.

She stared at him with bleak eyes. "No, I suppose not. Still, I've wondered why you were so vehement about not wanting to marry for money. You seemed to be protesting too much about what is clearly the logical choice for a man in your situation."

He turned away, feeling as drained as if he'd spent the evening pounded by an artillery barrage. And now he was going to have to reveal a wretched truth to explain his aversion to fortune hunting.

"I was raised to assume that wealth and rank and privilege would be mine by right," he said painfully. "Through a combination of bad luck and bad judgment, most of those assumptions were beaten out of me. While other young gentlemen raced horses and chased opera dancers, I learned that the world grants no rights beyond the chance to struggle for survival."

His mouth twisted. "In the army I was flogged, wore rags, and damned near starved to death. I was forced to face every flaw and weakness in myself, and to learn the harsh lesson that men born to whores and raised in the gutter could be stronger, braver, and more honorable than I."

Still not looking at her, he removed his cloak and folded it meticulously. "Now I've inherited the rank I once assumed was my natural due, but there's a very real possibility that I'll spend the rest of my life living hand to mouth, only a single step from disaster. Much of the fault is my own. But even though survival meant surrendering pride and hope and most of my youth, the one thing I refuse to yield is the belief that if I ever marry, I have a right to choose a woman I care about."

He thought he would suffocate in the ensuing silence. Then Rebecca said in a barely audible voice, "You're very eloquent. I'm sorry for saying what I did—getting caught was as much my fault as yours. More, probably, because I had less excuse for losing my head. But..." She drew a ragged breath. "Everything was going so well. Then it ended in an instant. I... I should have stayed in my attic and never allowed myself to be lured out." She turned and climbed the stairs, her back rigid.

He sank into an uncomfortable gilded chair and buried his face in his hands. She was right; they both should have stayed home. He had wanted to improve her life, and instead had caused greater damage. How many times did he have to learn the lesson that good intentions could produce terrible outcomes?

He could hardly blame her for her suspicions. She already knew that he was being less than fully honest; he'd told her so himself. From there it was an easy jump to believing he was a fortune hunter, especially when he had been so insane as to kiss her in what was virtually a public place.

Of course, he *had* been a little insane at the time. *Damn* Hermione. Though he'd known that eventually he would run into her, he had not been prepared for it to happen on his first venture into London society. He should have guessed that she would not respect the rules of mourning.

As much as he had always disliked his stepmother, he had still underestimated her viciousness. The best proof that she had deliberately seduced him was her brazen willingness to let Rebecca know about the incident. Bloody hell, had she told his father? The thought nauseated him.

Rebecca, bless her, had handled the revelation very well. Instead of running away in disgust, she had offered comfort and understanding. Thank God for her lucid, unconventional mind.

But now, because of his criminal carelessness, the two of them were officially betrothed. The hell of it was that, under other circumstances, he might well have asked her to marry him. He had never found such mental rapport with another woman, nor such intense desire. It would be very easy to fall in love with her. Instead, he was honor-bound to end the betrothal as soon as possible. He was in no position to marry. Even if he managed to resolve the mystery of Helen Seaton's death without Rebecca learning of his duplicity, a serious proposal would revive her suspicions that he wanted her for her money.

With a groan, he got to his feet and headed upstairs. He would change from his evening clothing, then go to his little studio and paint a furious watercolor of a battle scene. Perhaps that would relieve some of his turmoil.

~

As soon as Rebecca entered her bedroom, her shaky control dissolved. After locking the door—did she fear that Kenneth would follow her? Would she mind if he did?—she threw herself onto the bed. What a damned fool she had been. If she hadn't taken her distress out on him in the form of a stupid accusation, Kenneth would not have had to spell out that she was not a woman he could care for deeply.

Oh, he liked her in a friendly way, and he found her somewhat attractive, but those were superficial emotions. It was the beautiful, doomed guerrilla whom he had loved. She herself was not worthy of marriage even to save his estate and sister from ruin.

Not that she wanted to marry him, or any man. But she liked him. And—admit it—she desired him, and wanted him to desire her. To *burn* with desire, that only she could satisfy.

What would be the ideal relationship with him? Rebecca rolled over on her back and considered. To be lovers. That would be perfect. They would live in separate homes, and when she was in the mood, she would invite Kenneth over. They would make mad, passionate love, with no hurtful consequences.

What a pity that life was not so simple.

CHAPTER 18

Rebecca's first thought when she awoke was that she must tell her father what had happened. He would probably be half amused and half irritated. With a groan, she rose, washed, and put on an exceedingly respectable gray morning gown. Then she headed downstairs, praying that she would not run into Kenneth. She had no idea what to say to him.

Luckily, Sir Anthony was alone in the breakfast parlor. At her entrance, he glanced up from his newspaper. "Good morning. You're up early for someone who went to a ball. Did you have a good time?"

"Yes and no." She poured herself a cup of steaming coffee and sat down. "It was quite enjoyable at first. But then a sort of accident happened."

He laughed. "Someone stepped on the hem of your gown?"

Wrapping her cold hands around the cup, she said baldly, "Kenneth and I were caught kissing."

Before she could continue, her father's smile vanished.

"The devil you say! The idea was to reestablish you socially, not make your reputation worse."

"It was... an accident."

He glared at her. "You tripped and happened to land in Kenneth's arms?"

She gave him a look of annoyance. "Of course not. Something upsetting had happened to him. I was sympathizing, and a... a friendly kiss was exchanged." It was a good deal more than friendly, but she suspected that even a father as liberal as hers would not want to hear the lurid details. "We were in an alcove, and a dozen or so people came by on their way to the supper room. Some old trout saw us and became incensed. Lavinia happened to be part of the group. She saved the day by pretending that Kenneth and I are betrothed. Since she's well known as a friend of the family, no one questioned it."

"Thank heaven she was there and showed some sense," Sir Anthony said grimly. "Obviously you and Kenneth had none. I would have expected better of you both."

Clearly irritation was outweighing amusement. "It was an unfortunate incident, but harmless," she said defensively. "Everyone accepted the idea of a betrothal. We'll call it off in a few months, but in the meantime, formal notices will have to be sent to the papers to maintain the pretense."

"What do you mean, pretense?" He folded his newspaper and slapped it onto the table beside his plate. "I was willing to overlook your elopement with that imbecilic poet, but enough is enough. You'll simply have to marry Kenneth."

She almost choked on her scalding coffee. "Don't be absurd! Getting married because of a minor indiscretion is exactly the sort of foolish social convention that you are always railing about. Of course we won't go through with it."

Sir Anthony scowled at her. "I've been far too lax with you. It's time to rectify that. You're a grown woman and you should be respectably married. Kenneth will make a perfectly adequate husband. At least he recognizes a good painting when he sees it, unlike your poet."

Unable to believe what she was hearing, she sputtered, "What makes you think you can start ordering my life when I'm twenty-seven years old?"

"Better late than never." His eyes narrowed. "I am your father and it is my duty to guide you. You will do as I say, and I say you must marry Kenneth."

Rage exploded through her. Rebecca got to her feet and leaned over the table, planting her fists on the polished mahogany. "How *dare* you! You committed adultery with any attractive woman who caught your eye. You blandly accepted the fact that one of your best friends was your wife's lover. And now you claim the right to guide me? You... you *hypocrite!"*

Taken aback, her father stammered, "That has nothing to do with your situation."

"Nothing to do with it?" She crumpled her napkin into a ball and hurled it across the room. "With the example of marriage you set, I'd rather burn in hell than take a husband! If you don't like that, fine. I'll leave and set up my own establishment. I can perfectly well afford it."

"I told Helen it would be a mistake for you to inherit her fortune outright, but she was as stubborn as you are." He got to his feet, his expression ferocious. "If you set up your own household, I wash my hands of you. You are no longer my daughter. You can live alone, an outcast."

Too enraged to care, she shouted, "Fine! I look forward

to not having your lazy friends underfoot all the time. You can stretch your own canvases and make your own pastels and special oils. And if you think I'll tell you the formulae for my flesh tints, you're an even bigger fool than I thought!"

"You arrogant chit! I was mixing oils when your mother was still in the nursery." He swept his arm across the table, sending crockery crashing. "Go on, leave and good riddance!"

She was about to make another furious reply when a deep voice said sharply, "Enough! Both of you stop before you say something irrevocable."

Rebecca and her father turned to see that Kenneth had entered the breakfast room from the door at the far end. She flushed, wondering how much he had heard. After the heat came a chill as she realized how close she and her father were to a devastating rupture. If she lost him, she would be wholly alone.

Less reflective, her father snapped, "Mind your own business. This is a family matter."

Kenneth arched his brows eloquently. "That's the whole point. In theory, I am almost a member of your family."

"In that case, talk some sense into my daughter." Sir Anthony waved an exasperated hand at Rebecca. "She's being bullheaded, but surely you recognize that after being caught in a compromising situation you must marry, and soon."

"Not necessarily," Kenneth said calmly. "The consequences of a broken engagement would be minor compared to those of an ill-advised marriage."

Temper kindling again, Sir Anthony roared, "Damnation! I thought you were a gentleman, even if you were promoted from the ranks. I never should have hired you."

Beginning to feel a little giddy, Rebecca said helpfully, "You're forgetting that he's a viscount, he went to Harrow, and you've said yourself that he's the best secretary you ever had."

"All the more reason for him to do the right thing!" Her father glared at Kenneth. "Don't think you can get away with shirking your duty. You've compromised my daughter, and by God, you will damned well marry her or I'll take a horsewhip to you."

Rebecca stifled a giggle as she tried to imagine her slightly built father horsewhipping a man who outweighed him by four stone and who had fought through years of brutal warfare. The situation had gone from anger to farce.

Still calm, Kenneth said, "The decision whether or not to marry must be Rebecca's. If she wishes to go through with the betrothal, naturally I will oblige. But I will not force her to the altar. Neither you nor I have the right, or the power, to do so." His voice became dry. "I'm not much of a prize, so I can't blame her for preferring hell to having me for a husband."

Rebecca winced, sorry he had heard that.

"It's a perfectly eligible connection," Sir Anthony replied. "The more I consider, the better I like it. The house has ample room for the pair of you to stay on. Very convenient."

"For heaven's sake, Papa, I'm not going to marry merely so you can keep your favorite secretary!" Rebecca exclaimed.

Before her father could answer, Kenneth said soothingly, "The issue cannot not be decided now, when tempers are raging."

"Perhaps you're right." Sir Anthony stalked to the door. "But whether it is settled now or later, there is only one acceptable outcome. Kenneth, draft betrothal notices for the newspapers." Then he left, slamming the door behind him.

Rebecca folded her shaky body into a chair and covered her face with her hands. Kenneth's soft footsteps approached, and she felt the warmth radiating from his body as he knelt by her.

"Are you all right?" he asked.

"Don't worry, I'm closer to laughter than tears." She raised her head and gave him a slightly unsteady smile. "Of all the times for my father to decide that he should be a stricter parent! This whole situation is absurd."

He stood and went for the coffee pot, replenishing her cup before pouring one for himself. "Sir Anthony isn't taking this well," he agreed. "Am I about to be discharged?"

"I shouldn't think so. His tantrums don't last long."

"What about yours?" He served himself breakfast from the covered dishes, then sat down. "Will you really move out and set up your own household?"

"I doubt it will come to that."

"I hope you're right. I would hate to be the cause of a rift between you and your father."

As she took a grateful swallow of coffee, she realized that she felt no awkwardness with Kenneth. Her earlier unease seemed to have been burned away by the shouting match with her father. "If that happens, it will be our fault, not yours." She regarded him thoughtfully. "Did you mean what you said—that the decision whether or not to marry is entirely mine?"

"Of course." He cut his ham into neat squares. "Gentlemen are not allowed to end betrothals. It's a basic social rule."

She snorted. "I should hold you to the engagement as punishment for making me go to the ball."

He gave her a wry smile. "I've had worse punishments."

The intimate light in his eyes sent warmth cascading through her. Lord, if he wasn't careful, she really might make him go through with it. The thought was wickedly tempting. But she didn't want to lose him as a friend, and nothing would be more fatal to friendship than a marriage he didn't want.

Lightly she said, "Apart from publishing the announcement, do we have to do anything to support our false engagement?"

"Accepting a few invitations might be advisable, but that's all." He stabbed a piece of ham with his fork. "In a few weeks, life will be back to normal."

He might believe that, but she didn't. The events of the previous evening had caused a change in their relationship. She felt an odd mixture of intimacy and wariness and saw the same in him. Only time would tell how significant that change would be.

~

An hour later, Kenneth looked up guardedly when Sir Anthony came to the office for their morning business session. However, his employer was perfectly calm and made no reference to the scene at breakfast. After taking care of the usual correspondence and household matters, Kenneth silently offered the betrothal announcement he had drafted.

Sir Anthony read the brief, formal paragraph and handed the sheet back. "Fine, only use your title, not just your military rank." His voice became heavily ironic. "I want the world to know that my little girl has made a good match."

Kenneth laid down the notice, feeling acutely uncomfortable. "I'm very sorry for what happened, sir."

"You mean you're sorry you kissed my daughter?" Sir Anthony asked coolly. "Or sorry that you got caught?"

His employer was definitely looking for blood. Deciding on honesty, Kenneth replied, "I don't regret kissing her—Rebecca is immensely attractive. But doing so was wrong, and putting her in such an awkward position was contemptible."

"What are your intentions concerning her?" When Kenneth hesitated, the older man said irritably, "Come, Captain, surely I have a right to know."

"I don't deny that, sir." Thinking that he would rather face an army court-martial, Kenneth said carefully, "Before last night, I had no intentions. I have no right to take a wife when the estate I inherited is on the verge of bankruptcy."

"Rebecca is already in possession of a comfortable fortune. On my death, she will be a substantial heiress."

Kenneth felt a prickle of anger. "Are you trying to persuade me to marry her for her money? Because if you are, it's damned insulting to both Rebecca and me. She doesn't need a fortune for a man to want her, and I will not be bought."

Looking pleased, Sir Anthony said, "Keep your feathers down, Captain. No insult is intended. I am merely pointing out that if you want to marry her, it's foolish to let your pride stand in the way. Her fortune could set your estate to rights."

"It appears that you want to promote this match. Why?" Kenneth asked bluntly. "As I said at breakfast, I'm no great catch. I'm a secretary, for God's sake! There are any number of men who are wealthier, better educated, and better looking."

"Very true, but you're the only man Rebecca has shown any interest in since that damned poet," Sir Anthony said dryly. "That's a substantial qualification."

"But you know nothing about me. I merely appeared one day and asked for work. You have no evidence about my character."

"I don't need a sheaf of references to know what you are. A man's character is written in his face." Sir Anthony picked up a quill pen, drawing the vane through his long fingers. "I won't be here forever. My daughter has led an unusually sheltered life. She needs a husband who is kind and honest and capable. He must also appreciate art and respect her talent. Such men are not easy to find. You would do very well—*if* you care for her as a husband should."

For sheer humiliation, there was nothing to match being held in high esteem by the man he had been hired to destroy. All Kenneth could think to say was, "Rebecca would not agree that she needs a husband. She will do her own choosing, I think."

Sir Anthony gave him a gimlet stare. "You are not inexperienced with women. If you decide to exert yourself, I'm sure you could be very... persuasive."

" 'Persuasive,' " Kenneth repeated, incredulous. "Are you hinting that I should try to seduce your daughter into marriage?"

"A harsh way of putting it, but essentially correct," the older man said calmly. "I would be sorry to see a good match thwarted because of her stubbornness and your pride."

Kenneth took a deep breath. "Are all interviews between fathers and potential sons-in-law this harrowing?"

The other man chuckled. "I wouldn't know, since I eloped myself. When Helen and I returned from Gretna Green, her father informed me that her fortune would be put in trust for her children so I'd never get my greedy hands on it. I think he was disappointed that I didn't mind." His expression sobered. "A good soldier is a blend of honor and pragmatism. A man is nothing without honor—but it is often better to act from pragmatism. Rebecca is not a seventeen-year-old virgin. There is no need for you to behave as if she is."

With that paralyzing comment, Sir Anthony got to his feet and went to the door. He paused with his hand on the knob. "I am being frank because I believe you care for my daughter. But if you hurt her, by God, I *will* take a horsewhip to you, even if you are twice my size and half my age."

"Understood. But I suggest you avoid talking like this to Rebecca," Kenneth said dryly. "She would probably respond by moving out and telling us both to go to perdition."

"You understand her very well." Smiling, Sir Anthony left.

Kenneth exhaled roughly and rubbed his temples. He didn't actually have a headache, but he felt as if he ought to. Artists really were mad. It was the only explanation.

Yet in his heart he knew that if he weren't at Seaton House under false pretenses, he would be very tempted by Sir Anthony's suggestion that he seduce Rebecca.

CHAPTER 19

As the morning progressed, Rebecca was unnerved to receive several notes offering best wishes on her upcoming nuptials. The blasted betrothal was taking on a life of its own.

Then Lavinia dropped by and invited herself into Rebecca's studio. Rebecca looked up from her falling woman painting with a scowl. "I hope you're pleased with yourself. If you hadn't interfered, I would be safely ruined by now, with no more nonsense about rebuilding my reputation."

Lavinia laughed and settled onto the sofa with a flounce of skirts. "Sheath your claws, darling. You were glad enough to be rescued at the time. I thought you would fall into a dead faint when you were discovered." She gave the silky Persian carpet draped over the sofa an appreciative caress. "You really should have chosen a more private place to make a meal of Kenneth."

Face scarlet, Rebecca covered her canvas and lifted the Gray Ghost from a chair so she could sit down. Cuddling the cat on her lap, she said, "It wasn't exactly a matter of choice. It just happened. And I wasn't making a meal of him."

"No?" Lavinia said skeptically. "That was not a polite little kiss. It was a full-blooded, ready-to-rip-clothes-off kind of kiss, and I speak as one who knows."

"Lavinia!" Rebecca bent her head and concentrated on petting the cat. "You're embarrassing me."

Taking pity, Lavinia said more moderately, "Of course you can break the betrothal later, but think carefully before you act. You could do a great deal worse than Kenneth for a husband. Not only is he madly attractive, but a viscount, and he really fancies you. You're a credit to your sex. Few women could have accomplished so much in a single evening." She gave a gurgle of laughter. "And if you marry him, Hermione will become a dowager viscountess. She'll be enraged."

Rebecca glanced up. "You know Lady Kimball?"

"Yes, and a nasty bit of work she is. I noticed that it was after she cornered Kenneth that the two of you bolted from the ballroom. She must have been her usual dreadful self."

"Worse than dreadful. Wicked." Thinking that Kenneth would want to know, Rebecca continued, "What was her marriage like? Did she make Lord Kimball miserable?"

Lavinia considered. "I don't believe so. Hermione has a keen sense of which side her bread is buttered on, which meant keeping her husband happy and being discreet about her adulteries." She cocked her head. "How did your father take the news of your betrothal?"

"Not well," Rebecca admitted. "He started ranting that Kenneth must marry me."

"In that case, I'll say no more on the subject." Lavinia got gracefully to her feet. "There's nothing like being told to do something for one's own good to put one off doing it." With a smile and a flutter of her fingers, she left.

Rebecca returned to her painting, but had trouble concentrating. Instead, she found herself chewing on the end of a brush and wondering just how much Kenneth fancied her.

~

By the time Kenneth arrived for his midafternoon sitting, Rebecca had her unruly thoughts under control. It helped that he made no reference to their mutual dilemma. He simply scooped up the Gray Ghost and took his usual position on the sofa with the cat beside him. "How is the picture coming?" he asked.

"Quite well. All of the basic shapes, colors, and shadows are in place, so I can begin to lay in the details. In another week or two, you'll be a free man." She would miss these sessions, but they would still have the painting lessons. She lifted her palette. "Give me your wicked pirate expression."

"I'll never get used to this." He closed his eyes, then reopened them and looked at her with dark intensity. The effect was not so much dangerous as compelling. Profoundly masculine. It was an expression that would make Lavinia swoon on the spot.

Rebecca took a deep breath, then began detailing the corsair's face. She would show the pirate's haunted regret on the dark reflected profile, but that was for another session. Today she would concentrate on the jaded man who could love or kill with equal ease. Now that Kenneth was her friend, it was harder for her to see that menacing side of him.

She laid a narrow shadow along his cheek, then drew the

pale line of the scar over it with one delicate stroke. That mark gave silent testimony to a perilous life. More difficult was capturing the lucent clarity of his gray eyes. World-weary eyes that had seen everything, and trusted nothing. White highlights for the chancy sparkle. Charcoal rims made them piercing, as they were in real life.

She raised the brush for a last stroke, then halted. Half of being an artist was knowing when to stop.

She dropped the brush into the jar of turpentine and chose another to add the faint lines at the corners of the eyes. They gave maturity as well as proof of a life lived outdoors.

Shadows to define the chiseled cheekbones. Then the mouth. Immediately she ran into trouble. While outlining it, she had a vivid memory of what his lips had felt like on hers. A wave of heat went through her and the brush slipped. She made an exasperated sound.

Kenneth asked, "Is something wrong?"

"Just... just a misstroke." Avoiding his eyes, she wiped her damp palms, then scraped the paint off. Once again she tried to paint the mouth that had kissed her ear and made delicious nibbling bites down her throat....

Again she made a mistake. To her disgust, she realized that her hand was shaking.

Deciding to return to the face on a day when memory of his kisses was less immediate, she shifted her attention to the arm that lay along the back of the sofa. The white linen stretched at the shoulder, hinting at the strength of the body beneath the fabric. Only a little hardening of the shadows was needed. She did that, then studied the way the shirt fell around his torso.

She had pressed herself shamelessly against him, her breasts aching as they flattened against his hard muscles....

She dropped her gaze and swallowed against the dryness in her mouth. Being alone and private with a man, focusing totally on his body, was intensely erotic. Surely he must feel it, too, this dark, throbbing energy that charged the air between them, but she dared not look at his face to find out. She knew her own eyes would be too revealing.

Her gaze went to his legs, and the way the dark, skin-tight breeches pulled across his thighs. She immediately looked away. Impossible even to *think* about working on his lower body. She would detail the hand that rested on the Gray Ghost.

Telling herself to think like a painter, not a woman, she resumed work, glancing back and forth from her subject to her canvas again and again. Hands were almost as critical and difficult as faces. The strong bones defining his wrist turned out well, so she started on the hand itself.

His middle finger stroked across the cat's head, gentle and sensual. The gesture triggered a vivid memory of how that powerful hand had caressed her. The warmth. The feel of his palm cupping her breast....

Damnation, this was absurd! Yet she could not separate her awareness of him as a man from her professional perception.

Her face must have betrayed her turmoil, for Kenneth asked, "More problems?"

Hoping that she wasn't blushing, Rebecca thought quickly and said, "Please move your left hand an inch or so down the sofa." She moistened her dry lips and started to work on the hand that rested on the back of the sofa. The hand that had curved around her hip, pulling her close, sending tingles of liquid fire into deep, secret places....

With an oath, she banged her palette onto the table.

"That's enough for today," she said gruffly. "Let's take a tea break, then start your lesson."

"Good. I've had enough of sitting," Kenneth said with suspicious alacrity. He stood and stretched. Entranced, she watched the sleek, leonine flex of his body. Officially, she was betrothed to this man. In tomorrow's newspapers, they would tell the world that they intended to share a bed for the rest of their lives.

She jerked her gaze away and grabbed a rag to wipe her brush. A good thing this portrait was almost finished, she thought with exasperation. Otherwise she would need a new piece of studio equipment: a tub of icy water to cool the artist.

Kenneth was glad to stop posing, and even gladder that Rebecca stayed at the far end of the studio until the water boiled and the tea had steeped. It had always been difficult to sit still with nothing to do but admire Rebecca. Today it had been damned near impossible. His mind had ranged between remembering how enticing she had looked in amber silk and even more perilous thoughts of how she would look out of it.

After the tea, he reluctantly prepared for another painting lesson. He'd come to hate them because of his miserable lack of progress. He was no better than after the first lesson. Worse, if anything.

Rebecca's teaching was not the problem. Her comments were quiet and to the point, and she never sneered, no matter how dreadful his efforts. The fault was within him.

The focal point of his still life was a cast taken from the head of a Greek statue. It showed Zeus, the face full of wisdom and maturity. He'd chosen it because he'd liked the expression and weathered texture. By now, he loathed the blasted thing.

He painstakingly mixed the tints he would need. Then, expression set, he started to paint.

While he struggled with his canvas, Rebecca sat quietly at her worktable, grinding the pigments to make pastel crayons. After mixing in the binding solution with a palette knife, she rose and came to see how he was doing.

"The shadows on the bowl need to be sharper to indicate how reflective the surface is," she said after a brief study. "And the highlights should be warm to show that it's brass."

She was quite right. He understood those things, had rendered similar objects in pastel and watercolor. Why couldn't he get them right with oils?

Seeing his tight expression, Rebecca said, "It takes time, Kenneth. Don't be so hard on yourself."

Her sympathy was the last straw. With sudden fury, he slashed his brush across the width of the canvas, smearing the heavy oils. "There will never be enough time in the world for me to learn this," he said bitterly.

She frowned. "Your work really isn't that bad."

"But it isn't good. It will never be good." He slapped down the palette and brush and spun away from her, stalking across the studio in a blaze of frustration. The emotions churning inside him were explosive, too violent to be contained by a human body. Only Rebecca's presence kept him from smashing everything in sight.

"I can't do this, Rebecca. The oils won't go where I want. It's like trying to herd pigs. Even when I know what should be done, I can't get it right." He turned and gestured toward the ruined picture. "That's a waste of good paint and canvas. It's flat. Dead. Christ! I never should have tried to learn this."

He was heading toward the door when she said crisply, "The lesson isn't over, Kenneth."

"Yes, it is, and there won't be any more " Struggling for control, he paused with his hand on the knob. "I'm sorry, Rebecca. It was good of you to offer to teach me, but you're wasting your time."

"Come back here, Captain," she said, her voice whip-sharp. "I obliged you by going to that blasted ball, and you will oblige me by not giving up until we've at least tried to devise a different approach that will work for you."

It was an argument he could not ignore. He stared at the door, inhaling and exhaling with slow deliberation. When his emotions were tamped down to a safe level, he returned to his easel. Rather than looking at his travesty of painting, he watched Rebecca. Her intent expression and tousled hair were a far more pleasing sight. He asked tightly, "Did you have such difficulty when you were learning to paint?"

"Did, and sometimes I still do."

"Really?" he said, surprised. "I would have thought that you were beyond such problems."

"I don't think an artist ever gets entirely beyond," she said wryly. "Why do you think my father sometimes turns into a wild man and hurls things all over the studio?"

He gave a lopsided smile. "I have a lot more sympathy for such actions than when I first came here."

She perched on a stool and drummed her fingers on the tabletop as she thought out loud. "Oil paints are a *medium*—not an end in themselves, but simply a material that transmits ideas into visible images. In practical terms, that means that oils express your emotions. Because you want so much to master oil painting, you try too hard. You're as rigid as a marble statue, and that is transmitted to your canvas. Even though your basic drawing is fine, the overall picture is stiff, lifeless. You're crippling yourself and your work."

He had not thought in those terms before. "That's certainly true," he agreed. "But damned if I know how to stop doing it."

"Creative force is like a..." she searched for a phrase, "a river of fire. When it is in full flood, it blazes through the spirit with power and excitement. There are transcendent moments when an artist can do nothing wrong. Every stroke, every color is perfect. The image on the canvas comes very near to matching the image in the mind. Surely you've experienced some of that excitement when drawing."

"Occasionally," he admitted, thinking back. "That is what you feel when you paint?"

"Yes, though nowhere near all the time. I think the feelings must be similar for all creative work, whether it is writing or music or teaching, or even raising a child." Her tone switched from pensive to brisk. "When there is no creative flow, the oils reflect that and fight you every inch of the way. The colors are muddy, the shapes are wrong. There's no harmony."

He grimaced. "That part I recognize."

She studied him narrowly. "You have the talent. The trick is to find a way to release it. Part of the problem is boredom. It was a mistake to try to teach you like a novice when you're already an accomplished artist in many ways. You're simply not that interested in painting a still life. You must choose a subject that you care about—something that excites you so much that you can forget about your problems with the medium and get swept up in the river of fire."

"I wouldn't miss that blasted bust of Zeus," Kenneth

admitted. "But I can't imagine getting carried away by creative excitement when every brushful of paint is struggling like a company of French grenadiers."

She gave him a mischievous smile. "True. So we'll make the oils behave like a medium you've already mastered."

She turned and squeezed a dollop of azurite blue onto an empty palette. Then she slowly mixed in oil of turpentine, adding more and more until the paint was oozing like syrup. When she was satisfied with the consistency, she took a sheet of heavy paper and used a wide brush to lay a smooth wash of blue across the surface. "Thinned down, oils can be used almost like watercolor. You can work much more quickly and freely than when the oils are thick. Try it."

Doubtfully Kenneth accepted the brush and dipped it into the dilute azurite. Though the paint was heavier than watercolor, it flowed across the canvas with sensuous ease. Without conscious thought, he dipped and stroked again, creating shadings of blue like those he would use for the sky of a watercolor landscape.

He set down the brush and flexed his fingers wonderingly. "Interesting. My hand acted instinctively, as if I were working with watercolor." For an instant, he had not thought about the fact that he was using oil paint. His carefully honed manual skills had taken over.

Becoming intrigued, he squeezed burnt sienna onto the palette and thinned that. A few swirling strokes created a silhouette of Rebecca, her hair dancing about her shoulders.

She laughed. "You see the advantages?"

He frowned at the paper. "It's too easy. There has to be a reason why all oil painters don't work this way."

"The colors won't have the same depth and richness,"

she explained. "They'll also fade sooner than oils that have been built up more thickly."

"No matter." He added white lead to the burnt sienna and thinned it again. "I'm trying to learn, not create masterpieces for eternity." He used the tip of the brush to sketch a sleeping feline form, shadowing it with darker paint.

She gave an approving nod. "Another advantage is that dilute oils dry more quickly and can be worked over sooner. I suggest that you combine techniques. Lay in the background and general shapes with thinned paints. Then add details with thicker pigments. Wonderful oil sketches can be done that way. It's particularly good for informal portraits and landscapes."

Excitement began rising in him. He could do this. And if it wasn't classical technique, it was a long step in the right direction. "Ginger, you're wonderful."

Without thinking, he leaned over to give her a swift, grateful kiss. But as soon as his lips touched hers, the physical awareness that had been pulsing between them all afternoon crackled to life. He could no more have ended the kiss than he could have flown to the moon. Her lips opened and their tongues touched, sliding sensually together.

Her scent was intoxicating, a blend of rosewater and oils and woman, a fragrance as unique as Rebecca. He was hungry, famished, for the yielding warmth of female strength and mystery. She nourished him with her mouth as her fingertips curled into his back like a kitten's claws.

He wrapped one arm around her slim waist and held her close. His other hand skimmed her bodice until he cradled the gentle weight of her breast. He moved his palm in a circle. She gasped and arched against him, supple and seductive.

Their mouths worked slowly, rich with subtle nuance.

His hands molded her like a sculptor reveling in clay, learning the fertile swell of hips and the slimness of her waist. The delicacy of her nape and the strength of her graceful arms. The gentle curve of her belly. She gave a small cry as his hand slid lower, stroking the female tenderness hidden beneath layers of fabric. Then, chillingly, in his mind he heard Sir Anthony saying, *"I'm sure you could be very persuasive."*

Bloody hell, he was perilously close to the seduction Sir Anthony had suggested! The fact that he was not doing it in cold blood didn't mean the consequences would be any less profound.

Kenneth lifted his head and straightened, transforming his embrace from passion to protection. For an instant he felt the protest in Rebecca's body. Then she stilled, resting her head beneath his chin. She was so small. Fragile, almost. She deserved the strong, honest man that Sir Anthony thought he was, not the flawed, deceitful reality.

"If we aren't careful," he said unsteadily, "we might end up at the altar in truth."

"Heaven forbid that we fulfill everyone's expectations." Though her tone was acid, when she pushed away from him her expression was vulnerable.

Her hair was loose again. He was unable to stop himself from stroking his fingers into the thick tresses. Auburn silk, cool fire. "If I kiss you again, Rebecca, kick me. My willpower is nonexistent where you're concerned."

She gave a slow, pleased smile. A few feathers in her mouth and she would look like the Gray Ghost after a successful hunt. "My willpower isn't much, either. Remember, I've spent the last ten years as a ruined woman."

She lifted a hand to draw his head down. Hastily he caught it and pressed a kiss into the palm, maintaining his hold as a gentle way of immobilizing her. "We've rehabilitated you. Try to remember that you're respectable now."

She laughed and shook her head, sending her heavy hair tumbling down her back like rippling silk. The sensuality that he had sensed when they first met was no longer latent but scorchingly visible. As her father had said, she was not a seventeen-year-old virgin.

"Do I look respectable, Captain?" she asked with a touch of mockery.

His aching gaze went over her. Every time they kissed, he learned more about the body beneath her muslin gowns. His right hand, the one that had caressed her breast, involuntarily clenched. "You look like Lilith, the demoness sent to steal the souls of men. Wicked and irresistible." His mouth curved ruefully. "I'm sure she was a redhead."

Rebecca tilted her head, deliberately provocative. "Then you had better go before I steal your soul."

He kissed her hand again, then released it. As he started for the door, she said, "Better take this. You'll need more." She held out a jug of oil of turpentine.

He took it with a nod of thanks. But on his way out, he paused in the doorway for one last glance. She was lounging against the worktable, her hands resting on the edge as she studied him with a sultry gaze that was half artist, half woman. He had the sudden, unnerving thought that she might already have stolen his soul.

He turned and left, walking slowly down the stairs. Of one thing he was sure: He had found the subject for his next painting. A subject that excited him, and might sweep him into the burning depths of a river of fire.

Long after Kenneth left, Rebecca remained leaning against her worktable. She had wanted him to desire her, and he did. She did not trust love or marriage, could not see a future in which she and Kenneth would be together. He would certainly not be a secretary forever. If he managed to save his estate, there would be no room for someone like her in the life of a landed gentleman.

But for a little time, before Kenneth left Seaton House, she might be able to taste the forbidden fruits of passion. She wanted him, and the prospect of conceiving a love child did not frighten her. Indeed, she would welcome having someone to love, and love her in return.

And even if that didn't happen, at least she would have memories to warm her nights.

CHAPTER 20

Kenneth spent the evening and most of the night in his little studio, experimenting with dilute oil paints and burning a small fortune in candles. By the time he retired for a few hours of sleep, he had made a good beginning to the picture that had blossomed in his mind while talking to—and kissing—Rebecca.

The basic drawing was done and he'd laid in the underlying colors of the figure and background. The real challenge still lay ahead. He tried not to let himself hope too much. Nonetheless, he was beginning to feel a cautious optimism about his ability to become a real painter.

That morning it was hard to concentrate on secretarial work when his mind was buzzing with ideas and images, but he managed, eventually. He was working in the office in the early afternoon when Sir Anthony's friend Lord Frazier strolled in.

"Good day," Frazier drawled. "I saw in the newspaper that congratulations are in order." He raised his quizzing glass and examined Kenneth with exaggerated care. "So you're a viscount. Pray forgive me if I ever went through a door ahead of you. I didn't know you bear a title that has precedence over mine."

Though the remark was apparently intended as humor, there was a definite bite to the words. Kenneth suppressed a sigh; he had known that mentioning his rank would elicit this kind of response. It was the first time Frazier had ever addressed him as an equal rather than a menial. Kenneth would have preferred to stay a nonentity in the older man's eyes. "The title hasn't been mine for that long," he said peaceably. "Like a new pair of boots, it will take time to become comfortable."

Frazier tapped the quizzing glass against his palm. "So little Rebecca will become Lady Kimball. Have you introduced her to her future stepmother-in-law?"

Kenneth tensed inside. "We chanced to meet Hermione at the Candover ball. You know my stepmother?"

"Oh, yes." Frazier's knowing smile implied that he knew her very well indeed. "She has the most wonderfully wicked humor. Of course, you would know that."

"Absolutely," Kenneth said dryly. "Whenever I think of Hermione, I remember her wonderfully wicked humor."

Frazier lounged against the door frame. "You don't get along with your stepmother?"

Kenneth shrugged. "After so many years in the army, I don't really know her well. She was in good looks at the ball."

"Widowhood becomes her." Frazier's eyes narrowed. "You've done well to win Rebecca. She's quite a prize for a man who is down on his luck. A stroke of good fortune that you came to work for Anthony. Or was it chance? You never did reveal who sent you here."

Kenneth said coolly, "The next time someone hints that

I am marrying Rebecca for her money, I will break him in half."

Frazier blinked, as if surprised to find that the tabby he had prodded was really a tiger. "Sorry, no insult intended. Rebecca is so quiet that I really don't know her, even though we first met when she was a babe in arms. Tell me what she's like."

Uncertain how to reply, Kenneth said, "Shy but definite. Intelligent and talented." Thinking that Frazier might not know of her painting, he did not elaborate on that. "An excellent studio assistant and art critic. Her skills and comments are very valuable to Sir Anthony, I think."

"I had no idea she was so involved in his work," Frazier said with genuine surprise.

"As you said, she's quiet." Kenneth smiled involuntarily. "And lovely as a forest sprite."

"There speaks a man in love," Frazier said thoughtfully. "It sounds as if her marriage will be a great loss to Anthony." He glanced at the mantel clock. "Time I was going. Please give Rebecca my best wishes on her betrothal." He sauntered off.

With a shrug, Kenneth returned to work. He'd asked Rebecca to be excused from posing that afternoon. When he finished Sir Anthony's accounts, he would go to his studio and paint. Next to that, malicious aristocratic painters were of no importance.

~

As soon as Rebecca saw Kenneth at breakfast, she knew that his new approach to painting was going well. He positively vibrated with excitement. Understanding his mood, she was happy to allow him to skip their afternoon session.

His absence didn't interfere with her work. She spent the day on the shadowed background of the corsair picture, adding rich hangings in subtle Oriental patterns to enhance the exotic atmosphere. She also made the Ghost larger than life size and transformed him into a sleek Asiatic hunting cat with tufted ears. The result made her chuckle. She wondered what Kenneth would think of the painting when she finally showed it to him. He would be self-conscious at seeing what she had made of him. But the picture was good, the best work she had ever done.

She dined alone. Her father was attending some kind of Royal Academy function, and Kenneth did not appear at all. She considered going to the attic and reminding him that the house rule was that everyone must attend dinner, but she decided against it. If he was reveling in the first heady joys of successful painting, he should not be disturbed.

After eating, she returned to her studio and worked on the falling woman picture. Though the subject was emotionally draining, she felt driven to finish it. Perhaps when it was done, something dark and difficult would be exorcised from her soul.

Kenneth's studio had a wall in common with hers, and once or twice she heard faint sounds. But never an opening door. The man must be obsessed. Not sure whether she was worried or merely infernally curious, she finally decided to take him some food. Though his mind might have lost track of time, his stomach would surely welcome nourishment.

She went to the kitchen and piled a platter with sliced meat and cheese, added half a loaf of bread, a bottle of wine, and two glasses. Then she made the long climb to the attic again.

Balancing the tray with one hand, she tapped on his

studio door. Nothing. Beginning to feel real concern, she quietly turned the knob.

She needn't have worried. The light of half a dozen candles showed Kenneth working at his easel with utter absorption. Since he and the canvas were at right angles to the door, he did not notice her entrance. His brow was furrowed and his hair fell across his forehead as he wielded a narrow brush that looked absurdly small in his massive hand.

She smiled at the smudge of paint on his cheek. Red ocher, at a guess. He had taken off his boots, probably to avoid making noise that might disturb the servants sleeping in the rooms at the other end of the attic. He'd also removed his coat and cravat, and his open shirt revealed an inviting glimpse of chest. She studied him with frank pleasure. The muscular body and athletic grace made him a fine pirate or warrior. But the real Kenneth was far more complex and interesting than a Byronic hero. Aloud she said, "I thought you might want something to eat."

He pivoted with a soldier's swiftness, then smiled ruefully. "Sorry. You startled me." He glanced at the darkness outside the window. "I missed dinner, didn't I?"

"To say the least. It's about eleven o'clock." She set down her tray. "I gather the picture is going well."

"You were right. I needed a new way of working with oils, and a subject that interested me." He laid down his palette and brush and began to pace, the room too small to contain his brimming energy. "It was slow at first, but once I got going, it was exactly as you said—getting swept up in a river of fire. I've never experienced anything quite like it, even during my best moments of drawing. I love the richness of oils, the effects that are possible. I love the spring of the canvas under the brush, the slap of the paint."

She added a shovelful of coal to the fading fire. "I've been painting so long that I take things like that for granted. Hearing you reminds me how sensual painting is."

He laughed buoyantly. "It's everything I dreamed. For the life of me, I can't remember why yesterday it seemed impossible."

He was like a victorious soldier after a hard-fought battle, and his enthusiasm made her laugh with him. Curious to see his work, she crossed to the easel.

When he saw what she was doing, he spun about. "Christ, Rebecca! You can't look at that."

"Teacher's privilege," she said breezily. Then she came face-to-face with his painting and stopped dead in her tracks.

It was a nude picture of her.

She stared paralyzed at the canvas. He had used the diluted oil technique to loosely create a magical woodland glade in shades of green. In the foreground was the full-length figure of a woman. One of her hands rested on the trunk of a tree while the other held out an apple invitingly.

The woman's slim, naked body had been rendered with loving detail. Her peachy warm skin cried out to be touched and shining auburn tresses cascaded to the ground like dark flame. A few wisps made a teasing concession toward modesty in a way that reminded Rebecca of Botticelli's Venus when the innocent newborn goddess emerged from the sea.

But there was nothing innocent about Kenneth's vision. His naked lady radiated carnality. Her lips were full and wanton, her gold-flecked hazel eyes promised mysterious, dangerous delights to any man who dared accept the forbidden fruit from her hand. And she had been unmistakably modeled after herself.

Rebecca managed to wrench her gaze away and look at Kenneth. His face was starkly vulnerable, as if he expected her to shriek or faint or attack. Beyond that fear, he was also a newly fledged painter who desperately needed validation.

She had to swallow before she could speak. "It's... it's extremely good. You've done an excellent job of combining the different weights of paint. I supposed this is Eve?"

"Lilith," he said, his voice almost a croak. "The first woman God made, before Eve."

"Ah. Of course. You did say Lilith was a redhead. I think of her not as a demoness but the first independent woman, created as man's equal rather than his servant. Of course Adam hated that." She looked at the canvas again, trying to sound detached. "It works well as an idealized, mythic figure, though it wouldn't do as a portrait. Your Lilith is far more beautiful than I."

"No," he said intensely. "That is exactly what you look like. Beautiful. Sensual. Formidable."

In his eyes was the same blazing passion that had created the picture. She knew with absolute certainty that he wanted her, not casually but with fierce need.

His desire kindled the powerful yearning she had been trying to suppress. To hell with propriety. In his eyes she was beautiful, and the time had come to loose the river of carnal fire that could sweep them both into madness and searing joy.

Rebecca tossed her shawl over the single wooden chair. Her gown was secured by a row of spherical ivory buttons that ran down the center of the bodice. Amazed at her own temerity, she unfastened the first one, popping the small globe through its loop. "You must want to see how accurate your imagination is."

He stiffened as she undid the next button. "My imagination is fine, Rebecca," he said tightly. "I don't need you to model."

“No?” She smiled and released another ivory sphere. "I think that you have some of the proportions wrong." She undid another. His gaze was riveted to her fingers.

When the last button slid from its loop, she opened the gown and pushed it down her arms with provocative slowness before letting it slide to the floor in a whisper of wool. She had always disliked complicated clothing, so underneath she wore only stockings and a shift made of fine, translucent lawn that gave teasing hints of what lay beneath.

After stepping out of the crumpled gown, she kicked off her slippers and pulled out the pins that secured her hair. "A good artist works from nature whenever possible, Kenneth."

His scar a bone-white slash across his cheek, he said, "If you don't put your clothing back on, the horsewhip and the trip to the altar are going to become unavoidable."

She laughed and ran her fingers through her hair so that the curls rioted around her head and spilled wantonly to her waist. "Who said anything about horsewhips and marriage? For Lilith and the Corsair, surely desire is all that matters."

"Those are only fantasies," he said harshly, sweat filming his face. "It's wrong, Rebecca, in ways you don't understand."

"You're right, I don't understand." She perched on the chair and untied her garters, a process that meant raising her shift above her knees. She'd always thought her legs were nicely shaped. From the way Kenneth was staring, he must agree.

"You don't have to protect me, my darling corsair. I

know what I'm doing." She rolled off her stockings and crushed them into a ball, then lightly tossed them at Kenneth, aiming for the masculine bulge revealed by his breeches. "That being the case, give me one good reason why we should refrain from doing what we both clearly want to do."

Reflexively he caught the stockings, his hand clenching the gauzy fabric with a force that made the tendons stand out. In his eyes she saw the struggle between the gentleman and the pirate. Yes, he wanted her, but his damned sense of honor was winning.

Unable to bear the thought, she stood and moved toward him, her hands raised in supplication. "Please, Kenneth," she said starkly. "I want you so much."

She caressed his face, and his composure cracked like hammered marble. He put his hands over hers, trapping them against his cheeks. She was vividly aware of the strength in his fingers and the seductive masculine rasp of whiskers under her palms. "God help me, Lilith," he said thickly. "You win."

He drew her hands together and held them against his chest. She felt the pounding of his heart as his mouth came down over hers. With a rush of relief, she knew that there would be no turning back. They were caught in the river's inexorable current and would be carried by its fury until they shattered.

It was a pirate's kiss. Masterful. Devouring. She leaned into him, her arms sliding around his waist as his hands went to her buttocks. His clasp scorched through the thin fabric of her shift as he pulled her hard against him. Their loins pressed together with voluptuous promise. A hot, liquid yearning began to coil deep within her.

When he ended the kiss, she drew her breath in protest

until the touch of his lips on her ear transformed her objection into a rapturous sigh. Her head fell back and she swayed within his grasp, on the verge of falling.

"Lilith," he murmured, "with hair and soul of fire." He laid a trail of kisses from her jaw to the tender flesh of her throat, his mouth firm against her beating pulse.

Blindly she slipped her hands inside his shirt, hungry for the feel of his bare body. His neck and shoulders were dense with muscle. She gave an impatient exclamation when the garment could be opened no further.

Sliding her hands down his ribs, she tugged the shirt from his breeches.

She had just touched the taut warmth of his torso when his mouth closed over her breast. Lapping through the light fabric of her shift, he teased her nipple, circling it with his tongue before tugging with his teeth. She stiffened, paralyzed with an excitement that blazed throughout her body.

Paralysis dissolved in a fever that demanded release. She grasped the front opening of his shirt in both hands and ripped. The linen sundered all the way to the hem with a sharp tearing sound. She yanked the ruined garment down his arms and over his wrists, saying with satisfaction, "I've wanted to do that since the first time I saw you, my corsair."

His bare chest was magnificent. He shivered as she kneaded the hard planes of muscle, feeling the bones beneath the flesh, the dark sleek hair, the way his body narrowed to taut waist and lean hips. He would have made a superb model for a Greek sculptor seeking to portray an Olympic athlete, or a god.

She pressed her lips to the hollow above his collarbone. Saltiness tingled on her tongue as she licked and nipped downward to the flat velvety disk of his nipple. She kissed it as he had kissed hers, flicking with her tongue and teasing with her teeth.

He buried his hands in the heavy spill of her hair, his fingers opening and closing helplessly. "My God, Rebecca," he breathed, "you make me mad."

She laughed with delight and straightened, nuzzling her face into the angle between his throat and shoulder. His scent was musky and wickedly male.

Then she sucked in her breath as he caught handfuls of her shift and pulled the garment over her head. Her arms were lifted straight up, the material dragging over her elbows and wrists. She emerged from the lace-trimmed flounces acutely aware of her nakedness. For an instant she wanted to cover herself, to conceal her human imperfections.

But his gray eyes were glowing like winter stars.

"You are even lovelier than in my imagination," he said huskily as he cupped her breasts, his large hands molding the supple flesh and his thumbs stroking her nipples into taut peaks. He slowly massaged downward, learning every curve and hollow in a deeply sensual caress. Hot pulses raced through every fiber of her being. She was melting, eager to flow into whatever form would please him the most.

He scooped her up in his arms, then hesitated when she caught her breath in surprise. "You're so light," he said uneasily. "Delicate."

"But not the least bit fragile." Before his conscience could get the better of him, she drew his head down for another kiss, running her hands feverishly over any part of him she could reach. She was sharply conscious of the contact between her unclothed body and his bare chest, the way his powerful arms tightened under her naked back and legs as their kiss deepened. The liquid yearning inside her coiled tighter, ever tighter.

The half dozen steps to the narrow servant's bed in the corner were a zigzag path that ended when he laid her on the blanket that covered the sagging straw mattress. The scratchiness of the coarse wool on her back and thighs was one more sensation in a world that was all sensation. "I want to see the rest of you," she said tensely. *"Please."*

Fumbling a little in his haste, he unbuttoned his breeches and tugged them off. Then he peeled off his drawers, revealing himself fully to her gaze. She stared at his muscular thighs and rampant virility and thought of Greek gods again. Suppressing a nervous doubt about whether her body could accommodate him, she scanned slowly over his marvelous torso.

He sat on the edge of the bed and leaned over her. The craggy planes of his face were softened by candle glow, the scar almost invisible. She raised her hands and skimmed them over his shoulders and down his arms, enchanted by the way his broad frame filled her vision. She blinked against the sting of tears.

Seeing them, he asked softly, "Second thoughts?"

She shook her head, her hazel eyes luminous. "It's only that you are beautiful," she said softly. "So beautiful."

Kenneth had thought of himself in many ways, but never as beautiful. It seemed almost criminal to want to inflict his hulking male body on Rebecca's slim, delicate form. "I thought you had impeccable aesthetic judgment," he murmured. "It is you who are beautiful."

She gave him Lilith's smoldering smile. Though he was proud of his painting, he could never equal the enticing reality of her. "You are made for love," he whispered. "A feast for eyes and hands and mouth."

He lifted a handful of her hair and rubbed his cheek with the lustrous mass. "Extravagant hair spun of a thousand shades of red and bronze and gold."

He laid the shining strands across her shoulder, enjoying the contrast of hair and skin. "A pale, exquisite redhead's complexion that shows a faint tracery of veins." Then he smoothed his palms down her arms. "Flawless breasts. Not too large, not too small, crowned with dusky rosebuds." He bent his head and suckled her left nipple. It hardened instantly under his tongue. Her eyes closed and her breath roughened, causing her breasts to rise and fall.

When he had paid them due homage, he traced the circle of her navel with his tongue. His hand slipped between her knees so he could caress the satiny flesh of her inner thighs. She vibrated with response, her hips rocking against the blanket, her small hands fisted.

The feathery curls between her legs were a darker auburn than her glorious hair. He rested his palm on the gentle swell of her mound, marveling that the swift drumming of her blood was for him. Then he stretched out on his side next to her, holding her close with one arm while his other hand stroked through the moist, clinging strands to the luscious moisture of the folds hidden below.

She groaned wordlessly, writhing as he probed deeper and deeper into intimate heat. Before he could bring her to fulfillment, she reached out blindly, fumbling down his body until she found the hard, heated length of his shaft. Her hand curled around him and her thumb caressed the unbearably sensitive head.

Ravishing friction, intolerably sweet. He arched convulsively. *Oh, God, God, not yet.*

Mindless with urgency, he pulled away from her clasp and lifted his body over hers. His arms trembled as they braced his weight. He positioned himself, feeling her liquid readiness as his fingers prepared her for his entry. Then he drove into the blessed heat that would heal his madness.

There was an instant of sharp resistance, and he felt her stiffen. He damned himself for forgetting how small she was. His whole frame shaking with effort, he held still so she could adjust to him. He kissed her, using mouth and tongue to soothe away her tension.

She relaxed and her kiss became avid, as if she were trying to draw his essence into her. He began to move, first only fractions of an inch. Gradually he thrust harder, moving ever deeper and faster.

She twisted her head against the blanket, her breath coming in desperate gulps and her palms making circles on the small of his back. "Please, Kenneth, please..." she panted.

On the verge of shattering, he slid his hand between them until he touched her sensitive female nub. She gave a hoarse animal cry. Her hands curled into claws that bit into his buttocks, and her pelvis ground against him with frantic need.

Her climax triggered his own release. He groaned, driving into her again and again as harrowing pleasure flooded through him. A river of fire, more intense than anything he had ever known. And as the flames ebbed, he realized with wonder and despair that they had irrevocably seared his very soul.

CHAPTER 21

The bed was narrow, but there was room enough when Kenneth shifted to his side and cradled her against him. Rebecca's limbs trembled as if she had been fractured and reassembled into a different being. She hid her face against his sweat-slicked shoulder, knowing she would never have enough of his closeness. Or, God help her, of the pleasure that had pierced her hard-won reserve before warmly enfolding her heart.

Outside it was raining. There was something wonderfully intimate about lying warm and safe in Kenneth's arms only a few feet below the drumming raindrops. She dozed a little, coming awake when he raised himself on one elbow and kissed her temple.

Her eyes opened and she studied his face, thinking that the craggy planes were more appealing than Apollo's perfect features could ever be.

Seeing that she was awake, he gently brushed the hair from her damp brow. "I should burn my painting. No oil or canvas can ever do justice to you."

"Don't you dare," she said with a lazy smile. "It's a fine

painting. Just don't show it to anyone. Especially not my father." She shouldn't have said that, because a shadow darkened his eyes. Wanting to restore the tender mood, she continued, "There's a bottle of wine and two glasses on the tray I brought."

"An excellent idea." He levered himself up, then stopped, staring downward. She followed his gaze and saw that there was blood on both of them.

His head whipped up, and he stared at her with what was almost horror. "My God, you were a virgin. That's why it was difficult at first."

Her gaze slid away from him. "So I was."

He caught her chin and turned her face to him. His voice tight with barely controlled emotion, he said, "What about the elopement and the poet? All of your talk about being ruined?"

She wrenched her chin loose. "Ruination can be social without being physical. Frederick was willing to wait until we were legally married. By the time we reached Leeds, I knew that running away with him had been a terrible mistake. He wasn't in love with me, he was in love with the idea of himself as a dashing lover. And my future prospects, of course." She gave a shaky laugh. "The worst of it was discovering that he was *boring*. I realized I couldn't possibly spend the rest of my life with him, so I caught a mail coach back to London. But by then I had been gone for several nights, so my reputation was wrecked."

Kenneth took a deep breath. "Did your parents know that you hadn't lain with him?"

"It didn't seem relevant since I was ruined anyhow."

"Hell and damnation." He rested his forehead on her shoulder, his rough exhalation warming her breast. "You said you knew what you were doing, but you didn't. You *couldn't."*

For the space of a dozen heartbeats, there was silence. Then he lifted his head, his expression as grim as if he had just been condemned to the firing squad. "If it weren't for the fact that it would be a terrible mistake to marry, I would say that our betrothal has just gone from pretense to reality."

At a disadvantage flat on her back, she pushed up to a sitting position. "Having been raised among decadent artists, I have trouble taking virginity seriously. It really shouldn't matter."

He raised his brows expressively as he climbed from the bed and went to get the towel that hung on the small wash-stand. "Trust me, Rebecca. It matters."

After a brisk clean-up, he wrapped the blanket around her, casually pulled on his breeches and shirt, and poured them both wine. Then he sat beside her and leaned against the wall, his expression deeply troubled. "I deserve to be shot. I knew it was wrong to lie with you, and I did it anyhow."

She gave him an uncertain smile. "Since I almost assaulted you, it would have required an ungentlemanly amount of force to prevent it from happening."

He stared into his glass. "At my age, I should be able to control myself even when attacked by a ravishing female."

Ravishing? She liked the sound of that. "I'm glad you couldn't control yourself, and I'm vastly pleased with the results. I quite fancy myself as Lilith."

He smiled a little, but shook his head. "I'll grant that you aren't a naive girl just out of the schoolroom. But I was so mad with wanting you that I took no precautions against pregnancy. If you conceived..." His voice trailed off.

"That's unlikely after only one time, isn't it? And I shouldn't mind having a baby." She pulled the blanket more closely around her. "If my father couldn't bear the scandal, I can set up a household in some provincial city. Claim I'm a widow, perhaps. After all, I'm financially independent."

His hand clenched so hard around the goblet that she thought the stem might snap. "Do you seriously believe I would allow you to do that? It would be my child, too. It's one thing when circumstances force a mother to raise a child alone. It is quite another to have a baby for your own selfish reasons and deliberately deprive it of a father. If you have conceived, you are stuck with me for a husband." He took a deep breath. "And if that happens, God help us both."

She bit her lip and began finger-combing her hair to remove the snarls. She *had* been horribly selfish, thinking of her own wishes rather than the best interests of a child. She had also been criminally cavalier about Kenneth's feelings. Having seen the sensitivity and honor beneath his pirate exterior, she should have known he could not be casual about making love with her.

Had she unconsciously hoped to coerce him into marriage? No, she still had grave doubts about taking a mate. But she had been wild with desire, and that had made her reckless. She had forgotten that the consequences might bear more heavily on Kenneth than on her. Now his sense of duty might force him to marry a woman he didn't want. She would not have treated an enemy as badly as she had behaved with the best man she had ever known.

Wallowing in guilt wouldn't help. She tossed her hair back and said with measured calm, "I probably haven't conceived and we're worrying about nothing." She felt a knot form in her stomach. Knowing she shouldn't ask, she continued, "But if I did, why is the prospect of marrying me so dreadful? I know you don't love me the way you would a wife, but you seem to care a little. Is there someone else? If not, surely we would be able to rub along tolerably well. I swear I wouldn't plague you."

He swore under his breath and put an arm around her shoulders, drawing her close. "It isn't that I don't care for you, Rebecca, or that there is anyone else," he said quietly. "The problem with marriage is..."

He broke off. After a long pause, he said carefully, "I have an obligation to fulfill. When I have done so, there is a very real chance that you will want no part of me." His voice became wry. "Except for my head on a platter, perhaps."

She had a brief, gruesome vision of a silver tray with his severed head on it. An artist's imagination was not always a good thing. "I don't understand."

He rested his cheek on her head. "I certainly hope not. It is not something I can discuss."

Under her ear she could hear the steady rhythm of his heart. She wondered what his mysterious obligation entailed. Probably it was about the dreadful financial problems he had inherited. "Whatever happens, the fault is not yours. It was I who instigated what happened between us," she said softly. "And though it may have been wicked of me, I really can't be sorry."

"Neither can I, Ginger," he said with a rueful sigh. "Neither can I."

Rebecca found that it was easy to sin with a man who was living under the same roof—particularly in a household of mad artists who kept strange hours. No one noticed a thing.

Of course she and Kenneth knew, and tension thrummed between them the next morning. She was torn between wanting to apologize and wanting to rip his clothes off again.

It was hard to tell what Kenneth thought, but he was definitely not relaxed in her presence. Knowing that the intimacy of a sitting would be misery, she said brightly that for the next few days she would be busy with the background and clothing of the corsair picture, so he would not be needed for posing. He accepted that with visible relief.

Then, deciding that knowledge was better late than never, she invited Lavinia up to her studio for tea and a woman-to-woman talk. Specifically, she asked how to prevent conception.

Accepting the request as natural from a female on the verge of marriage, Lavinia matter-of-factly described several methods. She even promised to send over pieces of sponge suitable for soaking with vinegar and inserting. ("Not that I don't have the highest regard for your intended husband, darling, but when men become excited they sometimes forget to leave before they come. Much better for a woman to manage matters herself.")

Rebecca did not reveal that the question of marriage was still undecided. That was between her and Kenneth. But acquiring the means of preventing a baby made her feel wonderfully free. A second bedding would probably not make Kenneth feel any more remorseful than he already was, so perhaps, if the opportunity arose, she could try to ravish him again.

Because, blast the man, he had been right. She had not understood the difference between being a virgin and a woman who had tasted of Eve's apple. Before, she had yearned for Kenneth without knowing exactly what she wanted. Now her flesh remembered his feel and weight and scent with breath-catching precision. Now she understood how passion could intoxicate body and mind so that nothing existed except the lover. How desire could fill the emptiness inside her, and the touch of a man's hand could make her blood dance.

Yes, now she knew what she wanted, and she craved it with an intensity that unnerved her.

Most unnerving of all was the recognition that it wasn't sexual satisfaction in the abstract that she wanted. It was Kenneth. Only Kenneth.

~

Three days after the betrothal notices appeared, Rebecca found that she could proceed no further on the corsair picture without her model. The next morning she would have to ask Kenneth to sit again—and hope she could keep her hands off him. It was bad enough working on his image. The warm, solid physical reality might tempt her beyond her self-control.

She was staring at her corsair canvas, thinking depraved thoughts, when a knock sounded on the door of her studio. It was Minton, the butler, with a card on the tray. She frowned at him. "Why did you bring this up? You know that I am never at home to casual callers."

He cleared his throat meaningfully. "I thought perhaps you would wish to make an exception in this case, miss."

She took the card and her brows shot upward. *The Honorable Elizabeth Wilding.* "Is this a young lady, Minton?"

"Yes, miss. Escorted by a military sort of gentleman."

It must be Kenneth's sister, making a courtesy call on her brother's prospective bride. Rebecca hadn't known the girl was in London. And he was out running errands, blast him. She would have to carry the burden of pretending to be a happy fiancée alone. "Tell Miss Wilding that I'll be down in a few minutes."

She made a quick stop in her room to tame her hair and don a gorgeous Indian shawl that brightened her plain garb. Then she instructed Minton to send Kenneth in on his return and warily entered the drawing room.

Her guests were standing by the wall admiring one of Sir Anthony's paintings. Both turned when she entered. The young man was blond and attractive, with eyes that had seen experience beyond his years. His upright bearing and crippled left arm confirmed the likelihood that he had been in the army.

The girl beside him was slender and pretty, with a sweet face and Kenneth's striking gray eyes. She moved toward her hostess with the help of a cane. "Miss Seaton?" she said hesitantly. "I'm Beth Wilding, Kenneth's sister."

Recognizing a kindred shy person, Rebecca met her guest in the middle of the room. "I'm delighted to have the chance to meet you, Miss Wilding." She took her hand with a smile. "From what Kenneth said, I thought you were in Bedfordshire."

"Please, call me Beth since we will be sisters. When I saw the betrothal announcement in the newspaper I decided to come to London to welcome you to the family." She slanted a glance at her escort. "And we... we also wanted to speak with Kenneth about another matter. This is my friend Lieutenant Jack Davidson. He was in Kenneth's regiment."

Davidson bowed. "A pleasure, Miss Seaton. Please accept my best wishes on your betrothal."

Rebecca liked the look of him, though he seemed tense enough to ring like a bell if tapped. It was obvious from the way he and Beth looked at each other that they were rather more than friends. "You must both call me Rebecca."

Rather than ignore Davidson's injury, she glanced at his crippled arm and said matter-of-factly, "Waterloo?"

He nodded. "Kenneth—Lord Kimball—saved my life that day. If he hadn't put a tourniquet on my arm, I would have bled to death." The recollection seemed to make him even more tense.

Wanting to put her guests at ease, Rebecca invited them to sit down and rang for refreshments. After they took seats, she said to Beth, "I met your stepmother several days ago."

"And you survived?" Beth said promptly. Then she clapped her hand over her mouth. "Oh, dear. I shouldn't have said that. I meant to be on my best behavior."

Rebecca grinned, knowing she and Beth would get along very well. "Hermione is perfectly dreadful, isn't she? You must have great fortitude to have endured her."

"Luckily, I was usually beneath her notice. I lived quietly at Sutterton with a wonderful governess and did very well."

A tea tray and cakes were delivered. Rebecca noticed how deftly Beth arranged the cup and cake plate so Davidson could manage easily with one hand. They meshed together like clockwork gears. Not like her and Kenneth, who were circling each other as warily as two strange cats.

After several minutes of general conversation, Beth asked, "Do you know where we might find Kenneth?"

"He should be back soon. He's out doing some errands."

"He lives here?" Beth said with surprise.

"Yes, he's my father's secretary." Rebecca looked at her guest curiously. "You didn't know?"

"He's never mentioned where he was living. We've been sending letters to a postal receiving station."

Curiouser and curiouser. Rebecca wondered if the secretiveness had something to do with Kenneth's mysterious "obligation." Feeling an obscure desire to protect him, she said lightly, "He was probably afraid you would write to him as Lord Kimball. He's the most casual peer I ever met. Neither my father nor I knew about his title until his friends Lord and Lady Michael Kenyon met him here and revealed the dreadful truth."

After her guests laughed, Jack asked, "Do you know if Kenyon is still in London? I should like to call on him. He was in my regiment." He smiled, more at ease. "We humble lieutenants admired both him and Lord Kimball extravagantly."

"They have the same effect on me," Rebecca said.

As conversation flowed easily among the three, she listened closely for the sound of Kenneth's return. Her corsair was going to have some questions to answer.

CHAPTER 22

As usual when returning to Seaton House, Kenneth stopped to collect his letters. There was a sharp message from Lord Bowden, saying that he was about to go to his country seat, but that when he returned they must meet so he could learn how the investigation was proceeding.

Kenneth frowned as he tucked the letter away. He had continued making discreet inquiries of everyone who might have any knowledge of Lady Seaton's death. He had acquired a substantial file of notes. But he had yet to find anything that shed new light on what had happened. Perhaps there might be information in the Lake District. If not—well, when there were no more leads to pursue, the investigation would be over. Bowden would be furious, but Kenneth was guiltily aware that he himself would be relieved.

He walked through the afternoon drizzle, mentally going over everything he had learned for what seemed like the thousandth time. He could honestly say that he was doing the best he could. The fact that he had found nothing almost certainly meant that there was nothing to find.

If that was the case, his obligation to Bowden would soon be discharged, and in a way that meant Rebecca need not learn that he'd come to Seaton House to spy on her father. It was an open question whether Bowden would fulfill his side of the bargain; he might feel that he hadn't received his money's worth.

Kenneth would be in a quandary if Bowden balked at returning the Sutterton mortgages. Though they had signed a contract, he could not imagine taking the other man to court and letting the world—including Rebecca and Sir Anthony—know of the agreement. And while Kenneth was doing his best, it was true that he was finding the task increasingly distasteful. That would make it harder for him to demand payment.

If Bowden did not want to clear the mortgages outright, perhaps he would agree to a compromise such as letting Kenneth pay the debt off gradually. However the matter was resolved, at least the end was in sight—and after the investigation, Kenneth would be free to think about a possible future with Rebecca.

Now, he mostly thought about making love in the attic and wishing, rather desperately, that they could do it again.

He let himself into Seaton House and was shaking the raindrops from his cloak when the butler came and said, "Miss Seaton has asked that you join her in the drawing room."

Thinking that the Kenyons must have called, Kenneth went to join them. The sight of his sister and Jack Davidson rocked him.

Tart amusement in her eyes, Rebecca said, "Look who

has come to offer congratulations on our betrothal, my dear."

Beth rose and came toward him. "Hello, Kenneth," she said, her eyes anxious. "Are you sorry to see us?"

"Of course not. We still have years of separation to make up for." He enveloped her in a hug. "Though I'm surprised you came all the way to London. How on earth did you find me?"

Emerging from his embrace, she said, "Cousin Olivia saw the betrothal notice and said we should pay a call on your fiancée. She stayed at Sutterton because of a chill, but Jack and I had no trouble finding where Sir Anthony Seaton lives when we reached London." A touch of dryness entered her voice. "Finding you here was a lucky accident."

She had every reason to question his secretiveness. He was grateful that she didn't. His arm around his sister, he moved forward and took his friend's hand. "You look much better than the last time we met, Jack."

"Bedfordshire and Beth have worked wonders, sir."

As they shook hands, Kenneth observed that the other man looked as nervous as a mouse on a hot griddle. He was also being unnaturally formal. Perhaps there were estate problems so severe that his steward thought they must be discussed face-to-face.

Confirming his guess, Rebecca said, "Jack wants to speak with you privately. The small salon should be empty now."

Beginning to be seriously concerned, Kenneth ushered Jack from the drawing room to the small salon. As soon as the door closed behind them, he said bluntly, "More trouble at Sutterton?"

"Why, no." Jack paced across the room. "At least, not estate trouble. In that area, everything is going well."

"Then why do you look ready to jump out of your skin?"

Jack rubbed his crippled left arm, as if massaging phantom pains. "I... I've come to ask permission to marry Beth."

"When the time comes I'll be happy to give you my blessing," Kenneth said, surprised. "But when you wrote me about your intentions, you said it was too soon, and I agreed. You haven't known each other long, and the future of Sutterton is still undecided."

"I'm afraid we can't wait." Jack swallowed hard. "Or perhaps it would be more accurate to say that we *didn't* wait."

The silence was thunderous. Then Kenneth asked in a dangerous voice, "Are you saying Beth is with child?"

Looking miserable but resolute, the younger man said, "We think so." He met Kenneth's gaze steadily. "I'm sorry, sir. You must want to call me out, and you have every right to. It... it only happened once, and was certainly unintended, but that doesn't excuse me." His mouth twisted. "You saved my life, and I repay you by seducing your sister. All I can do is say that I love Beth from the bottom of my soul. I swear that she will always be loved and cared for, even if Sutterton is sold and I must find a situation elsewhere."

The first rush of Kenneth's brotherly anger was quickly followed by recognition of the irony. He could hardly take the moral high ground when there was a chance that he and Rebecca might also make a hasty trip to the altar. Heaven knew that he understood how years in the masculine maelstrom of war could make a man crave the healing warmth of a woman's arms to the point where desire overcame sense.

After taking a deep breath, he said, "It isn't what I would have chosen, but I suppose there is no harm done. I suspect that the seduction was mutual. Beth has a mind of her own."

Jack's wry smile showed that Kenneth had hit the mark. Beth and Rebecca obviously had certain similarities, though Kenneth doubted that his sister was as wonderfully brazen as Rebecca. After a brief, dizzy memory of his Lilith shaking her flaming hair provocatively over her naked shoulders, he said, "Shall we return to the drawing room and break the news to the ladies?"

Looking enormously relieved, Jack said, "You're taking this very well, sir. Better than I deserve."

"You and I have both seen our share of the world's misery. The impetuousness of love is a minor problem by comparison." Kenneth gave the younger man a stern glance. "But for God's sake, stop calling me sir!"

Jack smiled sheepishly. "Under the circumstances, using your Christian name seemed like insult after injury."

"Since we're going to be brothers-in-law, you'd better go back to calling me Kenneth." As they went to the door, he asked, "What would you have done if I'd refused permission?"

"Married her anyhow. Beth is of age." Jack held the door open for Kenneth. "But neither of us wanted to start our life together by becoming estranged from you."

A good, practical point of view. As they retraced their steps to the drawing room, Kenneth found that his pleasure in his sister's marriage outweighed the inconvenient timing. Beth and Jack both had steady dispositions, and they seemed deeply in love. He only hoped that he would soon be able to provide his sister with the dowry to which she was entitled. He did not want to see the young couple forced to live hand-to-mouth, especially with a baby on the way.

They entered the drawing room. Kenneth said to his sister with a smile, "Jack has asked for your hand, and I intend to see the two of you spliced before he discovers what an imp you are. Since we're both here in London, how about marrying by special license within the next few days?"

"Oh, Kenneth!" Beaming with relief, Beth hurled herself into his arms. "You are the best of brothers."

"I'm not, you know. Jack will take much better care of you than I did." He hugged her back, his mind busy with ideas for making her wedding memorable despite the haste and his lack of money. It was time to ask for a favor or two.

Releasing his sister, he said, "Michael and Catherine Kenyon are staying at Ashburton House, and he has mentioned several times how large and empty the place is. I think they would be happy to have you both as guests for a few days."

"If they are willing, it would be far more convenient than staying in an inn," Jack said with a pleased smile.

Rebecca said hesitantly, "Of course you scarcely know me, Beth, but if you don't have a friend in London who can stand up with you, I would be honored to do so."

Beth instantly accepted the offer. As wedding planning began, Kenneth sent a note to see if Michael and Catherine would take two guests. Michael replied within the hour, saying that any officer of the 95th and any sister of Kenneth's would always be welcome under their roof. The note was delivered by a handsome carriage that awaited the orders of the expected guests.

Somewhere in the midst of the bustle, the tension that had been between him and Rebecca evaporated. There was another kind of tension that came when he speculated about what kind of bride she would make. As he watched

Beth and Jack climb into the carriage, he wondered wryly if weddings were contagious.

The next day, George Hampton came by with a trial engraving of Sir Anthony's third Waterloo picture. The two men had a noisy discussion before agreeing on several areas that needed work. Sir Anthony returned to his studio and Hampton was preparing to leave when Kenneth approached him. "I'd like to talk to you sometime, sir. When would be convenient?"

"I have a few minutes now." Hampton clapped the younger man on the shoulder. "By the way, congratulations. I think you and Rebecca will suit each other very well." He chuckled. "I was amused to learn I had been ordering a viscount around, but I expect I would have done so even if I had known."

Feeling more nervous than when waiting for a French cavalry charge, Kenneth said, "I... I have something to show you."

He led the way to the office and produced a portfolio containing a dozen drawings he had selected from his Peninsular work. Hampton's bushy brows shot upward when he saw the picture of the mortally wounded soldier that had so affected Rebecca.

The engraver studied it for a long time, then wordlessly flipped through the other sketches. When he was done, he glanced up, his gaze keen. "Where did you get these?"

Knowing he was taking a significant step, Kenneth took a deep breath. "I drew them."

"Really! I had no idea you were an artist."

"I have drawn my whole life," he said simply.

"Have you shown Anthony your work?"

"There was no reason for him to see it. However, Rebecca thinks the drawings have merit."

"She's quite right. You and she will suit each other even better than I realized." Hampton closed the portfolio and laid one hand on the leather cover. "Would you allow me to make engravings of these? Even though the war is over, there is still considerable interest in military subjects."

"I was hoping you would want to." Kenneth hesitated, trying to find the right words to make it clear that he was interested in money as well as the honor of having his work published. "Though I've kept Sir Anthony's accounts, I have no idea what the financial arrangements should be for pictures by an unknown."

"Mmm, a good question." Brow furrowed, Hampton produced and lit a cigar. "I suppose I should exploit your ignorance and offer you ten pounds for the lot, take it or leave it. But that would be a shabby way to treat my goddaughter's future husband."

Quashing his guilt about the falseness of the betrothal, Kenneth said, "Actually, I've heard that you are notoriously generous to the artists whose work you use."

"Merely good business. Ensures that I get first choice of the best work," Hampton said, scowling as if he had been accused of theft. "You have a distinctive style. What is the best way to take advantage of that?" He drummed his fingers on the desk. "Perhaps a series called something like 'An Officer's Views of the Late War.' We could issue most of the engravings individually, then put out a book with new ones added. That way people would have to buy the book to get the other pictures."

A series. A book. Trying to control his excitement, Kenneth said, "You'll need more pictures. What kind?"

The engraver blew out a thin trickle of smoke. "Certainly more battle pictures—as many of the major engagements as possible. And views of the people and towns and landscapes as well as military subjects. Can you do that?"

"I was at almost every significant battle, and I have a good memory for details." Too good, Kenneth had often thought, but it seemed that ability would now be valuable. He liked the idea of a series. His first attempts to release his darkest memories on paper had given him a desire to do more. After he had chronicled his personal war, perhaps he would finally be free of it.

More smoke rose as Hampton considered. "How about two hundred pounds advanced against a percentage of total sales? If I'm right—and I usually am—over the next few years you could earn a nice little income from this project."

It was far more than Kenneth had hoped, enough for a decent wedding gift for Beth and Jack. "Done. And thank you." He offered his hand.

"We shall do well for each other, Kimball." After shaking hands, the engraver got to his feet and tucked the portfolio under his arm. "Make me a list of the scenes you want to do. I'll draw up a contract and send a draft for the two hundred pounds." He surveyed Kenneth's broad frame, a smile lurking in his eyes. "You don't look like an artist, but then, neither do I. So much for appearances." He donned his hat and left.

Dazed with excitement, Kenneth wandered from the office, not thinking about where he was going until he found himself knocking on the door of Rebecca's studio. Of course he had come here. Who else would understand what Hampton's offer meant to him?

Rebecca called permission to enter and he went inside.

She glanced up from her easel. "You look like a cat who has dined well on fresh canary."

He laughed. "I've just gone from amateur to professional. George Hampton is giving me two hundred pounds to engrave a series of my sketches. It will be a chronicle of the war, with perhaps a book coming from it later."

"That's wonderful!" She set down her palette and came toward him, hazel eyes glowing like new-minted gold coins. "But no more than you deserve."

She was irresistible in her generous pleasure. He swooped her up in his arms and whirled her around exuberantly.

She laughed, her head barely missing the slanted ceiling. "You're a lunatic, Captain."

"But a happy one." She was like a flame in his arms, vividly alive. When he stopped spinning, he found that he could not let her go. He lowered her back to the floor slowly, her body sliding along his. Soft. Feminine. Erotic.

The few days since they had made love seemed like an eternity. He bent his head and kissed her. Her arms tightened around him and her lips clung, sweet as the first strawberries of spring.

He was on the verge of carrying her to the sofa when a wisp of sense intruded. Reluctantly he ended the kiss. "I keep forgetting that we're not supposed to do that."

"So do I," she said unevenly as she detached herself from his embrace. Her lips had a ripe, just-kissed fullness.

Trying to regain his control, he glanced around the familiar studio. It was so thoroughly Rebecca. He'd missed it. "Hampton approves of our betrothal. I wince whenever someone congratulates me. They all seem so happy about the prospect."

"Probably because it was assumed that I was a hopeless

spinster," she said with light self-mockery. "You are much admired for your courage in taking me on."

"Rebecca," he said quietly. When she looked at him, he continued, "If a jewel is concealed in the attic, the world has no chance to appreciate it. I think I am envied for being the lucky man who discovered a hidden treasure."

A shimmer of what almost seemed like pain showed in her eyes. "What a lovely romantic thing to say. Utter nonsense, of course, but lovely." She drifted toward her easel. "This is definitely your lucky day. I've learned there will be no baby."

Surging relief was tempered by a surprising pang of regret. A small part of him that was all feeling and no sense would have welcomed a situation in which marriage was the only choice.

But not a marriage where he risked having Rebecca despise him if he learned something that harmed her father. Schooling his face, he said, "About the sitting this afternoon. The usual time?"

Not looking at him, she lifted a brush and drew the point across her palm experimentally. "Usual time."

He left, wondering if the day would ever come when he could speak freely to her. Even more, he wondered what he would say if that happened—and how she would respond.

CHAPTER 23

As they waited in the salon of Ashburton House for the carriage that would take the bridal party to the church, Rebecca circled Beth for a last-minute check. Kenneth's sister looked enchanting in a cream-colored silk gown. It had been a gift from Lavinia, who adored all weddings. Rebecca paused in her orbiting to make a minor adjustment to the train.

"You're more nervous than I am," Beth said with a smile.

"Probably. I've never been part of a wedding before." Rebecca was enjoying the combination of high spirits and hysteria that surrounded the event. Hiding from the world had caused her to miss a great deal of fun.

But she was still impatient to be off. Kenneth and Catherine had gone to confer with the cook about the wedding breakfast, which the Kenyons were providing here at Ashburton House. Michael and Catherine had both been wonderful. Though Kenneth might not have accumulated much in the way of worldly goods, he had certainly acquired friends beyond price.

"Soon you'll be doing this, thought not on such short notice," Beth remarked. "Have you and Kenneth set a date?"

Rebecca glanced away. "Not yet. There's no hurry."

"Unlike Jack and I." Beth's hand slid protectively over her abdomen. "Though it's wicked of me, I can't be sorry."

Rebecca stared, wondering if she was misinterpreting the gesture. "Are you saying that... that..."

"That I'm in the family way?" Beth said cheerfully. "I thought Kenneth would have told you, since you're his fiancée. I guess he was being a very discreet big brother, but it's not the sort of thing that can be kept secret very long. When the baby is born, anyone who can count will wonder, even if the dates are not wholly impossible."

No wonder Kenneth had agreed to an immediate marriage. Rebecca was not surprised that he hadn't told her. Though he had done another sitting, they had both been on rigidly good behavior. It took so little to set passion blazing between them. Even friendly conversation was dangerous.

The door opened and Kenneth and Catherine entered. He was carrying a sizable parcel. "Beth, this was delivered a few minutes ago, addressed to both of us." He set the package on the table beside her. "A wedding gift, I presume, though I don't know why my name would be on it."

Beth unwrapped the package and found an elaborately gilded casket. She unlatched and lifted the lid, then gave a gasp of astonishment. Inside was a gleaming trove of jewelry with a sealed note resting on top.

"Good God!" Kenneth exclaimed. "The Wilding jewels. I don't believe it."

He removed the note and tore it open. As Rebecca and Catherine converged on the table, he read,

. . .

"To Beth and Kenneth: I've decided that the Wilding family pieces belong with you. Best wishes on your wedding day, Beth. Hermione Kimball."

Eyes wide, Beth picked up a pair of sapphire earrings, cradling them gently in her palm. "I never thought I would see these again. How wonderfully generous of Hermione."

"I don't believe it," Kenneth said flatly. "She never had an unselfish impulse in her life."

"Nonetheless, the proof is in front of our eyes." Beth frowned as she returned the earrings to their velvet-lined compartment. "And I didn't even invite her to the wedding." She glanced at her hostess. "It's too late for her to come to the ceremony, but may I invite her to the wedding breakfast?"

"Of course," Catherine replied. "There is paper and ink in the writing desk in the corner. Write a note, and I'll have a footman deliver it right away."

As Catherine and Beth went to the desk, Kenneth folded the note and tucked it inside his coat. "I still don't believe it."

"Nor do I," Rebecca said quietly. "The woman is a snake, and while snakes may shed their skins, they don't change their spots. She must have had an ulterior motive."

Kenneth frowned. "I wish I knew what it was, but I can't imagine any way she would benefit by giving these back."

Rebecca touched the brilliant diamonds of the magnificent necklace Hermione had worn to the Candover ball. Someday Kenneth's wife would wear it. "Are all the heirlooms here?"

He surveyed the contents of the casket. "I think so. There are some pieces I don't recognize."

"Perhaps she included some of her personal jewelry in a fit of remorse for the way she looted your family," Rebecca suggested. When Kenneth gave a disbelieving snort, she chuckled. "Or perhaps Hermione got wildly drunk last night and acted while the balance of her mind was disturbed. Whatever the reason, don't look a gift horse in the mouth. Now that the jewels are in your hands, they are yours."

An arrested expression appeared in her companion's eyes. Before Rebecca could ask what he was thinking, Beth rose from the desk and Catherine rang for a servant.

When the footman arrived, he accepted Beth's letter and added, "The carriage for the bridal party is ready, my lady."

Catherine turned to the others. "Shall we go? I'll ask the butler to put the casket in a safe place until later."

"In a moment." Kenneth lifted a beautiful multi-strand pearl necklace from the box. "You can be married in Mother's pearls, Beth. They were always meant to come to you."

"What a wonderful blessing for the day," Beth said softly as her brother fastened the pearls around her neck. "Now I regret all the unkind things I've said about Hermione. She really does have a heart under her glittering surface."

Rebecca wasn't so sure. Kenneth's stepmother had a glittering surface, all right, but it was composed of reptilian scales. There had to be an interesting story behind the casket of jewels. She hoped someday to learn it.

A few minutes' ride brought the bridal party to the small

church where the wedding was being held. Kenneth helped the three ladies from the carriage. Then, with his sister on his arm, he entered the church. They were greeted by a joyous cascade of organ music that made the old stone walls resonate.

Catherine hugged Beth, then went into the sanctuary to take her place with the handful of other guests. While they waited for the ceremony to begin, Kenneth studied his sister, feeling a little sad. He was losing her before ever having a chance to become really close. There was too great a difference in age, too many years when he had been gone.

His mood must have shown on his face, because Rebecca said briskly, "Take heart, Kenneth. You're not losing a sister. You're gaining a steward." Then she peered through the double doors to check the progress of events. "Almost time, Beth. Jack looks wonderfully handsome. Also ready to expire on the spot. Michael is fulfilling his groomsman's duties by standing ready to catch Jack if he swoons. Ah. Jack is smiling now that he knows you're here. I think he'll survive after all."

Rebecca waited for the processional music to begin. Then she clasped her flowers in front of her and walked down the aisle with slow grace. She wore the amber silk gown again and looked almost as radiant as Beth.

His sister leaned her cane against the wall and took hold of his arm. When he raised his brows, she said decisively, "I'm not going down the aisle with a cane." She smiled up at him, her face luminous with love and certainty. "Besides, I won't need it. I have you to lean on now, and Jack later."

Kenneth smiled back. "You look lovely, Beth." He was struck by a pang of grief and deep regret. "I wish Mama could be here to see you."

Beth gestured at the vaulted ceiling and the glowing

stained-glass windows with her bouquet. "I think she is, Kenneth."

Then she locked her hand firmly around his elbow and they proceeded to the altar, and into Beth's future.

~

After the ceremony, the newly married couple and guests returned to Ashburton House for the wedding breakfast, all of the females except Rebecca wiping away happy tears. There was a period of buoyant confusion in the vast foyer. The process of removing cloaks and hats was not helped when Louis the Lazy, the Kenyon hound, decided to nap on Beth's train. Eventually the party went on to the dining room.

Kenneth lingered behind with Michael to say, "My thanks to you and Catherine for making the day special."

His friend made a deprecating gesture. "Who doesn't like a wedding? I've always thought well of Jack Davidson, and your sister is a darling. Seeing her safely wed must be quite a burden off your mind."

"I suppose this is good practice for when Amy gets married."

Michael groaned. "Don't talk about it. I'm afraid that I will break the neck of any beastly young man who dares ask her to walk in the garden."

Kenneth smiled, thinking that his friend had taken to the role of stepfather very thoroughly. They were walking toward the corridor that led to the dining room when the knocker smashed furiously into the front door. Michael went to open it. "A late guest, perhaps? I can't think who is missing."

The door swung open and Hermione barreled into the

foyer. Ignoring Michael as if he were a footman, she charged straight at Kenneth. "How dare you!" she shrieked. "First you break into my house to steal my jewelry. Then you have the unmitigated impudence to make Beth write and thank me for 'giving' the jewels back! You... you beast! You contemptible villain!"

This was the stepmother he recognized. As she slashed at his face with clawed fingers, he caught her wrist in an iron grip. "It's too late to change your mind, Hermione," he said coolly. "I have proof that you returned the jewels of your own free will, so wild accusations will do you no good."

"Liar! I did no such thing." She wrenched her wrist free. "I'll have the magistrates on you for theft!"

"Oh?" Kenneth withdrew from his coat the note that had come with the casket. "This looks like your handwriting to me."

Hermione opened the note with shaking hands. "It's a forgery!" she gasped. "I never wrote this."

"Perhaps you did in a fit of absentmindedness, then forgot." Wanting to keep the note in case it was needed as evidence, he plucked it from her nerveless fingers.

As Hermione prepared for a new explosion, a musical voice said guilelessly, "Lady Kimball, how lovely that you've come to the wedding breakfast. Beth will be so pleased."

Catherine sailed into the foyer, every inch the gracious hostess. "I'm Lady Michael Kenyon. We've never been introduced, but of course I recognize you as one of the great beauties of London society." She smiled a thousand-candle smile. "I was deeply touched when the jewels were delivered this morning. It does you great credit that you put the claims of tradition and sentiment over personal gain."

Hermione stared, stunned speechless by so much lavish charm.

"As soon as the jewels arrived, I wrote about your unselfish gesture to my brother-in-law, Ashburton," Catherine continued. "Of course, you must know him."

A calculating gleam appeared in Hermione's pale blue eyes. "I've never had the privilege of meeting the duke."

"Then I shall invite you to dine with us when he returns to London. Just a private gathering, of course, since he is in mourning for his wife, but I should like you to meet him. It is *so* important that he make the right choice when he remarries."

There was a long, meaningful silence as the two women regarded each other. Then Hermione's lips curved into a predatory smile. "Since I have also been recently bereaved, I'm sure the duke and I shall have much in common."

Catherine beamed. "Come join us for the breakfast. Beth will be anxious to thank you for making it possible for her to wear her mother's pearls on her wedding day."

"I can't stay, but I do want to offer my best wishes to dear Beth." Hermione gave a tinkling laugh. "So absurd that I have a stepdaughter only a year or two younger than I! I was the merest child when I married Kimball, you know."

After the two women left the foyer, Kenneth said with awed respect, "Correct me if I'm wrong, but I think I have just seen your saintly lady wife defang a serpent by promising to promote a match with the most eligible man in the marriage mart."

Michael chuckled. "Catherine is a dangerous woman, isn't she? I give thanks daily that she is on my side."

"She could give Wellington lessons in generalship. But I thought you liked your brother. It would be cruel to deliver him into Hermione's clutches."

"Stephen has too much sense to be attracted to a harpy like her," Michael said reassuringly. "By the time she realizes that she hasn't a chance to become the next duchess, it will be too late for her to claim that the jewels were stolen."

Suspicious of how neatly Catherine had intervened, Kenneth said warily, "You didn't burgle Hermione's house, did you?"

Michael arched his brows with aristocratic disdain. "Of course not. What would I know about housebreaking?"

"Not much, I suppose. But wasn't one of your Fallen Angel friends some kind of government spymaster? A man like that might have some interesting skills."

Amusement gleamed in Michael's eyes. "It's possible that I mentioned your stepmother's disgraceful behavior to Lucien. He has a keen sense of justice. Perhaps in his indignation he alluded to the situation with some of his less reputable acquaintances."

"Which probably include forgers as well as burglars."

"No doubt," Michael said blandly.

Kenneth grinned. "I don't think I want to know any more. Please give my deepest thanks to whom it may concern."

"What are friends for?" Michael put his hand on Kenneth's shoulder. "Come along now. You and I are needed to offer toasts to the newly wedded couple."

~

Like all good wedding breakfasts, Beth and Jack's lasted until well into the afternoon. The celebration finally broke up in a happy babble of good-byes, thank-yous, and hugs. As Lavinia pulled on her gloves, she said to Rebecca and Kenneth, "I'm going your way. Can I take you in my carriage?"

Kenneth shook his head. "Take Rebecca home. I want to walk and enjoy the fine weather."

"May I come?" Rebecca asked. "I need to clear my head after the champagne."

"I shall be glad of the company."

He offered his arm with a smile. She took it, thinking that he looked very fine today. A pirate polished up for a wedding.

She gave a sigh of relief as they stepped into the street outside Ashburton House. "It's been a delightful day, but peace is very welcome after so much bustle. I don't want to go to any more social events for at least six months."

"Then this is probably not the time to remind you that next week we must go to another ball."

"That's right, the Strathmores. I'd forgotten." She made a face. "I suppose I'll be able to face a crowd again by then."

As they strolled through the Mayfair streets, she studied Kenneth from the corner of her eye. Even though she had been working on his portrait for weeks, she hadn't tired of looking at him. Moments like this, she rather wished she could keep him.

Pushing aside the dangerous thought, she said, "What happened with Hermione? Ever since she showed up smiling like a rabid hound, I've been perishing to know."

A smile lurking in his eyes, Kenneth described how his stepmother had burst raging into Ashburton House and been deftly tamed by Catherine.

When he finished, Rebecca broke into laughter. "Marvelous! Because Hermione is venal, she assumed Catherine is, too."

"Catherine venal?" he said, looking intrigued. "I thought at the time that I was missing something in the exchange between her and Hermione. What was it?"

"When Catherine said she wanted Ashburton to choose the right wife, she was implying that she wants him to marry a woman who won't bear him an heir," Rebecca explained. "That way, her own son would be in line to inherit the dukedom."

"Ah," Kenneth said, enlightened. "Since Hermione was married for years without conceiving, there's a good chance she is barren. At the same time she is beautiful enough to attract a duke, which makes her perfect for Catherine's alleged purposes."

"Exactly. The cream of the jest is that Catherine told me herself she's not keen on seeing young Nicholas inherit." Rebecca laughed again. "Naturally Hermione can't imagine anyone turning down wealth and power."

"So that is what was going on. Catherine is even more devious than I realized."

Rebecca gave him a slanting glance. "Nothing will convince me that your stepmother relinquished those jewels voluntarily. Did someone send a death threat in your behalf?"

He grinned. "I think Michael asked a friend with nefarious connections to arrange for the jewels to be stolen from the house and the note forged. Not that I asked for confirmation of that."

"Justice over law. I approve." She raised the bouquet she carried and inhaled the sweetness of the blossoms that had come from the Ashburton glasshouse. "Can the jewels be sold for enough to get you out of debt?"

"Probably not enough to pay off everything, but God willing, I'll realize enough to restructure the mortgages."

"So you're saved from bankruptcy. That's wonderful!"

"It's too soon to say that," he said cautiously. "I'd say the odds are about even." He paused to let a carriage to pass in front of them. "But there is one thing I can certainly do. In my grandfather's time, a neighboring manor called Ramsey Grange was added to the estate. The house, which is quite handsome, was let, and the land is farmed with the rest of Sutterton. Since Ramsey Grange was mortgaged separately from the other property, I can clear the debt and sign it over to Beth and Jack."

"So they will be provided for even if Sutterton is eventually lost," she said quietly. "How very generous you are."

He shrugged. "It's merely the dowry Beth is entitled to."

Perhaps, but not all brothers would do so much when their own finances were critical. What a thoroughly decent man her pirate was. She sniffed the flowers again, thinking vaguely romantic thoughts. It must be the champagne.

"Isn't that the bouquet Beth carried?" he asked.

Rebecca made a face. "She said that since I was the next to be married, she would give me the bouquet directly rather than throw it at random."

He gave her a smile of rueful understanding. "A false betrothal has unending repercussions."

"It's not false, it's quite official. We merely intend to break it before reaching the altar."

"But not for a while." He came to a halt and dug something from his pocket. "Take off your left glove."

Obediently she stripped off the white kid. He lifted her hand and slid a lovely antique ring onto the third finger. There was a brilliant flash as sunlight caught the exquisite diamond.

Rebecca stared at her hand. She knew that, traditionally, great care was put into ensuring that a ring was the right size because it was considered an omen for a harmonious union. This one fit perfectly. She swallowed, wanting to cry and not knowing why. "It's... it's very pretty."

"The ring has been in the Wilding family for generations," he said gruffly. "I found it in Hermione's casket and thought it would be useful for maintaining the pretense of betrothal."

Her hand curled protectively shut. "I'll take good care of the ring until the time comes to return it." She raised her gaze to his and saw a reflection of her own feelings. There was something too intimate, too full of promise, about a ring.

Rebecca pulled her glove on again, snagging the thin kidskin on the diamond. Then she took Kenneth's arm and resumed walking. Preferring to talk of business rather than more personal matters, she said, "Handing-In Day is in about three weeks."

"What is that?"

"The last day to submit work for the Royal Academy exhibition." She fingered her bouquet pensively. "Midnight of April tenth. That should be enough time for you to prepare a painting. Though not the one of Lilith, of course."

"What?" He stopped dead. "Me, submit to the academy? That's absurd!"

"It most certainly is not," she retorted. "It may be hard to accept, Captain, but you are now a professional artist. The finest engraver in Britain is going to produce your drawings. Getting hung at the academy is the next step. It's the best way to bring your work to the attention of potential patrons."

Looking as if she had clubbed him with a fence post, Kenneth said weakly, "But even if I can paint well enough, what I want to do might be too radical for the academy."

"As my father says, an artist must do what an artist must do," she said, not giving an inch. "Hundreds of painters have their work hung every year, and many of them are no better than mediocre. With your talent, you have an excellent chance of being selected. If your pictures are too radical... so be it. Keep painting and submit again next year."

He stared at her for a long time, his face taut. Then his expression changed. "I'll submit a painting if you will."

"Me!" Her voice was almost a squeak. "Nonsense! There is no reason for me to exhibit."

"Feels different when the shoe is on the other foot, doesn't it? Though you have no financial need to sell your work, I think it's important for you to exhibit." His eyes gleamed wickedly. "You have a gift. Honor it."

Her words had come back to haunt her. "I do honor my work," she said defensively. "I'm always trying new techniques and striving to improve my skills."

He took her by the shoulders, his expression intense. "That isn't enough. Remember the biblical parable of the man who hid his talent in the ground rather than using it? That is what you are doing. You are an immensely gifted artist, and you have a moral obligation to share your gift. Give others the opportunity to be moved and uplifted or even angered by your work."

Rebecca tried to look away, but Kenneth's piercing gray eyes had snared her.

"What are you afraid of?" he said softly. "Surely not failure. Your paintings are superb, and you know it."

Her work had recovered from the weakness of spirit that had diminished it after her mother's death. Why, then, did the thought of exhibiting her paintings make her heart pound like a frightened hare? What was the real reason?

Dredging the words from deep inside, she said, "I... I'm afraid of exposing so much of myself to strangers."

"I understand, but get over it," he said bluntly. "Every

artist exposes himself. Every writer. Every musician. At least, the ones who are any good. Do you think I relish knowing that my own private horrors are going to be available to anyone with a few shillings to spare? Yet if I don't put myself into the drawings, they will have nothing to say. The same is true for you. If you continue to bury your talent, it may eventually wither and die. Oh, you'll always be able to paint pretty pictures, but you risk losing the ability to touch the soul."

On some deep, intuitive level, she recognized that there was truth in his words. "You know the most vulnerable place to put your lance, Captain." She took an uneven breath. "Very well. I'll submit if you will."

"Done!" He bent and brushed her lips with the lightest of kisses. "Here's to our mutual success."

She shivered at his touch. What was it about Kenneth that threw her mind into such disarray? Before he had come to Seaton House, she had been resolved never to exhibit her work. Now, as she took his arm again and they walked the last blocks to her home, she felt a sense of humming excitement at the prospect.

Kenneth was right. It was time for her to dare.

~

When Kenneth went to his studio after dinner, he spent several minutes studying the Lilith painting. It was done except for the final varnish. A pity it could never be shown to anyone. The painting would always be close to his heart, and not only because it had freed him of his mental paralysis over working with oils. His gaze strayed to the bed for a moment. More important, the image was Rebecca in all her seductive power.

He covered Lilith and set the painting against the wall. Then he placed another canvas on the easel. He had primed it with a red ground in preparation for the picture he must paint now. It was not a project that would require lengthy sketches and experiments in composition, for the image had been seared into his mind years before.

To do the subject justice he would have to reawaken much of the old agony. The technique would be reckless, a swift, passionate howl to the heavens, and the red ground would add an undertone of fury. The result would be quite unlike the cool, detailed historical subjects the academy loved. Everyone, with the possible exception of Rebecca, would hate it.

Yet it was a picture he must paint.

Deliberately he summoned up the image, and the piercing horror that came with it. The pain that had diminished but never gone away.

Then, tears glinting in his eyes, he lifted his charcoal to the canvas and began to sketch.

CHAPTER 24

Using an extra-fine brush, Rebecca darkened a faint shadow at the corner of the corsair's eye. She studied the result and was about to make another stroke when she stepped back with a rueful smile. It was easier to start a painting than to finish it. There was always an itchy desire to do more, to keep going until perfection was achieved. It was hard to accept that perfection was impossible, and that trying to reach it might destroy whatever had been accomplished.

She felt a touch of emptiness in finishing a work that had absorbed her so completely. At least in this case, completion meant she would no longer be driving herself mad by thinking constantly about Kenneth and his magnificent body. Instead, she would think of him only... oh, perhaps ten or twelve hours a day.

The door opened with a squeal and Lavinia swept in.

Rebecca sighed. "You really must learn to knock."

"I did. Three times. You didn't hear me."

"Oh. Sorry." Rebecca glanced outside. Late afternoon.

She seemed to have missed luncheon. "Would you like a cup of tea?"

"Thank you, but I haven't the time. I came to drop off the gown my maid altered for the Strathmore ball. I gave it to your girl, Betsy. She shows real promise as a lady's maid. She certainly has more interest in fashion than you do."

"Sorry again. Things are always rather disorganized this close to Handing-In Day."

"I've noticed. With four major historical canvases to perfect, Anthony is barely civil." Lavinia cocked her head. "Why are you busy? Don't tell me you've finally decided to submit your work!"

Rebecca nodded bashfully.

"Well, hallelujah! It's about time. What will you submit?"

"Probably this one I've just finished, and one other." She gestured at her easel. "Would you like to see my corsair?"

"I'd love to." Lavinia came to the easel, then gave a low whistle of appreciation. "Ye gods. What does Kenneth think?"

"He hasn't seen it yet. Naturally I won't submit it if he objects."

"If that happens, ignore him and exhibit it anyhow. All women who love art and men will thank you."

Rebecca frowned. "What do you mean?"

"You've captured the essence of maleness," Lavinia said with a wicked smile. "Your corsair is every woman's dream lover who comes to her in the shadows of her mind. Dark. Dangerous. Irresistible. Yet when she looks into his eyes, she knows that she is the reason he breathes." She began fanning herself with her reticule. "In short, my dear, it is pure passion."

Rebecca winced. "Tell me you're joking."

"Exaggerating a bit, but not joking." The older woman pursed her lips as she studied the canvas. "You really will have to marry if you see him that way."

"Lavinia, it's a *painting*! Oils on canvas. A romanticized portrait of a former army officer. It is not a declaration of love everlasting."

"That's what you think. I haven't spent half my life around artists without learning a thing or two. Most of you don't know your own emotions unless you have a pencil in your hand." She fanned faster. "If you don't want him, can I have him? Please?"

Rebecca laughed. "Kenneth is not a shawl that I can lend or give away. And at the risk of being tactless, you once made an advance that he didn't accept."

"I didn't expect him to, but he was so serious that I couldn't resist teasing." Lavinia grinned. "Mind you, if he had said yes, I shouldn't have hesitated to follow through."

Rebecca shook her head. "You're irredeemable."

"Probably." Lavinia studied the canvas again. "All joking aside, it's a wonderful painting. The best thing you've done yet. What else will you hand in?"

Rebecca hesitated, not wanting to talk about the falling woman picture. "I'm not sure yet."

"As long as you submit something. The academy would benefit by exhibiting more female artists. Someday they will have to accept women as members again. When they do, you must be ready." Turning from the easel, she added, "When you go to the ball, don't get caught in any more compromising situations. I won't be there to rescue you that night."

"Having already been ruined and betrothed, I can't imagine what more damage I could do to my reputation."

Lavinia sniffed. "Coming up with a new way to disgrace

yourself would be child's play for a woman of your creative talents. Try to restrain yourself."

"I make no promises," Rebecca said with a laugh.

After the other woman left, Rebecca studied the picture again. Pure passion? She realized uncomfortably that there was truth in that. As she had told Kenneth, paint was a medium, and it had faithfully transmitted her hidden desire for her model. Luckily, few people would see that as clearly as Lavinia.

Rebecca thought of the night that she and Kenneth had made love, and liquid warmth stirred deep within her. A vivid image of his body braced above hers made her turn away from the canvas, her lips tight. She wanted, with fierce intensity, to celebrate the completion of her painting with the man who had inspired her. A single taste of passion had not been enough.

Yet she dared not surrender to desire, no matter how much they would both enjoy it. It would be too easy to become addicted to the pleasure of mating with him. Already her judgment was warped. If they became lovers, she would end up at the mercy of her emotions.

And if her emotional control ever cracked, she would be destroyed. Better to be only friends.

But as a friend, she could go to his studio and see how his work had progressed. After all, Handing-In Day was tomorrow. They had both better be ready.

~

A knock at the studio door was accompanied by Rebecca's voice saying, "It's me. May I come in?"

"Of course." Kenneth set down his palette and rubbed

his tight neck muscles as she entered the room. She looked quite delectable in a navy blue dress with a scarlet ribbon tying back the thick waves of her hair. Red shouldn't have looked so good with auburn, but she had chosen exactly the right shade. He studied the tendrils that curled around her face and emphasized the slim line of her throat, then made himself look away. "You're a sight for sore eyes."

She glanced around the room. "It's interesting how we imprint our personalities on our studios. Father's is elegant. Mine is cozy. Yours has a kind of military neatness that's rare in an artist, but useful when the studio is so small." Her amused gaze returned to him. "You, however, look as if you've hardly slept in a week. How is your work going?"

He thought of the harrowing effort he had put into his painting since Beth's wedding. How gut-wrenching it had been to revisit his nightmares. Deciding to let the work speak for itself when the time came, he replied, "I can sleep after Handing-In Day. I'm devoutly grateful that Sir Anthony has been so busy with his own submissions that he hasn't needed me much. Otherwise, I never could have completed my paintings in time."

She glanced toward his easel, but didn't try to see the work in progress. Since the Lilith picture, she had treated him as a fellow artist rather than a student. That as much as anything had given him confidence.

She asked, "You're submitting more than one picture?"

"Two—a related pair." He sighed. "The first is surely unacceptable to the academy, and I don't know if the second is much better. Still, they say what I wanted to say."

"Every now and then the academy surprises us by recognizing what is powerful and new. Perhaps that will happen with you." She hesitated. "After dinner, let's ask Father to look at our work. He still doesn't know that either of us intend to submit to the exhibition."

"We can't put it off any longer." He gave her a quizzical glance. "Do I finally get to see the corsair?"

"Right now, if you like." She glanced toward the easel again. "May I look at your work?"

Kenneth shook his head. "I'd rather wait and show you and your father at the same time. You might be too kind."

"You overrate my charity," Rebecca said with a laugh as she strolled across the studio to the window. "I have said nothing about your work that wasn't honest."

He watched her surreptitiously as he covered his canvas. The fabric of her gown moved fluidly, as if she wore little beneath. Like many of her dresses, it buttoned in front. Convenient for her, and a major temptation. She had such lovely little breasts....

His body tightened and he looked down at his brushes. A good thing he had been so busy lately, or God only knows what might have happened. "Lead on. Am I going to hate the picture?"

"I don't know." As she went out the door, she said over her shoulder, "Lavinia just saw it. Her reaction was rather alarming, but she did like it."

When they entered Rebecca's studio, she wordlessly indicated the easel by the north window. It was turned away from the door so that the light fell full across the canvas. Eager to see what she had made of him, he circled around to see it. Then he stopped cold in his tracks.

As the silence stretched, Rebecca said in a small voice, "You hate it."

Trying to match the detachment she had demonstrated on seeing herself portrayed as a naked demoness, he said,

"Not at all. It's a superb painting. I just find it a bit... unnerving to see myself rendered so dramatically."

He must separate his judgment from the fact that it was his own eyes staring back at him. He began analyzing the picture piece by piece.

The Oriental hangings and the Persian carpet tossed over the sofa were luxuriant but muted, creating an exotic atmosphere without detracting from the main subject. He studied the brushwork with admiration. Rebecca was wonderful at giving a sense of rich texture with only a few fluid strokes.

The Gray Ghost made a splendidly haughty hunting cat. Though tufted and striped and doubled in size, the supercilious feline expression caught the Ghost to the life.

Feeling more objective, Kenneth brought his attention back to the pirate who dominated the canvas. The powerful, arrogant figure sprawled back against the sofa like a waiting tiger, challenging the viewer with charcoal-edged eyes. Looking at the corsair as a stranger rather than as himself, he said slowly, "You've captured the essence of someone who has lived by violence. Hardened. Brutal, even. A man of no illusions who has had to kill or be killed. It's riveting.

"But this is what makes the painting great." He gestured at the profile reflected darkly in the wall that angled behind the corsair, its surface as smooth and black as polished obsidian. "This image shows the cost of violence to your pirate's soul. He has lost much of what makes life worth living. Now, knowing the price he paid for survival, he is haunted by the question of whether it would have been better to let death take him."

"Is that how you see yourself, Kenneth?" she said softly.

He thought of the aftermath of battles, and of Maria. "There were moments when I felt like that. Yet it isn't really me. Rather, you found a buried facet of my nature and distilled it into something universal and compelling. You are going to hand it in tomorrow?"

"You wouldn't mind?"

"I'm not enthralled about exposing my tattered soul to fashionable London, but I'll survive. For those who have the perception, the painting will be deeply moving." He glanced from the canvas to Rebecca. "What was Lavinia's reaction?"

She laughed. "You know Lavinia. She said the picture was pure passion, and that if I felt that way, I really would have to marry you. Utter nonsense, of course."

He suppressed a sigh. A pity that Rebecca was so set against marriage. Because the more he thought about it, the better he liked the idea.

When dinner that night was almost over, Kenneth said, "Sir Anthony, I have a favor to ask."

Her father looked at Kenneth with surprise. Rebecca guessed it was the first time his secretary had ever asked for anything.

Kenneth continued, "I don't know if Rebecca has ever told you, but I... I'm something of an artist myself."

Rebecca was delighted that his confidence had increased to the point where he could say that. Sir Anthony, however, had the wary expression of a man who had been too often approached by amateur artists with exaggerated notions of their ability.

To reassure him, she said, "He's very good, Father. I

suggested he use one of the empty attic bedrooms as a studio."

Sir Anthony's brows rose. "It seems that much has been going on behind my back. No wonder you're so insightful about painting, Kenneth. What kind of favor do you want?"

"I'm thinking about submitting two pictures to the Royal Academy." Kenneth fiddled with his fork with uncharacteristic nervousness. "I think it unlikely that they'll be accepted, but would... would you be willing to look at them and tell me if I'd be humiliating myself to try?"

Sir Anthony set his napkin on the table and got to his feet. "If you wish, but I warn you, I'm a harsh critic."

"Even of his daughter," Rebecca said with feeling as she thought of her early lessons. Her father had never accepted less than her best. She also rose from the table. "While you're in the attic, Father, you can look at the two paintings I intend to hand in."

"So you're finally going to submit! It's about time." Sir Anthony glanced at Kenneth. "Your influence, I presume. Betrothal obviously suits you both."

She really ought to repeat that she had no intention of marrying, but that was an argument for another day. "We did encourage each other to make the attempt."

"Very good. Now let's do the viewing so I can return to work." Her father left the table and headed for the stairs.

Kenneth bowed politely for Rebecca to go first. His expression was opaque, but it was obvious that his nerves were taut. Not surprising when painting meant so much to him and he was about to be evaluated by one of the finest, and most exacting, artists in Britain. Whatever confidence he had developed might be crushed if her father was too critical.

Well, she was anxious, too. She had never asked her

father for this kind of professional judgment. Worse, her pictures were deeply personal.

They reached Rebecca's studio first. She indicated the portrait of Kenneth on the easel by the window. "Behold *The Corsair.*"

Sir Anthony studied it narrowly. "Excellent. The picture is both heroic and human. Kenneth, you will never look better. This will certainly be hung. It will also be a great popular success." From the amusement in her father's eyes, it was clear that he saw some of the same sensuality that Lavinia had. Luckily, he did not comment on that.

He looked around. "What else are you submitting?"

Feeling considerably more nervous, she led him to the falling woman picture, which was on another easel. "I think I will call it *Transfiguration.*"

Both of the men stared at the canvas. A muscle jerked in her father's cheek.

Most viewers would see the painting as a romantic depiction of an exotic culture. The setting was inside the crater of a Pacific island volcano. The lower canvas was a seething hell of molten lava and billowing smoke.

On the lip of the crater high above, a group of brilliantly clothed islanders watched as a young woman gave herself to the pagan gods of the volcano. She was falling freely, her arms outstretched and her black hair and bright sarong swirling about her slim body. On the girl's face was an expression of rapture, an utter surrender that was also the invincible strength of being beyond human malice and desire.

The picture had been inspired by Kenneth's remark about feeling no fear when death seemed inevitable. Rebecca had wanted to portray unconquerable spirit in the face of death; serenity in the heart of tragedy. Some mysterious mental alchemy had transmuted her grief for her mother into this pagan princess. But though she had succeeded in artistic terms, she had failed to find the inner peace she craved.

Sir Anthony swallowed hard. "It will not be fully understood, but it will be much admired. You have surpassed yourself. Kenneth, it's your turn."

As her father turned and headed toward the door, she saw him blinking back tears. She should have known he would understand.

Kenneth paused to say quietly, "It is transcendent." Then he went after Sir Anthony.

She glanced at the corsair painting. Heroic yet human. Not a bad description of Kenneth. Then she followed the men to the small back attic studio. She arrived as Kenneth finished lighting two branches of candles. A quick glance around confirmed that Lilith was not in sight. She wondered what her father's reaction would be if he ever saw it. Probably a volcano would form in Mayfair.

Kenneth lifted a painting and set it on the bed, tilting it back against the wall. For an instant she remembered that she had given him her virginity on that bed. Then she looked at the canvas, and all personal thoughts vanished.

He had painted an execution. It was a night scene, most of the canvas shadowed while an unholy light illuminated half a dozen Spanish guerrillas who were being slaughtered by a French firing squad. She guessed the painting had been done swiftly, for the style was as free as a watercolor, with the haziness of nightmare. Yet it had deep and profoundly visceral power.

The menacing French soldiers were anonymous in their

blue uniforms, their faces shadowed by shako headdresses. But the Spanish guerrillas were individuals, each so distinct that she could have recognized him in a crowd. Several men lay dying on the ground, including a priest clutching a crucifix in his hand. The focal point of the picture was a young man whose arms flung outward as the French balls tore into his flesh. Already his white shirt was stained with gouts of blood. To look at the painting was to rage at the savagery of war.

"I understand your compunctions about whether it will be accepted," Sir Anthony said. "The academy is not usually fond of blatantly emotional works. What do you call it?"

"Navarre, the Fifth of November, 1811," Kenneth replied, his expression stark.

Sir Anthony said tersely, "Show me the other one."

Rebecca glanced at her father with surprise. Though his own style was classical, surely he saw the quality of Kenneth's work.

"The scenes are related." Kenneth took the canvas from his easel and set it on the bed beside the execution scene "I call it *Spanish Pietá."*

It was even more riveting than the first painting.

Pietá was Italian for "pity," and the term was used to describe one of the classic images of Christian art—the Virgin Mary supporting the body of her dead son across her lap. Rebecca saw that Kenneth had chosen to copy the pose of the famous sculpture Michelangelo had done for St. Peter's Cathedral.

However, his version had none of the classical restraint of his model. Working with more tightness and detail than in the execution scene, he had portrayed a middle-aged Spanish woman cradling the body of the youth who had been in the center of the previous painting. Her head was thrown back as she gave a mother's raw cry of agony for her murdered child.

The image was timeless and haunting, and it sliced through Rebecca's defenses into the anguished core of her own grief. She stared, literally paralyzed by her reaction, terrified that she would begin to weep and be unable to stop.

She wrenched her gaze away and looked at her father. He was studying the canvas without expression. She wanted to hit him for not speaking. Couldn't he feel Kenneth's anxiety?

Finally Sir Anthony broke the taut silence. "You have much to learn before you become a great painter, Kenneth. But you are already a great artist." Then he turned and left the studio.

Kenneth watched him go, his expression stunned, as if he were unsure how to interpret Sir Anthony's comment.

When Rebecca was sure her voice would be even, she said, "Congratulations, Captain. You have received a rare accolade."

He exhaled and rubbed the back of his neck wearily. "What do you think of the pictures, Rebecca?"

"Extraordinary," she said honestly. "They will inspire both love and hate. The pietá is so powerful that I can barely endure looking at it. But these are pictures that need to be seen. I hope the academy has the sense to accept them."

"Even if they don't, I'm going to ask Hampton to engrave these for the Peninsular war series. One way or another, they will be seen."

She looked at the paintings again, her gaze passing quickly over the pietá to linger on the execution. "You saw these things happen." It was not a question.

"They are two of the prime images from my gallery of nightmares." The scar on his face whitened. "As a reconnaissance officer, I spent much of my time riding across Spain, always wearing my uniform so that if I was captured, I wouldn't be shot as a spy. It worked, too." He nodded toward the execution painting. "Part of my job was visiting guerrilla bands to gather intelligence. I worked most often with this group, and was captured with them when the French surrounded us. As a British officer, I was treated with great respect. The French gave me wine and said they envied the fact that I'd be sent to Paris if an exchange couldn't be arranged." He halted, his eyes so dark they appeared almost black.

"And they made you watch your friends die," she said softly.

"I wasn't forced to watch. But not to see would have been..." he searched for words, "dishonorable. Cowardly. I had to bear witness to their courage and sacrifice."

"And they have haunted your dreams ever since." She indicated the painting. "This is a noble memorial, Kenneth."

"They would have preferred their lives," he said bleakly.

Her reluctant gaze went to the pietá again. She had repaired her defenses a little and was able to view the picture with a modicum of detachment. Even so, the grief of the picture cut close to home, perhaps because she was a woman. She wondered what it would be like to carry a child in one's body, birth it with pain, raise it with love—and then see that child murdered. Even imagining it was almost unbearable.

Throat tight, she said, "This young man was a particular friend of yours?"

"Eduardo was Maria's youngest brother," he said quietly. "Only seventeen when he died."

Rebecca studied the boy's face, seeing a resemblance to the pastel sketch Kenneth had done of his mistress. "You said Maria was killed by the French. She was also shot?"

"No." His eyes closed and a spasm of pain crossed his face. "Someday I will paint that scene. Then, perhaps, I will no longer have nightmares." He opened his eyes again. "You were the one who taught me that pain might be transmuted through art. It is another debt I owe you that can never be repaid."

She turned away. There was too much emotion in the room. Too much dangerous warmth in his expression. "You owe me nothing, Kenneth. I've also benefited from our friendship."

Perhaps also wanting to retreat from intensity, he said, "I know that all paintings have to be delivered to the Royal Academy by midnight tomorrow. Then what happens?"

"The justly named Hanging Committee is made up of several academicians. They decide what to accept—usually around a thousand pieces. Work is submitted for judging, except for academy members like Father and Uncle George and Lord Frazier. Their pictures are always hung."

"They are also academicians? I didn't know that."

"Uncle George is one of the two engraver members. Frazier is only an associate. I suspect that he resents having been passed over several times when vacancies have opened up for full members, but he has too much pride to speak of it."

"A pity Frazier's talent and discipline don't match his pride," Kenneth said dryly. "How will we find out if our work has been accepted? Is a list posted?"

"Nothing so civilized," she said ruefully. "After the selection, artists must go to the academy and ask the porter about the fate of their work. There is a great queue of people, and the porter loves to bellow out 'Nay' for the pictures that haven't been accepted. Very embarrassing."

Kenneth made a face. "I expect that will happen to me."

She gave him a level look. "Rejection won't mean that your work is unworthy."

He smiled. "Having received approval from you and Sir Anthony, I can survive the academy's lack of appreciation."

Once again, she saw that disquieting warmth in his eyes. It reminded her too much of when they had made love. She drifted across the small room. "One learns where one's work has been hung on Varnishing Day, when artists can make last-minute changes." She smiled. "Mr. Turner has been known to practically repaint a whole canvas from wonderful to even more wonderful."

"How do they hang a thousand paintings?"

"Very closely. The frames almost touch. The Great Exhibition Room is enormous, too. A painting hung near the ceiling is practically invisible. They call that being 'skyed.' Better than nothing, I suppose, but it doesn't do much to advance an artist's career."

"Obviously acceptance is only the first hurdle of what turns out to be a whole steeplechase." Kenneth's expression became pensive. "It feels odd to be talking about painting and exhibition so naturally. I was raised to be a landowner, and fate made me a soldier. I could not have imagined living an artist's life even three months ago."

She looked at his craggy features and powerful body and thought of the corsair. Perhaps he wasn't every woman's secret romantic fantasy—but he was certainly hers. Knowing she must leave, Rebecca put her hand on the doorknob. "Perhaps a pattern that you didn't recognize brought you to art in a roundabout way, Kenneth. You had the talent to learn despite having no formal teaching, and war has given you the material for great art. The result is: a unique vision."

Then shc turned and left swiftly, before she gave in to the temptation to walk into his arms.

CHAPTER 25

Kenneth whistled softly when he and Rebecca entered Somerset House. "You weren't exaggerating about the number of people queuing up to learn if their work will be hung."

Rebecca edged closer to him. "Think how much worse it would have been if we had arrived first thing this morning."

"It's bad enough now. There must be fifty or sixty men jammed in here." He smiled at her. "And about three women."

More artists were arriving steadily, some of them jostling about in their anxiety. Knowing how much Rebecca disliked crowds, he aimed his best officer glare at those who came too close. He and Rebecca were always granted more space.

The porter who was consulting the list of paintings boomed out "Nay!" to the man at the head of the line.

"Poor devil," Kenneth murmured as the artist turned and left, his face white.

She took hold of his arm. "I'm seriously regretting this."

He patted her hand where it rested on his forearm. Her fingers were icy. "I would tell you the truth—that you will be accepted—but it wouldn't make you feel any better, would it?"

She gave him a wry smile. "You must feel the same way."

"Worse," he said feelingly. "My chances are much poorer."

"I have better technique, but you have more substance."

"Your work has every bit as much substance, it just isn't as melodramatic."

They looked at each other and broke into laughter at the same time. Rebecca said, "We're in a terrible state, aren't we?"

He had never felt closer to her. Apparently shared worries were as powerful a bond as shared passion. He hoped devoutly that her work was accepted. He was resigned to the fact that his paintings would be rejected, but it would go harder with her. After all, she was Sir Anthony's daughter, not an unknown.

"We need a change of subject, or we'll both have a fit of the vapors." He tried to think of an innocuous topic. "Let's talk about the Gray Ghost. He's in fine condition for a cat that you reckon must be ten or twelve years old."

She gave a glimmer of a smile. "He should look good. He's only been awake for about two of those years."

He chuckled. They managed to maintain a pretense of conversation as the line moved forward, but he doubted either of them would remember a word that was said. He did notice that about three out of four artists had their work rejected. He guessed that Rebecca was aware of that, too.

An interminable wait later, only one man separated them from the porter. "Frederick Marshall," the artist said hoarsely.

The porter rustled through the much-thumbed papers,

his lips moving a little as he read the names. Then he peered over his half-glasses. "Marshall. Nay."

Marshall slammed one fist into the opposite palm. "Damn the academy! What do those old fools know of real art?" Eyes blazing, he pivoted and stalked away.

Rebecca's turn. Kenneth put his hands comfortingly on her shoulders. A tremor in her voice, she said, "R. A. Seaton."

The porter gave her a disapproving glance, then bent to his papers again, his finger moving slowly down the page. "Seaton. *The Corsair.* Aye. *Transfiguration.* Aye."

Rebecca seemed to light up like a candle under Kenneth's hands. She spun to him, her eyes shining. He wanted to kiss her, but settled for saying warmly, "Wonderful, and deserved."

"Your turn," she said. In her eyes, he saw how much she wanted for him to succeed as well.

He stepped forward. "Kimball."

The porter seemed to be getting slower with every artist. He fumbled through the pages. "Kimball. Nay."

Kenneth's heart froze. Though he had told himself he would be rejected, the reality still hurt. It hurt like hell. Rebecca's hand caught his and squeezed hard.

Then the porter muttered, "Nay, that was Kimbrough. Let's see, you're Kimball?" He peered at Kenneth, who managed a nod.

The porter looked at his list again. "Navarre, the Fifth of November, 1811. Aye. Spanish Pietá. Aye."

With a rush of pure joy, Kenneth caught Rebecca up in his arms and whirled her around. She hugged him, laughing with equal delight.

The man behind them pushed by impatiently and gave his name. Brought to his senses, Kenneth carefully set

Rebecca down again. Their gazes caught and held with dangerous intensity.

He should know better than to touch her when they were both in an emotional state. That was what got them into trouble before. If they hadn't been surrounded by people, he couldn't have vouched for the consequences.

He tucked her arm in his elbow and led her away. "We did it, Ginger. We did it!"

She almost danced down the outside steps. "Even if our pictures are skyed up to the rafters, we'll always be able to say that we've exhibited at the Royal Academy!"

He smiled at her exuberance. For today, at least, they shared the camaraderie of soldiers who had fought and won a battle, side by side.

~

Varnishing Day was chaos. Not only was the exhibition hall full of artists prepared to make last-minute changes to their work, but gawkers who had used influence to get in for an early look were underfoot. Rebecca instinctively pressed closer to Kenneth. He was such a comforting presence in a crowd.

Eyes wide, he glanced around the gigantic room. "You told me that every wall was covered with paintings floor to ceiling, but the reality is still a shock. I feel overwhelmed."

"So do I. I've attended exhibitions my whole life, but I've never had to look for my own work amid the confusion."

"We had better do this methodically. Let's start at that corner and go around until we find our work."

"All the while praying that we've been hung somewhere near the line." When he gave her a quizzical glance, she explained, "The line is that ledge that runs around the room. It's about eight feet high, so pictures hung near it are the easiest to see. The line is usually reserved for paintings by academicians, with whatever is left going to the best work by outsiders."

She took his arm and they started around the room, dodging artists carrying ladders and supplies. Though Kenneth had brought a portmanteau filled with paints and brushes, they had both decided not to make any changes to their work unless they noticed some truly horrifying detail.

"Look!" Rebecca halted, stopping Kenneth as well. "Father's Waterloo paintings. Don't they look magnificent?"

The four great canvases hung side by side on the line, dominating a whole wall. An awed group of people had gathered to admire the works.

"Sir Anthony has achieved his goal," Kenneth said quietly. "Generations from now, people will look at these pictures and know what it meant to be at Waterloo."

She pointed at the line-of-battle picture. "There you are with your regiment, a little left of center."

"Actually, I'm there." He indicated the scarred veteran guarding the regimental colors in the foreground. "Sir Anthony repainted the sergeant to look like me, just as he threatened."

"You are going to be a London celebrity after this exhibition," she said with a wicked smile.

He groaned. "My identity isn't obvious in your father's picture. As for the corsair—forgive me if I hope that it has been hung up by the ceiling."

"Out of my hands," she said cheerfully. "It's a pity there are no women on the Hanging Committee. That would guarantee the picture a good spot."

Laughing and teasing, they continued around the room.

There was much to see and discuss. Too much. Rebecca knew from experience that it would be necessary to come back again and again to fully appreciate the works displayed.

They had surveyed two walls and narrowly missed being hit by a palette dropped by a nervous young man on a ladder when Kenneth said in a voice of suppressed excitement, "Look. There."

Their paintings had been hung side by side, and right above the line where they were readily visible. Kenneth's pair were on the right and Rebecca's on the left.

"Thank heaven," she said fervently. "Your career is made, Kenneth. How much do you want to sell the paintings for?"

He looked surprised. "I hadn't really thought beyond getting my work exhibited."

"Well, it's time to start thinking. After all, the purpose of exhibition is to sell."

"Have you set your prices?" he retorted.

She glanced at the corsair and the falling woman. "These two paintings are not for sale. I wouldn't mind if I got some portrait commissions out of this, though."

A fashionable couple stopped to look. The man exclaimed, "Look at those Spanish paintings. Such power! Such realism!"

The elegant lady on his arm shuddered. "I think they are hideous. Art should be about beauty, not squalor." She gestured at Rebecca's paintings. "Now, *these* are beautiful. Look at the exaltation on the face of the girl as she sacrifices herself for her people. Most affecting." Her gaze went to the corsair. "The pirate is rather scandalous, but certainly striking." The tip of her tongue touched her lips. "I wonder who the model is."

Rebecca muffled her laughter with one hand as she pulled Kenneth away. "That was a fair sample of what we will hear about our work. And you, my lord corsair, are going to awake the day after the exhibition opens to find yourself famous."

He winced. "I'll have to leave London immediately."

When she laughed again, he said sternly, "You're enjoying this entirely too much. I should have submitted Lilith. Then men would pursue you the way you claim women will pursue me."

"Nonsense." She batted her lashes demurely. "No one would believe that such a sensual demoness had been modeled after a prim creature like me."

"You vastly underrate your charms, Ginger." Kenneth's gaze shifted to something beyond her. Raising his voice above the babble around them, he said, "Good day, Frazier."

Lord Frazier said genially, "Good day, Kimball, Rebecca. Anthony said you've both had work accepted."

"Those four." Rebecca indicated their pictures. "We were fortunate to be hung in a good location."

"No doubt Anthony used his influence." Frazier's gaze went to *Transfiguration,* and his expression became utterly still.

After a long silence, his gaze passed over the other pictures, ending on Kenneth's pietá. "Interesting, though a bit modern for my taste, I'm afraid. A pity you haven't been properly trained, Kimball. If you intend to continue painting, you must apply yourself to historical subjects. One cannot claim to be a serious artist without knowledge of the antique, and of the Grand Manner so ably described by Reynolds."

Rebecca was not surprised that he didn't comment on

her paintings. Frazier was the sort who believed that female artists could never equal males.

Kenneth said politely, "Did you submit a painting this year?"

"Yes, but I haven't located it yet." Frazier scanned the crowded walls. "I chose to portray Leonidas at Thermopylae. I consider the Greek victory over the Persians to be one of the seminal moments of Western civilization."

"I agree—a noble subject. I saw a picture that might be Leonidas over there. I doubt it's yours, though, because of where it's hung." Kenneth indicated a painting on the opposite wall, about halfway between the line and the ceiling. While not impossible to see, it was far from a choice spot.

Frazier's gaze went to the picture, and his face went rigid. "That is my painting," he said tightly.

The note in his voice alarmed Rebecca. The man looked ready to have an apoplexy. "Obviously it was hung in error," she said. "Remember several years ago they made a similar mistake with one of Father's paintings." Unobtrusively she nudged Kenneth's ankle with her toe.

Understanding, he said, "Disgraceful that such mistakes are made with the work of an academician." He gestured toward the canvas. "An immensely complex composition, Frazier. It must have taken a very long time to paint."

Frazier's expression eased a little. "I've been laboring on it for over two years. It's one of my finest works."

"You must go and see that the picture gets hung properly," Rebecca said sympathetically.

"Yes. I'll take care of that at once. The fools." With no other farewell, Frazier left.

Under his breath, Kenneth said, "Was it an error?"

Rebecca shrugged. "As an associate of the academy, he should have automatically been hung on the line. He's not well liked by his fellows, though. Too arrogant. Other artists only tolerate arrogance if it's coupled with genius. Perhaps someone on the Hanging Committee decided to even an old score with him."

"Either that or the Hanging Committee made its judgment based on the work itself."

Suppressing a smile, Rebecca said, "That's unkind. It's technically very competent."

"But forgettable." Kenneth contemplated the dozens of naked, sword-wielding and shield-bearing figures. "And highly illogical. All of the soldiers I know prefer to wear clothing when fighting battles."

"Hush," Rebecca said with a laugh. "It's in the classical mode, not modern realism."

"Even two thousand years ago, soldiers would want to protect vulnerable body parts," he said firmly.

Smiling, she took his arm so they could continue their tour of the exhibition. Only as they moved away did she realize that Lord Frazier had been waylaid by someone a few feet away from them. All she could see was his stiff back, but it was possible that he had overheard Kenneth's criticism.

She hoped he had not. After all, being mediocre did not make an artist any less sensitive.

CHAPTER 26

The day of the Strathmore ball had arrived, and Kenneth and Rebecca were sharing a light meal in the drawing room to take them through until the late supper. As he took another piece of spice cake, he said, "I'm looking forward to the ball tonight. Now that the exhibit has opened and we are both certified successes, we're entitled to a night of frivolity."

Rebecca smiled indulgently and divided the last of the tea between their cups. "I must admit that I'm looking forward to it, too."

He studied her fondly as he sipped his tea, thinking that she looked as delectable as the cakes. Now that he wasn't working himself to exhaustion, his desire to bed her was rapidly getting out of hand. He had better start work on his engraving series. That should absorb some of his unruly energy.

His thoughts were interrupted when Sir Anthony came into the drawing room, resplendent in full evening dress.

Rebecca glanced up. "Hello, Father. I thought you had left for dinner already."

"George and Malcolm will be here to collect me in a moment, but I wanted to pass on some news," he replied. "Rebecca, today at the exhibition, two people asked if you did portrait work. Expect to hear from them. There have also been several outrageous offers to buy *The Corsair,* all from women. I assume it is not for sale?"

"You assume correctly. Still... how outrageous?"

"Five hundred guineas."

She spilled her tea. "That's a fortune!"

"That was the highest firm offer," he continued. "A certain elderly duchess said she would give a thousand guineas for it, but I believe she was jesting."

Rebecca grinned at Kenneth. "You're famous, Captain."

He stared gloomily into his cup. "Perhaps I'll grow a beard so no one will recognize me."

"There was also considerable interest in your two paintings, Kenneth. I advise you not to accept less than three hundred guineas apiece. You should be able to get more."

"You think they're worth that much?" Kenneth said, amazed.

"A painting is worth what someone wants to pay. Don't undervalue yourself." As Sir Anthony opened the door to leave, he said with regret, "I assume I'll need a new secretary soon."

Kenneth thought of his still unfinished investigation. "Yes. But not just yet."

At that moment, Hampton and Frazier arrived. Since the drawing room door was open, they came to say hello.

Hampton said, "You two young people have done brilliantly with your exhibition pieces. Rebecca, your pictures are superb." His gaze went to Kenneth. "I feel vastly pleased with myself for having contracted you to do the Peninsular series. Any chance that when the first prints are offered, I can borrow *The Corsair* to hang in my shop window? It would do wonders for sales."

While Kenneth groaned and Sir Anthony laughed, Rebecca said firmly, "I think not, Uncle George."

"A pity," Hampton said, his eyes twinkling. "A fine marketing opportunity lost."

Lord Frazier watched the interplay with a faint expression of distaste. The man needed a sense of humor, Kenneth decided.

"Time we were off. We're dining with Benjamin West tonight." Sir Anthony paused, his expression commanding everyone's attention before he continued, "West wishes to talk about my succeeding him as president of the Royal Academy."

There was a moment of profound silence. Kenneth noted that Hampton looked surprised and Frazier looked downright shocked.

Then Rebecca exclaimed, "That's wonderful!" She bounced up and went to hug her father. "With the backing of the current president, your election is assured when the time comes."

"That's still a few years away, I trust. I'm fond of West and in no hurry to see him die." Sir Anthony smiled. "But when a new president is needed, I would be honored to serve."

"Perhaps Tom Lawrence will have something to say about that," Frazier drawled. "Still, if West makes his preference plain, your chances are excellent."

"Anthony is by far the best choice," Hampton said warmly as he shook his friend's hand. He glanced at Rebecca. "Who knows? Perhaps someday Kimball will head the academy in his turn. There's already talk of making him an associate when the next vacancy occurs.

You'll have the distinction of being both daughter and wife of presidents."

It was a flattering thought, but Kenneth saw a look of authentic rage in Frazier's eyes. He said deprecatingly, "Such talk after only two pictures exhibited is highly premature. Besides, my artistic education is deficient in many areas."

"I'm glad you're aware of that," Frazier said acerbically. "It would be a pity if your head became turned when you are still the merest novice."

Hampton gave the other man an annoyed glance, but said only, "Time we were going. Good night, Rebecca, Kimball."

After the door closed on the three men, Rebecca said, "Poor Frazier—he obviously resents the fact that his star is in eclipse when everyone else's is rising." She danced over to Kenneth, who had just resumed his seat, and threw her arms around him exuberantly, almost spilling the teacup he had just lifted. "But the rest of us are so wonderfully successful that I can scarcely believe it."

Faced with a choice between cooling tea and a warm armful of femininity, the decision was easy. He set the cup aside and pulled her onto his lap. "I owe this all to you, Rebecca. If you hadn't bullied me into painting, I would never have tried."

He gave her a kiss that was intended to be light, but which swiftly turned serious. Her arms slid around him and her mouth opened under his. She tasted of spice cake and delight, a heady, intoxicating blend that aroused him in seconds.

He pulled his head away and tried to pretend that he was unaffected by the embrace. "We really shouldn't do this in the drawing room. Or anywhere else, for that matter."

Briefly he saw his own indecision in her. Then her expression changed as exuberance transmuted into reckless passion. "You're right. My studio is a much better place." She raised her hand and caressed his cheek with sensual promise. "Lavinia said *The Corsair* depicts every woman's dream lover, dark and dangerous and irresistible. That it is pure passion."

It was becoming hard to breathe. He set her on her feet and stood. "Lavinia has a colorful imagination."

"On the contrary, she's very acute." Instead of moving away, Rebecca stepped so close that her breasts almost touched him. As he stared at them, mesmerized, she continued, "Lavinia said the painting shows how I see you, and she's right."

He should move away. He didn't. "How do you see me?"

"Dark." She slid a cool hand around the back of his neck and caressed his nape, her fingertips tangling in his hair and her breasts a warm, insistent pressure against his chest.

His pulse began hammering with desire and dismay.

"Dangerous." Standing on tiptoe, she lightly nipped the lobe of his ear.

Sensation blazed through him, tingling in his limbs and pooling in his groin.

"Irresistible," she murmured against his throat. Her lips feathered across his cheek and her mouth slanted over his.

He exhaled roughly and drew her into his embrace, thirsting for the rich liquor of her mouth. She was like ginger wine, soothing and sizzling all at once. Lilith, the demoness of desire. His hands glided down her supple spine and came to rest on the sculptured softness of her hips. He drew her against him, feeling every lovely feminine curve.

It had been hard enough when he had only guessed what lay beneath her gown. Now he knew, and the knowledge was physical pain. He wanted to bare her shapely limbs to his hungry gaze. He wanted savagery and tenderness. To sink into her welcoming body. To see the wildness blazing in her eyes, and the deep contentment that would come later.

No.

"Lilith the demoness indeed. Sent to steal my soul and succeeding admirably." Aching with regret, he set her away from him. "To be fools once might be forgivable. Twice would not."

"What is so foolish about making love?" She reached back and jerked loose the ribbon that secured her hair so that it fell about her shoulders like a sun-gilded auburn veil. "And let us have no nonsense about you being a lowly secretary. You are a viscount and a rising young artist."

He tried to think what other barriers he could put between them, apart from the truth of his duplicity. "Having escaped a forced wedding once, we'd be fools to risk our luck again. I can't swear I would be able to withdraw when I should." He stroked the delicate arc of her cheek with the back of his hand. "You are too intoxicating."

She caught his hand and pressed the open palm to her breast. He went rigid, unable to pull away.

"If that's all, you needn't worry. Lavinia explained how to prevent unwanted consequences." Color rose in Rebecca's face, but she didn't drop her eyes. "I have what I need to... to... protect myself upstairs."

His fragile control collapsed like a house of cards. Why should they deny what they both wanted so much? His responsibility to Beth was fulfilled, his obligation to Bowden nearly so, and he'd found no evidence that Sir Anthony had killed his wife. Within a matter of weeks, perhaps only days, his life would be his own again. The return of the jewels should save him from bankruptcy no matter what Bowden decided to do with the mortgages. Though there would still be debts, he would finally be Kimball of Sutterton in a meaningful way.

When that happened and he could speak freely... Well, he was willing to rethink his feelings about heiresses if Rebecca would reconsider her distaste for marriage.

As for this present moment, they both burned, and there was only one way to quench the flames.

This time he would not allow the swift madness of their first mating. She knew how to give; he must teach her to receive. He took her face between his hands. "If the corsair is a dream lover, you are a dream mistress. Passionate. Open. Lovely beyond belief." He gave her a long, soul-draining kiss. When he broke for breath, he whispered, "Prepare yourself, Lilith, for you are impossible to resist."

"Good," she said huskily. "I'll join you in the studio."

They left the drawing room a demure yard apart, though anyone watching would guess what they were about to do. The message was in her glowing eyes and unbound hair, and surely on his own face as well. Luckily, no one saw them. He went directly to the studio. There he took the knee rug from the sofa and spread it on the carpet by the fireplace. He also built up the fire, since the air would be cool on bare skin, and he intended to see every glorious inch of her.

By the time he had removed boots, coat, and cravat, she had arrived. He met her in the middle of the room and swept her into another drugging kiss.

She pulled up his shirt and laid her hands on his bare ribs. Her palms were cool against his fevered flesh. "I've wanted this so much," she breathed.

"So have I. Dear God, so have I." He undid the small buttons of her bodice with impatient clumsiness. The upper part of the garment fell away, revealing the creamy swell of her breasts. The little witch had removed her undergarments so that she wore nothing under the gown. Her audacity was shockingly erotic. He knelt to take one dusky nipple in his mouth. She whimpered and wrapped her arms around his head. Her scent was ripe roses, like full-blown blossoms baking in the sun.

As he suckled her nipples to vibrant tautness, he raised her hem and caressed her bare leg. She exhaled rapturously when his hand moved from her firm calf to the supple skin behind her knee. He stroked higher, gliding over the satiny flesh of her inner thighs.

He had meant only to tease, to hint of what was to come. Then his fingertips brushed the damp warmth between her legs and he was lost. He slid his fingers possessively into the silky curls, searching for the most sensitive places in the secret labyrinth of folds.

She gasped, "Oh, yes, yes," her body swaying.

He got to his feet and tugged off her gown while she watched him with dazed, passion-darkened eyes.

When he straightened, she said huskily, "Let me see you."

He complied, yanking his clothing so roughly that two buttons popped off and bounced across the floor. Her ardent gaze made him feel like the irresistible dream lover of her painting.

She said with a touch of laughter, "You're a magnificent nude. I'm torn between drawing you and kissing you."

"Drawing can wait." He swooped her up in his arms for the sheer joy of holding her. Her hair fell over his arm, sweeping almost to his knees in a tantalizing cascade. He nuzzled his face into the angle between her throat and shoulder. "We have better things to do."

She took advantage of his closeness to nibble provocatively on his ear. He groaned, feeling as if every nerve ending in his body were on fire. He went down on one knee and laid her on the yielding pallet before the fire. She was flame and ivory, a feast for all the senses. He stretched out beside her, raining hot kisses over her throat and breasts and belly as once more he caressed her intimately.

She opened to him, arching her back as her slim frame trembled helplessly. *"Now,* Kenneth."

Her questing hand found his rigid, pulsing shaft and clasped tight, the ball of her thumb stroking the acutely sensitive flesh. His hips heaved uncontrollably.

Beyond thought, he rolled between her legs and buried himself in the hot silk of her body. He was lost, lost, in a savage rhythm of possession and surrender. She met and matched him, thrusting and clashing as frantically as he. They were carried helplessly in the river of fire until they reached a shattering climax that fused them, for an instant, into one spirit and one flesh.

Consciousness returned in fragments as the convulsive shudders faded away. They collapsed together in an exhausted tangle of limbs. As he gulped for breath, he shifted to his side and tucked her against him. She seemed too small, too fragile for the fury of passion she carried within her. Yet his body was still shaking from the force of their mating.

The only sounds were the ticking of the clock, the faint crackle of burning coals, and the harshness of their labored breathing. He slid his fingers into the damp auburn cloud of her hair. Lilith. Ginger. Rebecca. She was a collection of paradoxes, both kind and fierce, sharp and tender.

He hoped to God that when the right time came she would have him, because he doubted he would have the strength to let her go.

Rebecca dozed a little, cradled spoon-style against Kenneth's powerful body. Impossible to imagine any greater contentment. But time was passing. When she felt his weight shift, she murmured, "Must we really go to the ball?"

"I'm afraid so." Kenneth lazily stroked from her shoulder to her hip. "I think that Strathmore is the man who arranged for the Wilding jewelry to be returned. I'd like to say thank you, even if it has to be oblique."

"A good reason to go." She rolled onto her back to admire him. Her corsair. Everything Lavinia had seen in the painting, and so much more. "For a soldier, you don't have many scars."

"Luckily, I never received any major wounds. If I had, I wouldn't be here. Serious battlefield injuries almost always result in amputation or death." He smiled. "Except for Michael, who is indestructible."

She sat up and glided a hand along his back. "I can feel faint ridges here. You said once that you had been flogged?"

He nodded. "Very early in my army career. Common soldiers can be flogged for any number of reasons. In my case, it was insolence. I was sentenced to a hundred lashes."

"Were you guilty?"

"Absolutely." He gazed into the fire. "Though I was an enlisted man, I still had the arrogance of my breeding. I let the officer see that I thought he was an ass. He neither knew nor cared that I was the Honorable Kenneth Wilding, heir to Viscount Kimball. I was tied to a pair of crossed pikes while a whip stripped away a fair amount of my back." His expression turned thoughtful. "I'll have to sketch that for George Hampton's series. A drummer does the flogging, you know. They have very strong arms. The other drummers mark time, one beat for every stroke of the lash."

She winced at the vivid picture he had conjured up. "You could have been killed."

"Not at all. The regimental surgeon stands by to stop the flogging if the soldier appears to be in dire straits," he said dryly. "When the poor devil has recovered sufficiently, the rest of the strokes are administered."

"That's barbaric."

"Perhaps, but effective." He glanced at her with a faint smile. "I learned that being nobly born counted for nothing when I stepped outside my place in society. It was the first step toward becoming a decent soldier."

She studied the rugged planes of his face, thinking that it was this breadth of experience that made him different from any man she had ever known. He had lived with privilege, and with harsh repression. With brutality and danger, and with a deep appreciation of beauty. Such contrasts might make him a great artist. They had also made him a matchless lover; she did not need wide experience to know that. "When you became an officer, did you order floggings yourself?"

"When necessary. If one is dealing with hard men, sometimes hard measures are required." He got lithely to his feet. "Time to return to the mundane world, Ginger."

More interested in his naked body than his words, she took a tablet and charcoal from a nearby table and began to sketch. "If you think that is too dramatic, wait till I portray you as Hercules. Your proportions and muscle definition are superb. I'll ask Uncle George if he would like me to do a series of engravings of tasteful, classical male nudes."

Seeing her sketchbook, he began to stalk toward her

menacingly. "Do that and Lilith will become the centerpiece of next year's exhibition."

"No gentleman would show that picture," she said loftily.

"Who said anything about a gentleman? You wanted a pirate, and that's what you've got. A dangerous corsair who lives to assault innocent maidens."

She chuckled. "Then I should be safe."

"No one is safe from a corsair." He suddenly dived at her.

She gave a small shriek and tried unsuccessfully to escape. He tossed the drawing materials aside and wrestled her down to the blanket, kissing every giggling inch of her.

"No one is safe from Lilith, either," she panted as she fought back, nipping his shoulder and touching him in the ways she had learned drove him mad.

She'd learned her lessons well. He groaned and pinned her wrists to the blanket. Then he spread her legs with his knees and impaled her with one powerful thrust.

They stared into each other's eyes, both of them laughing. Her heart constricted. She loved seeing him so happy. She had not known that playfulness could exist side by side with desire.

As he began moving inside her with provocative slowness, she uttered a silent wish that they could stay like this forever, safe from the harsh demands of the world.

Yet even as she fell tumbling into rapture, she knew with a chilly touch of premonition that her wish would not come true.

CHAPTER 27

Despite their amorous encounter, Kenneth and Rebecca arrived at the ball at a reasonable hour. He was amused by her demure expression as they greeted their hosts. Anyone who didn't know her might think she was a meek creature without an opinion to call her own.

As they walked toward the ballroom, she glanced up and their gazes met. He felt a wondrous sense of closeness, as if they were inside each other's skin.

She gave him a teasing smile. "What are you thinking?"

Taking advantage of the noise to speak without being overheard, he said softly, "That you transformed yourself from a naked demoness to an elegant lady with remarkable speed. That I would like to take you into an empty room and ravish you. And that I would dearly love to spend a whole night with you."

Her cheeks pinkened charmingly. "Will you act on your thoughts?"

"Alas, I shall have to settle for dancing with you several more times than is proper." The music was striking up for a waltz, so he led her onto the floor. He supposed that if he couldn't ravish her, a waltz was the next best thing.

When the music ended, they drifted around the ballroom greeting new friends. Rebecca was far more at ease than at her first ball and her dances were spoken for quickly. On the previous occasion, that had happened because Michael had asked his friends to make sure she was not ostracized. This time, men came to her because they wanted to.

Since Rebecca was among friends, Kenneth went off for a private word with his host, Lord Strathmore. After an exchange of pleasantries, he mentioned his stepmother's miraculous change of heart about the Wilding heirlooms, and his own fervent gratitude for the result. Strathmore grinned, the mischievous light in his eyes confirming his part in what had happened.

Hoping he would someday have the opportunity to do a good turn for Strathmore, Kenneth strolled around the room, talking to friends and occasionally dancing. He calculated that he would reach Rebecca just in time for the supper dance, which he had reserved for himself. Several times he saw her dancing, looking slim and winsome. He didn't begrudge other men the chance to dance with her. After all, he was the lucky devil who had spent half the afternoon in her arms.

Michael Kenyon hailed him, and Kenneth went to say hello. After an exchange of greetings, Michael said, "Catherine and I went to Somerset House today. You've come a long way from charcoal sketches of Louis the Lazy."

Kenneth grinned. "A dog who never moves is an easy subject."

"I hope your paintings aren't spoken for yet," Michael

continued. "Would you accept a thousand guineas for the pair?"

Kenneth's jaw dropped. "That's absurd! Or is it charity?"

"I knew you'd say that," his friend said imperturbably. "On the contrary, my great-grandchildren will give thanks for my foresight in buying two magnificent early Wildings. The price I paid will look like theft on my part."

Kenneth smiled, but still felt doubtful. "Are you sure you want them that much?"

"Catherine and I were in Spain, too," Michael said quietly. "Those pictures speak to both of us in a special way."

"In that case, they are yours." Kenneth offered his hand. "And I'll even be able to visit them now and then."

"I certainly hope so. I must tell Catherine. She was worried that the pictures might have been sold elsewhere." With a parting nod, Michael went in search of his wife.

A little dazed by his good fortune, Kenneth turned to look for Rebecca. Instead, he almost collided with Lord Bowden.

Though Bowden was not a large man, his thunderous expression made him formidable. "I hoped to find you here, Kimball," he snapped. "You have refused to meet with me or to answer my letters, but you will certainly talk to me now."

Kenneth winced inwardly. He had forgotten the date that Bowden was due back in London. In fact, in the last fortnight he had thought of little except painting and Rebecca. "Sorry. I really haven't been trying to avoid you. For the last several days I've been too busy to collect my letters. I agree that it's time we met. When would be a good time for you?"

"You will talk to me *now,*" Bowden said through gritted teeth. "In the middle of this ballroom, if necessary."

The man was on the verge of explosion, and Kenneth couldn't blame him. Luckily Rebecca was dancing and wouldn't notice if Kenneth left the ballroom. "I think both of us would prefer privacy. Let's find an empty room."

Bowden gave a grim nod and together they moved through the laughing crowd. Kenneth's mind was working at top speed, but to no effect. He had nothing to say that would satisfy a man who wanted Sir Anthony destroyed.

~

The quadrille ended, and Rebecca breathlessly thanked her partner. Then she looked around for Kenneth, who was to lead her out in the next set. To her surprise, he was leaving the ballroom with another man who seemed vaguely familiar. She strolled after them, cooling herself with the ginger kitten fan. It was dearer to her than the Wilding diamond ring, because the ring would have to be returned eventually. But the fan was *hers.*

She emerged from the ballroom in time to see the men disappear through a door down the corridor. Curious, she followed. The door swung open silently, admitting her to a long, narrow library. The room was divided by an arch. Her end was shadowed, but lamplight and the flicker of a fire came from the far end, along with the murmur of male voices.

She hesitated. Kenneth was probably engaged in some sort of business, perhaps selling his paintings. She really shouldn't interrupt. Since she was not visible to the men, it would be easy to withdraw quietly and wait for him in the ballroom.

She turned and put her hand on the doorknob. Then an unfamiliar voice rose sharply, saying, "Damn you, Kimball! I hired you to find evidence of Anthony's crimes, not marry his daughter! Did he buy you off with the girl and her fortune?"

Rebecca froze. Surely she had misunderstood. She turned away from the door, her ears straining.

Kenneth's deep voice replied, "The betrothal was something of an accident. It has nothing to do with Sir Anthony."

She knew their betrothal was false. Still, they were lovers, and his casual dismissal of their relationship hurt. She crept toward the arch and took a position just out of sight, so that she would miss none of the conversation.

The other man snorted with disgust. "Then you're playing a double game of your own. When I returned to London and learned from my wife that my unknown niece had become betrothed, I made inquiries. A suspicious mind might think you schemed with that slut Lavinia Claxton to get caught in a compromising situation with the chit. After all, she inherited Helen's fortune. I should have guessed that an aging heiress would be irresistible to a man with your financial problems."

"Lord Bowden, you insult both Lady Claxton and Miss Seaton," Kenneth said sharply. "Do not do so again. You also have a penchant for seeing conspiracies where none exist. I repeat: My relationship with Miss Seaton has nothing to do with my investigation."

Bowden? Dear God, Kenneth's companion was her father's brother. He had the same build, a similar way of moving. But why, after decades of estrangement, would he want his younger brother investigated? The man must be mad.

But if he was mad, Kenneth was his tool. Shaken to the core, she rested her forehead against the cool brocaded wall.

"Have you had as much success with your investigation as with your courtship?" her uncle asked coldly.

"Not the kind of success you hoped for. I'll send you a report, but I've talked to everyone who might have knowledge of what happened and there is simply no evidence of foul play. Perhaps in the Lake District I will learn something, but I can make no promises."

"There must be proof, Kimball," Bowden growled. *"Find it."*

Light footsteps, not Kenneth's, moved across the room. Then a door opened and closed with a bang. Rebecca closed her eyes for a moment, wondering what on earth Kenneth was investigating. It was absurd to think of her father as a criminal. He was a famous painter with all the wealth he needed, not a thief or a corrupt government official. No wonder Kenneth could find no evidence of wrongdoing.

But that did not mitigate Kenneth's deceit. He had entered the house under false pretenses. His vague explanation of having been sent by an anonymous friend had seemed amusing at the time, but no longer. He had ruthlessly taken advantage of her father's trust to gain free access to the household and all of Sir Anthony's private papers.

She had a sudden, vivid memory of her first glimpse of Kenneth. Feral intelligence. Almost brutal. A pirate in Mayfair. No wonder he hadn't looked like a secretary; he was really a spy. How many times had he asked her seemingly casual questions? And she had always answered. Her stomach churned with nausea at the realization that he had been using her in his attempts to gather evidence against her father.

For the length of a dozen heartbeats, she leaned shaking against the wall. Then rage gave her strength.

She stepped into the open archway. Kenneth stood by the fireplace looking down into the coals. Her corsair. Powerful, compelling. She had thought him heroic.

She was a thrice-damned fool.

Her voice a hiss, she said, "You are *despicable."*

His head jerked up and he stared at her, his face going white. "You heard that conversation?"

"Yes, I heard it." Her mouth twisted bitterly. "If I were a man, I would kill you, but I suppose I'll have to settle for burning your portrait and telling my father that his favorite secretary has betrayed him, and me as well."

"Rebecca..." He raised his hand and took a step toward her.

She had the sudden, horrible thought that if he touched her she would melt into a mindless adoring female and accept whatever deceitful explanation he offered. "Don't come near me!" she said furiously. "I don't ever want to see you again."

She turned and bolted from the room before he could come closer. He called her name again, but she ignored him and fled down the corridor. She had to get out of this house.

Not wanting to call attention to herself, she slowed to a walk and schooled her face to impassivity before entering the ballroom. Her progress was complicated by the fact that most of the guests were moving in the opposite direction, toward the supper room. Luckily, she was small enough to slip through a crowd easily. Several people called her name, but she ignored them. She was only here because Kenneth had wanted her to become respectable. To improve her value as a wife? To hell with the lot of them. She had lost all interest in joining his world.

As she neared the foyer, she remembered that their carriage would not return for them until midnight. Nor did she have money to hire a sedan chair or hackney coach. She would have to walk. Seaton House couldn't be more than a mile or so away, and Mayfair should be safe enough.

She considered going for her shawl, but changed her mind when she glanced over her shoulder and saw Kenneth grimly working his way through the crowd. Her pulse jumped with alarm. She swiftly went to the front door. As the footman swung it open for her, she indicated Kenneth's advancing form. "That so-called gentleman has been bothering me," she said imperiously. "Don't let him follow me to my carriage."

The footman bowed. "Yes, miss."

Though the servant was a hefty fellow, she doubted he would be able to stop Kenneth for long. However, that should be enough.

She caught up her skirts and darted down the steps. To the right, a line of carriages waited for the Strathmore guests, the drivers talking or dicing together. She turned left and went toward the corner at a near run, not caring what onlookers might think.

A turn, a short block, another turn, a long block. She ran until a cramp in her side forced her to stop. She halted and clung to a set of rusting iron railings, her hand pressed to her side as she gasped for breath. The damp night air was bitingly cold on her bare arms and neck.

She should have known better than to confront Kenneth. Of course he would try to use that treacherous tongue to convince her that black was white. She should have quietly returned to the ballroom and asked one of her new acquaintances for the use of a carriage to go home. But whom could she have asked? They were all Kenneth's friends, not hers.

For a moment she thought of Catherine and Michael and the others she had met through Kenneth. Her heart quivered at the knowledge that she would lose them as well as him.

Furiously she quashed the reaction. She didn't need Kenneth's friends, and her experience of balls had been flat-out catastrophic. She was better off alone.

But how would she ever be able to use her studio and not think of him? Kenneth sprawled on the sofa in the corsair's languid, sensual pose. Kenneth making tea and the easy conversation that followed. Only a few hours earlier, he had made passionate love to her in front of the fireplace, acting as if she was the most desirable woman in the world.

Acting was the key word. She had been available—dear God, how available she had been!—so he had bedded her. Obviously he was the fortune hunter Bowden had claimed. What better way to convince her of his integrity than to vehemently protest that he found the very idea of fortune hunting loathsome?

Desperate to escape her thoughts, she began walking again. Where the devil was she? Everything looked different at night, and she had not paid much attention during the drive to Strathmore House. The neighborhood was rougher than she would have expected. Vaguely she recalled that Hanover Square was on the edge of the fashionable district. She must have turned in the wrong direction when she left Strathmore House.

At the next intersection she looked at the corner tablet, but didn't recognize the street name. Beginning to feel nervous, she halted and tried to decide which direction to go. She didn't like the look of the street ahead; the neighborhood was definitely getting worse.

Her decision was made when she saw several men sauntering toward her. From their loud voices, they had been drinking. She pivoted and walked back the way she had come, acutely aware of her skimpy evening gown and expensive jewelry. Her mother's jewelry. She put her hand over her opal pendant protectively.

One of the men behind her called in a slurred voice, "Hey, dollymop! There's three of us here. No need to go all the way back to Covent Garden to find customers."

Heart pounding, she quickened her pace. Wasn't there anyone respectable on the streets tonight? She moved closer to the wall of the building on her left, hoping the men would pass her by.

The footsteps behind her grew louder. Suddenly a heavy hand caught her arm and swung her around. The man was tall and disheveled and he stank of gin. "You're a pretty little thing," he said with a drunken leer down her décolletage. "We'll give you a guinea each, eh? That's more than fair."

"You quite mistake the matter," she said in her coolest, most ladylike tones. "I am not the sort of female you want."

The man holding her was momentarily nonplussed. Then one of his companions said with a coarse laugh, "Now, ain't she the little lady? But as my guv'nor always said, if it walks like a whore and dresses like a whore, it's a whore."

Encouraged by the comment, her captor pulled her into a revolting kiss, his hand clamping over her breast. Gagging from gin fumes, she shoved at him wildly. Her struggles had no effect at all. Near panic, she raised her hands and scratched his face, just missing one eye.

He howled and jerked his head back. "Damned little slut! I'll teach you manners."

He slammed her back against the wall and pinned her there, his hand tearing at her gown. She tried to scream, but he leaned forward, smothering her face against his coat. Fear such as she had never known blazed through her. She, Sir Anthony Seaton's daughter, could be casually raped by these beasts, and she was utterly helpless to stop it.

Then suddenly the devouring mouth and clawing hands were gone and her assailant was hurtling through the air. As he crashed to the ground, she sagged against the wall, struggling for breath. In front of her the powerful, unmistakable form of Kenneth loomed black against the night.

"Stay out of the way," he ordered. Then he spun to confront the two men who were charging forward to avenge their friend.

Making it look laughably easy, Kenneth knocked one down with a blow to the jaw and flattened the other with a kick in the belly. Undeterred, the first man rose with an angry shout and lurched into another attack. Kenneth smashed a fist into the middle of the drunk's face, breaking his nose. The man collapsed again, blood streaming down his shirt.

Kenneth turned to her. "Come on. We should leave before one of them produces a knife or pistol."

"Thank you for saving me." Rebecca stared at him, shaking violently. "But I still despise you."

"Understood." He peeled off his coat and draped it over her shoulders, then took her arm and hurried her away. "We're just around the corner from Oxford Street. We should be able to find a hackney there."

"It must be very comforting to know that you are more

vicious than anything else that stalks the night," she said through chattering teeth.

"It is," he said imperturbably. "I assume you also learned that there is no joy in being a victim."

The fact that he was right made her even more angry. She would have given his coat back, but she needed the warmth. She pulled it tightly around her shoulders, loathing the intimacy of being enveloped by his lingering body heat and scent. Yet she could not deny that those qualities soothed her.

Despairingly she recognized how far she had allowed this man, her father's enemy, to penetrate her defenses. She was going to pay a bitter price for her weakness.

Rebecca didn't say a word as Kenneth found a hackney and gave the orders to take them home. Her face might have been carved from ice. He stayed as far away from her as was possible in the small vehicle.

Thank heaven he'd found her before she was injured. But if it hadn't been for him, she would never have been in danger.

Bleakly he stared out the window at the empty streets. He had known that matters were going too smoothly. How could he have been stupid enough to believe he could painlessly extricate himself from his dilemma? Nothing in his life had ever come easily, and in the space of minutes, he had gone from happiness and hope to utter disaster.

He tried to remember exactly what he and Bowden had said. Enough to damn him in Rebecca's eyes forever.

At Seaton House, he paid off the hackney and followed

her up the steps. She banged the knocker viciously against the door.

While waiting for a servant to admit them, she turned and snapped, "Collect your things and leave. If you aren't gone in fifteen minutes, I'll have the servants throw you out."

"There is no one on the staff capable of throwing me out," he said mildly. "Furthermore, the servants have been taking their orders from me for weeks. Don't put them in the position of having to decide whom to obey."

For a moment he thought she would strike him.

"I was hired by your father, and it is his place to discharge me," he said in a conciliatory tone. "I have every intention of making a full confession, and I'll go quietly when he tells me to leave. But first, I must talk with you."

Before she could reply, the butler opened the door. Rebecca swept into the house as if it were normal for her to be wearing a ruined gown and a man's coat. "Is my father home, Minton?"

"Not yet, Miss Rebecca." The butler's eyes widened at their appearance, but he asked no questions.

Her back like a ramrod, she turned and climbed the steps. Kenneth followed. As soon as they were out of Minton's earshot, he said, "I suppose your studio is the best place to talk."

"No!" She pulled off his coat and hurled it at him.

As he caught it reflexively, she tore off her left glove and wrenched the Wilding diamond ring from her finger. She threw that also. More by luck than skill, he caught the ring after it bounced off his chest.

Clamping down on the pain, he said, "It's either your studio, mine, or a bedroom. But we most assuredly will talk."

Recognizing his determination, she pivoted and marched up the stairs to the attic, picking up a candle along the way. When they reached her studio, he built up a fire while she lit the lamps. He didn't waste time planning what to say; he had already decided that nothing less than the whole truth would do.

When Kenneth finished with the fire, he stood and saw that she had found a worn shawl and wrapped it around her shoulders. She looked like a small and very dangerous child.

"Do you think anything can mitigate your deceit?" she said in a low, furious voice.

"Probably not, but I must try." Praying that he could make her understand, he continued, "I want you to believe that I didn't like coming here under false pretenses, but I had little choice. It was investigation or ruin. I've hated the deception more with every day that passed."

"Which is why you seduced me—because you hate deception," she said bitterly.

He caught her gaze. "I seduced you? Think back on what happened, then see if you can honestly say that."

Her face turned a deep, humiliated red. "Very well, I seduced you. But no honorable man would lie with me when he was here to destroy my father's life."

"I told myself that, repeatedly," he said quietly. "The simple truth, Rebecca, is that I couldn't help myself."

Her mouth twisted. "What a convenient answer. You're a good enough actor to live a lie day and night for weeks, but lack the self-control to resist the pathetic advances of a spinster."

"It was Bowden who made that stupid remark about aging heiresses. Believe me, you are not pathetic," he said wryly. "I think you are the most formidable woman I've ever met. And the most desirable."

Again she looked as if she wanted to hit him. "Don't try to flatter your way out of this! Your mind was in control of your body, and it decided that I was rich and available."

He experienced a flare of anger that equaled hers. With one step, he was beside her. He caught her shoulders in his hands and kissed her fiercely. Her mouth crushed under his. For an instant, she resisted violently.

Then the passion that was anger's blood twin flared between them. She gasped and her mouth opened under his. As her body became pliant, he had a nearly overwhelming desire to continue, to seduce her in truth and let passion bridge the chasm between them. After they made love, she would be more open to reason.

Then he recognized his insanity. Rebecca's body might be willing, but if he bedded her while she despised him, it would be emotional rape. She would hate him forever.

He released her and stepped away. "Do you still think that the mind always controls the body?" he said hoarsely.

She pressed the back of her hand to her mouth, her eyes wide and stark. "You've made your point, Captain." She took a chair by the fire and wrapped the shawl tightly around her. "What the devil are you supposed to be investigating? My father is no criminal. He isn't interested enough in money to steal it."

So she had not heard everything. Bluntly he replied, "Bowden believes your father murdered your mother."

Her jaw dropped in utter shock. "That's insane. Either Bowden is mad or you're a liar. Probably both."

"Bowden is obsessed, but I don't think he's mad." Tersely Kenneth explained the financial proposition that Bowden had made, and the thinking that lay behind it.

When he finished, she said, "You've found nothing

because there is nothing to find. It's inconceivable that my father would injure anyone."

Kenneth arched his brows. "Have you forgotten his tantrums? His tendency to throw things when enraged?"

She bit her lip. "That means nothing. He would never hurt any woman, much less my mother."

"Can you really say that for certain?" He sank onto the familiar sofa, wishing fervently that he did not have to discuss such things with her. "I agree that Sir Anthony is unlikely to be a cold-blooded killer. But he could have caused your mother's death without intending it. By all reports, they both had fierce tempers. A fight, an angry shove, or a misstep as she tried to get way from him—it would explain a great deal."

"No!" she cried in anguish. "That wouldn't have happened. Yes, they argued, but not violently. Why can't you accept that my mother's death was an accident?"

"Accident is still the most likely explanation," he agreed. "Yet no one can come up with a good reason for her falling off a familiar cliff in broad daylight, and I find it damned suspicious that everyone close to your mother is evasive about her death. You, Lavinia, Frazier, Hampton, Tom Morley—every single one of you tightens up in a way that seems to be more than simple grief. It makes me suspect that there is something to hide. Do you all fear that Sir Anthony was involved?"

"No!"

"If not that, then what?" he said implacably.

Rebecca got to her feet and paced across the room in agitation. Then, as if reaching a decision, she swung around to face him.

"Very well, if you must know," she said savagely. "The secret fear that no one will discuss is not foul play, but suicide. If my mother did not fall accidentally, she must have killed herself. If that became known, she would have been condemned by church and man, forbidden a grave in holy ground."

She closed her eyes and said in a raw whisper, "Do you blame us for not wanting to talk about her death?"

CHAPTER 28

"Suicide!" Kenneth stared at her in shock. "I heard that Helen was emotional, but never that she was self-destructive."

Taking bitter satisfaction in having managed to surprise him, Rebecca returned to her pacing. "Mother was usually so animated that most people would not have believed it. Only her intimates knew about her terrible spells of melancholia. Winter was the worst time. Sometimes in the darkest months she would stay in bed weeping for days. Papa and I never knew what to do. We both feared that if the melancholy became too deep, she would kill herself rather than endure the misery. Nothing seemed to help but time. As the days became longer, her mood improved. Summer was much easier for us all."

"Yet she died in high summer." He frowned. "Had she ever made an attempt on her life?"

"I... I'm not sure. There was an incident that made Papa and me wonder." She drew a shuddering breath. "And once at Ravensbeck, when the three of us were on a ridge trail, she got this odd expression and looked out across the valley, saying that it would be very easy to simply walk off a cliff."

He considered. "You may be reading too much into a casual comment. I've had similar thoughts while standing on cliffs and high buildings, and I haven't a suicidal bone in my body."

"I might agree it was casual, except for the fact that she died exactly that way," Rebecca said sharply.

"But not necessarily by suicide. Was she in low spirits before her death?"

"She seemed happy enough, but her moods were very volatile." Feeling chilled, Rebecca went to stand by the fire again. "If she was struck by a sudden spell of melancholia, she might have decided on impulse to... to end it all."

"Perhaps," he agreed. "But it's pure supposition. From what you say, there's no evidence that her mood was self-destructive at the time of her fall."

Rebecca hesitated. Discussing her mother's death was almost unbearably painful, but she needed to convince Kenneth that he was wrong about her father. Then he would go away and leave them alone. "There is one piece of evidence. I've never told anyone, even Papa, about this."

She went to her desk and removed the golden ring from the drawer where she kept it. "Are you familiar with gimmal rings? Two or more separate bands are designed to fit together and form a whole. I believe that in medieval times a man and woman who were pledged would sometimes each keep a band, then combine them into a wedding ring at the ceremony."

She gave Kenneth the ring. "This one is an antique that Papa found somewhere and bought as a curiosity. He gave it to my mother when they eloped. Later he got her a proper wedding band, but she continued to wear this ring from sentiment. It fascinated me when I was a child."

He examined the ring, which showed two hands clasping, one larger, the other smaller and more feminine. She wondered if he would recognize what was wrong.

He glanced up. "The two bands don't fit together very well. They seem too loose."

He was observant. She supposed it was an essential skill for a spy. "This particular ring has three bands. When the clasping hands are separated, a heart is revealed underneath." She separated the bands and returned them. "When they brought my mother's body up from the bottom of the cliff, she was clutching the ring in her hand instead of wearing it. It... it had to be pried loose. I kept the ring and didn't realize until later that the heart band was missing."

He looked at the two empty golden hands. "And you decided that it was a message from her—that your mother had lost her heart for living."

Again she was reluctantly impressed by his quick perception. "Exactly. She wore the ring always, so the heart couldn't have been lost by accident. It had to have been removed deliberately."

He toyed with the gold bands, his expression abstracted. "Intelligence work is a matter of fitting odd pieces together and looking for patterns. What you're saying doesn't fit the pattern of a suicide."

Her mouth twisted. "Perhaps not, but it was also difficult to believe her death was accidental."

"I gather no suicide note was found, which would make sense if she didn't want to distress her loved ones. But in that case, it seems strange that she would leave any clue at all. Did you ever find the missing heart?"

"No, though I did look." Rebecca tried not to think of how close she had come to breaking when she searched her mother's jewelry case and vanity table. "I wanted the ring to be intact in case my father ever asked about it. If he saw the heart was missing, he would think the same as I did. He didn't need that extra grief. But he never asked."

Kenneth fitted the gold hands together. "Let's assume that she didn't kill herself and that she didn't die by accident. That would mean someone else was involved in her death."

Rebecca's eyes narrowed. "Not my father!"

"I'm inclined to agree." His hand tightened over the gimmal ring. "There's something chilling about a person who would leave such an oblique, mocking message. I can imagine Sir Anthony hurting someone in a rage, but not cold-bloodedly taking the ring apart and throwing his wife off a cliff."

She shuddered, wishing he had used less graphic words. "You're relying on logic to explain an illogical situation. There's no more evidence of murder than for accident or suicide."

"There are hints. For example, the signs of struggle at the top of the cliff. That tends to rule out the possibility of suicide. And the missing heart doesn't fit with an accident."

She bit her lip. "Maybe that band wore through and broke."

"One would think the middle band of three would be the last to wear out." He held up the two remaining bands. "Nor is there any significant wear on these."

He was right about the ring, but she was still unconvinced. "Who would want to kill my mother? Everyone liked her."

"Perhaps not everyone. Over the past weeks, I've thought about the possibilities. Perhaps your mother decided to end her affair with Hampton and he became violent."

"Not Uncle George," she protested. "I think that Mother loved him because of his kind, steady disposition. He would be the last person to turn murderous from obsessive love."

"Lady Seaton seemed to inspire intense feelings," Kenneth pointed out. "Almost thirty years after their broken betrothal, Bowden cares enough about her death to spend a fortune trying to determine how she died. Your father's last secretary, Morley, was in love with her even though she was old enough to be his mother. Having seen the portrait in the study, I can understand why. Who knows what other men have become obsessed with her?"

She rubbed her temple. "I've sometimes wondered if she might be the reason Lord Frazier never married. Mr. Turner and Sir Thomas Lawrence are other painters who claimed half seriously that they would never take a wife since 'the beauteous Helen' was unavailable. I could easily name a dozen other men who admired her intensely. But I can't imagine any of them murdering her."

He shrugged. "An army officer is often a de facto judge for what happens among his men. I learned that most crimes are motivated by passion or a desire for gain. In your mother's case, passion is the most likely since the only person to gain financially from her death was you."

Outraged, Rebecca interrupted, "You can't possibly think I injured her!"

"Of course not," he said dryly. "You see why I prefer passion over gain as a motive? Although a possibility that combines both would be if your father's mistress of the time wanted to eliminate Helen to clear the way for a second wife. Do you know who he was sleeping with then?"

She shook her head. "I never wanted to know such things. However, I think his mistresses were always women he had painted. I've also suspected that they usually pursued him rather than vice versa."

"He becomes enamored of their beauty, and they become intoxicated by the fact that he sees them as beautiful," Kenneth said meditatively. "The bond between artist and subject is an interesting one, isn't it?"

Under other circumstances, she would have enjoyed discussing his comment. This time, she said only, "I don't know about the philosophical implications, but a good way to identify possible mistresses would be to look at my father's daybook for that spring and see who his clients were."

"That particular daybook got left at Ravensbeck in the confusion of your mother's death and the early return to London." He considered. "Would Lavinia know who he was bedding then?"

"Ask her if you wish. I wouldn't want to." Rebecca hesitated, then added, "Despite Lavinia's lurid reputation, I don't think she ever lay with my father while my mother was alive. She mentioned once that she didn't believe in sleeping with the husbands of her friends."

"An interesting woman, Lavinia."

Seeing his expression, Rebecca said forcefully, "She's not a murderer, either. The idea that someone killed my mother is bizarre. Why can't we all let her rest in peace?"

"I'm sure she is at peace," he said softly. "But if someone murdered her, he is still at large. Do you want that?"

She took a deep, calming breath. "Of course I would

want to see justice done—*if* she was murdered, which I don't believe."

"Justice was part of the reason I accepted Bowden's proposition," Kenneth said dispassionately. "Yes, I wanted to save myself from bankruptcy. But it was also true that finding a murderer seemed like a worthy mission."

She turned away, not wanting his words to soften her anger. "You don't seem to have had much success."

"True. But it wasn't until tonight that I've come to believe there really was a murder." He got up to put more coal on the fire. "Something you said earlier interested me —that there had been an incident that made you and your father fear that Lady Seaton was suicidal. What happened?"

Rebecca sighed. "Toward the end of the winter before she died, she fell into a kind of coma. The physician said she had taken a massive dose of laudanum. When she finally awoke, she didn't remember clearly what had happened, but thought she'd mixed a sleeping draft incorrectly. She was very convincing when she said it was an accident, but... Papa and I had our doubts."

Not that they had ever discussed it. For the whole of Rebecca's life, there had been a tacit conspiracy of silence about Helen's problems.

Kenneth's eyes narrowed. "Interesting. Like the fall that killed her, a drug overdose could be an accident, attempted suicide, or a murder attempt."

She stared at him, chilled. "But if someone tried to kill her with laudanum, the person must have been in our household."

"Many people wander through here," he replied. "For someone who knew where medications were kept, it wouldn't be hard to make a quick substitution. And I gather that a large part of your father's circle goes to the Lake

District every year. A killer who failed in winter could have made another attempt in the summer."

"Perhaps... perhaps you're right," she said with deep reluctance. She went to the window and gazed into the dark street. The idea of murder was distant, shadowy, compared to the terrible reality of her mother's absence. A mother was the glue that held a family together. Without Helen, Rebecca and her father were not a family but two isolated individuals, living under one roof and separated by pain.

An ugly thought insinuated itself into her mind. Was it possible that her father, in a moment of anger, really had...

No! She rejected the thought violently. Her father would not have been able to conceal his guilt from her. What she did feel in him was a terrible regret, a belief that he had failed his wife by not preventing her from killing herself. She recognized that guilt because it echoed her own.

In the silence, the clatter of a carriage could be heard pulling up in front of the house. Her father was home.

Kenneth said, "Shall I go down and confess to Sir Anthony?"

She turned from the window and regarded Kenneth gravely. Her father would be deeply distressed to learn that a man he liked had betrayed his trust, and even more infuriated by the suggestion that he had killed his wife. She hated to think that his pleasure at the prospect of becoming the next president of the Royal Academy would be spoiled so quickly.

Almost as if he read her mind, Kenneth said, "If you think it would upset him unnecessarily, I could simply say that my financial situation has changed and I am needed at my estate."

In a matter of moments he would walk out of her life forever. It was exactly what she wanted. Wasn't it?

Lips dry, she said, "That might be the best solution."

"What about the possibility that your mother was murdered?"

She rubbed her temple again, feeling a headache coming on. "Perhaps I'll hire a Bow Street Runner to investigate further."

"Bowden did. The Runner learned nothing. That is why I was enlisted—because as a secretary I would have better access to the household than an outsider."

She frowned at him. "You have something in mind. What?"

"If there is any evidence of what really happened, it is likely to be in the Lake District, where she died," Kenneth said soberly. "Perhaps a clue in your father's daybook, or something that a local person might have seen. Since an accident was assumed, no inquiries were made then."

"You're saying you want to carry on as if nothing happened and go to the Lakes with us," she said flatly.

His mouth curved without humor. "Pretending nothing happened will be impossible, but the rest is true. I'd like to see this investigation through to the end."

"For the sake of justice and your mortgages?" she said with heavy irony.

"Exactly." He hesitated. "And perhaps to help you and your father learn what happened. I owe you that. As soon as I came here, I realized that something was wrong. Your mother's death in ambiguous circumstances injured all who were close to her. The truth, no matter how painful, might come as a relief."

He sounded so blasted reasonable. So kind. She leaned against the wall and closed her eyes. Part of her didn't want to see him go, but another, larger part was terrified at the thought of living under the same roof with the shadow of his treachery between them. It would be better if he left.

Yet if anyone could solve the mystery of her mother's death, it was Kenneth. Tonight he had demonstrated a kind of deductive skill that was alien to her. Surely she owed it to Helen's memory to let him finish his investigation.

As she weighed the choices, he said quietly, "I concealed my true reason for coming to this house, but that was my only deceit. Everything I told you about my past, everything that happened between us, was true. *Everything.*"

She caught her breath as pain lanced through her. She wanted so much to believe him, but her emotions had been too badly mauled. Her gaze went to the carpet in front of the fireplace. A few hours earlier, she had known pure happiness. But he had sounded just as sincere and believable when he had talked with Bowden.

"You kept too many secrets, Captain," she said tightly. "You concealed your station in life, your artistic ability, your very reason for coming to this house. I've run out of trust."

The scar across his cheek whitened. "If you allow me to stay, I'll keep out of your way as much as possible."

"See that you do."

It was permission, and the signal for an armed truce. Kenneth nodded and silently left the studio.

When he was gone, she went to the sofa and curled up against the Persian silk carpet, wrapping her shawl around her like a cocoon. Too much had happened in this disastrous evening. Passion. Treachery. Assault. The possibility of murder. She was too drained even to go down to her bedroom.

Where did deceit end and truth begin?

Kenneth's talent was real. His military experience and

sister were also real. His friends were real and loyal, and the quality of those friends reflected well on him.

But that didn't mean he wasn't a fortune hunter. It didn't mean that he had felt anything beyond lust when he bedded her. It didn't mean she could trust him.

Eyes starkly open, Rebecca watched the dying coals slowly crumble into ash.

Exhausted, Kenneth stripped off his clothing and went to bed as soon as he reached his room. The first edge of Rebecca's fury had been blunted, but the chasm between them was still catastrophically deep. Perhaps it could not be bridged.

She was such a contradiction. Her unconventional upbringing had given her a misleading air of sophistication. She had acted as if virginity were no more than a minor nuisance, and insisted that she had no interest in marriage.

Yet he suspected that at heart she was a romantic who yearned to believe in love and faithfulness. Otherwise she would not disapprove so much of her parents' infidelities. Nor would she have waited until the age of twenty-seven to trust a man with her body and at least a small part of her heart. She had been gradually opening up to him. He had hoped that by the time his financial affairs were sorted out, she would be willing to trust him with her hand as well. But tonight she had bolted back into her shell, possibly forever.

Ironically, the catastrophic evening had finally produced something significant to report to Lord Bowden. The missing heart band from the gimmal ring was a small thing, but it had crystallized vague suspicions into a firm belief that Helen Seaton had been murdered. He couldn't prove it yet. But now that he was convinced there had been foul play, his chances of finding her killer were greatly enhanced.

As Kenneth drifted into restless sleep, he pondered the irony of his situation. Without his secret mission to Seaton House, he never would have met Rebecca. Yet those same secrets might have doomed any chance of building a future with her.

CHAPTER 29

Two days after the Strathmore ball, Rebecca received a note from Lady Bowden saying that her newfound aunt would be walking near the Serpentine in Hyde Park later that morning. She fingered the paper doubtfully. She had thought of Lady Bowden several times since their meeting. A day earlier, she would have welcomed this discreet invitation to further their acquaintance.

After hearing of Lord Bowden's desire to prove Sir Anthony a murderer, she was not so sure. It would be hard to keep that from Bowden's wife. Then again, perhaps this was a heaven-sent opportunity to learn more about her father's brother.

Pragmatism won, and two hours later Rebecca and her maid Betsy went to the park. Relatively few people were about at this unfashionable hour, so it took only a few minutes to locate her aunt's slight, elegant figure.

"Good day, Lady Bowden," Rebecca said as they approached each other. "It's good to see you again."

Her ladyship gave her maid a glance. The woman fell back out of earshot and walked with Betsy. Lady Bowden smiled. "I'm glad you could come on such short notice, Rebecca. We're leaving for the country tomorrow. Even though it is only a few miles from your father's summer home, I don't think it will be possible for us to meet there."

"Someone would surely notice," Rebecca agreed. She looked around her. "I'm glad to have an excuse to come out on such a fine day. I've been so busy I've scarcely noticed the weather."

The two women talked of inconsequential things as they strolled toward the narrow end of the lake, which was busy with splashing waterfowl. When they reached it, Lady Bowden opened her large reticule and brought out two chunks of bread.

After handing one to Rebecca, she broke a corner off her own bread and tossed it into the water. Ducks and geese darted forward from all directions, honking hopefully.

Rebecca smiled and threw out a piece of bread. "Why is it so soothing to feed waterfowl?"

"They're so much more direct than humans," her aunt replied. "By the way, my felicitations on your betrothal. I gather Lord Kimball is that splendid specimen who escorted you when we met?"

The Candover ball seemed a long time ago. "You mean the gentleman with whom I was caught misbehaving. To be honest, Aunt Margaret, the betrothal was a pretense to avoid scandal. We intended to break it quietly after a discreet interval."

Her aunt gave her a look of bright-eyed curiosity. "From the way you speak, you sound as if you're considering making it a real betrothal. After all, misbehaving with a man generally indicates a certain fondness for the fellow."

"The situation has changed. Perhaps I shouldn't say this, for I don't want to cause you pain. Still, in a way it concerns us both." Rebecca hurled a piece of bread as far as she could. A great mute swan swooped majestically into the water and stole the tidbit from a goose. "I recently learned that your husband hired Lord Kimball to enter our household as a secretary in order to seek evidence that my father killed my mother."

"Oh, my. I see why you were reluctant to speak." Lady Bowden's eyes widened with shock. "Oh, my... I presume you are concerned for your father and furious with your young man."

"He is *not* my young man. Especially not now."

"Men are imperfect creatures, aren't they? But they are the only opposite sex we have, so we must make the best of them." Her aunt sighed. "Strange how even after almost thirty years, my husband can't get Helen out of his mind."

"I'm sorry, Aunt Margaret," Rebecca said softly. "I know the knowledge must be hurtful."

"Only a bit. He does love me, you know, though I understand that better than he does himself." She tossed out several small pieces of bread, her face a little sad. "We've had a good marriage. Our two sons are a great joy to us both. But I think that because he loved Helen when he was young, she represents the lost dreams of his youth. He doesn't want to let them go."

"I can sympathize, but not if his regrets lead him to falsely accuse my father." Rebecca flipped a piece of bread over a fat Canada goose so that a small female mallard could snatch it. "Forgive me for asking, but... is there any chance that your husband's hatred would lead him to manufacture evidence to support his belief in my father's wickedness?"

"No chance at all. Marcus can be very fixed in his opinions, but he is rigorously honest." Her aunt gave her a slanting glance. "How did you learn of my husband's scheme?"

"I overheard him talking to Kenneth at the Strathmore ball."

Lady Bowden grimaced. "Perhaps I should have attended instead of crying off. Did you confront Lord Kimball?"

"Yes. If I'd had a weapon, I would have assaulted him."

"Did he brazen it out?"

"Not really. He said he regretted the duplicity." Her mouth hardened. "But that doesn't change the fact of his lies."

"Once he became embroiled in the situation, he could hardly come out and tell you the truth," Lady Bowden said reasonably. "He was truly caught on the horns of a dilemma."

"A dilemma of his own creation," Rebecca said bitterly.

A sudden flicker in the air over the lake was followed by a brief, tortured avian shriek as a pigeon exploded in a flurry of feather and bone. A falcon had knifed down and slaughtered its hapless prey, then carried it off. Rebecca caught her breath, shaken by the suddenness of the strike.

Lady Bowden's gaze followed the feathers drifting down to the water. "You're angry, and you have reason to be." She tossed out the last of her bread, then brushed the crumbs from her gloves. "But if you care for the young man, my dear, I suggest that you not rule out the possibility of forgiveness."

"Is it possible to restore trust once it is gone?" Rebecca asked painfully.

"Love can heal broken trust. Love can heal a great many things. If it weren't true, the human race would have died out long since." Lady Bowden took her niece's arm. "Shall we go have an ice? I've found that ices are very good for dark moods."

As Rebecca obediently went with her aunt, she wondered if she would ever have such tranquility. Probably not. But she appreciated being around it.

For Kenneth, the two days following Rebecca's discovery of his deceit passed with hellacious slowness. As he had promised, he did his best to stay out of her way. She barely looked at him. His own misery was increased by the terrible ache he sensed inside of her, but he could do nothing to ease it. So he kept busy. The drawings for the engraving series benefited.

The one positive event had been Lord Bowden's reaction to the news of the missing band of the gimmal ring. He'd understood the implications immediately. Of course, he was still convinced that Sir Anthony was the killer, but at least he was satisfied that some progress had been made.

Kenneth spent the second evening sketching in his studio, which had the advantage of sparing him the sounds of Rebecca preparing for bed when she retired. Perhaps he should sleep on the narrow bed in the studio. The night before, the knowledge that she lay only a few feet away had made rest impossible.

It was well past midnight by the time he was ready to retire. The rest of the house was silent. He set aside his sketchbook and went to the window. It had rained earlier, but now a waxing moon was shining through fitful clouds. Perhaps he should do a painting of a night skirmish, with moonlight sliding coldly along rifle barrels and the edges of slashing sabers. It could be eerily effective.

Seaton House stood on a corner, and his attic view let him see a man walking along the side street just outside the garden wall. Kenneth's gaze sharpened when the man halted. There was something oddly purposeful about the action.

Then the man made a swift, hurling movement. A spark of light flashed through the air toward the house, ending in the sound of shattering glass somewhere below Kenneth. A few seconds later, an explosion rocked the building.

"Jesus Christ!" Kenneth bolted from his studio.

As he ran down the narrow hall, he pounded on the servants' doors. Then he raced down the steps three at a time. He reached the floor below as Rebecca and Sir Anthony were emerging from the bedrooms in their night-clothes. With Sir Anthony was Lavinia, obviously spending the night with her lover.

"My God, what has happened?" Sir Anthony gasped.

"There's a fire!" Kenneth called over his shoulder as he headed for the next flight of steps. "In your studio, I think. Make sure the servants are awake! We must evacuate the house."

Lavinia headed for the attic while Rebecca and her father followed him down the stairs. Both were only a few steps behind when Kenneth threw open the door to the elegant studio.

Choking smoke billowed from the room. A great fire snarled and hissed, already nearly out of control, and smaller blazes were beginning to take hold in the carpets and furnishings. Kenneth swore as a jug of linseed oil exploded, hurling more burning fragments around the room. A houseful of priceless artwork was on the verge of utter destruction.

"Oh, God, my paintings!" Sir Anthony cried with

anguish. He darted toward the portrait of the twin countesses and their husbands, which stood on an easel below some burning draperies.

The draperies began to collapse with unholy majesty. Rebecca screamed, "Father!"

Kenneth yanked Sir Anthony to safety an instant before the blazing fabric dropped onto the painting. "For God's sake, take pictures that are farther from the fire!" He seized a small carpet and began beating savagely at the leaping flames.

Sir Anthony seized two paintings from the wall and carried them from the room. A moment later he returned for more, Rebecca at his side. Kenneth would have laughed if he could have spared the breath. Leave it to artists to ignore danger to save art.

The two young footmen thundered in, carrying pitchers of water collected from various nightstands. Kenneth yanked off his cravat and soaked it before tying it around his mouth. Then he and the footmen splashed the pitchers onto the largest blaze.

Smoke billowed up in eye-stinging clouds, but the fire was cut in half. Kenneth retrieved his carpet and attacked the remaining flames and managed to beat them out.

But fires still blazed around the room. The dancing flames illuminated the studio and the adjoining salon with a hellish orange and yellow light. From the corner of Kenneth's eye, he saw Rebecca and her father carrying *Horatius at the Bridge* from the salon. Only a few small tongues of flame had crept into that room, so Kenneth beat them out, then closed the double doors.

The butler, Minton, appeared with a long hooked pole usually used for opening upper windows. He used the pole to smash several glass panes, then began hooking smoldering furnishings and tossing them out into the rain-soaked garden.

Several female servants appeared with pails of water lugged up from the kitchen. Kenneth ordered, "Pass the buckets to me."

He drew as close to the blistering heat as he dared, then hurled water over the largest remaining blaze. Without looking, he handed back the bucket and took another as it was put into his hands. Lift. Throw. Lift. Throw. Again. *Again.*

They were winning. When there was water, he threw it, choosing targets carefully. When there was none, he fought with his scorched carpet. The taste of charcoal filled his mouth, and he was half blind from smoke and tears. But one after another, the fires were being drowned or pounded into oblivion.

After an interminable hell of smoke and flame, the last flame was finally gone. Kenneth lurched into the corridor and folded onto the floor, gulping the cool air into his lungs.

Almost unrecognizable in his blackened nightclothes, Sir Anthony gasped, "We did it. Or rather, mostly you did it."

Kenneth coughed, his throat painfully raw from smoke. "More water should be put on anything still smoldering."

Lavinia quietly gave orders for more water to be brought up, though at a less furious pace. Rebecca knelt beside Kenneth, a basin of water in her hands. Her delicately embroidered nightdress was smudged with soot and her bare feet were black. "Are you burned, Captain? Your hands don't look good."

He glanced down and saw soot, red skin, and blisters. The sight made him aware that his hands hurt like the devil.

Wincing, he flexed his fingers. "I think the damage is minor."

She lifted a wet cloth and sponged his right hand. Then she spread a salve over the blistered area, never lifting her eyes.

Her loose muslin gown fell away from her body, revealing the curve of her breasts. The skin was creamy white compared to the sooty haze where she had been exposed to the smoke. His reaction to the sight was clear proof that he was not seriously injured.

He looked away. She finished his right hand and began treating the left with the same cool, impersonal competence.

Sir Anthony returned from a survey of the studio. "The furnishings are completely ruined and five paintings were incinerated. Trivial compared to what might have been. But how did it happen? No candles or fires were left burning. Surely the linseed oil didn't explode spontaneously."

"It was arson," Kenneth replied grimly. "I happened to be in my studio looking out the window when a man threw some kind of incendiary device at the house. At a guess, he filled a bottle with black powder, plugged it with wax, and devised some sort of fuse that would burn for a few seconds before setting off the gunpowder. It wouldn't have been difficult."

"But *why?*" Sir Anthony said with bewilderment.

"Who knows? An art critic. A jealous rival. An angry husband. A Bonapartist who doesn't like your Waterloo pictures." Kenneth got wearily to his feet. "I recommend hiring a couple of guards to patrol around the house all night for the indefinite future."

"All excellent ideas," Lavinia said. "But for tonight, I suggest brandy all around. Then back to bed."

Kenneth's gaze scanned the servants who were standing in the hall, their faces revealing the same blend of fatigue and triumph that he felt. "Without the efforts of everyone here, Seaton House would have burned, and possibly half the block with it. In recognition, you will all receive bonuses."

Sir Anthony gave a nod of approval as a small buzz of pleasure went through the bedraggled staff. Then he went off with Lavinia's arm around his waist. Kenneth watched as Rebecca followed, her gaze still avoiding him.

He dismissed all the servants except the footmen and the butler. Together they policed the studio to make sure there was nothing to ignite new fire. Then he told the servants that they could go to bed while he kept watch until morning.

Minton said, "I shall take that duty, my lord. Your efforts were greater than everyone else combined. You are reeling with exhaustion."

When Kenneth tried to protest, the butler said firmly, "Go."

He smiled crookedly. "In the army, that would be insubordination."

"This is not the army, my lord, and the most you can do is discharge me."

"Small chance of that." Kenneth rested his hand on the butler's shoulder for a moment. "Thank you."

Then he went tiredly up to his bedroom. He opened the door, and found Rebecca waiting for him. To his regret, she had donned a heavy robe that thoroughly disguised her figure.

Her cool expression made it clear there was nothing romantic about the visit. She got to her feet and gave him a filled glass. "I thought you could use some brandy."

"You thought rightly." He took a deep swallow. The brandy first scorched, then numbed his raw throat. His water pitcher had been returned full, so he washed the soot from his face and hands before turning to his visitor. "Events have moved from the realm of vague possibilities to undeniable violence."

She bit her lip. "Then you think there is a connection to my mother's death."

"Perhaps not, but it's more likely than the possibility that your family has two deadly enemies." He piled his pillows against the headboard of his bed and sprawled heedlessly across the counterpane, muscles and throat aching. "So far, there have been three incidents: your mother's overdose of laudanum, her fatal fall, and tonight's incendiary device. Each had been more dramatic and deadly than the one before."

Her eyes darkened. "Anyone who risked killing a dozen innocent people over a private feud is utterly vicious. You said an enemy of my family, but my father must be the target. No one knows me well enough to want to do murder." Her mouth twisted. "Except you, perhaps."

He said soberly, "Believe me, Rebecca, I have never had any desire to harm you."

She glanced away. "Perhaps we should tell Father your theory that the fire is part of a larger pattern."

He thought, then shook his head. "There's no real advantage. After tonight, it should be easy to persuade him to be careful even if he doesn't know my suspicions."

"Very well." She got to her feet. "Good night, Captain."

He had an almost unbearable desire to take her into his arms and draw her down to the bed. Not to make love, but to be able to hold her. To be in harmony again.

No chance of that. With a sigh, he set his empty glass

on the nightstand. "Do my efforts tonight do anything to allay your resentment of my past actions?"

She paused by the door. "I never doubted your courage, Captain. Only your honesty." Then she was gone.

Her unhappiness was so intense that he wondered if she was suffering from something more than anger toward him. Perhaps his duplicity had triggered some deeper source of pain. Her first youthful love had proved disastrous, and her father, though much loved, was not exactly a model of parental care and steadiness. It must be easier for her to believe that men were unreliable than that they could be trusted.

If that was true, he might never be able to win her forgiveness, for he was far from a paragon himself. It was a profoundly disturbing thought.

Kenneth forcibly turned his attention to the arsonist. What had the man looked like? In the darkness, he'd seen nothing distinctive. Medium build, perhaps a bit above average height.

He was on the verge of going to bed when a soft knock sounded on the door. "Come in," he said tiredly.

Lavinia entered. He started to get to his feet, but she waved him back to the bed.

"Sorry to disturb you," she said, "but since you and Rebecca are still feuding, I thought you wouldn't mind."

"You notice too much," he said wryly.

"Someone around here needs to be normal."

"Won't Sir Anthony wonder where you've gone?"

"He's fast asleep." She closed the door behind her, then asked bluntly, "Is Anthony in danger?"

"I think he might be."

She perched on the edge of his only chair. "What can I do?"

Realizing that Lavinia, with her perception and wide circle of acquaintances, might be helpful, Kenneth asked, "Can you think of any enemies who might want to physically harm Sir Anthony?"

She shivered and pulled her robe more tightly around her ample curves. She looked her true age, her stark expression very unlike her usual flamboyant manner. "A man as successful as Anthony is bound to be resented, but I can't think of anyone who would want to burn him alive, along with his whole household."

Kenneth said quietly, "You're in love with him, aren't you?"

"Since the day we met," she said simply. "I was seventeen when I first modeled for him. I was tempted to try to seduce him, but I didn't want to be merely another passing affair. I thought that friendship would last longer, and it has." She sighed and leaned back in her chair. "Helen said once that if anything happened to her, I should take care of Anthony. She didn't want him to fall into the hands of some dreadful harpy who was interested only in his fame and wealth."

Thinking this a good time to get the answer to another question, he asked, "At the time of Lady Seaton's death, who was Sir Anthony's mistress? I heard a rumor that he was very serious about the woman—perhaps to the point where he might consider ending his marriage. If he wished, he could have divorced Helen over her affair with Hampton."

"He would never, ever have done that," Lavinia said firmly. "And certainly not for that creature he was bedding then. She probably spread the rumor herself from vanity, since she had a husband and couldn't have married even if Anthony did get a divorce."

"The woman was?" Kenneth prompted.

Lavinia hesitated, then shrugged. "Your stepmother."

He felt only a small jolt of surprise. Hermione's portrait had been painted by Sir Anthony about then, she was beautiful, and wanton. He hoped his father hadn't known. "Now that she's a widow, does she have designs on Sir Anthony?"

"He ended the affair at the time of Helen's death and has had nothing to do with Hermione again," Lavinia said with obvious satisfaction. "Helen would have been so pleased. Your stepmother is exactly the sort of creature Helen was concerned about." She grinned. "Hermione is about to get her comeuppance. I have it from a reliable source that she's going to marry Lord Fydon, very quietly since she's still in mourning. He's enormously rich, but absolutely loathsome. She is going to regret this."

So Hermione had decided not to pin her hopes on the Duke of Ashburton; a rich earl in the hand was worth two dukes in the bush. "I hope your source is right. I assumed Hermione would never remarry because it would cost her too much. Under the terms of my father's will, everything but her widow's jointure will revert to the estate if she takes another husband. That means the London house and a number of government consoles that are in trust will come to me."

"Oh, she'll marry Fydon. Not only is he very, very rich, but the Fydon jewels are stunning, and Hermione is in desperate need of jewels." Lavinia's eyes twinkled. "I don't know how you managed that, but you have my congratulations."

"I did nothing," he assured her before returning to the early subject. "Are there any women who might be dangerous to Sir Anthony because of unrequited love?"

Lavinia shook her head. "His affairs were always light

and friendly, and I speak as one who has watched very carefully over the years. There are no crazed Caroline Lambs in his life."

"Perhaps the daybook at Ravensbeck will have some clues," Kenneth said pessimistically.

"A better source of information might be Helen's diaries."

He sat bolt upright. "She kept a journal? I had no idea."

"I'm not sure that Anthony and Rebecca knew. Helen kept them more to record feelings and impressions than events."

"Where are they?"

"I have them," Lavinia said calmly. "At the same time she told me to look after Anthony, Helen said that if she died I must burn her diaries. I wonder if she had a premonition."

"But you didn't burn them?" Kenneth said hopefully.

"No." Lavinia hesitated. "Having them is a connection with Helen. To burn them would sever another link. Yet I haven't had the courage to read them, either. It would be too painful."

"Let me see them. Perhaps I can find some clue as to who might have set the fire tonight."

"It's worth a try." Lavinia got to her feet. "I'm sure that you're an excellent investigator, though you've not had an easy time with this situation."

Kenneth regarded her warily, wondering how much she had guessed. "You're an alarming woman, Lavinia."

She gave a seraphic smile. "I merely watch the world around me. Good night, Captain." Then she slipped out the door.

Kenneth's mind was whirling as he took off his sooty

clothing. If Hermione remarried, his personal fortunes were saved. Finally he would be in a position to take a wife.

But first he must find the villain who might have killed Helen and was now threatening Sir Anthony. He uttered a silent prayer that Helen's diaries would provide the necessary clue. Perhaps saving her father would soften Rebecca's anger.

Yet in his heart he knew that wouldn't be enough. It would be easier to find a murderer than to heal a broken trust.

CHAPTER 30

In the morning light, the studio looked even worse than the night before. Kenneth stopped on the way down to breakfast and found Sir Anthony already there, surveying the damage.

"This makes my blood run cold," the older man muttered. "What if it had happened while I had the Waterloo pictures here? I could have lost the best work I've ever done."

"But you didn't, thank God." Kenneth looked around the room assessingly. Besides new plaster, paint, and furnishings, most of the floorboards would have to be replaced. "It could have been much worse. If the incendiary device had landed in your bedroom, you and Lady Claxton might not have escaped alive."

"Believe me, I've thought of that," Sir Anthony said grimly. "How can we find the villain who did this?"

"I don't know. A Bow Street Runner could be engaged, but such a crime leaves few clues. It will be almost impossible to investigate if the Runner doesn't have an idea where to start looking. Do you know of any deadly enemies?"

"Of course not," Sir Anthony said irritably. "The trouble is the ones I *don't* know of. A man in my position can easily cause an unintentional slight. Perhaps I made a derogatory remark about a bad painting at the exhibition, someone reported it to the artist, and the fellow is out for revenge. Painters are an unstable lot."

"I take your point. If you can think of any possibilities, let me know." Kenneth studied the charred rubble. "What pictures were lost?"

"Portraits in various stages of completion. The most significant was the second Strathmore and Markland painting. The Marklands' version had already been delivered. I shall have to redo the one for the Strathmores." He rattled off the names of the other four clients. "Send letters to each of them about the delay. They'll have to come in for more sittings. Obviously I can't work here. I suppose the salon will do."

Kenneth opened the scorched doors that led to the salon. "There's quite a bit of smoke damage here, and last night I noticed water damage in the drawing room below." An idea struck him, one that might take Sir Anthony out of harm's way. "Why not go to the Lake District now instead of waiting until your usual departure date? The damage can be repaired over the summer."

Sir Anthony's expression brightened. "An excellent idea. You can stay in London until the rebuilding arrangements have been made, then join us there."

Kenneth hesitated, not liking the idea of Sir Anthony going off without his protection. On the other hand, the enemy was obviously here in London, and probably would be for a while. Kenneth could get the rebuilding started and be on his way north in less than a week. "Very good, sir. If packing is begun right away, you could leave day after tomorrow."

"Give the orders."

Kenneth nodded and went downstairs. In the front hall, he met Lord Frazier, George Hampton, and other friends of Sir Anthony who had heard of the fire. He studied the faces, looking for hints of satisfaction or disappointment, but saw only curiosity and concern. As he went for breakfast, he wondered if any of them would leave to summer in the Lake District sooner than originally planned.

For the next day and a half, Seaton House was in an uproar of packing. By the time the carriages and baggage wagon rumbled away, Kenneth felt as if he had organized the whole Peninsular army for a major crosscountry march.

As the carriage that carried the family pulled away from the house, he had a sudden, horrific memory of the last time he had seen Maria alive. He had felt deep foreboding about her departure, but she had laughed at his fears and ridden away.

Logically, he knew there was no comparison. Maria had been a known guerrilla traveling through a war-torn land; Rebecca was journeying with her family along modern roads. Moreover, she would be safer away from London and her father's enemy. Yet even knowing that, the departure triggered irrational fear. Perhaps because he and Rebecca were emotionally estranged, he didn't want to let her out of his sight.

"Excuse me, my lord, are you unwell?"

It was Minton speaking, his brow furrowed. The butler

would stay in the city all summer to supervise the rebuilding and the small staff that would remain in the house.

Kenneth took a deep breath. "Only sorry to see Miss Seaton leaving."

Minton relaxed. "The impatience of young love. Don't worry, my lord. You shall be with her again in a few days."

As Kenneth went back into the house, he told himself to stop brooding. Rebecca would be fine. With luck, she might even decide that absence made the heart grow fonder.

Yet his foreboding persisted while he visited the London fabric and furniture warehouses. It was a tiring business, but he did find suitable furnishings.

Much of the evening was spent dealing with Sir Anthony's correspondence. It was late before he could look at the diaries Lavinia had quietly given him that morning. He hesitated before opening the first of the thick volumes. Helen Seaton might not have wanted her words read. But neither would she have wanted her husband to be killed, nor her own death to go unpunished.

He skimmed the earliest diary to get some sense of what she considered worthy of recording. As Lavinia had said, it was a series of reflections and opinions, often undated. But Helen Seaton's voice came through with warmth and wit.

The diary started when she was seventeen and had recently lost both her parents to a virulent fever. After her mourning ended, her guardian sent her to London for presentation. She was a great success, *"despite my dreadful red hair."*

His eye was caught by Lord Bowden's name. The next few pages sketched out the story of her engagement and elopement.

. . .

Marcus Seaton, Lord Bowden's heir, has offered marriage. I accepted, for I like him better than my other beaux. In fact, I think I am in love, though not quite sure since the state is unfamiliar to me. But Marcus is adoring and charming and intelligent. I quite like being adored. He and I shall do very well. Next week we will travel to his family seat in the Lake District to meet other relatives and see my future home.

The next page began:

Seaton Manor is very fine and the countryside is magnificent. I shall enjoy being mistress here. Today I met a neighbor girl called Margaret Williard. Not beautiful, but pretty and sweet and with speaking eyes. I think she is in love with Marcus, because she becomes so quiet when he is near. He is oblivious. So like a man! Margaret must surely resent me, yet she is always gracious. I hope we can be friends. Perhaps she will marry Marcus's younger brother Anthony, the mad artist. He and two of his friends shall arrive tomorrow. I look forward to meeting them....

The mad artists have arrived. Young Lord Frazier is very handsome and a bit full of himself, but most gallant. He sketched me as Aphrodite. George Hampton is of humble birth and a little shy around so many people of superior station. But he is a dear, with a natural dignity that will serve him well. As for Marcus's brother Anthony—

Dear God, I don't know what to say of Anthony.

The next entry, a week later, was stark:

. . .

Anthony has asked me to elope with him. To even consider it is indecent—yet how could I bear to be his sister-in-law? And would it be fair to marry Marcus now that I know I do not love him? What a fool I was to say that I thought I was in love. If one has to think about it, one isn't.

A day later she wrote:

Anthony and I are going to elope. We can be in Gretna Green in a day. I don't care about the scandal, or the fact that I shan't be Lady Bowden and mistress of Seaton Manor. We shall have a roof over our heads and each other. Nothing more matters. May God, and Marcus, forgive me for my wickedness.

He continued reading, absorbed by the story of her life as a wife and mother. He smiled when he read:

I think Anthony was a bit disappointed at first that I did not bear a son. But now he is quite enraptured by his tiny daughter with her red curls. Already he has filled half a sketchbook with pictures of her sleeping and gurgling and doing what all infants do. One would think she was the first baby ever born.

The first volume of the diary ended there, so he got up to stretch and take a break. To his surprise, it was after midnight. Time for bed.

But before he retired, he spent a few minutes with his

pastel crayons to sketch a picture of a baby with bright red curls and grave hazel eyes.

~

For at least the fiftieth time, Rebecca thought gloomily that the worst thing about the Lake District was its distance from London. Her father paid heavily for post horses, which kept travel time to a mere four days. Four long, bruising days, when nothing could be done but hold on to a strap and think.

Since her mind circled between thoughts of Kenneth and of the danger to her father, the process was not a pleasant one. Nor did she relish the prospect of returning to the place where her mother had died. Would it be possible to stay at Ravensbeck and not see Helen at every turn? She hoped that after a few days the pain would dissipate. It would be cruelly unfair if her pleasure in the Lakes was permanently ruined.

The coach hit a large bump and she lurched toward Lavinia. A quick grab at the strap prevented her from crashing into the older woman.

Sir Anthony said from the opposite seat, "Is it my imagination, or are the roads worse than usual this year?"

Rebecca had to smile. "You say that every year. Your memory mercifully obscures what a wretched trip it is."

"And you say *that* every year. It's coming back to me now."

Lavinia said lightly, "At least traveling at this speed gets us there quickly."

"That is what Helen always said," Sir Anthony commented.

There was a short, uneasy pause. Rebecca looked from

her father to Lavinia. Once she had thought their relationship casual, but no longer. They had been friends for decades. The trust and easy companionship they had always shared was now supplemented with what Rebecca suspected was a very satisfying physical relationship. She had learned to recognize the signs since her own recent discovery of passion.

But her father, who carried the guilt of his wife's ambiguous death, might be incapable of reaching out for happiness. A push was necessary. Besides, it would be nice if *someone* was happy. "The mourning period for Mother will be over soon," Rebecca said. "Why don't you two get married?"

The silence congealed like a rice pudding as the older couple stared at her, thunderstruck.

After a long moment, Lavinia said in a voice that wasn't quite steady, "He hasn't asked me, dear."

Rebecca turned her gaze to her father. "Why haven't you asked her? The two of you are virtually living together. You ought to make an honest woman of her."

Sir Anthony gasped. "I can't believe that I am hearing this from my own daughter. Have you no respect?"

"I learned outrageousness under my father's roof," Rebecca said, unrepentant. "Remarrying wouldn't be disloyal to Mother. She would not have wanted you to be alone. There are precious few women who would be as patient with an eccentric artist as Lavinia. She'll do a good job of managing the household after Lord Kimball leaves."

Looking on the verge of explosion, her father snapped, "If you say one more word, I will put you out to walk."

"At least my backside wouldn't be so sore," she said tartly.

Her father gave a snort of disgust and turned to look

out the window at the unremarkable green fields through which they were passing. At least a mile went by before Lavinia said in a small voice, "I didn't put Rebecca up to that, Anthony."

"I know," he said gruffly. "You would continue to put up with my selfishness indefinitely."

Speaking as if they were alone in the carriage, Lavinia said softly, "Of course I would. I've always loved you, you know."

"I know that. I've loved you, too, ever since you appeared in my studio when you were seventeen and modeled for the most delicious Jezebel ever painted."

He swallowed hard. "But I don't deserve the love of a generous, giving woman. I loved Helen, too, but I was a bad husband to her."

"You were the husband she wanted. And you are the husband I want." Lavinia's tone turned wry. "I've made a vocation of being outrageous, and I slept with a lot of men over the years because I couldn't sleep with the one I wanted. We're neither of us perfect, Anthony. It's better that way."

She reached across the coach. He grasped her hand convulsively. Rebecca turned her head discreetly to the scenery, ignoring the sounds of Lavinia shifting to the seat next to Sir Anthony and the soft murmurings between them. It sounded as if they were sorting matters out to their satisfaction.

Cheerful Lavinia would be an easier partner than Helen with her volatile moods. In fact, Rebecca realized, perhaps the reason her parents had indulged in affairs was because they were both so intense and emotional that they had needed relief from their marriage. Helen had found peace with steady George Hampton. Her father would do the same with Lavinia. It would be a different love than the tempestuous bond he had shared with Helen, but nonetheless valid.

She was happy for them. She really was. Yet as she stared sightlessly at the green countryside, she ached from the emptiness inside her. The brief happiness with Kenneth seemed like a mirage, one she would never see again.

Kenneth spent the day after the Seatons' departure looking for carpenters, painters, and plasterers. Luckily, an army friend who now worked for the Duke of Candover was able to refer him to reliable craftsmen. Kenneth also called on his solicitor to let him know of Hermione's likely marriage. The solicitor cordially loathed Lady Kimball and could be trusted to look out for the Wilding family interests.

After dinner, Kenneth wrote out detailed specifications for the remodeling job to guide Minton. The butler had turned out to be a very capable manager. Sir Anthony's next secretary would not have to be as involved in household matters as he himself had been.

When he finished the instructions, he opened the next volume of Helen Seaton's diary. The closer he came to the present, the more carefully he looked for hints of a secret enemy. She had recorded instances of jealousy, backbiting, and politics. However, he found no anecdotes that suggested possible danger.

Still, he enjoyed the reading. Helen was an excellent writer, amusing and able to skewer pretensions with a phrase. She had created a vivid portrait of almost three decades of English painting and painters. When he returned the diaries, he would suggest they be published in fifty years, when most of the people mentioned would be dead.

But there were parts that the family might want to edit out as being too personal. He was struck hard by a description of a miscarriage when Rebecca was about two years old.

The baby would have been a son. Oh, God, why can't I weep? I miss my mother desperately. At every major event of my life—my betrothal, my marriage, Rebecca's birth—I miss her almost as if she had died yesterday. Yet, still, I cannot weep. Perhaps there is a season for proper grieving, and mine has not yet arrived. Or perhaps I missed the right time and am now doomed to mourn forever, incomplete. My sorrow is like a vast, endless interior ocean, yet I cannot release it with tears.

Her words touched something deep inside him. He laid the diary down, his face rigid.

He had known his share of grief. Like Helen, for a long time his misery had been bottled up in his heart, almost forgotten except for a dull, chronic ache. It had taken Rebecca to teach him how to release his private horrors.

Ironically, she had given him the key to freedom while remaining trapped in her own grief. Like Helen, she mourned her mother's loss, and he guessed that, like Helen, she had never wept. Certainly he had never seen a sign of tears, even when her eyes were haunted by anguish.

Perhaps, when he saw her again, he would be able to help her find consolation. But for now, he knew beyond doubt that the time had come for him to paint his own last haunting image.

He headed upstairs to his studio. Watercolor would be best because of its fluid swiftness. He prayed that after he committed the image to paper, he would finally be free to use the emotions of his past as he chose rather than be crucified by them.

Kenneth worked until dawn to paint his last nightmare. Though it was not yet complete, in the process he found a weary sense of peace. The picture could be a commercial success, he supposed. Certainly it was dramatic. George Hampton would be delighted to add it to the Peninsular series. But some things were too private to reveal to the world. Rebecca was the only person he could imagine showing the picture to. The thought that they might never be on close terms again was chilling.

Again, most of the day was taken up in making arrangements for Seaton House. He pushed himself hard, hoping that in another two days he would be able to head north.

Though tired from lack of sleep, after dinner he started reading the third and last of Helen Seaton's diaries. In the early part, she revealed a growing sense of melancholia.

Why is it that the same things that make me happy in May are like ashes in January? This past week, life has been such an active horror that I have wondered if it would be best to go to sleep and never wake up. Certainly Anthony and Rebecca and George would be better off without me. Only the knowledge—gray, without hope, but undeniable—that things will get better keeps me from acting on my cowardice. That, and the fact that I lack the determination even to put an end to myself.

He shook his head after reading that passage. No wonder those close to her had worried about the possibility of suicide.

As the years passed, she ceased to make entries during the winter months. He guessed that writing took more energy than she possessed. Either that or she could not bear the misery of her own thoughts.

Yet he still found no clues as to who might be a lethal enemy. From sheer doggedness he kept reading.

Then, only a few pages from the end, he found an entry that shocked him into full wakefulness.

Anthony has painted the most wonderful portrait of me, laughing and looking wicked on the Ravensbeck lawn. He says that I am his muse. He put the portrait in the drawing room so that everyone could admire it after dinner tonight. Malcolm had an odd expression as he looked at it. He said the most absurd thing—that I was Anthony's heart. That without me, Anthony would no longer be a great artist.

Kenneth stared at the line as the pieces clicked grimly into place. The heart missing from the gimmal ring—that had not been a message from Helen, but from Frazier. He had removed the woman that he thought was Sir Anthony's heart and inspiration.

Great things had been expected of Frazier when he was young, but he had never fulfilled his early promise. His work had been stunted by the smallness and rigidity of his soul. For almost three decades, he had been condemned to watch as Sir Anthony's star had risen higher and higher.

What had started as a friendship of equals must have become warped by Frazier's jealousy and resentment. Kenneth remembered Frazier saying sorrowfully that Sir Anthony's work had not been the same since his wife's death. That had been wishful thinking, and the wish hadn't survived the exhibition success of the Waterloo pictures.

The final insult had come when Sir Anthony announced that he was Benjamin West's choice to become next president of the academy. In effect, he would be the head of the profession in Britain, while Frazier languished as an associate who had never been judged worthy of becoming a full academician.

Kenneth remembered that Frazier had been shocked and not particularly gracious when Sir Anthony announced the news. The firebomb had been thrown two days later. Frowning, he visualized the brief glimpse he had of the arsonist. It could have been Frazier.

He pulled out his watch and checked the time. Not quite midnight. Late, but not too late to confront a murderer.

He wouldn't mind if Frazier resisted; it would be a pleasure to beat the truth out of a man who could kill an innocent woman. Nonetheless, he loaded the small, sleek pistol that he kept in his wardrobe and tucked it into an inside pocket. Frazier was not the sort who would fight fair if he could avoid it.

To a fast walker, it was only fifteen minutes to Frazier's house. No lights visible, but Kenneth did not become concerned until he climbed the steps and reached for the knocker.

The knocker was gone.

He caught his breath as the anxiety he had been fighting for days erupted. Removing the knocker was the usual way of indicating that the owner was not in residence.

The bastard had left town.

CHAPTER 31

Rebecca was glad they had reached Ravensbeck after dark, for it meant that fatigue dulled her grief at the return. Luckily, Kenneth had sent a message that arrived in time for the staff to have prepared the bedrooms and a hot supper. The travelers ate, then went straight to bed.

After an exhausted sleep, Rebecca woke early. She slid out of bed and went to the window. She had been coming to the Lakes her whole life. Even so, the first view after months of absence was always breathtaking. Mist lay in the valleys with only peaks of the rugged hills rising above, like islands in a cloudy sea.

Though she had lived most of her life in London, she was always happiest in the country. Fewer people, fewer problems, cleaner air, and less noise. It suddenly occurred to her that there was no reason not to stay at Ravensbeck all year round.

She turned the idea over in her mind consideringly. Her father and Lavinia would have the London house to themselves, which would be appropriate for a new marriage. As for herself, she would have no shortage of subjects to paint. The landscape was worthy of a lifetime's work, and the local residents had wonderful strong, weathered faces. It would be as interesting as doing portraits in London.

Best of all, she would not have to see Kenneth. He was well on his way to becoming established as an artist; if she lived in London, he would be hard to avoid.

Heart a little lighter, she went down for a breakfast of coddled eggs, toasted bread, and strong tea. Her father and Lavinia had not come down yet. She was glad, for she wanted to go on the first of two private pilgrimages.

After cutting a bouquet of spring flowers, she rode a pony down to the village. There she tethered her mount by the church and walked to her mother's grave. The grass had grown into a delicate green blanket in the past nine months. The headstone her father had designed had also been installed. It read *Helen Cosgrove Seaton, 1768-1816. Beloved Wife, Mother, and Muse.*

The words brought an almost unendurable stab of pain. Rebecca laid the flowers on the grave, then stood with her head bowed for a long time, hoping for a sense of her mother's presence. But she felt nothing except her own grief.

She whispered, "No more melancholia, Mama." Then she turned and walked away.

As she came within sight of her pony, she was surprised to see Lavinia standing by another of the Ravensbeck mounts.

"I didn't want to disturb you," Lavinia said quietly.

Rebecca smiled a little at the bouquet the other woman held. "The gardener is going to be very cross with us."

"We can tell him to plant flowers here to spare his

garden." Lavinia hesitated. "You truly won't mind if I marry Anthony?"

"I truly won't," Rebecca assured her. "My father needs someone to take care of him when he becomes too involved with his work. It won't be me, since I'm no better."

"And of course you'll be marrying soon yourself."

Rebecca's face froze. "I doubt it."

The other woman's brows drew together. "The situation with Kenneth is that bad?"

"Yes," Rebecca said shortly. Not wanting to discuss Kenneth, she looked out across the vividly green valley. "Strange to think the Seaton family estate is less than ten miles away, yet I've never set foot in it. I met Lady Bowden this spring. She was nice in spite of the family feud."

"Margaret has always been a gracious lady. The feud is entirely by Bowden. I think Anthony would be glad to end it."

"You know Lord Bowden?"

"A little. He despises me." She smiled faintly. "He'll set another black mark against Anthony when we marry."

"The more fool he." Rebecca gave a parting nod and mounted her pony so Lavinia could have the same privacy she herself had wanted. Then she rode back to Ravensbeck. The first pilgrimage was over. Tomorrow she would make the second, more difficult one: to the cliff where her mother had died.

~

A ride in the black and maroon Royal Mail coaches made flogging look merciful. Dedicated entirely to rapid delivery of the mail, their creature comforts were nonexistent. The passengers were jammed together like herrings in a barrel, and stops for food were brief and infrequent. But passengers tolerated the discomfort because the Royal Mail was by far the fastest way to travel.

In a burst of extravagance brought on by his improving finances, Kenneth bought two seats for himself because the only way he would fit into the standard sixteen-inch width was if he were cut into pieces. The discomfort was worth it, for he would reach Kendal, the town nearest Ravensbeck, in a mere two days—only a day and a half after the Seatons themselves arrived.

Throughout the long journey, he told himself that he was starting at shadows. There was no reason to believe Frazier had gone to the Lake District to cause more trouble. So far, his campaign against Sir Anthony had been sporadic, to say the least.

But the amateur bomb that had set fire to Seaton House had seemed like a declaration of war. The risk that Rebecca might be caught in the crossfire was not one Kenneth wanted to take.

His anxiety built steadily as he traveled north. At Kendal's largest inn, he used his title and military manner shamelessly to hire the landlord's own horse. It was a powerful beast, easily able to carry Kenneth and his modest luggage. He set off immediately for Ravensbeck.

He had never been in the Lake District before, and he was fascinated by the desolate splendor of the countryside. On any other trip, he would have been stopping to admire the views, perhaps to sketch or do a swift watercolor. This time, he pushed on as quickly as he could. There would be time to enjoy the scenery after he knew Rebecca was safe.

Lady Bowden finished the last of her tea and set the cup down with a delicate chink of porcelain. Then she raised her head and regarded her husband gravely. "I'm told that Anthony and his daughter have arrived at Ravensbeck for the summer."

Bowden froze, his teacup halfway to his lips. "And what concern is that of yours, Margaret?"

Lady Bowden linked her hands in her lap. "It's a lovely day. I am going to drive over to Ravensbeck to offer my condolences on Helen's death, as I should have done last summer."

Her husband slammed down his cup. "We will have nothing to do with any member of that household!"

"Perhaps you will not, but I will," she said in a steely voice. "For all of the years of our marriage, I have ignored your obsession with Helen and your hatred for your brother, but no longer. Anthony and Helen fell in love and married. That was unmannerly, but hardly a crime. It was pure malice to hire that nice young man to try to prove that Anthony is a murderer."

His jaw dropped. "How did you learn about that?"

"Your own impatience gave it away." She got to her feet. "You never really knew Helen. She was a tempestuous woman who would have made you very uncomfortable. She had affairs, you know. Would you have wanted that in a wife? Hardly. It is time to stop mooning after her like a boy of seventeen."

He rose, sputtering, "I forbid you to go to Ravensbeck!"

"Will you hold me prisoner, my lord husband?" she asked with delicate sarcasm. "Will you bar me from my own house after I visit your brother? I don't think so."

"Have you been pining for Anthony all of these years?"

he said savagely. "Visiting him secretly like his other whores?"

Her voice turned to ice. "Don't be an utter fool, Marcus. You can accompany me or not, but you cannot stop me."

She turned and left the room, her hands shaking. In all the years of her marriage, she had never tested her influence over her husband. It was quite possible she had exceeded whatever small power she had. But twenty-eight years was long enough to live in the shadow of another woman. It was time to gamble in the hopes of bringing her marriage into the sun.

~

Lord Bowden sank into his seat, feeling as if the floor beneath his feet had cracked and he was on the verge of falling into the abyss. How could Margaret betray him so?

Yet weren't his years of obsession for another woman a kind of betrayal of his wife? Occasionally he had seen Helen in the distance in London. He had stared avidly, wondering what their life would have been like if Anthony hadn't come between them. Yet if Margaret was right about Helen's temperament and affairs, it was true that he had never really known her.

He thought of Helen and her beauty, and realized that what he felt was not love but the memory of love. The woman of his dreams would not have abandoned him for another man. That woman existed only in his imagination.

Anthony and Helen fell in love and married. That was unmannerly, but hardly a crime.

If Anthony had caused Helen's death, it was certainly a crime. But had there been a murder? Once, he had been convinced of it. The missing portion of the gimmal ring that Kimball had discovered had seemed proof positive. Now he had to wonder. How much of his conviction had stemmed from a desire to punish Anthony for being Helen's choice?

Too much.

A spasm of pain ripped through him. Who in his life had brought him the greatest comfort and happiness? Margaret. He had known her since she was a sweet-natured infant. Through the years of their marriage, she had wrapped him in a cocoon of kindness and comfort. Now, in a handful of words, she had withdrawn the love and loyalty he had always taken for granted.

Sometimes, Bowden realized, one doesn't know what one values until it's gone.

He went to the stables and ordered his horse to be saddled. Then he set off after his wife, not knowing if he was going to try to stop her or join her.

At breakfast Rebecca announced, "I'm going to take a picnic and spend the day drawing."

Sir Anthony glanced up absently. "What direction shall we send the search parties if you forget to return for dinner?"

"West. I thought I might walk to Skelwith Crag."

He gave a nod of understanding. She guessed that he would make his own pilgrimage to the cliff when he was ready.

Rebecca packed a basket with drawing supplies, bread, cheese, and two small jugs, one holding cider and the other water for watercolor painting. Then she set off.

It was cooler in the Lake District than London, and

snow was still on the highest hills. She took a shawl for warmth. The crisp air was bracing. More and more she liked the idea of living permanently at Ravensbeck.

In no hurry to reach her destination, she walked at a leisurely pace and collected wildflowers on the way.

But finally, filled with trepidation, she arrived at Skelwith Crag.

Despite the name, it was not a high, bare mountaintop but a tall hill crowned with birches. One face was sheered away, which created a breathtaking view over a fertile river valley.

She emerged from the birch grove and set her basket on the ground. Then, as the wind whipped through her hair, she took note of each familiar landmark.

Six mirror-smooth lakes and tarns were visible, and several tumbling little rivers, full now from the snowmelt. Rugged hills beyond counting, with well-cultivated dales in between. It was a lovely view for the last moments of one's life.

Then she deliberately studied the crag itself. Rather than a sharp drop-off, the cliff had a slanting brow that sloped gradually at first, then with increasing sharpness until it reached the final, fatal drop. It would not be impossible for someone to absently walk farther than was safe.

Accident? Suicide? Murder? She doubted they would ever know for sure. She felt a deep ache, and wondered if she would ever be able to weep for her mother.

One by one, she threw the flowers over the edge and watched them drift on the wind to the valley far below. Then she found a sunny, protected corner and settled down with her back against a convenient stone. Rebecca thought that a religious person might have prayed for her mother's soul. She opened her watercolors.

Helen Seaton would have understood.

~

Frazier went to an attic window of his leased house and raised his telescope to scan the river valley. His gaze went automatically to Skelwith Crag. He expected to see nothing, but someone was there. A woman in a dark blue gown, sitting.

He caught his breath with sudden excitement when he realized that Anthony's damned daughter was there sketching. Perfect.

He went to his room for the slender gold band, then down to the stables. The ride would take about an hour. Since she was drawing, she should still be there when he arrived.

But she wouldn't be for much longer.

~

Kenneth arrived at Ravensbeck by late morning, his horse lathered with exertion. Ignoring the charms of the weathered gray limestone house, he took the front steps three at a time. The door was unlocked, so he walked in.

A footman who had come from London emerged to greet him. "Lord Kimball, you're here early," he said with surprise. "Impatient to see Miss Rebecca, I've no doubt."

"Exactly. Where is she?"

"I believe she's gone walking in the hills."

Kenneth swore. "What about Sir Anthony? Or Lady Claxton?"

"They're in the gardens. Shall I take you there?"

Barely curbing his impatience, Kenneth said, "Please."

Sir Anthony and Lavinia were enjoying the pale sunshine when Kenneth arrived. His employer said jovially, "You've completed the rebuilding arrangements already? If you'd been in charge of the army, Napoleon would have been defeated in six months."

After dismissing the footman, Kenneth said, "I came because I'm concerned for your safety. Is Frazier in the neighborhood?"

"Not that I know of."

"Perhaps he is," Lavinia remarked. "One of the local maids said this morning that all the Londoners seemed to be coming early this year. I didn't think much about it at the time. But Frazier has a summer house only a few miles away. Perhaps the girl was referring to his arrival."

Kenneth swore again. "I believe he threw the bomb into Seaton House and that he killed Lady Seaton last summer."

There was a moment of frozen silence. Then Sir Anthony sputtered, "That's absurd! Helen's death was accidental. It's insane to say she was killed by one of my oldest friends."

Kenneth shook his head. "It was an improbable accident. I gather that her intimates suspected suicide, which is why no one will speak of her death."

Sir Anthony's face paled. "You've been talking to Rebecca."

He nodded. "From what she said, if Lady Seaton were to take her life, it would probably have been in the winter, when her melancholia was at its worst. Not in the summer."

Lavinia laid her hand over Sir Anthony's. "Listen to him, my dear. He's making sense, especially about Malcolm Frazier. Frazier's voice is always edged when he speaks of you. His resentment of your success might have overcome his friendship and made him capable of doing what Kenneth said."

While Anthony stared at his mistress, Kenneth said impatiently, "I'll explain later, but first I want to find Rebecca. Do you know where she went on her walk?"

"To Skelwith Crag, where Helen died," Sir Anthony replied.

Lavinia's brows drew together. "I think the crag is visible from Frazier's house. If he is in residence, he could see her there. But surely he would have no reason to hurt Rebecca."

"Why would he kill Lady Seaton?" Kenneth retorted. "I think he's more than a little mad, and I don't want to take chances. Is there a groom who can guide me to the crag?"

"I'll take you there myself." Sir Anthony got to his feet. "Though I don't believe you, your concern is infectious."

"Then let's go *now*. By horseback."

Ten interminable minutes later, they set off at a brisk canter. As the men rode, Kenneth began to give terse explanations. When he described Lord Bowden's assignment and his own covert role, Sir Anthony said dryly, "So Marcus is the one responsible for finding me a secretary. I think I'll write him a thank you note. He'll hate knowing he did me a service."

Surprised, Kenneth said, "You can forgive my deceit?"

Sir Anthony gave him a shrewd glance. "You may have entered the house falsely, but that doesn't mean you're treacherous."

"I wish Rebecca were so tolerant."

"Ah. So that's why she isn't wearing your ring."

"I didn't realize you had noticed that."

"I notice a great deal, but thought it better not to

meddle any further." They came to a fork in the trail and Sir Anthony turned onto the left branch. "My daughter has a problem with trusting, I fear. It's easier for her to believe the worst of people."

"I've given her cause," Kenneth said grimly.

Sir Anthony sighed. "She was such a quiet little girl. She never seemed upset by the irregularities of the artistic world, or by her mother's volatile moods, or my self-absorption. It wasn't until she ran off with that idiot poet that I realized we had failed to give her the stability a child needs. By that time, it was too late to really repair the damage. I worry about her. Except for her work, she has become so closed in. That was why I thought you would be good for her. She needs a man who is steady. Someone she can rely on, no matter what."

Sir Anthony's analysis of his daughter certainly explained why she had taken it so badly when she learned that Kenneth had violated her family's trust. It had been easy for her to think the worst, and his own guilt and confusion about his future hadn't helped. But, by God, Kenneth knew now what he wanted.

Putting the thought aside, he described why he believed Frazier was a murderer and arsonist. As Sir Anthony listened, his doubtful expression changed to shocked acceptance.

When Kenneth finished, the painter said, "If Helen didn't kill herself..." His voice broke. "You can't know what that means to me." His face showed grief and anger, but also relief that a terrible burden had been lifted.

They fell into silence. Kenneth pushed the pace hard across the rough countryside. The anxiety he had first felt when Rebecca left London had intensified to near panic even though his head told him he was worrying needlessly.

Rebecca would be painting a landscape and snappish at being interrupted. She would tell him acerbically that he was a fool to carry on so.

He would never be so happy to be wrong if he lived to be a hundred.

CHAPTER 32

"Good day, Rebecca."

She almost jumped from her skin as a familiar voice sounded from a dozen feet away. Her concentration and the constant soughing of the wind had kept her from noticing his approach.

She glanced up, holding her sopping brush to one side so it wouldn't dribble onto her picture. "Good day, Lord Frazier," she said coolly. "I didn't know you intended to come north so soon."

"I came on impulse." He gazed at the vista, tapping his thigh idly with his riding crop, every inch the London gentleman.

She thought dryly that it was a pity he hadn't stayed in London. It was tiresome to have him underfoot all the time. The man seemed to have no independent life—he existed as a satellite of her father. But he must be treated politely. "The lake country is a welcome relief after the city."

He dug into his waistcoat pocket. "I had a mission—to give you a small gift."

Not wanting anything from him, she said, "If it's a

betrothal present, I must decline. Lord Kimball and I have decided we shall not suit."

"It's not a betrothal present." His lips curved into something that was not a smile. "At least, not for *your* betrothal. Here."

He extended his hand. She reluctantly reached out and he dropped a small object into her palm.

It was the missing heart band from her mother's gimmal ring.

She stared at the slim band, feeling a chill that struck to her bones. Kenneth had been right. Her mother had been murdered, and by her father's friend.

In the wake of understanding came suffocating fear. *Pretend ignorance.* "What a pretty ring. Thank you, Lord Frazier."

"Put it on," he ordered.

Uneasily she slipped the band onto the ring finger of her left hand. "It's a little loose." She started to remove it.

"Leave it on," he commanded. "Helen was larger than you, but no matter. The ring is necessary."

Desperate to leave, she said brightly, "I'll tell my father you've arrived. I'm sure he'll want you to dine with us tonight. I'll see you then."

She started to pack her drawing supplies in her basket.

"Don't bother with that," he drawled. "You don't need your watercolors to join your mother."

The most frightening thing was his utter calm. He might have been discussing the weather.

Still dissembling, she said, "I don't understand."

He flexed his riding crop between his hands. "I think you do. You're a mousy little creature, but not stupid. Still grieving over your mother's sad end, you will join her in death. No one who saw your *Transfiguration* painting will be surprised. A pity the significance of the ring will not be understood. It's the details that make a picture."

Her chances of escape were almost nil; he was tall and strong, and his coolness increased the menace. Perhaps if she could discompose him, it might work to her advantage. "If you kill me, Kenneth will know. He deduced that Mother was murdered. He'll realize that the same thing happened to me."

Frazier only shrugged. "Kimball must be more clever than he looks, but it won't do him or you any good. I had already planned to eliminate him. The man irritates me, preening over the shallow praise for his ugly paintings."

"You can't hurt him," she said scornfully. "He's a soldier, a man of action. He could break you in half with his bare hands."

"Even men of action die when they take a bullet in the heart," he said imperturbably. "I may not be a soldier, but I am an excellent marksman." He started toward her.

Her heart clenched with fear. "Why are you doing this?" she cried. "My father has been your friend! How can you let your jealousy turn you into a murderer?"

Frazier paused. "Anthony *is* my friend—my dearest friend in the world. The only thing I love more is art. My actions have not been aimed at Anthony, but at the wicked influences that have corrupted his work."

She stared at him. "Corrupted his work? He is the finest painter in England. His portraits, his landscapes, his historical paintings—all are brilliant."

Frazier's face twisted with the first emotion he had shown. "It's all *rubbish.* Helen ruined Anthony as an artist. When we were students at the Royal Academy Schools, he had a passion for all that was highest and best in art. His early paintings in the Grand Manner were glorious—full of nobility and refinement."

"They were beautifully executed but not very memorable," she shot back. "It wasn't until he finished his schooling that he developed a distinctive style and vision."

Frazier's knuckles whitened on his riding crop. "Helen *destroyed* him! To support her, he turned to tawdry portraits and vulgar paintings that Hampton could engrave and sell to any fishmonger with a shilling in his pocket. Anthony could have been the equal of Reynolds! Instead, he dishonored his talent."

Horribly fascinated by his warped thinking, she said, "Do you consider *Horatius at the Bridge* to be a disgrace?"

Frazier spat on the ground. "A perfect example of what is wrong with his work. A resonant classical theme, superb execution. It could have been brilliant—but he spoiled the picture with blatant emotionalism. A pity it didn't burn in the studio fire. The ideal of the Grand Manner is to transcend nature, not wallow in it."

"My father transcends the Grand Manner," she said dryly. "He and other real artists show the world in fresh ways. They don't regurgitate the same tired scenes over and over."

"Kimball was right when he said you had great influence on Anthony's work." He angrily slapped his riding crop into his left palm. "I had thought the real problem was Helen, that after her death he would return to more worthy painting. But how could he, with you spouting stupid female ideas about art? When I saw your work in the exhibition, I realized what an insidious influence you have been on him. A pity that foolish poet I sent after you wasn't more competent."

It was another stunning shock. "Did you hire Frederick to seduce me?" she said incredulously.

"Nothing so formal. I merely pointed out how romantic red hair was, and how wealthy you would be someday. His own fevered imagination took care of the rest." Frazier shook his head. "If you'd married him and moved from under your father's roof, it wouldn't have come to this. You have only yourself to blame."

"That is the most ridiculous thing you've said yet." Rebecca rested her hand on the water jug used for rinsing her brush, and tensed in readiness. "No wonder you're such a poor painter. You have terrible judgment and no sense for truth. Your Leonidas was pathetic. I was a better artist when I was ten."

Her words were the final straw that snapped his control. He lunged at her furiously. She screamed at the top of her lungs on the chance that a shepherd or walker might hear. At the same time she lifted the water jug and hurled it at Frazier. It smashed into his face, water spraying into his eyes. As he howled with pain, she bolted from her sitting position and ran to the right, away from him. When she was clear of the rocky ledge she had been sitting against, she pivoted into the birch grove.

She had barely made it to the first trees when he recovered and came after her. His long strides closed the distance in seconds. He grabbed and caught her shawl. She let it slither from her shoulders and kept running even though she knew escape was impossible. A moment later he caught her arm and jerked her around. Blood streamed down his face and his handsome features were distorted in a mask of rage. She screamed again and slashed at him with clawed fingers.

"Damn you!" He slammed his fist into her midriff with

stunning force, knocking her to the ground. Her head banged into the soil and her breath was blasted from her body, leaving her dizzy and incapable of movement.

As he loomed over her, she lay eerily helpless, able to see and hear but without strength to resist. She was at the mercy of a madman, and in a few moments she would become the falling woman who had haunted her nightmares.

Sir Anthony pointed ahead. "This is Skelwith Hill. The crag is on the other side of that birch grove."

A woman's scream cut through the air, followed an instant later by a masculine bellow.

"Christ! Rebecca!" Kenneth kicked his horse into a gallop and bolted ahead of his companion. He entered the trees first and drove his mount through at a lethal speed, flattening along the beast's neck so he wouldn't be knocked off by a branch. As he wove through the trees, Rebecca screamed again.

He emerged from the grove almost on the edge of the precipice. As he wrenched the terrified horse to a halt, he saw a scene that scorched his mind like a brand of fire. A bloody Frazier was half-carrying, half-dragging Rebecca toward the cliff. Her limp body hung like a broken doll, her red hair and blue dress whipping in the gusty wind.

It was a tableau of death.

He reacted instinctively, vaulting from his horse and shouting furiously to rattle his opponent. As he charged forward, he pulled his pistol from inside his coat and cocked it.

Frazier took two long steps toward the brink and raised

Rebecca before him like a shield. "Stay away from me, Kimball!"

Kenneth stopped in his tracks. Then he lowered the pistol, his heart hammering with fear. If Frazier made one false step, he and his captive would both go over the cliff. "If you kill Rebecca, you're a dead man, Frazier. Let me have her. You can go free." He took a wary step toward the other man.

"Stop or I'll take both of us over," Frazier said wildly. His eyes were crazed, like a cornered boar.

Kenneth halted again, unsure how to deal with a madman. Frazier's facade of normality had disintegrated, and the first victim of his panic would be Rebecca. She was disheveled and seemed stunned from her struggle. But Kenneth saw awareness in her eyes. She knew how close she was to death.

In the tense silence, Sir Anthony rode from the woods. He reined in his horse, his face white with horror when he saw his daughter. Dismounting, he said with attempted calm, "The joke has gone far enough, Malcolm. Bring Rebecca to me."

A muscle jerked in Frazier's face. "This isn't a joke, Anthony. I had hoped to persuade you to return to real art, but I've bungled it. There is no going back." He glanced down at Rebecca, his face indecisive. "At least she'll pay for her part in ruining your work. You should have avoided becoming entangled with women, Anthony. They're good only for bedding and forgetting. Listening to them is poison to a serious artist."

Sir Anthony shook his head. "No woman poisoned my work. Not Helen, not Rebecca, not Lavinia. Any failings are my own."

"If you had been allowed to develop naturally, without

the pressures of supporting a family, you could have been another Raphael!" Frazier said stubbornly. "Instead of a handful of great works, you have produced a mountain of rubbish."

"We will never agree on this." Sir Anthony began to move cautiously toward Frazier. "For God's sake, don't take your disagreement out on my only child! If you must throw someone off this damned cliff, let it be me, not Rebecca."

The other man said in an agonized voice, "I could never hurt you. You're my friend. My best friend."

In Frazier's face was a dawning realization that he had already lost everything he cared for—his friendship with Sir Anthony and his position in the art world. He was a coward and a bully, and Kenneth knew with absolute certainty that in another moment, he would escape from his unbearable dilemma by jumping and taking his captive with him from sheer vindictiveness.

There was no time to waste. While Frazier's attention was on Sir Anthony, Kenneth smoothly raised his pistol and sighted on Frazier's head. Though he ran the risk of hitting Rebecca, shooting her captor was her best hope.

At the same instant Kenneth squeezed the trigger, Frazier made up his mind and took an ungainly step toward the precipice, changing the position of both him and his captive. Kenneth watched in horror as the bullet slammed into Frazier's shoulder so close to Rebecca's head that it might have struck her, too.

Frazier gave a shriek of pain and spun around, dropping his captive. Rebecca fell farther down the slope, hitting the ground hard.

Then slowly, inexorably, she began rolling down the angled brow of the cliff toward the final drop-off.

CHAPTER 33

As Sir Anthony gave an agonized cry that echoed across the rocky hills, Kenneth sprinted toward the cliff and dived down the angled surface. He landed hard on his belly with his right arm reaching for Rebecca. She was just beyond his grasp, her limp body on the verge of tumbling over the brink.

He propelled himself forward and managed to catch her slender wrist. She stopped with a jerk that strained his arm. For an instant they were still, both of them flattened on the slanting surface like starfish. Then they began sliding slowly downward, drawn by the implacable force of gravity.

As he dug his toes and left hand into the rough ground, the wind whipped her hair sideways and he saw with horror that dark crimson blood was saturating the auburn strands. If the bullet had struck her before hitting Frazier, she might already be dead.

But he would not let her fall. He made a wide sweep with his left arm and caught a scrawny shrub. It pulled up in seconds but held long enough for him to grasp another stronger bush.

Temporarily they were safe, but it was a precarious balance. The angle of the slope was so steep that they would slide downward without his hold on the bush, and already his left arm was shaking from the strain of supporting their weight.

He glanced to his left. The next suitable handhold was a couple of feet beyond his reach. If he were alone he could probably have scrambled up to it, but that was impossible when Rebecca's weight was dragging him downward.

Though he doubted she could hear, he said through gritted teeth, "Trust me, Ginger, we're not going over."

But it was bravado. A tremor ran through the shrub that was his handhold. When it broke, they would both go over the edge. Perhaps Sir Anthony could help—but he was a light man. Unless he found a secure grip, he would be pulled down with them.

Then suddenly the wind gusted violently, shoving against their prone bodies. It shouldn't have made a difference—but for an instant Kenneth was relieved of most of Rebecca's weight. At the same moment he got a burst of extra strength. He released the failing shrub and kicked against the sloping surface, driving himself upward until his clawing fingers caught a deep-seated rock two feet farther from the brink.

Panting with exertion, he pulled Rebecca toward him until he could wrap his right arm around her. Then he dragged them both upward, the muscles of his left arm shaking with the strain of supporting two bodies.

When he was as high as he could go, he rested for a moment, drawing great ragged gulps of breath. Then he reached for another handhold. The angle was becoming shallower, and each foot was easier to achieve than the one before.

It took half a dozen more moves up the rough slope to reach the safety of level ground. Too exhausted to stand, he lay gasping for breath, Rebecca's limp form cradled against him as if sheer proximity would ward off harm. But Christ, where was her pulse? He felt her throat and couldn't find it. Despairing, he sat up and laid his hand in the center of her chest. There he found the steady, blessed beat of her heart.

Weak with relief, he looked up. Though it had seemed like a terrifying eternity, very little time had passed since he had fired his pistol. Sir Anthony was racing toward them while Frazier stood swaying in shock, his right hand pressed to his bleeding left shoulder.

As Sir Anthony dropped to his knees by his daughter, he said furiously, "You'll hang for what you've done, Malcolm. Before God, I swear it!"

Frazier jerked as if he had been struck. Then his expression changed to cool arrogance. "I lived and painted in the Grand Manner," he drawled, "and I shall die that way as well."

He turned, straightened to his full height, and walked off the cliff.

He did not cry out as he fell. If there was a sound when he hit the stones below, it was carried away on the wind.

"The fool," Sir Anthony swore. "The stupid, bloody fool. He had talent and wealth and a passion for art. Why did he become a murderer?"

As Kenneth examined Rebecca's wound, he said tersely, "Frazier's real passion wasn't art, but imposing his ideas on the world."

He had also loved Sir Anthony too much and in the wrong way, Kenneth thought, so his unadmitted resentment had been turned against the women who were close to his friend.

Sir Anthony drew his daughter into his arms, her blood staining his white shirt. "Did... did the bullet strike her?"

"No. She gashed her head when she hit the stone. Scalp wounds bleed like the very devil, but her breathing and heartbeat are strong. I think she'll be all right." Kenneth pulled out his handkerchief and folded it into a pad, then yanked off his cravat and bound the fabric tightly to her head.

He stood, then bent and lifted Rebecca in his arms. She looked heartbreakingly fragile. Yet she had managed to fight off a man twice her size long enough to save her life. Indomitable Ginger. He brushed a tender kiss on her forehead. "Time to take her home."

When they reached Ravensbeck, Kenneth carried Rebecca directly into the drawing room and laid her on a brocade sofa while Sir Anthony shouted for medical supplies and for a doctor to be summoned posthaste. Chaos ensued, with servants running every which way, the more excitable ones weeping.

Lavinia appeared and imposed order, then efficiently cleaned Rebecca's wound and put on a better bandage. Kenneth sat on the arm of the sofa and kept a hand on Rebecca's shoulder, unable to bear having her beyond his reach.

Sir Anthony was pacing anxiously about the drawing room when a startled male voice said, "Good God, what has happened? Have you been shot, Anthony?"

Kenneth glanced up to see Lord and Lady Bowden standing in the open door. Probably the front door had been left open and they had walked in. But why were they at Ravensbeck?

As Sir Anthony stared at the visitors in shock, Bowden strode toward him, his alarmed gaze on the blood-soaked shirt.

Sir Anthony ran trembling fingers through his disordered hair. "I'm fine, Marcus. My daughter has been hurt, but Kenneth says she should be all right."

Bowden looked across the room to where Rebecca lay unconscious. "What the devil happened?"

"One of my oldest friends went mad and tried to kill her," Sir Anthony said tersely. "He had already killed Helen."

There was an appalled silence. Bowden's gaze went to Kenneth, who said, "It's true. Lord Frazier was the villain."

Recovering his irony, Sir Anthony said, "To what do I owe the honor of this highly unexpected visit, Marcus?"

Bowden said stiffly, "Margaret told me in no uncertain terms that I've been a stark-raving idiot where you and Helen were concerned and that it was time to make my apologies."

"You know I would never use such intemperate language, Marcus," Lady Bowden said with gentle reproach.

Sir Anthony smiled. "You haven't changed, Margaret. It's good to see you." He took her hand and squeezed it affectionately before turning to his brother. "She's made you a much better wife, you know. Helen was not at all biddable. She would have driven you mad."

Bowden's face worked. "I'm a lucky man." He gave his wife a look of mingled love and apology. "And a thrice-damned fool for not having realized it sooner."

"Things happen in their own time, my dear. Before, you were not ready to hear what I had to say." Lady Bowden touched his arm gently. Her expression made it clear that she was supremely content with her husband's new attitude.

Bowden swallowed hard. "After the way I have behaved, will you allow me under your roof, Anthony?"

His brother said quietly, "You would always have been welcome, Marcus. Always." He extended his hand.

Bowden took it in a grip that started tentatively, but quickly became heartfelt.

Thinking it was time to leave the brothers to become reacquainted, Kenneth said to Lavinia, "I'll take Rebecca to her room. She needs peace and quiet."

Lavinia gave a nod of agreement. "I'll show you the way."

Kenneth carefully lifted Rebecca. Still unconscious, she gave a small sigh and rested her head against his shoulder.

Lord Bowden turned to study her pale face. "She is very like Helen," he said with a note of wonder.

"Helen's looks, and my talent." Sir Anthony took the knee rug from the sofa and tucked it over his daughter. "Yet in temperament, she resembles you more than she does Helen or me. Strange how these things happen."

Bowden smiled wryly. "My younger son is very like you. Charming. Clever. Maddening. I'm trying to be more understanding than Father was with you."

Sir Anthony glanced at Lavinia and said with a challenge in his voice, "I believe you know Lady Claxton. We intend to marry when I am out of mourning."

That might have been too much for Lord Bowden, Kenneth thought, but not his wife.

Lady Bowden took Lavinia's hand and said warmly, "How wonderful. Helen once said that if anything happened to her, she hoped you would marry Anthony, since you were her best friend and the only woman she knew who would take proper care of him."

Her husband said with horrified fascination, "You and Helen were in communication?"

His wife's lashes swept enigmatically over her soft blue eyes. "Our paths sometimes crossed in town."

Bowden shook his head, then said with determined graciousness, "Please accept my best wishes, Lady Claxton."

"Thank you, Lord Bowden," she said sweetly. "And don't worry. I'm not half so wicked as you think." Then she escorted Kenneth from the room.

He carried Rebecca up the stairs, his spirits lighter than they had been in weeks. An estrangement that had lasted nearly three decades had been healed.

Perhaps there was hope for him and Rebecca.

~

Rebecca awoke to darkness and a throbbing head. She blinked muzzily and realized that she was lying in her bed in a room illuminated by a small fire and a lamp shielded to keep the light from her eyes. The faint, familiar scratch of a steel drawing pen came from her left.

She turned her head and saw Kenneth sitting in an upholstered chair a few feet from the bed. He had a drawing board across his lap and was carefully adding detail to what appeared to be a watercolor. He looked tired, and the planes of his face were harsh in the dim light.

She wanted to go to him and kiss the shadows from his eyes. She settled for swallowing against the dryness of her throat, then whispering, "Trust an artist to stop and sketch the flames when Nero is burning Rome."

He glanced up with a smile that transformed his expression. "You sound remarkably clear-headed." He set the drawing board aside. "How do you feel?"

"Fragile." She ran her tongue over dry lips. "Thirsty."

He poured a glass of water. When he brought it to her, she pushed herself to a sitting position and drank, sipping slowly until her mouth felt normal again.

Feeling much better, she mounded the pillows into a backrest. "How long have I been unconscious?"

"About ten hours."

"What... what happened?"

He took his seat again. "What do you remember last?"

She thought. "Lord Frazier hitting me in the midriff so hard that I couldn't move. A very strange and unpleasant sensation. He was hauling me toward the cliff when you thundered up like a regiment of cavalry. You're a fearsome sight, Captain."

"I've had a lot of practice," he said modestly.

"Papa came, and a gun fired. You shot Frazier, didn't you? I don't remember anything after that." Gingerly she touched the bandage on her head. "Was I hit by the bullet?"

"No, but Frazier was, and he dropped you on your head." Kenneth smiled a little. "Luckily, that's stone hard. According to the doctor, there is no serious damage. Frazier wasn't critically wounded, but when he realized that his sins were about to catch up with him, he stepped off the cliff."

The image of a falling man crossed her mind. Her mouth tightened. "If I were saintly, I might feel sympathy for his madness. Instead, I'm glad he's dead. If I'd had a pistol and known how to use it, I would have shot him myself."

"Personally, I would have liked to see him hang. Very publicly. But this spares you and your father the strain of a trial, so perhaps it's for the best." Kenneth glanced toward the fire. "There's soup warming on the hearth. Would you like some?"

She nodded, and he went to ladle soup into two mugs. Only then did the realization sink in that her mother had been murdered. *It hadn't been suicide.*

Helen Seaton had not taken her own life because of inner demons; Rebecca and her father had not failed her mother. The knowledge produced a rush of relief so intense that it left Rebecca shaky.

When Kenneth brought her a warm mug of soup, she accepted it gratefully. It was a creamy potato leek blend. Delicious. Warmth and strength began flowing through her.

Suddenly aware of the incongruity of his presence, she asked, "Why are you here?"

"I came up from London because of something I found in your mother's diary." Between sips of his soup, he gave a succinct explanation of what he had discovered and his trip north, then continued, "The specific reason I'm in your bedroom is that I ruthlessly intimidated Lavinia, your father, and Lady Bowden, all of whom wanted to stay with you until you awoke. Luckily, I'm far larger than they are."

She blinked. "Lady Bowden?"

"The other main event of the day was Bowden and your father reestablishing relations."

"What!"

He chuckled as he sat down with his own mug. "I suspect that Lady Bowden told her husband it was time to grow up, and threatened to kick him out of bed if he didn't."

She smiled at the thought of her elegant aunt saying any such thing. No doubt Lady Bowden had been more subtle, but after so many years of marriage, she must have known what notes to strike. "I'm so glad. I think Papa regretted the estrangement. There was a wistful note in his voice whenever he mentioned his brother."

"I wonder if Bowden ever really believed your father was a murderer," Kenneth said pensively. "Since he had too much pride to end the estrangement, his desire for an investigation was a way to stay connected to Helen and Sir Anthony. To be indifferent would have been to lose them both."

"A classic example of how love and hate are opposite sides of the same coin." Images began flickering through her mind. "There's a painting in that somewhere."

"Now who's drawing the flames while Rome burns?" he said with amusement.

She finished her soup and set the mug on the bedside table. "Bowden must be pleased with the outcome of your investigation."

Kenneth nodded. "He's canceling the mortgages. It seems far too great a payment for what I did, but he insists on fulfilling the terms of the original agreement."

"You found the murderer and indirectly paved the way for Lord Bowden to reconcile with Father," she said quietly. "I think he got a bargain."

"Ah, but I also met you, which would never have happened otherwise. That would have been payment enough."

Kenneth set his mug aside and leaned forward, his face taut with emotion. "Now that I'm in a position to marry, I give you fair warning. I'm going to do my damnedest to coax you to the altar. I can't change the reason I came to Seaton House, but I hope it counts for something that I love you rather desperately." His eyes darkened. "I... I didn't fully realize how much until I came so close to losing you forever."

He reached into his pocket and brought out the gimmal ring. "I found the heart band on your finger and joined it with the other pieces." He handed it to her. "The ring is whole again."

She stared at the ring, almost suffocated by the chaotic emotions that his words triggered. Terrified by their intensity, she set the ring aside and said in a frantic attempt to change the subject, "What were you drawing?"

The scar on his face whitened at her blatant rejection. After a moment, he said, "I was inking in some details on a watercolor, but I don't think the picture is suitable for showing a convalescent."

"That sounds irresistibly interesting," she said lightly.

He shrugged and lifted the drawing board. "It's a picture of what used to be my worst nightmare," he said as he set the board across her lap. "I have a new nightmare now—the sight of you being dragged toward a cliff by a madman."

His watercolor picture strikingly depicted a massive tree set in a sun-seared Spanish plain. It was dawn, the sky was clear and delicately tinted—and from the branches hung the bodies of a man and a woman. The woman's long black hair floated in the wind, mercifully obscuring her face.

Rebecca felt a visceral shock of understanding. "Maria's death?"

He nodded, his face rigid. "About the only comfort I had after I was captured and the rest of the guerrilla band was executed was knowing that Maria was a long way off, and her older brother Domingo was with her. I was put in chains and sent across country to the French headquarters. We rode until well after dark, then stopped at a campsite by a tree. It was too late to build a fire, so we had bread and cheese and wine in the dark, then rolled up in our blankets.

"But I... I couldn't sleep. I knew something was horribly

wrong, but had no idea what. Finally I woke the officer in charge of me and made him move thirty or forty paces away. It wasn't quite as awful there, though I still didn't sleep. Then the sun rose and... and I saw Maria and Domingo."

"How horrible for you!" Her throat was so tight she could barely speak. "I wonder that you didn't go mad."

"I did for a time." He closed his eyes with a spasm of pain. "Two days later, I managed to escape. I went back to my regiment and refused to do reconnaissance work again. It was Michael who saved my sanity. I never spoke of what happened, but he recognized desperation because he had experienced it himself, I think. He was always there, knowing when to talk and when to be silent, until the madness had passed."

Rebecca reached across the distance that separated them and took Kenneth's hand. Touching him was like an electric shock, intensifying the emotions that pulsed through the room.

"Maria died for Spain," she said softly. "Her country is now free, and surely she and her brothers are at peace."

His hand closed fiercely over hers. "I hope to God that's true."

She felt the pain in him, and it found the matching pain in her, dissolving the frail barriers that protected her from unendurable sorrow. She was a grown woman; she should be able to accept the loss of her mother and carry on with her life. Yet inside her was a vast reservoir of grief that scalded like lava.

Voice agonized, she asked, "Do you believe in God? And in heaven?"

He hesitated, then said slowly, "I believe in a creative power beyond anything we can comprehend, and that spirit cannot be destroyed. Maria and your mother are not only at peace—somewhere they are as alive and real as you and I."

The tears she had suppressed since her mother's death erupted into a shattering paroxysm of grief. She began to weep violently. She had feared that if she ever began to cry, she would never be able to stop, and now she knew that her fear had been real. That no one could survive such anguish.

The bed sagged under Kenneth's weight. He shoved the drawing board from her lap and drew her into his arms, holding her tightly against the tempest that racked her. She burrowed against him, shaking uncontrollably and gulping for breath, as helpless as when Frazier had been taking her to her death.

But then she had been calm, beyond fear. Now she was reliving every sorrow she had ever known. She was a small girl yearning silently for attention, an older child confused by adult infidelities. She suffered again the misery of social condemnation, and the bleak belief that she was unimportant to her parents compared to the high drama of their own lives.

Most of all, she felt loneliness, and a desolate certainty that she would never be loved. That she was not worthy of love.

But she was *not* alone. Kenneth's arms cradled her, protecting her from the disintegration she had feared. Under her cheek, she felt the steady beat of his heart. Though their relationship had begun under false pretenses, he had never been anything but brave, kind, and honorable. Loving. Even the most terrible loss of her life was countered by the warmth and understanding she had found only in him.

As she clung to him, shaking, she slowly recognized the extent to which grief had paralyzed all her emotions. Now that her sorrow was released, other feelings were gushing free like a river in the spring thaw. She had not known her own capacity to love until now, when every fiber of her body thrummed with the power of her feelings for Kenneth.

And because of his love, she could recognize other love. Earlier that day, her father had offered his life for hers. And her mother had loved her, too. Not always perfectly, but with the best that was in her intense, troubled nature.

An image blossomed vividly in her mind. "My mother was there today, Kenneth," she whispered in a raw voice. "I saw her when I was unconscious, I think. She was all light, like an angel, and she was trying to save my life. Is that possible?"

"Life-and-death circumstances can thin the veil between the seen and the unseen, Rebecca." He caressed her back with infinite tenderness. "Frazier dropped you when he was shot. You began sliding toward the edge of the cliff. I managed to catch you, but the slope was too steep for me to go back.

"We were both flattened on the rock, on the verge of falling, when a fierce gust of wind struck us. Somehow it shifted the balance so that I was able to get us both to safety. It seemed unnatural—and I swear it was the difference between living and dying. Perhaps it was your mother, lending her strength to save us both."

A seed of warmth took hold in her heart, swiftly growing into a serenity that flowed throughout her body. So this was faith, she realized with quiet amazement. Love and peace and immortality were real, and she had learned them from a corsair.

She raised her face. "I love you, Kenneth," she said huskily. "Don't ever leave me."

A slow, intimate smile lit his face. "I can't promise not to die—but I will always be with you, Rebecca, in spirit if not in body. I swear it." He bent his head and pressed his lips to hers, murmuring, "Always."

His kiss was like nectar, imparting a sweet strength that miraculously healed the ragged holes of her spirit.

After sweetness came fire. She lay back on the pillows and pulled him down beside her. "Make love to me, Kenneth. Please."

He stroked her gently, but his brows drew together in a frown. "That was quite a blow on the head you received today."

"When you kiss me, my head doesn't hurt at all." She pressed her lips to his throat, feeling the hard beat of his pulse. He tasted salty, and his long journey north had resulted in a pleasant rasp of whiskers. She slid a hand down his body. "If the physician were here, I'm sure he would agree that you're the best medicine for a headache."

He caught his breath as she caressed him. "You win, shameless wench." He caught the hem of her nightgown and worked the garment up over her head. "I foresee a marriage where you will always get whatever you want."

She laughed as she emerged from the muslin folds. "That will be easy, since what I want is you."

His garments joined her nightgown on the floor. He touched her as delicately as if she were made of spun glass, but her ardent response soon changed that. For the first time, the passion that had always joined them was allowed to run free, without doubt or reservation.

It swiftly became their own private river of fire, shot through with currents of warmth, tenderness, even laughter. All of the myriad facets of love. At the height of fulfillment she wept again, this time with joy, for she had never dreamed that in surrender she would find such wholeness.

After the storm they rested peacefully in each other's arms, lit only by the warm glow of the dying fire. His head was a warm, reassuring weight on her breast.

She ran her fingers through his dark hair, the silky strands curling around her fingers. "I shall paint you as Vulcan, god of the forge," she murmured. "He was all strength and physical mastery, like you."

"And he was married to Venus." He sat up, marveling at her loveliness and his own absolute happiness. "You could have modeled for Botticelli's Venus—slim and elegant and achingly desirable." He kissed her between her breasts, then climbed from the bed and dug into the pocket of his crumpled coat.

She made a small sound of protest that ended when he rejoined her. He lifted her hand and slid the Wilding betrothal ring onto the third finger of her left hand.

"I'm getting this all backward, my love." He kissed her hand, then linked his fingers through hers. "Betrothals should begin with a ring, not a bedding."

She smiled. "Artists are allowed to be different."

"I may be an artist, but I have a very conventional belief in fidelity," he said firmly. "No mistresses, no lovers. Just one man, one woman, and one bed. Forever."

She gave him Lilith's enchanting smile as she drew his head down for another kiss. "I wouldn't have it any other way."

The End

AUTHOR'S NOTE

As always, history provides marvelous texture and detail to help the author. Wellington did indeed use reconnaissance officers who rode fearlessly across Spain during the Peninsular War, gathering intelligence, working with guerrilla groups, and sketching enemy fortifications. The fate of Kenneth's mistress was taken directly from the tragic death of Juana, lover of Captain Colquhoun Grant, most famous of the reconnaissance officers.

Kenneth and Rebecca's success with their first Royal Academy Exhibition was inspired by two young pre-Raphaelites, John Millais and William Holman Hunt. At age nineteen and twenty-one, they worked on their exhibition paintings almost nonstop for days, finishing an hour before the deadline on Handing-In Day. No doubt the canvases they rushed to the academy were more than a little wet. That year, Hunt's picture was accepted and Millais's rejected. The next year, though, both were successful and their pictures were hung side by side "on the line." If Millais and Hunt could do that, why not Kenneth and Rebecca?

I shamelessly combined traits of real artists in my

fictional characters. I thought of Sir Anthony as a cross between Jacques-Louis David and Sir Thomas Lawrence. Rebecca was intended as a sort of proto-pre-Raphaelite, with a dose of feminism added. Kenneth's work bears more than a passing resemblance to Goya, with maybe a dash of Thèodore Gèricault. According to my *Oxford Dictionary of Art,* Gèricault was an "archetypal Romantic artist," and "virile and inspiring."

What more could one ask for the hero of a romance?

Thank you for taking the time to read *River of Fire*. I hope you've enjoyed it—and if so, please consider helping other readers find it by leaving a review of the novel at your favorite online bookstore or reader website. The final novel about the Fallen Angels is *One Perfect Rose,* in which Stephen Kenyon, the new Duke of Ashburton, becomes entangled with a wandering theater family and enchanted by their spirited daughter.

Readers of the Fallen Angels series might also enjoy my Silk Trilogy. It begins with *Silk and Shadows,* when Peregrine, an exotic prince who fascinates London with his wealth, mystery, and dangerous allure, seeks retribution for an appalling crime. Nothing and no one can stop him—except perhaps Lady Sara St. James, whose fragile beauty conceals a gentle heart, genuine goodness, and a soul of steel.

Finally, if you would like me to let you know when my upcoming books are published, you can join my newsletter by visiting my website at MaryJoPutney.com.

Happy reading!

—Mary Jo Putney

ALSO BY MARY JO PUTNEY

The Bride Trilogy

The Wild Child, #1

The China Bride, #2

The Bartered Bride, #3

The Fallen Angels Series

Thunder & Roses, #1

Dancing on the Wind, #2

Petals in the Storm, #3

Angel Rogue, #4

Shattered Rainbows, #5

River of Fire, #6

One Perfect Rose, #7

The Silk Trilogy

Silk and Shadows, #1

Silk and Secrets, #2

Veils of Silk, #3

Other Historicals

Dearly Beloved

Uncommon Vows

The Rake

The Bargain

The Marriage Spell (paranormal)

Putney Classics (Sweet Regency Romances)

Carousel of Hearts

The Diabolical Baron

Lady of Fortune

The Dark Mirror Trilogy

(Young Adult fiction, written as M. J. Putney)

Dark Mirror, #1

Dark Passage, #2

Dark Destiny, #3

Fallen From Grace (A Dark Mirror Short Story)

The Guardian Trilogy

A Kiss of Fate, #1

Stolen Magic, #2

A Distant Magic, #3

The Lost Lords Series

Loving A Lost Lord, #1

Never Less Than A Lady, #2

Nowhere Near Respectable, #3

No Longer A Gentleman, #4

Sometimes A Rogue, #5

Not Quite A Wife, #6

Not Always a Saint, #7

Rogues Redeemed Series (A Spin-Off of the Lost Lords)

Once A Soldier, #1

Once a Rebel, #2

Once A Scoundrel, #3

Once A Spy, #4

Once Dishonored, #5

The Circle of Friends Trilogy

The Burning Point, #1

The Spiral Path, #2

An Imperfect Process, #3

A Holiday Fling (novella, also published in *Christmas Revels*)

Shorter Works

Weddings of the Century: A Pair of Novellas

The Christmas Cuckoo (novella, also published in *Christmas Revels*)

The Black Beast of Belleterre (novella, also published in *Christmas Revels*)

The Dragon and the Dark Knight (written as M.J. Putney)

Christmas Collections

Christmas Revels

Christmas Candles

Mischief and Mistletoe (contributor)

The Last Chance Christmas Ball (contributor)

Christmas Roses (contributor)

Seduction on a Snowy Night (contributor)

ABOUT THE AUTHOR

A *New York Times, Wall Street Journal,* and *USAToday* bestselling author, Mary Jo Putney is also a recipient of RWA's Nora Roberts Lifetime Achievement Award. She was born in Upstate New York with a reading addiction, a condition for which there is no known cure. Her entire romance writing career is an accidental byproduct of buying a computer for other purposes.

Her novels are known for psychological depth and intensity and include historical and contemporary romance, fantasy, and young adult fantasy. Winner of numerous writing awards, including two RITAs and two *Romantic Times* Career Achievement awards, she's had a number of her books listed as top romances of the year by *Library Journal* and *Booklist,* the magazine of the American Library Association.

You can visit her online at MaryJoPutney.com.

COPYRIGHT

PANDAMAX PRESS

River of Fire

Fallen Angels Series: Book 6

ISBN: 978-1-948880-02-2

Published by Pandamax Press, a division of Mary Jo Putney, Inc.

Cover by Kimberly Killion of The Killion Group.

Pandamax logo by Elizabeth Person.

Printed in Great Britain
by Amazon

18462289R00263